SCANDALOUS

MARTEL MAXWELL

ISIS
LARGE PRINT
Oxford

Copyright © Martel Maxwell, 2010

First published in Great Britain 2010
by
Penguin Books Ltd.

Published in Large Print 2011 by ISIS Publishing Ltd.,
7 Centremead, Osney Mead, Oxford OX2 0ES
by arrangement with
Penguin Books Ltd.

British Library Cataloguing in Publication Data
Maxwell, Martel.
  Scandalous.
  1. Celebrities - - Fiction.
  2. Sisters - - Fiction.
  3. Love stories
  4. Large type books.
  I. Title
  823.9'2–dc22

ISBN 978–0–7531–8814–9 (hb)
ISBN 978–0–7531–8815–6 (pb)

Printed and bound in Great Britain by
T. J. International Ltd., Padstow, Cornwall

For my mum, Anne Maxwell-Stevenson.
Thank you.

Late Edition:
Let's Get this Party Started

Max's body was pumping with adrenaline. Somehow, she'd managed to scale halfway up a twelve-foot pole — the only thing between her and Hollywood's man of the moment, Kirk Kelner.

Sheer determination had got her this far. Well, that and three eye-watering gin cocktails from the free bar. Just a few feet more, she thought as she hoisted herself up the pole, then who knows? The biggest scoop of the night — maybe the biggest scoop of her career. Showbiz Reporter of the Year had Max's name all over it.

She could hear legendary newsreader Sir Trevor McDonald now: "And the next award goes to a young woman who brings you the stories the stars hope you will never read. Ladies and gentlemen, Maxine —"

"Nice view."

What? Who the hell? Max's thoughts returned to the present as the voice carried up to her precarious position. Oh bugger, had she remembered to put pants on? She had read in *Glamour* last week that it was healthy to let in a bit of air down there and since then she had sometimes gone commando.

Quickly, she took one hand off the pole and patted her pleated grey-velvet Armani skirt which only just covered her bum. Thank God, she had remembered. A teeny La Perla pink thong, but knickers nonetheless. Just enough material to cover her landing strip. Getting that done had really hurt. But she thanked her lucky stars she'd kept her waxing appointment the day before.

"Thanks, boys," Max shouted down to the two men who had a bird's-eye view, one of whom, she noted, was rather fit. Tousled blond hair, twinkling blue eyes, slight tan, oh and no wedding ring . . .

Stop it, not the time or the place, she told herself and focused on making a final hoist over the pole, one of dozens holding together a temporary canvas wall shielding the VIP enclosure at the after-party for the premiere of *Man of Steel 4*.

Pity she had no one to admire her landing strip. Being single was such a waste as Max had felt decidedly horny for the past few days. Perhaps it was the summer heat. They said men think about sex every few seconds. Max was beginning to realize how disabling this was as her mind drifted constantly during work to thoughts of one of the messenger boys, a boy in his early twenties, and she pictured him bumping into her in the corridor, pushing her into a conference room, pulling her skirt up and pants down in an expert move. He groaned as he felt how wet she was . . . and then Max's thoughts would come crashing back to the real world in which the singer at the end of the phone had been silent for a while. Shit, what bollocks had he said about the American Billboard charts?

Focusing on the matter in hand — gatecrashing this celebfest of a party — Max spotted a ledge halfway down the other side of the wall. She used it as a footrest for the toe of her tan leather Miss Sixty cowboy boot before jumping down. She noted a few odd glances as she landed, but only from bemused guests more interested in the champagne and canapés. Fortunately, there was not a security guard in sight.

Just twenty minutes earlier, Max had been turned away from the VIP entrance by a burly black security guard called Mike.

Mike was a regular bouncer on the London showbiz circuit and was used to Max's attempts at sneaking into the VIP section of A-list parties.

Despite her biggest brown-eyed Bambi look, he had refused her entry. Max asked him to check the list.

"My name is most definitely there, Mike."

"I don't need to check, Max. All journalists are banned. Orders from above. Kirk Kelner can't stand you lot. Says all those stories in the papers about his affairs will cost him millions in his divorce."

Mike was already looking over Max's shoulder, preparing himself for three girls standing behind her.

Max was relieved to note they did not belong to the competition — the tabloid showbiz writers on rival columns who wanted the same thing: a scoop on Kirk Kelner. The *Mirror*'s 3a.m. girls hunted as a twosome, as did the *Star*'s Goss team, while the Bizarre editor on the *Sun* was usually with one of the largely unknown

3

members of his team. Those writers had their airbrushed pictures at the top of their columns while only Max's name appeared, with those of a few other showbiz reporters, under her boss's picture. Max liked it that way — it gave her the freedom to be a chameleon and adopt a whole new identity if the fancy took her. Fuck, concentrate. What kind of a journalist would she be if she rolled up for work tomorrow with a stonking hangover and no story on Kelner? And God, the thought of the roasting she'd be in for if the rival front pages had some juicy exclusive on him made her shudder.

"Come on, Mike, no one will know."

"No, Max. Nice try, but not even your old phone trick is going to work."

Ah, the phone trick. It had served Max well in her three years as a showbiz reporter for the *Daily News*, Britain's second biggest-selling daily newspaper. Only the mighty *Sun* sold more copies.

She would pretend to be on her mobile and march straight into the VIP section of a premiere with all the presence of an A-lister.

Normally, Max grabbed her opportunity to waltz in when the regular guards who knew her were on a break or had gone to the toilet.

When a guard grabbed her arm, she would give him a venomous look and hiss, "Can't you see I'm on the phone? Anyway, I've been in already."

Sadly, tonight Mike's bladder had remained resolute.

The *Daily News*, along with the other newspapers' showbiz desks were always given one pass, sometimes two, for premiere parties. The PRs were paid to make sure the film was talked about, after all. But she had learned within weeks of starting her job that a premiere ticket meant little if you wanted to mix with the big stars. Sure, some old-timer soap actor or struggling singer might have a ticket to join the main crowd at the after-party.

But the big names always insisted on a VIP enclosure with a strict no-entry rule for journalists. They were happy to pick up their £5-million pay cheques for filming but didn't want some hack witnessing their drunk and debauched behaviour.

With a natural beauty, petite frame, long chestnut hair and big brown eyes, Max was prettier than many of the stars she wrote about. In the dog-eat-dog world of tabloid journalism, every reporter used what they had to get a scoop.

One girl from the *Sport*, a tall, slim brunette with a slight acne problem, was renowned for sleeping with male stars' security guards — normally after the celeb had turned her down. She got her monthly quota of stories during warm-up cocktails, and warm-down pillow talk.

Max had never gone there — and never would, no matter how pressurized she felt to bring in stories. She had simply learned to play on her looks and wit, and nine times out of ten flirted her way past security guards into the VIP enclosure. But tonight she had been unceremoniously knocked back by Mike. Max had given it ten minutes before deciding to climb her way to the A-listers.

And here she was, mingling with the cream of Hollywood. Yes, her unorthodox arrival had gone largely unnoticed, aided no doubt by the never-ending supply of pink Laurent-Perrier circulating in the room.

Guests outside the enclosure were being offered cheaper rosé Cava, served on trays by ultra-toned, tanned girls in khaki-coloured bikinis with camouflage paint on their cheeks — in keeping with the action theme of the movie. Mini pokes of chips with battered fish were offered up by rugged men with bulging biceps and rippling six-packs hidden under *Die Hard*-esque string vests and combat trousers.

Outside, hundreds of partygoers chatted and looked over each other's shoulders to spot a star, talking over some up-and-coming rock band, while a few tipsy guests attempted an assault course set up for the evening.

Max surveyed her new surroundings in the VIP area. She stifled a giggle when she saw three women wearing identical bright green Versace frocks spattered with orange sunflowers. How embarrassing — the hottest ticket in town and they had chosen the same outrageous number. Must remember to dig out their pictures tomorrow at work. The headline "Frocky Horror Show" for a picture feature would be perfect.

The outfit wasn't all they had in common. Max wondered if they shared the same double-F boob-job specialist. At £3,900 a pop (the dresses, not the boobs), only the rich could afford Versace's latest number.

Since these silicone-enhanced "beauties" were balancing their mounting overdrafts with growing coke problems, Max had no doubt they had asked their rich sugar daddies to cough up for the latest must-have. Having forked out the cash, the married men were supplied with blow jobs on tap during their twice-weekly visits, while their wives did their credit cards some damage on Bond Street.

What went over the girls' highlighted heads, Max thought, was that class or style can't be bought. Madonna might have worn the dress ten days ago but no A-lister worth her salt would go near them now the wannabes had them.

Max grabbed two flutes of bubbly for Dutch courage from the nearest waiter and drained the first in two gulps before smoothing down her skirt. She checked that her black-satin Vivienne Westwood corset was showing just enough cleavage but no trace of her boob-boosting Wonderbra.

Max then shook her mane of glossy hair, tinged with auburn in certain lights and cascading over her shoulders in heavy waves, and told herself she belonged with the stars.

They were no better than her. OK, so the women looked like they'd taken two days to get ready. Manicured, hair-extensioned and fake-tanned to the max, they certainly turned heads. But they also managed to look near-identical.

Holding on to her remaining full glass of bubbly, Max strode into the crowd. The mix of champagne with the gin she'd already drunk had the desired effect of numbing her nerves.

Now she wanted a cigarette. As she negotiated her nicotine craving Max recognized a woman she'd seen on the red carpet earlier that night: Kirk Kelner's mum, Daphne. Good spot. Kirk had charmed the camera crews by telling the pretty reporters his mum was his date for the night. Daphne, in her mid sixties, clearly loved every moment and took to it like a duck to water yet she was full of grace and didn't try to steal the limelight. She spoke only when spoken to on the red carpet but never failed to give reporters quick, witty replies to their questions.

Jesus, was that the new-season Prada dress in scarlet she was wearing? The richly coloured, velvet, floor-length dress cost £7,000 and she made it look worth every penny. It covered her breasts but plunged low at the back, revealing flawless skin, and finished with a fishtail skirt.

Sexy but refined. Demure and elegant.

It looked better on her than on the girls a third of her age in the magazine ads. Daphne Kelner reminded Max of veteran Bond girl Honor Blackman. She was one classy lady.

"Hello, Mrs Kelner," offered Max. "I just wanted to say how lovely you look."

On the surface Max had no hesitation in talking to anyone at a bash like this. Aside from the bouncers, no one had a clue who she was. The more confident she acted, the more important people assumed she was. In truth, Max was often terrified to strike up conversations with stars. But a few vodka Red Bulls, or whatever was on offer, always did the trick.

Daphne gave Max a quizzical look but hardly missed a beat before breaking into a welcoming smile. "Why, thank you, darling. How very kind of you. My son bought me this dress for tonight." Then, as though confiding a secret with her best pal, she leaned in close and placed a perfectly painted long scarlet fingernail on Max's arm. Whispering loudly, she said: "Having a famous son has a few bonuses, you know."

They giggled like new schoolgirl pals. Then, as silence fell upon them, Max prepared to ask where her celebrated son was.

"Ah, here he is. Kirk, darling. Come give Mommy a kiss."

Swaying slightly, the movie god that was Kirk Kelner lurched between them, stooping to give Daphne a peck on her cheek.

Max couldn't believe it. The superstar voted sexiest man in the world for three years running by *GQ* — ahead of Brad Pitt, George Clooney and Russell Crowe — was standing beside her. She looked up into his smooth tanned face and found the twinkling blue eyes that had graced thousands of magazine and newspaper covers. Wow. He really was as handsome in the flesh. Almost flawless. Like a waxwork.

"Kirk, you must meet this lovely lady, Miss . . .?"

"Alison Brown." It was the first name that came to mind — hell, better safe than sorry. If he was anything like most celebrities, he'd spend hours Googling his name and know the names of all showbiz reporters on the nationals.

The eyes of the impossibly dashing actor glistened as the corners of his mouth lifted. "Well, it's good to meet you, Alison."

Max held his gaze, a mass of nerves inside but a vision of calm on the outside. He was drunk. But still, was one of the most famous men in the world flirting with her? Max wondered if she was about to have a heart attack. It felt like a drummer on acid had crept inside her chest. Oh God, maybe he was looking at something on her face. Did she have lipstick on her teeth?

Max could picture the amazing six-pack from the poster beside her desk at work. It was hiding under that dinner suit and it was just a few feet from her. Those fabulous bronze thighs that had glistened with sweat when he played a gladiator in *Land of the Strong* were so close she could touch them.

Stay cool, she told herself, smiling and widening her eyes.

"Fucking journalists," Kirk sneered at Max. "Blood-sucking parasites the lot of them."

Oh shit, who's told him, Max thought. Was he about to have her seized and dragged outside?

Kirk Kelner drained his champagne flute and burped. "Oops, excuse me." Looking Max straight in the eye, he said: "You know what? My bodyguard says one hack has just been thrown out trying to get in here. Doesn't matter, she'll just make up some bullshit anyway. Those bastards give vultures a bad name. If I had my way —"

Having been introduced to Kirk by his mother, it seemed as though Max had been "vouched for" by the Mafia boss. Kirk was not holding back.

"Kirky, wash your mouth out. There is no need for that sort of language — and in front of this beautiful girl. What must she think of you?"

For a second Kirk looked like a little boy who'd been smacked. "Yeah, sorry, ladies. I've just had a hard time from the gutter press these last few months. And I've had a few drinks. I hit a bar while you watched the film. I've seen it so many times . . ."

Composing himself, Kirk straightened up to his full six foot two inches, flashing that all-American dazzling smile.

Was this actually the Kirk Kelner who had made it on to her laminated list? The mental list Max had compiled of her three chosen men, whose names she had written down on a card and laminated so she couldn't change it. If she got married, she would tell her husband she would always be faithful . . . unless the opportunity arose with any of the three stars she had chosen.

Max had finalized her dream team during a drinking game with her best pal, Suzie, and settled on Nicholas Cage (not your typical hottie but there was something deeply sexy about him), fellow Scot Ewan McGregor and Kirk Kelner. Because he was perfect.

Suzie, a school pal from home and the only girl Max knew who could drink her under the table, had opted for Colin Farrell on account of his looks and Irish accent, Brad Pitt and Kirk Kelner too.

And here he was. Undeniably sexy. And so charismatic. Even now, slightly the worse for wear, he made every other man in the room look unremarkable, dull. His skin was smooth, flawless and tanned. Not a wrinkle in sight and yet no sign of the frozen Botox look.

Kirk brushed a subtly manicured hand through his dark blond hair. "So, Alison, what is it you do?"

Oh God. What to say? Max was normally honest about her job but sensed this was no time for the truth. "Oh I'm one of those parasite hacks who have followed your every move since you split from your wife" probably wasn't what he wanted to hear. And who was Max to spoil Kirk Kelner's big night?

Maybe he would like to hear about her laminated list. Oh God, maybe she'd actually shag him. She'd never seriously thought she'd meet any of her Top Three. Max was certain he'd be well hung. No one that sexy could be packing a chipolata.

"Me? I'm a writer." She felt his gaze beating down on her. Quick, be convincing. "Of . . . children's books."

The smile was back. "Oh yeah? Cool." Just then they were joined by a short beer-bellied man with a red face, whom Kirk introduced as his attorney.

Keep calm, Max told herself, you can't go to work in the morning and tell the boss you actually chatted to Kirk Kelner without getting a kick-ass story. You're here to work. And anyway, his type was the blonde, huge-breasted variety.

12

While he was undeniably beautiful, Max couldn't help but be a little disappointed at meeting Kirk. Seeing him drunk made him human, as annoying as any guy who'd had too much. He was arrogant too, his jaw a little rigid, making Max wonder if he'd taken coke. How disappointing to find the god that was Kirk Kelner wasn't quite what he seemed on the cover of *GQ* and billboards promoting his movies. But he was beautiful. And, of course, she still absolutely would.

"Hey, Al, this young lady writes children's books. What do you think? Maybe she could write one for my wife — she's a big fucking baby, isn't she, Al?" His slurring had increased. "A big baby who's throwing all her toys out of the pram to get her hands on my millions — that I worked for. So I slept with the nanny. Who doesn't?"

Bingo! Oh yes, yes, yes, thank you, Kirk Kelner. Not only had he saved the planet in *Man of Steel 4: The Final Frontier*, he'd also landed himself on the front page of the *Daily News*.

Less than two minutes later Max was dialling her news desk. She had excused herself, telling Kirk she had to make a quick call to make sure her friend who had just split from her fiancé had arrived at the party — lies tripped off the tongue in this job — and found a quiet place beside the canvas wall.

"Hello, is that the night news editor?

"Yes, Max?"

"Hi, James, I've got a corker for you on Kirk Kelner."

13

"Go ahead, I'll take it down myself. If it's worth it, I can get it in the late edition."

"OK, ready?"

"Ready."

"'EXCLUSIVE by Maxine Summers: KIRK CHEATED WITH NANNY. We can today reveal the real reason for Hollywood heart-throb Kirk Kelner's divorce . . . he cheated on his supermodel wife, Alanna, with their nanny. Now the thirty-nine-year-old star of *Man of Steel 4* faces a bitter court battle over his £500-million fortune.'"

"Fuck me, Max, that's brilliant. That'll be the front-page splash. Does anyone else have a sniff of it?"

"No, I was the only journalist talking to him. It's all ours, definitely an exclusive."

It might have been Max's story but James, as night news editor, would get the kudos of calling the paper's editor at home and telling them a great story had come in and he'd like to put it on the front page.

Closing the porn site he'd been surfing, his voice was full of cheer. "Well done. Carry on, I want every juicy detail."

Exclusive:
Beauties Go To War

"Lucy, darling, you look wonderful," Clarissa gushed, stepping away from her guest and taking in her Chanel lemon-linen dress. Lucy did look wonderful, as always. Like her sister Max, she took pride in her appearance at all times even though their individual styles were very different.

She had been flattered by Clarissa's invitation to join her and her fiancé, Clive, in the Royal Enclosure at Ascot. Clarissa was one of London's most prominent socialites, her little black book reading like a who's who of the capital's aristocracy.

Lucy's boss had stared in wonderment when the invitation landed on her desk, her beady eyes settling on "Clarissa Appleton-Smythe". Through gritted teeth Genevieve said, "Oh lucky you. I hadn't realized you knew Clarissa so well."

In truth, Lucy didn't really know her. And of course she was aware of the reason for the socialite's sudden interest in her. It had little to do with Lucy herself and everything to do with her new boyfriend. For Lucy had recently started dating Hartley Balmyle, the fifth Earl of Balmyle — pronounced Bal-mile — and one of the most eligible bachelors in the UK.

In the three weeks since they had met, she had been on half a dozen dates with Hartley. Naturally, she had been welcomed into Team Clarissa with open arms when Clarissa met her a week after she'd stepped out with Hartley to a charity luncheon. Their picture had appeared in some magazine and Clarissa recognized Lucy at a fashion show in Mayfair. The Appleton-Smythe set laughed loudly at Lucy's jokes, even when she said something she didn't think particularly funny, such was their desire to meet Lucy's new beau. At the end of the fashion show Clarissa had asked Lucy to join her at Ascot. She looked crestfallen when Lucy explained Hartley wouldn't be able to make it and that she would be coming on her own. Lucy didn't mind one bit, though. Clarissa's warmth was contagious and, anyway, knowing her could only be useful for work.

Clarissa was well versed about the Balmyles. The fifth Earl of Balmyle was Scottish. His family had a huge estate on the outskirts of Edinburgh. This was the famous Balmyle Hall, surrounded by thousands of acres of land which was rich for farming. The Queen Mother had often visited the family on the estate when staying at Glamis Castle during the summer. It had been passed down the generations and was now run by Hartley, his father having died five years ago. The family had also kept a considerable property portfolio in the city, which had grown vastly in value with the opening of the Scottish Parliament in the capital. The *Sunday Times* had put the family at the top of their Rich List for Scotland. They were in the Top Twenty Rich List for the UK.

"Darling, what scent is that? Is it the new Jo Malone? Oh it's delicious, Lucy. Quite the trend setter."

Clarissa was thirty-two, a generous size 14 and on such days out she seemed always to wear garish pink or purple taffeta skirt suits, topped off with a similarly outlandish hat. Lucy wondered if her attire was a calculated attempt to stand out in the society photos that graced the back of her magazine. Or perhaps it was just a sign of her eccentricity.

Without coming up for breath, she whispered conspiratorially in Lucy's ear: "Straight ahead, twelve o'clock, powder blue, Lady Chalmers. You know the one, the American heiress. She's had at least three glasses of Cristal since she got here an hour ago."

Following Clarissa's directions Lucy noted the pretty blonde who seemed to be enjoying herself, throwing back her head in laughter with her friends.

Lucy couldn't help but giggle at Clarissa's army-like precision when it came to spotting the rich and famous. Lucy was preparing to compliment Clarissa's outfit — well, it would be rude not to make the hostess feel special — but she was cut off.

"Lucy, darling. What bad luck Hartley couldn't make it. I was just saying to Clive that we simply must have you over for one of our Friday suppers. You'll love it. Jasper Whitaker — you know the jockey who hangs out with the royals — and Philippa Bonner of the Bonner publishing empire are regulars."

Clarissa suddenly took a sharp intake of breath and her face flushed.

"Oh no, I think Philippa knows Hartley's ex." Looking over her shoulder, she lowered her voice almost to a whisper. "God, I hear she's an utter b-i-t-c-h. Have you met her?"

Lucy shook her head. Thankfully she never had encountered Lady Bridget Beames but had seen her splashed across the society pages of the glossy magazines, looking so perfectly put together but severe and skinny.

And she had heard plenty about her. As soon as the girls at work had discovered she was dating Hartley, they relished telling Lucy the numerous dreadful stories they had heard about how rude she was.

Lucy smiled back at Clarissa. "Don't worry if one of your guests knows her. It's no big deal. I'll survive."

"You'll do more than survive, darling," Clarissa laughed, squeezing Lucy's hand. "Your debut at my Friday-night supper will be the talk of parties for months to come."

Lucy warmed to the theme, putting on her poshest voice. "Yah. London's finest will be begging for an invitation to one of your gatherings but you shall have to turn them away, such will be the demand to attend."

Clarissa clasped her hands in delight. "Exactly. And Bridget will hear of your mesmerizing beauty and impeccable manners and choke on her carrot stick."

Lucy looked relieved. Yes, Clarissa had ruthless ambition but, unlike so many other girls, she was upfront about it. There was something undeniably likeable about Miss Appleton-Smythe. She thrived on

18

making friends, fussing over them and gossiping at her Friday suppers.

As far as Lucy knew, Clarissa didn't have a job, no doubt being provided for by rich parents and her fiancé, and so arranging her social calendar had become something of a career, at which she excelled.

She had become known within certain London sets as a bit of a fixer. "Oh you want to go to the March Ball? Let me give you Clarissa Appleton-Smythe's number." "You want a minor royal to attend your charity auction? You really should talk to Clarissa."

She was still talking. "So I'm planning a supper in three weeks and I won't accept no for an answer, Lucy. I'm giving you plenty of notice; please say you'll both come." Noting a slight panicked look, Clarissa squeezed Lucy's hand. "Darling, I know I'm an utter pain in the whatsit, but it's how I get my own way. I promise I'll be utterly lovable when you get to know me."

Lucy found herself laughing and nodding her assurances to her new friend, not knowing what else to do. Somehow Lucy wanted to please Clarissa, to allow her the thrill of telling her set Hartley was the guest of honour at her Friday supper. It was like giving a small child the key to the gingerbread house where everything inside was delicious and edible.

She hoped Hartley wouldn't mind.

Clarissa was visibly excited and started a mental list of her best-connected friends. Oh and what to eat? Chateaubriand, perhaps. The seating plan — Hartley would have to sit next to her.

As her hostess thought dreamily of becoming the Earl of Balmyle's new confidante, Lucy excused herself to the restroom.

She could never understand the ruthless determination of so many girls in London. None of her close friends were like them but working at the magazine had opened up a new world of women. Being in the company of the "right" people at the most sought-after social events seemed to be somewhat of an obsession.

Most of these girls were cold and snooty. Clarissa, at least, was refreshing in her honesty and more than a little comical. She seemed less self-deprecating with others in her set of friends than she was with Lucy. Somehow, inexplicably, Lucy and Clarissa clicked.

Lucy had landed on her feet at *Trend*, a glossy fashion and celebrity magazine which counted *Vogue* as its main rival, and established a name for herself on the editorial team as a leading fashion writer, taking charge of styling fashion shoots as well as putting words to them. Despite what the outside world thought writers at the top-end glossies earned, she spent most of her salary on a mortgage for the two-bedroom flat she had bought a year ago with her sister. Victorian terraced flats did not come cheap in Kensington and when her half of the mortgage was paid she spent what was left on clothes, for which she had always had a passion, and her contribution to the monthly lease payments of the sports car she shared with Max, a nifty black Z4. It never failed to astound her how judgemental the girls in her office were when it came to wearing the right labels, living at the right postcode. No doubt her boss and other girls in the office thought she was dating Hartley because of his wealth and connections. That's why they would date him.

But no, she could never be with someone she didn't love. She wasn't sure how she felt about Hartley yet, but she had been pleasantly surprised, impressed even, so far. He seemed so kind, funny and generous — all the things she really admired in a man. Hell, maybe she was sure but was too scared to admit it to herself; after all, it was such early days. She could remember how perfect John had been at the start and how broken she felt when she realized what the real man was like.

"Oh my God."

A high-pitched voice interrupted Lucy's thoughts. A breathless Clarissa, so excited she could barely get the words out.

"Lucy . . . darling . . . hurry. Lady Bridget Beames is here. Hartley's ex."

Lucy's head was swimming.

"Oh Lucy, come and look. She's making a terrible scene outside. Let's find her, darling. She'll be hopping mad when she sees you."

Lady Bridget 0 . . .
Lucy Summers 1

Lady Bridget was not amused. Some buffoon had spilled a glass of beer all over her new cream Burberry summer coat. It wasn't even in the shops yet and she'd pulled every string to get one. Daddy had paid. And now this cretin, with a bulging belly and red face that screamed high blood pressure, had ruined it. She was so angry she had no control over a shrill shriek escaping her thin, scarlet-painted lips.

"You idiot. You absolute imbecile."

Lady Bridget's raised tones had attracted the attention of several guests gathered in the Royal Enclosure. But not the one she wanted.

"You," she spat as she thumped the unsuspecting man on his left shoulder. "Do you know what you've done? Do you know who I am? Do you know how much this cost?"

The bewildered man turned to see a woman staring down at him, pointing at a wet mark on her coat.

Focusing his beer-goggled eyes on her angular ivory face framed with a jet-black bob he stuttered an apology.

For the first time Bridget became aware she was causing a scene. People had stopped to listen. That wouldn't do, she chided herself. Some diary writer would hear of it and dub her a diva in their newspaper.

"Oh look at me, what a frightful bore. Who cares about a silly coat?"

Bridget smiled down at the man's balding head, touching him lightly on his shoulder.

"Do forgive me," she cooed.

"Oh OK, sorry," said the man, not sure if he'd imagined the hostility he'd just witnessed.

"Oh come, please, not a word of it."

Mission accomplished, thought Bridget. I turned the situation round to look thoroughly ladylike, which I am.

The coat was gorgeous, knee length and pure cream silk, with a matching belt in velvet tied tightly, showing off her twenty-four-inch waist. Obviously it didn't have a trace of that awful checked pattern turned into a badge of honour for wannabes and chavs.

It probably cost more than the cretin beer-spiller earned in a month . . . no, two months. God, they'd let anyone in the Royal Enclosure these days.

Bridget turned to ask a girlfriend to get her a glass of champagne, but an unfamiliar face was in her way.

Clarissa managed to look surprised at bumping into Lady Bridget.

"Oh hello. Lady Bridget, is it not? My name is Clarissa Appleton-Smythe. Pleased to meet you."

The name rang a bell with the socialite, who was not in the mood to make friends but offered her hand anyway. It wouldn't do to be rude to someone who was often mentioned by her set, especially someone who might prove to be useful to her.

"A pleasure." She smiled thinly.

"Allow me to introduce my friend, Lucy Summers," Clarissa gushed triumphantly, turning to her beautiful new friend. Bridget's cold green eyes shifted immediately to the blonde girl beside this plump thing in pink.

This was the tart who was dating Hartley? Her handsome Hartley. The man she had been so sure she would marry. The love of her life.

"Delighted, I'm sure," Bridget purred, holding out a bony white hand.

Lady Bridget Beames was as blue-blooded as Hartley. She had skied with the royals since she was a child and was no stranger to showing *Tatler* round the Mayfair townhouse Daddy had given her for her twenty-first.

Daddy provided a generous monthly allowance. And there was the interest from her great-aunt and grandmother's estates. There really was no need to work. A lot of time went into looking the way she did, lunching in the right places with the right people and so on. It was like a full-time job. And anyway, helping to organize a charity ball or two a year for free was more than enough to keep her busy.

So busy, she had been known to cancel a lunch here, a shopping spree there with a girlfriend. All in the name of work. She hoped people appreciated her help; attaching her name to a ball attracted the right people.

24

"Lovely to meet you too." Lucy met Bridget's gaze and was chilled by its coldness. More than that: its venom.

Bridget drew herself up. Lucy was tall but found herself looking up into Hartley's ex's stony face. Her complexion was perfect but almost white, made all the starker by her painted lips.

"Ah! So you are Hartley's latest conquest." Lady Bridget pronounced each word as though Lucy might be hard of hearing and had to lip read, or was it so her crowd of friends could hear?

To her side was a strawberry blonde, freckled girl who looked so fragile and timid she would blow away if her Ice Queen friend blew on her. And beside her, a robust brunette with rosy cheeks and eyes that drank Lucy in, who had the smug look of someone who'd eaten an entire cream cake and blamed it on someone else. Both girls were well groomed but it struck Lucy that their clothes, expensive but unimaginative ill-fitting suits, were made for women twenty years older.

Behind Bridget, a delicate-looking, thin-faced man in a charcoal-grey suit and lemon cravat was bobbing up and down, craning to see what was going on over her shoulder.

Lucy was taken aback but more than a little amused by the hostility that was so obviously on show. She opened her mouth but no sound came out.

Bridget kept her gaze as she unfastened her beer-stained coat, slipping it carefully off her ivory shoulders to reveal a high-necked, emerald-green-satin Stella McCartney sleeveless blouse and matching knee-length skirt, which clung to her long thin thighs. She handed her coat dismissively to the strawberry blonde.

So this was the little tramp. The "beauty" the *Independent* and *Daily Telegraph* reported had stolen Hartley's heart. She could see why her darling Hartley's head had been turned. This "Lucy" was undoubtedly pretty, if you went for that kind of bland look. And her dress was this season's Chanel. Perhaps her family was wealthy. But she was still a commoner. Was she an equal to Hartley? Did she have a title? No.

Just six months ago, all of Bridget's friends had assured her Hartley would propose soon. They had been to Paris for a wonderful weekend and had agreed they were of an age when they should be thinking of settling down. Well, she had told Hartley this, but he seemed to feel the same way.

At last she would have the man she had wanted to propose for the twelve months and ten days they had been dating. Her social standing would rise even further and they would have children straight away. At thirty-six, Bridget was painfully aware that her biological clock was ticking.

Then, just two days after they had returned, Hartley had taken her to the ever-fashionable Wolseley for supper. Over lemon Dover sole and Sancerre he had finished it, explaining he needed some time alone, leaving her an utter wreck.

After months of going over and over what could have gone wrong, she decided that her darling Hartley merely needed time to sow his oats, get it all out of his system, before he came back. She was the only woman for him and she would get him back at any cost.

"Ah yes. I can see what Hartley might see in you . . . in the short term."

A cruel smile spread across her face, making her look like a cross between the Joker and Cruella De Vil.

Lucy's bright blue eyes widened as she took in Lady Bridget's words, spoken in her cutting upper-class tone. The girls by her side were clearly amused, biting their lips and looking at the ground. How clever they must think their important friend was.

"I hear you write for a magazine. How lucky. When Hartley and I get back together I'll be sure to come to you first with the photo shoot. Don't you think we'd look wonderful on your front cover?"

Lucy was shell-shocked. How could anyone be so vile and yet have friends who were hanging off her every word? She felt Clarissa's cushioned hand clasp her own.

"Let's get back to our friends," Clarissa said, with the emphasis on "friends".

Lucy was touched by Clarissa's loyalty in putting her friend's feelings before befriending the famous socialite who outranked Lucy's status a thousand-fold.

"Well?" Bridget's shrill voice was tinged with victory and impatience as it cut through Lucy's thoughts. "Don't you think we'd look wonderful?"

Lucy calmly looked out towards the racecourse, smiled, then met Bridget's stare once more.

"Oh yes, perhaps a few years ago. You were very attractive. But my, haven't you let yourself go?"

Revenge is a Dish
Best Served . . . Now

Bridget had left Ascot immediately. The bitch would pay, she thought as she pulled away in her black Range Rover. She was so angry she almost ran into a child running across the car park as she left. The little brat.

Who was she anyway, this Lucy? This little bloody upstart who had felt she had the right to talk to her like that? Bridget was furious she hadn't known more about her. Some secret she could have embarrassed her with, instead of being the one who was left red-faced.

She was the only woman for Hartley; she knew exactly how to behave in their circle. It came naturally to her. She chided herself for occasionally confiding too much to him. In the last few weeks of their relationship she had been rather honest about certain friends in their group. Well, it was hard to be Miss Perfect all the time. She had acted so sweetly when they first met, charm personified, saying only nice things about everyone and everything. But being sugary-sweet was exhausting — and boring. Bridget had no doubt her friends admired her honesty and drive, but all the same she wished she had been a little less vocal. Hartley never seemed to say a bad word about anyone. Never mind, she would behave like a delicate mouse when she got him back.

She had called her mother as soon as she returned from their trip to Paris and told her to dig out the family tiara she had worn on her wedding day. Indeed the heirloom had been in the family for generations and now it was Bridget's turn. She'd told Daddy that nothing other than a Vera Wang dress, top of the range, thank you very much, would do. After all, it would be the society wedding of the year and feature in *Tatler*, *Hello!* and *Harper's Bazaar*. Perhaps Jimmy Choo shoes for the bride were a little played out. Bridget made a mental note to call Manolo Blahnik and ask for their bridal range.

And then suddenly Hartley had ended her dream. She had had to contend with her mother, Lady Barbara Beames, rolling her eyes and tutting. She had been married when she was twenty and had both Bridget and her brother, Boris, before she was thirty. Boris was two years younger than Bridget, Barbara had reminded her daughter with a look of disdain, and was married with eighteen-month-old twins. Didn't she realize time was ticking?

Fucking twins, Bridget thought. The golden boy and his mousy little wife, Miranda, had produced not one but two sprogs while she had none.

Miranda, or Plain Jane as Bridget and her mother had taken to calling her behind her back, didn't like Lady Barbara being too hands-on, or "interfering" as she had whined to Boris. It would be so special for Barbara if her only daughter had children she could fawn over and show off to her friends, who had taken to talking about their grandchildren all the bloody time.

Her mother also made no secret of her desire for Bridget to marry Hartley.

"Such a gentleman," she repeated ad nauseam, "and an earl, Bridget. Really, why did you let him go?"

Bridget screamed at her mother that she hadn't let him go and that she would get him back. She just had to remove his little girlfriend from the picture.

She had overheard someone in the crowd whisper how pretty Lucy was. Idiot. Bridget looked at her hands gripping the steering wheel. She was shaking with rage.

Yes, Lucy Summers would pay dearly. By the time she was finished with her, Hartley wouldn't want her, and no one else would either.

Exclusive:
Gotcha!

Lucy had risen at 9 a.m., two hours after she normally got up, but she allowed herself a lie-in because it was Sunday.

She showered leisurely, lathering on Jo Malone Nectarine Blossom and Honey shower gel and Thalgo skin exfoliator.

She rubbed a generous amount of Crème de la Mer over her face and blasted dry her long blonde hair before smoothing on just a touch of gloss serum. Perk of the job: an endless supply of cosmetic samples. Some of the girls in her office displayed an unattractive greed when it came to freebies, constantly dropping unsubtle hints to designer houses that they'd love their new-season bag . . . and there was such a good chance they'd include it in their "must have" section.

Lucy cringed at their phone conversations: "Yah, yah, darling, the new Westwood tweeds are to die for. If you have any spares, don't be shy — send them over. That way I can, like, show them to my boss and she might go for an entire feature on them."

Lucy found some of her colleagues' blagging embarrassing, and she was given plenty of freebies anyway, as well as generous discounts and bits and pieces from sample sales. For a genuine fashion lover, it was a dream come true.

Lucy often wondered how the girls at the magazine could afford an entire wardrobe of the season's designer must-have clothes and different accessories every day. She wondered if there was a secret closet and they all had a key, although that was doubtful given that no one in the office could keep a secret if their Prada baguettes depended on it. Perhaps they were all trust-fund kids with a rich daddy on speed-dial. A few of the nicer girls had told Lucy her outfits were the cause of envy at work — where did she find the little vintage Westwood and Dior numbers and how did she match everything so perfectly with new-season stock?

The truth was that Lucy knew every vintage and second-hand shop in a five-mile radius. She could never afford to drape herself in full-price designer gear. She had a talent for spotting worn pieces and restoring them lovingly with fabric she picked up, or paying her favourite seamstress at a tiny shop near her flat to work her magic. Lucy refused to be a labels snob and proudly told the girls her shirt was from Marks & Spencer or Topshop rather than a named piece which cost ten times as much.

Lucy picked out her favourite Marc Jacobs summer dress. The silk fabric felt wonderful as she pulled it over her head and let it slide over her body. The muted green floral pattern was feminine and fresh, perfect for her date with Hartley. They were going for cream tea at Claridge's that afternoon.

She brewed some fresh Columbian coffee. Lucy normally stuck to green tea, but treated herself to a little caffeine on weekends. She squeezed several oranges and grapefruit into a jug and poured a glass before remembering to pick up the Sunday papers which would have been dropped outside the flat door.

News of the World for gossip, the *Sunday Times* for every supplement known to man and the *Mail on Sunday* for something in between.

Lucy's heart stopped as she took in the front page of the *Mail* staring up at her.

BATTLE OF THE SOCIALITES AT ASCOT

Below the headline was a flattering head shot of Lucy — taken two weeks earlier at a charity ball — and one of Lady Bridget. A most unattractive shot with her eyes half closed and lips pursed.

"Oh my God," Lucy whispered.

Her heart raced as she turned to page thirteen for the main story — a commentary by the social editor, Gerard Bosworth, renowned for his outspoken opinions and lack of interest in making famous friends.

We knew competition was stiff to win the heart of Britain's most eligible bachelor, Hartley Balmyle, but we didn't realize society beauties were prepared to fight over him.

Yesterday's events at Ascot took a nasty turn when the Earl's former girlfriend, Lady Bridget Beames, was introduced to his new love interest.

33

The green-eyed monster became guest of honour in the Royal Enclosure as Bridget tried to ridicule her fairer (and dare we say it, more beautiful) rival.

Despite her title, it was fashion writer Lucy Summers who behaved like a lady on the day, smiling pleasantly throughout Bridget's verbal assault.

But the blonde butterfly proved she is more than a pretty face, delivering a deadly put-down that outclassed bitchy Bridget.

One to Lucy Summers . . . nil to Lady Bridget Beames.

As Lucy took in the words on the page, her alarm washed away and a smile of relief spread across her face. She had come out well. How funny. Lady Bridget, for all her connections, money, title and standing, appeared bitter and rude. Who said the newspapers always got it wrong, she chuckled to herself.

What about Hartley? Would he think this was all her doing? Oh God, he hated publicity. What if he was furious? What if he blamed her?

Bloody hell, I'm on the front page of the *Mail on Sunday*. Lucy hated being at the centre of attention, but had to admit it felt rather pleasant to read an accurate description of Lady Bridget.

"Max, Max, wake up. You have to see this."

Armed with fruit juice in one hand and the newspaper in the other, Lucy used her right hip to push open her sister's bedroom door.

"Jesus," Lucy said as the stench of alcohol overpowered her. "Max, I can smell you before I see you. Good night, then?"

Max wasn't quite ready, or able, to respond as her sister's voice cut through her semi-comatose drink-induced sleep. As she raised her head slowly from her pillow and opened her eyes, Max registered with depression two sure signs she was in for a terrible hangover.

First, she had dry-eye syndrome. So severely was her body dehydrated the moisture had drained from her eyes.

Secondly, her tongue felt like a mouldy slice of bread which had put out a thousand cigarettes. Must stop bloody smoking when pissed.

"Oh Max, you look dreadful."

"Thanks, Luce," Max croaked with as much sarcasm as she could muster.

"No really, Max, you look bloody awful. One of your eyes is closed."

"Oh fuck. Right. Don't worry; it normally opens after I've had a shower."

As Max focused on her sister, she noted with a mix of admiration and envy just how radiant she looked.

Like a vision out of a Herbal Essences shampoo ad, her fresh-smelling, white-blonde hair was clipped effortlessly at the nape of her long elegant neck.

Her figure-hugging, knee-length floral dress was both refined yet sexy, an understated Marc Jacobs. How come she always smelled so good?

Envy aside, most of all Max felt love for her big sister, who was always there in her time of need. Even if 90 per cent of the time that meant offering her fluids to alleviate her hangover. Who would ever think they were sisters, Max thought as she forced a lopsided smile to reassure Lucy.

Well, half-sisters, as they had different dads. But with no other siblings, Max had never entertained the thought they were anything other than sisters and best friends.

Max was full of life and always in trouble, as wild as Lucy was sensible. Max was beautiful, like a petite doll, while Lucy was graceful and refined. Each sister longed a little to be like the other. Each sister adored the other.

Lucy stood at five foot eight, a good four inches taller than Max. She was elegant, poised and always immaculate. At thirty-one she was two years older than Max. Her natural blonde hair turned almost white in summer and at its darkest was a light honey in the cold winter months. Her eyes were a mesmerizing piercing blue.

Something was different, Max thought. Lucy was normally so calm, so relaxed, but today she looked excited. The younger sister propped herself up on her elbows, avoiding eye contact with the mirror opposite her bed.

"So, how was Ascot?"

Lucy bit her lip. "Oh you know . . . Ascot. I met Hartley's ex, Lady Beames. Max, wait until you see the newspaper. I don't think she'll ever forgive me."

Shagger Sheri Saves the Day

"Sheri has called three times already," Emma told Max as she sat down at her desk.

Shagger Sheri was the nickname the paper had coined after publishing a string of her lurid kiss-and-tell sex stories. Once a promising topless model, reputable photographers wouldn't touch her now after five ops had left her with comically huge tits.

Oh good, just what I need to kick the day off, Max thought as she negotiated yet another hangover. Last night she had reviewed the opening night of Arctic Monkeys' European tour at the Carling Academy. The band's after-party with free bar got the better of her plans for an early night.

One too many Jack Daniels and Cokes had clouded her judgement and somewhere around 2 a.m. she made a booty call to Phil, a guy she had seen for about a month before ending it a few weeks back when she realized that other than an animalistic sexual attraction they had nothing in common.

She never did quite figure out what he did for a living — a bit of bar work, the odd gig DJing at his local club in Camden, which is where they had met. At thirty-three, he was living a Peter Pan existence, poised always for the next phone call to party. Mind you, so was Max, but then that was her job. He had piercing blue eyes, broad shoulders and wispy brown hair that curled slightly over his forehead. Max was, at base level, hugely attracted to him and the sex was amazing. That and the fact he made the infamously well-endowed Tommy Lee look like a button mushroom had kept her interested. But Max found him intensely boring — and a bit whiffy. He was into "nature" and despite drinking like a fish — and Max had no doubt he had a fondness for the white stuff (though he had never indulged in front of her) — he loved to talk of his love of everything organic. This included no deodorant, with Phil preferring to smell the way nature intended. But at 2a.m., with blurred vision, which made it difficult to find his name in her phone, and impaired logic, Max invited him to her flat. Twenty minutes later he was inside her.

Phil was on top, Max pulling his firm bum into her. Biting her lip, Phil told Max he had been dreaming of fucking her since they split. Drunkenly, Max told him she had wanted him badly too, but even as she said the words they made her cringe and she knew she had lost interest. She tried to concentrate on him inside her, grabbing his peachy buttocks so he was as deep as possible. She didn't want love with Phil. He was good for wild sex, for making her abandon her senses momentarily. But tonight it wasn't working. Even his perfected skill of rubbing her nipples, the part of her body she found most sensitive, between his saliva-moistened thumb and first finger was having no effect. She'd had too much to drink to climax and had caught a whiff of his body odour, sour and pungent after vigorous missionary. Turning her head to the side, she let him thrust away, making small groans in the right places until she felt his spasm and heard his breathless grunts.

"Wow, babes, that was awesome."

"Sure was," Max said, lacking conviction.

"I was thinking, babes, me and you . . . we make a great team. I miss you."

Get the fuck out of my flat, you malodorous twat, Max wanted to scream but instead feigned exhaustion.

"Let's talk in the morning, Phil. I'm really tired." She smiled, squeezing his hand before turning from him and curling into the foetal position. Within seconds she was fast asleep, her last thought a daydream of finding her soulmate: in a scene a decade from now she was eating tapas and drinking wine on holiday with a man she loved and their children.

Come the shrill tone of her alarm at 8.30 a.m. and a killer headache, Max felt almost sorry for Phil, who was gazing into her eyes as she woke. Perhaps there was something wrong with her. Why was it she behaved more like a boy — losing interest in guys, preferring to be by herself than with someone she didn't adore, fancy, love? Did the man of her dreams even exist?

Max smiled as she remembered her phone call with Suzie the day before.

"Guess what?" her friend had screamed so loudly Max had to hold the phone away from her ear.

"You've slept with one of your laminated three?" Max asked. She'd never heard her sound so excited and had more than an inkling of what was coming.

"I'm engaged. David proposed!"

Everyone at the showbiz desk had heard. Max laughed.

"I've got to go — I think David's mum is trying to get through — but you'll be my bridesmaid?"

"Of course. I'm so happy for you."

And she was. Rarely had she seen a couple as suited or as in love as Suzie and David. He put up with her getting so drunk he had to carry her home; but that was a monthly occurrence now as opposed to twice-weekly when they first met a few years ago. But she looked after him in so many other ways, driving him on at work, giving him more confidence than anyone ever had.

Another school friend had got engaged a few weeks ago. Max wondered if this was the start of the deluge. Being fussy was one thing, but what if Max was still ignoring calls after a second date a decade from now? Maybe she'd end up like some Patsy from *Ab Fab*: fag in mouth, bottle of Jack in hand, slouched on a sofa while all her girlfriends bounced their babies on their knees at the monthly book club. Fuck, what a thought.

She and Suzie, Max's height and frame with tousled mousy-brown shoulder-length hair and green eyes, had been partners in crime ever since school. Suzie had studied fashion design at Dundee University's Duncan of Jordanstone and moved to London around the same time as Max. For years they had met every week or two at the Italian restaurant chain Strada near Oxford Circus, sometimes joined by other friends, and made their way through bottles of house red and packs of Marlboro Lights.

After Suzie had met David, they still kept their Strada appointment. But when David was offered a new job as an accountant in Glasgow, she agreed to move back to Scotland with him. Since then, Max had seen Suzie only every couple of months. Sometimes she craved her company. But it was always the same when they met up. Time or distance could never touch a great friendship.

So there Suzie was with the man of her dreams while Max was still looking for love after more than a decade. She had tasted love after falling passionately for Alfie when she was just seventeen. He was two years older. They dated for three years and split because Max's feelings had weakened and she wanted so much to experience the world. She knew that by staying with him she would end up resenting him for clipping her wings. Alfie did not share her drive to succeed and had started to question why she spent so much time working at the local paper, the Dundee *Courier*. He wanted to settle down with Max and have babies, but at just twenty Max knew she had to live her life fully first. Taking a job on a local Manchester paper had signalled the end of their relationship. She knew she had broken his heart and in truth she too was devastated, but she knew it was what she had to do.

Since splitting with Alfie, Max had dated for six months here, a year there, with no shortage of flings in between. But nothing had come close to the attraction, then raw love she had first felt for Alfie. He had inherited his Brazilian mother's grace — those beautiful big brown eyes, her silky black hair and creamy caramel skin. His broad back and muscular tall frame came from his father, who had grown up locally in Lochee in Dundee and had won some acclaim as a boxer in his youth. A delicious mix, unlike anyone Max had known. Perhaps, she often thought, he was the love of her life and she would never match it again. Everyone had laughed when she said she was in love; they said she was too young. But Max knew it had been real. If she found such happiness with another man now she would have no hesitation in making a commitment, but she didn't want to settle for less.

Looking at Phil beside her, she smiled faintly, kissed him on the cheek and said she had to rush. Watching as he pulled on his jeans, she caught another whiff. She hoped she would never call him again, no matter how wasted she was. When he left moments later, she was overcome with guilt, with a grubby feeling the shower did not wash away. She was on the pill — mainly to regulate her over-frequent periods — but he could have given her chlamydia, which she always thought sounded like a posh girl's name, or worse. And what about him? He deserved better too. He deserved someone who wanted to be with him come the morning. Panic overcame Max as she hailed a taxi to work, a feeling of intense self-loathing rising within.

But here she was, bang on 10a.m., at the large rectangular desk which accommodated another three showbiz reporters, Derek, Simon and Jade, and their editor, Claire, and secretary, Emma. Professional hat on, she got down to the business of finding stories.

"Max, did you hear me?" Emma's voice cut into Max's thoughts. "Sheri's called for you three times."

"Thanks, Emma," Max said, wondering what star Sheri would have slept with last night for another juicy kiss-and-tell to fund her Champagne Charlie lifestyle. Or maybe she was just chasing payment for her last story.

Max smiled as she logged on to Facebook and noted Suzie's status update: "Suzie is . . . engaged!!!!"

"Oh and these came through from Splash agency in LA," Emma said, reaching over her computer to hand Max a pile of A4-size photos.

"Jesus, Emma," Max groaned, glancing at them. "You want to see last night's tequila make a comeback?"

Emma laughed while filing her nails and Max studied the pictures of the latest celebrity heiress exiting a car wearing a short skirt and no knickers. By the time the snaps made it into the paper, a little fig leaf would cover her privates. But for now Max had full view of the unedited version. Eugh. Disgusting. But Max couldn't help squinting to see her bits. Wow. No hair. Wonder if she waxed. Oh God, the pain. Was it worth it, to have bits that looked like ludicrously inflated collagen lips? She shouldn't be looking at a stranger's bits, but what the hell? It was no doubt a PR stunt to get some publicity. Like so many stars who moaned about their privacy being invaded, she actually loved the attention and judged her success on how many column inches she took up. Why else live in the paparazzi centre of the world that was Los Angeles and holiday in that other paparazzi magnet, London? Why else choose to stumble out of a club known to have hundreds of photographers waiting outside to snap stars and flash your undercarriage in its full glory?

Right, on to Shagger Sheri, another woman who was economical with ladylike positions when getting out of cars. Max didn't need to look up her number, she knew it by heart. Dabbing Touche Éclat concealer under her eyes as she punched the number into her desk phone, she thought about Sheri.

She must have paid Sheri at least twenty grand in the last six months, ever since persuading her to change allegiance from a rival daily paper to which she normally sold her kiss-and-tell stories. How easily loyalty could be bought in the vacuous world of Z-list celebrity when you offered to pay more.

Max pulled down her white DKNY summer dress so it was a little closer to her knees than her bottom and buttoned her pastel-green Urban Outfitters cardigan at the top. There was still an old-fashioned "time and place" logic on the editorial floor among the middle-aged male reporters, although showbiz writers, unlike news reporters, were not expected to look like they were suited for a funeral.

Max waited for Sheri to pick up.

"Hello?" came a croaky voice.

"Hi, it's Max."

"Awright, darlin', 'ow are you?" Sheri's Essex whine grated at the best of times. But with the taste of vodka and tequila still in her mouth Max found it almost unbearable.

"Wait till you hear this, darlin'. Guess who I shagged last night. Go on, you'll never get it."

"David Beckham?"

"Na, one day, Max, then you'll give me fifty grand, right?"

"Sure will, Sheri. Listen, I've got an interview in a minute," Max lied. "Sorry to hurry you, but . . ."

"OK, OK, mate. I only bloody had sex with Kirk Kelner."

Really? Kirk Kelner?

Now that was a result for Shagger Sheri. She had slept with so many famous football players and soap actors she had become a marked woman, avoided like the plague by any British star who ever read a newspaper.

She'd been in so many tabloids, showing off her 32GG falsies, that men knew their wives or girlfriends would find out and they stayed away no matter how much dirty sex they wanted.

But of course American Kirk Kelner would have had no idea who this big-boobed beauty with dead coke-fuelled eyes was when they met at whatever party they had been at the night before.

It made sense. Kirk had stayed on in London after promoting *Man of Steel 4* to start filming his next movie, some romantic comedy with Jennifer Aniston.

He would be keen to sample the single life with a string of obliging English girls. Sheri was hardly girlfriend material. But she was just right for a one-night stand for the Hollywood star.

Max thought of her scoop that had landed Mr Kelner on the front page of the paper.

"WORLD EXCLUSIVE: Kelner Cheated With Nanny" had been the headline. The story told how the movie star admitted to friends that he had slept with his children's nanny behind his wife's back.

The picture desk had dug out a snap of their nanny, a twenty-two-year-old Spanish girl called Maria, and tracked her down to her mum's house in Madrid where she had fled, no doubt with a wad of money from Kirk to keep quiet. It hadn't been enough because the nanny had broken down in front of the paper's Spanish correspondent and told how used and dirty Kirk had made her feel . . . with the help of a cheque from the paper for £10,000. He had declared his undying love for her, promising to leave his supermodel wife. But he had dropped her the instant his wife found out.

Thankfully, Max's picture hadn't accompanied her name in the first exposé. So if Kirk had read the paper that day he'd have had no idea "Alison the children's author" was in fact Maxine Summers, tabloid hack.

Although the reporter in Spain had his name on the nanny's confession, Max was credited within the office for bringing in the original story.

Max had been the toast of the showbiz desk after the stories broke. Her ability to work a room, get in any VIP enclosure and talk to anyone was becoming legendary among her fellow journalists. She'd been given a pay rise and told to make the most of her expense account by taking pals to dinner, so long as they went to the right restaurants, like Nobu, the Ivy, the Caprice or the Wolseley, where she might see stars misbehaving. Far better to be there with a chance of getting a story than in front of the television at home, her boss, Claire, had told her.

But her last front page, on Kelner, had been two weeks ago and she hadn't had a big hit since. For all the perks of her job, her boss expected at least one big exclusive every week in return.

"Ten grand. Minimum." Shagger Sheri's whining voice cut through her thoughts. For her, life was about fame and money. That and getting on the guest list for China White, Funky Buddha, Penthouse, Embassy, Boujis, the Wellington or any other club in which she could snare a star. The likes of Soho's Groucho Club for media movers and shakers or Maddox, full of wealthy Arabs, trust-fund kids and the rich Euro set, were, however, too discerning and off-limits.

But Maddox was a place she'd like to go every night. Even if there were no stars, it was heaving with money. Sheri had managed to get in once, when a rich Arab spotted her at China White and invited her, along with three other girls. Tables competed for the highest bar bill. Rich Russians would think nothing of ordering jeroboams of vodkas for £800, while the fabulous-looking girls they'd invited gyrated in their tiny dresses to the blaring music.

47

Sheri was expert at letting men know what the night had in store if they chose her over the dozens of other wannabes grinding to the R 'n' B music beside their table. She would sit opposite them, lick her collagen-enhanced top lip smeared with Bobbi Brown pink gloss and open her legs. With her micro dress hitched a few inches, it was easy to see she was commando and completely shaven. After that, the men would go over to their male pals, nudge, wink, point at Sheri and escort her out of the club.

Then it was back to a nearby hotel — often the Sanderson at Sheri's request because she'd already tipped off a photographer to get there for a snap of her and her famous pull — and fuck each other senseless. Well, when the men weren't too wasted on drink and drugs to get it up.

More than once Sheri had woken feeling raw, her mind flashing back to the previous evening's debauchery. To hungry, hard sex where he threw her on the bed, made a feeble attempt at foreplay by squeezing her inflated breasts and entered her angrily.

Sometimes they asked to take pictures of her naked on their mobile phones. She knew it would flash on the phones of dozens of footballers or soap stars. She liked that thought.

Sometimes they asked if a friend could join them. Sheri, fuelled by a few lines and expensive champagne, always agreed. She wanted to please them and she wanted a killer story to sell the next day. Sometimes they didn't ask. Their friends would just happen to turn up at the hotel room and join in. Of course, they'd been text messaged on their mobile phones by their pal with details of the hotel, room number and positions that had been done so far. Sheri pretended not to know any of this.

She never said no. Occasionally, she wondered what they would do if she refused. She had no doubt some would take what they wanted anyway, some would find someone who would give it to them and others would return home to their wife or girlfriend and wake them.

Rarely did these guys call her again. When they did they were fuelled with champagne and cocaine and wanted a debauched night of sex, sometimes with other girls they'd picked up. So why shouldn't she make some cash through the stories? They were using her as much as she was using them.

"Sheri, I'll see what I can do," Max told her. "You know you get the best rates from me. Whatever you do, don't tell a soul. Where are you?"

"I've just left his hotel room. I'll be back at my flat in twenty minutes."

"OK, I'll see you there in half an hour. Have a think about the juiciest details from last night. You know the score — the juicier it is the more cash I can get you, OK?"

"Right, doll. See you then."

God, this job could be sordid, Max thought. But she was grateful to get out of the office and into the warm summer's day.

Hold the Front Page

Max went over to Bermondsey, just south of the Thames, and made her way to the flat that Sheri shared with a gorgeous black topless model called Envy.

"Awright, darlin'," Sheri said, air-kissing Max's cheeks as she led her through to her sitting room.

Max had sat on Sheri's sofa several times. Each time she admired the surprising taste with which the flat had been decorated, with wooden floors, cream sofa and chair, matching cream walls and a huge brown rug as a centrepiece.

The surroundings said a lot about Sheri. Yes she was an airhead, caught up in the hedonistic world of celebrity. Having developed a dependence on coke — a few years back it was once a week, now it was most nights . . . and days — making money from sex stories had become an obsession, with Sheri feeling it was the only thing that validated her. But beneath it all was a reasonably intelligent young woman. In a different life she would have gone to college or university and had a good career. She would also have had a natural beauty untouched by the surgeon's knife.

As Sheri sat on the floor like a child, with her knees under her chin, Max noticed how awful she looked.

With sunken eyes framed by dark circles and the remnants of last night's heavy eyeliner, she had aged ten years from the Sheri the world knew. The brazen, perfectly made-up girl with huge boobs and dripping in bling looked a mess this morning.

As if reading her mind Sheri said: "I feel awful, Max. Not been to sleep — so much coke I was buzzin' all night. You want a coffee?"

Max said yes and Sheri, unrecognizable from her kiss-and-tell pictures in a baggy navy tracksuit, disappeared into her kitchen.

"Thank God you ain't brought a photographer, Max. I'd have said no," Sheri shouted through to Max. "I've got some right nice shots from a lads' mag shoot a few months ago. You can use them, yeah? I don't want no snapper taking pictures of me looking like this."

"Should be fine, Sheri," Max assured her as Sheri placed two steaming mugs of instant coffee on the small table beside the sofa.

"Ready to start?"

"If you're ready to pay," Sheri said automatically. She was in the grip of the familiar paranoid comedown of a cocaine hangover.

"You know the score, Sheri. I'll get you as much as I can. If there are great details it will make the front page, then you're looking at up to ten grand. Can't say fairer than that."

Sheri looked reassured. As she clasped her mug of hot coffee, the shaking seemed to subside.

They both knew the questions and answers inside out. Stick to complimenting the star — huge penis, rampant appetite for sex — and they rarely sued.

As Kirk Kelner was a single man, he had nothing to lose and everything to gain from the world knowing how hot he was in bed. His film company would be happy with the publicity; his female fan base would grow. And so would Sheri's bank balance.

Max tied her long brown hair back with the elastic hair-band she always wore on her wrist, crossed her tanned legs and clicked on her tape recorder.

"Tell me how you met Kirk, Sheri."

"Well, Wednesday's a good night at Kabaret club in the West End so I went along to meet me mates."

"And Kirk was there?"

"Yeah, he was at a private table that was roped off."

"So how did you get to meet him?"

Sheri cast her mind back to the night before. She knew the security man guarding the club's VIP section — a tiny area with four private booths. She couldn't remember his name, but he was in his mid thirties with a beefcake build and tanned face,

When he told her to get lost she politely reminded him that he hadn't been so quick to get rid of her when she'd given him a blow job in the staff toilets a few months back — in return for instant access to the VIP enclosure where football players were celebrating some victory.

The guard narrowed his eyes and took her in.

"Fuck, it's you. You've changed your hair. Listen, my boss is here tonight. I can't let you in." A slow smile crept across his face. "And, sadly, I can't escape for some fun."

"I wasn't offerin'," Sheri retaliated. "Now let me in before I tell your boss how you swap favours for oral."

The guard was suddenly deadly serious.

"Shit. You bitch." With that, he lifted the red rope to his left and let her in.

Sheri suddenly snapped out of the flashback. To get in the paper she had to paint a far more glamorous and romantic picture of what had happened.

She smiled at Max. "How did we start talkin'? There was an instant attraction as soon as our eyes locked. Kirk is unbelievably sexy in the flesh. He took one look at me and told the guard to invite me over to his table."

"And how did things progress?"

The truth was that Sheri asked Kirk whether he minded if she joined him and two male friends while she waited for a mate.

Through his beer-and-champagne-goggled eyes Kirk had smirked as he took Sheri in. Huge tits, like overripe watermelons, were almost totally on display, spilling out of a black PVC corset that was teamed with a black denim miniskirt barely covering her pert arse. Her orange fake tan made her look bronzed and toned in the dim light of the club.

Winking at his pals, Kirk had slurred his approval and asked the waiter to bring another glass so she could share their rosé Taittinger champagne.

Sheri made it clear who she was interested in, homing in on the movie star and ignoring his pals.

Sharing a dirty joke, she discreetly took his hand and placed it carefully under her skirt. Kirk's eyes suddenly came into focus and brightened as he felt her smooth damp pussy. Excusing herself to go to the ladies, she told Kirk to follow so they could leave.

That was what actually happened, but who wanted to hear the callous version of how she marked her man and got him? Sheri pushed her hair behind her ears as she readied herself for the airbrushed version, the one both she and Kirk would rather the world read.

"Progress? Well, we chatted for hours about his career. He was such a gent and treated me to lovely champagne. We had so much in common and I felt he was crying out for company. Even the sexiest man in the world gets lonely sometimes and he's had such a hard time. Kirk insisted his chauffeur drop me off so I got home safely. But as soon as we were in the car we couldn't keep our hands off each other."

"And then you went back to his hotel?"

"Yes, we were like animals. Sometimes he was full of passion, sometimes so tender and loving."

In truth, Kirk had barely been able to make it to his penthouse suite at the Dorchester, stumbling all the way. Drunkenly they entered his room and she led him over to the biggest bed she had ever seen. It was covered in the finest white Egyptian cotton.

Sheri undressed him quickly, realizing he was so drunk he could crash out at any second. But she kept his attention by pulling her enormous boobs over her PVC corset. Slipping out of her skirt, she stood before him in her thigh-high black leather boots with her corset around her stomach.

Kirk sat up, grabbed her breasts and stared at them intently. With an expert efficiency, she manoeuvred herself on top of Kirk to straddle him. His medium-sized cock already hard, he entered her, his eyes rolling skywards as he let out a groan of pleasure. Kirk never once looked at Sheri's face, transfixed by her gravity-defying breasts.

Grinding down on him, she lifted herself up before plunging down, sitting upright and throwing back her blonde mane of extensions alluringly, in case he looked up from her breasts. He was full of desire, transfixed by her. And yes, Sheri was making Kirk bloody Kelner feel this way, she thought. But barely a minute had passed before Kirk let out a loud grunt and flopped his head on the bed, signalling the end of their session.

Sheri took a sip of her coffee then smiled at Max.

"His lips were so soft and kissed every part of my body. I still have tremors when I think about how he made me feel. Like I was the most beautiful thing he had ever seen. After hours of foreplay he entered me. I have to say he's a big movie star in every way. He was insatiable and we made love non-stop throughout the night. His body is incredible — rippling with muscles. Kirk is all man."

Sheri stopped and sighed.

"He poured champagne all over my body and licked every drop off, making me squirm in ecstasy. I came at least ten times. Eventually, our bodies spent, we fell asleep in each other's arms."

"And in the morning, what happened then?"

In the morning what really happened was that while Kirk had snored off the booze, Sheri had lain awake for hours, buzzing from the cocaine she had taken for courage to blackmail her way to Kirk Kelner. She was also buzzing from perhaps her biggest conquest yet. The footballers she'd slept with had netted her between £2,000 and £5,000 here and there. But Kelner was a global superstar. She would make a fortune — from Max then from some magazine for a follow-up.

Around 10a.m. Kirk had woken with a start as his alarm buzzed.

As he turned to face her, Sheri took in for the first time how utterly beautiful he was. Like a Greek God wrapped in the white sheet. She could just make out his rippling stomach muscles under the cotton.

"Hi, honey," he croaked. "Erm, listen, this is a bit embarrassing but I can't remember a goddamn thing. What's your name? . . . Right, Sheri, babes, I don't mean to be rude but my manager will be here in ten minutes. Can I give you some money for a taxi? Thanks, honey. Would you mind leaving, like, now?"

Sheri looked at Max with a dreamy smile. "In the morning Kirk woke me with fresh coffee and a croissant. We kissed tenderly before I had to leave. Maybe I'll see him again but he works so hard I'll understand if we don't. Whatever happens, neither of us will forget that amazing night for the rest of our lives."

After a pause to make sure Sheri was finished Max smiled, clicked off her recorder and drained her mug.

"Great! Thanks, Sheri. One more thing. Did you remember to get evidence? It's so complimentary he'll never sue . . . but better to be safe."

"Oh yeah, I took a picture of us at the club on my mobile. And one of him sleepin' with me next to him. Oh, and one of his dick — couldn't resist."

As Sheri showed her the pictures, Max couldn't help laughing. "OK, Sheri, that should be fine."

The next morning, Sheri was delighted to see the front page of the *Daily News*.

WORLD EXCLUSIVE:
SHERI: KIRK IS THE BEST I'VE EVER HAD
(AND SHE'S HAD A FEW)

Today glamour girl Sheri Jones lifts the lid on her night of passion with Hollywood heart-throb Kirk Kelner.

In an explosive interview Sheri, 28 (pictured, left, in raunchy lingerie), tells how the muscle *Man of Steel 4* star:

SATISFIED her like never before

LICKED champagne from her famous curves

WAS unstoppable in bed and carried on ALL night.

Turn to page 7 for Sheri's full story.

Max was once again the toast of her paper. But as she stared down at the front page she was aware that the buzz she had once got was diluted. She dismissed the thought . . . Parties every night, mixing with stars, a huge salary and expense account. And she did love socializing and meeting new people, always seeing the fun in a party. The relentless free bars helped give her the confidence to speak to the celebs most people only got to glimpse through the pages of *Heat* or *Grazia*. Young, free and single. This was the time of her life to party hard and write celeb stories. And that's what the public wanted. She was living the life . . . So why was she feeling so underwhelmed, so indifferent? Perhaps she just needed another great story.

When Lucy Met Hartley

It was funny, Lucy considered, that when you were in those first magical months of a relationship, boredom vanished. All those times alone — tedious tube journeys, impatient waits for late appointments — no longer existed when your mind kept floating off to replay every detail from the night before.

Lucy found herself thinking about the night she met Hartley just a few weeks ago, one Friday sometime after midnight at Annabel's members' club for London's elite.

It attracted a different crowd from the trendy celeb hangouts. There were more of the well-to-do blue-suit brigade than must-be-seen designer-label junkies.

On the night Lucy had met Hartley, she had been for dinner at Nobu with Amy, her best friend from Oxford University, whose Kashmiri parents had gifted her the most exquisite looks. Lucy could never tire of hearing her soft but distinct Manchester accent, from the city her parents had moved to shortly before she was born. Amy, with her sparkling skin, shiny black bob and wide hazel eyes, had graduated with a First but had never taken up the high-salary job she had always imagined her degree would lead to.

She had hooked up with a politics student called James de Vosse in their second year and now they were engaged. James was an old Etonian whose upbringing was poles apart from Amy's. Somehow they seemed to work together but Amy had confided that she was worried about becoming a Stepford Wife like so many of the women in James's set. Lucy was sure this would never happen. They had known each other for thirteen years and Amy hadn't compromised who she was one bit. She had her own mind, roots and style, which would never leave her.

After seeing off a bottle of Chablis over edamame, tuna sashimi and black cod, they giggled as they looked around the restaurant and tried to figure out what cupboard Boris Becker had chosen for his famous quickie with a stranger, which had lasted all of two minutes and resulted in his love child.

Instead of winding down with green tea, they had decided on a nightcap at Annabel's. Amy called James, who had membership, and asked him to phone ahead to ensure the girls were not turned away.

Once inside, Lucy found herself surrounded by the set she had become so used to at the magazine: the aloof group of girls who had known each other from birth. Most of them were born with a title, or would marry someone who could give them one. Their outfits ranged from understated black Miu Miu dresses decorated with a string of pearls, to long flowing skirts with tight angora or cashmere cardigans.

"Do you think that, in the eyes of the law, wearing anything by H&M would be a crime?" Lucy whispered to Amy at the bar, where they ordered two vodka martinis.

Lucy looked so different to the other girls, like she'd just stepped out of a magazine spread, yet somehow she was also the most natural-looking woman in any room.

Other girls provided the background to a scene in which she seemed always to be bathed in a radiant spotlight. Most enchanting of all was that Lucy seemed to have no knowledge of her magnetic presence. She was elegant and dignified but never cocksure or blasé.

Lucy's calf-length Matthew Williamson berry-pink-satin skirt clung to her curves in the style of a glamorous fifties star, and a crisp fitted white shirt from Zara was virtually indistinguishable from the new Prada range — even to the most cynical fashionista's eye.

A fashionable thick black belt which covered her entire midriff, matched with black Manolo heels, completed the flawless look.

On the inside, Annabel's was surprisingly similar to many clubs in cities up and down the country. After walking down a narrow corridor Lucy and Amy came to the square bar, where Hartley and his friends were gathered round an ice bucket of champagne. In front of the bar were cosy booths framing a dance floor.

The mood was relaxed and low-key, the room bathed in dim orange light, giving an intimate air.

Lucy knew exactly who Hartley was when she spotted him at the bar. She had read a piece in her magazine a few months earlier on the country's most eligible bachelors and he had topped the list.

Hartley lived in London, where he ran a charitable foundation, but spent at least a week each month in Scotland. Lucy's own family lived in Broughty Ferry near Dundee; it was on the east coast, like Edinburgh, and was just over an hour's drive from the capital. Of course, it was no wonder they hadn't met before. They may both have boarded at English schools and called Scotland "home" but their worlds were so different. Hartley probably didn't have a single friend outside the blue-blooded set he had grown up with.

Lucy stood back and talked to Amy while a gaggle of girls tittered and vied for his attention. She noted that in the flesh this sought-after young man was rather attractive.

He had the classic physical characteristics of the upper class. Standing at six foot, Hartley had dishevelled dark blond hair framing a cheery, rosy-cheeked face. His eyes held a boyish charm, and even the dim lights failed to hide a jovial twinkle. He reminded Lucy of a man in a grand painting — the kind you see in castles. He could have come straight out of the seventeenth century with an old-fashioned aura no amount of trendy clothes or haircuts would transform. He looked like he'd just finished riding on a chilly day and come inside for a whisky to warm up. Hartley's clothes were the staple Ralph Lauren casual uniform of chinos, open-necked shirt, V-necked fine wool jumper and Missoni boat shoes, mirrored on his old school chums.

Lucy thought he looked rather kind; but he was probably pompous, like so many of the over-privileged twits she'd met on the London fashion circuit, accompanying their stony-faced girlfriends who were on their fifth "gap year" since leaving university.

62

Lucy turned to chat to Amy, who was asking for fashion advice about an outfit to wear to an ex's wedding. What girl wouldn't want to look good enough to eat on an ex's big day?

Turning her full attention to Amy, Lucy assured her friend she would look nothing short of mouth-watering for the occasion and she had just the dress at home for her.

Lucy's indifference to Hartley, mixed with her natural beauty, attracted him. Within twenty minutes of her arrival, Hartley had introduced himself. This was most out of character for the Earl of Balmyle, who was used to sharing jokes with his chums or making polite chit-chat with the girls in their circle, most of whom he had known since he was a boy.

Hartley was unpractised at the art of approaching "new" people, preferring the easy comfort of old pals.

"Hello, are you having a good evening?"

"Yes, thank you."

"Good. I'm Hartley. Pleased to meet you."

Accepting his hand, Lucy smiled, tilting her head slightly. "Hello, Hartley. I'm Lucy. And this is my good friend Amy."

Buoyed by a few glasses of Krug, he realized he was having fun chatting to Lucy. Amy was utterly unaware of who their new companion was. She smiled politely after shaking hands and excused herself to go to the Ladies.

When Amy returned, Lucy and this chap Hartley were laughing. Encouraging, Amy thought. Lucy had been single for over a year since finishing with John, a disarmingly handsome professional rower who used his boyish charm to seduce her. He had adored Lucy. Well, for the first few months. Then his restless nature had surfaced. By their first anniversary, his rowing times had reached a worrying low, while his betrayals and boozy nights out were at an all-time high. Lucy was devastated when she learned of the other girls and told him it was over. She had been down for months afterwards, her confidence at a low.

It was time Lucy had some male attention; it was just what she needed. And this guy looked respectable and sweet. Amy winked knowingly at her friend and announced she had to leave for fear of being a terrible wreck at a breakfast meeting.

Lucy decided there was no harm in staying a little while and settled into an easy conversation with Hartley. She had been prepared to find him arrogant but he had an unexpected warm magnetism. There was something about his slightly bumbling character she found endearing. Lucy was fascinated to hear how he tried to be self-sufficient when at home on his family estate in Scotland; she found it strangely sexy that he could work the land to live, that he didn't need anything from anyone else.

Hartley stopped suddenly and smiled. Catching Lucy's confusion he leaned in close. "What a pleasure it is to meet someone who wants to listen. Don't you find so many people want only to talk about themselves?"

Lucy laughed.

"So, do you live in London?"

"I do." Lucy smiled. "In Kensington. But I'm actually from Scotland too. My family live in Broughty Ferry. Do you know it?"

"Of course — the little seaside place next to Dundee? It's beautiful. It used to be a fishing village, no?"

"That's right."

"I went out to Fat Sam's nightclub in Dundee once when I was staying with my friend Robbie over the water in Fife."

"Ah Fat Sam's — it used to be my regular haunt during uni holidays."

"Ha! You sound about as Scottish as me," Hartley teased. "What happened to your accent?"

"I grew up there but moved to Kent, to boarding school, when I was thirteen. I guess I just adopted the accent around me."

Hartley nodded. "It's a bit of a bugger speaking like this in Scotland; no one believes you're a bloody Scot, more like a Sassenach. And it takes me an age to get served at the bar — too posh to be understood apparently."

Lucy threw her head back and laughed at the thought of the Earl repeating himself over and over again in Fat Sam's. Out of the corner of her eye she noticed the girls at the bar look over to see who had caught the Earl's attention.

Touching Lucy lightly on her arm he whispered conspiratorially: "I love London, Lucy, but it's nice to meet someone who doesn't think life starts and ends here."

Lucy nodded. "And London is kept wonderful by having other beautiful places to escape to."

"Exactly." Hartley clinked his glass with Lucy's and caught her eye for a few magical seconds.

Checking her watch, Lucy realized she had been talking to Hartley for almost an hour.

"I really must be off. Like Amy, I too have work in the morning."

"Well, it's been a pleasure meeting you. I only hope I haven't been too much of a bore."

Flicking her golden hair, Lucy laughed, dazzling him with her white smile. "Not at all, it was lovely to meet you."

When he asked gingerly if he might call her, Lucy obliged with a calm smile, which hid her elation at Britain's most eligible bachelor wanting to add her number to his little black book. She corrected herself inwardly, knowing the real reason she was happy was that she liked him and wanted to see him again.

Lucy couldn't help but feel flattered. Hartley must be so used to girls hanging on his every word. He had his pick of the women who socialized in his circle.

But maybe, just maybe, he liked her . . . well . . . for her and not for trying desperately to impress him with talk of members' clubs and skiing in Aspen.

Oh God, wait until she told her boss. Lucy considered the possibilities. Either Genevieve would insist Lucy became her new best friend and ask her to be her "plus one" for all the big parties. Or she would spread it around their offices that Lucy was social climbing. Maybe she shouldn't tell her. After all, it might seem a little boastful. Then again, watching Genevieve, who was a tremendous snob and name-dropper, choke on her celery stick ("it contains less calories than you use to digest it") over lunch might just be worth it. Anyway, Hartley may tire of her. He could be overwhelmingly underwhelmed by her lack of travel, multiple gap years and inherited titles. Yet, so far, he seemed to like her just the way she was.

Max Draws the Short Straw

"Let's get this straight." Max was addressing her boss, who was sitting at the other side of the showbiz desk at the *Daily News* offices. "You want me to walk down the Kings Road — one of the busiest places in London, littered with restaurants and shops — wearing only my bra and pants?"

Her boss stifled a laugh. "Sorry, Max, it's not funny."

"Yes, it is. It's fucking hilarious," piped up Simon, Max's fellow showbiz reporter.

A few minutes earlier Claire had come out of morning conference with the various heads of department — news, features, sport, online — and the big boss, the editor of the paper, and gingerly told Max her name had come up.

"There's some woman in Sheffield," she'd explained to Max. "She's in the paper today."

Claire thumbed through the paper and opened it at a picture of a woman who looked like she'd seen better days. She was in a lacy black bra and pants in what appeared to be a changing room.

"This woman, Betty, swears that the only way to go shopping for your summer wardrobe is to wear just a bikini or underwear — with a coat on top. That way she doesn't have to take all her clothes off then put them all back on again every time she gets into a changing room."

Max took in her words. "OK, so they want me to be the girl who tries out her theory?"

"Correct."

"Why me?"

"All the paper's glamour girls are on location in Spain for a photo shoot and they want it in tomorrow's paper so . . ."

"Anyone will do?"

"Yes, I mean no . . . you have the best figure in the office."

"Oh please." Max rolled her eyes skywards. "Well, it won't be so bad — you said this woman wears a long coat to cover up, so I can too."

"Not exactly. As you know, the pictures have to tell the story and the best snaps will be of you in your bra and pants with all the builders ogling you."

Not quite what Max had had in mind when she became a showbiz writer for the country's second biggest-selling paper.

But she was smart enough — and fearless enough — to realize that, on a staff of hundreds of reporters, saying no to such a task would only count against her.

Not a black mark as such, but refusing would put her in the same category as the vast majority of writers who would never dare to do the daft things she found herself being asked to do on a weekly basis.

"OK, I'll ask the picture desk to assign a photographer and head down in a cab now."

"Good girl. Best of luck." Claire was suddenly business-like again. Max was gone from her mind, replaced by thoughts of how she could prove that Madonna wanted to adopt her fifth African baby.

It was fine for Claire. Come tomorrow, it wouldn't be her arse staring up at millions of readers around the country.

Butterflies Over Cream Tea

Hartley had been such a sweetie about the whole Ascot affair. On the day Lucy found herself front-page news, she had met him at Claridge's.

She and Max had squealed like children over the story.

"Luce, Bridget is the bloody queen bee of London's society girls," Max had told her. "No one does this to her. But my butter-wouldn't-melt sister has stuck one to the po-faced cow. Luce, I'm so proud."

Carlos, Lucy's best friend at the magazine, could barely contain his excitement. Lucy had met the one and only Carlos Santiago on her second-ever styling job for the magazine. He was a renowned PR, having made his name working for a large company that represented the likes of Madonna, Sir Paul McCartney and Kylie Minogue in Los Angeles before starting his own firm — Why Not? — with his boyfriend, Raymondo. They specialized in representing up-and-coming models, and keeping damaging headlines about their wild antics out of the papers.

The publishing house that owned Lucy's magazine and a few others — a lifestyle monthly and upmarket interior design quarterly among them — had made Carlos an offer he couldn't refuse to look after the PR for all their publications. So he worked from Lucy's office four days a week while Raymondo took charge of their other clients.

Lucy was astounded by how gorgeous Carlos was when they first met. From the stories she had heard about his reputation for getting results she had expected a gruff, ageing tyrant. You didn't get to be known as the best damage-limitation PR in London by being a pushover.

But he looked more like a male model. His body could pass for a footballer's: neat but solid and muscular. His clothes looked effortlessly thrown together yet immaculate. Carlos Santiago wore the labels, not the other way round, unlike so many women and men desperate to get the look of the moment.

Everyone wanted to know him and yet feared him in equal measure. With his name, Lucy thought he might have been Italian or Spanish but he was a black New Yorker who took no shit. Lucy guessed (Botox or face peels aside) he was not yet forty. Everything from his Armani pinstriped charcoal suit to his baby-pink Prada cravat and tan leather Gucci lace-ups looked perfect on his solid yet understated frame. He wasn't all bulk and biceps like the gym goons but there was no denying that even under a suit Carlos was in shape.

His features were a curious mix of great-looking guys, Lucy had decided. There was a hint of a young Denzel Washington, with a smattering of Jude Law — though neither comparison did him justice. And Carlos's eyes were simply mesmerizing, an impossibly bright green. He insisted they were entirely natural, nothing to do with coloured lenses, but Lucy noted the slight playful tone to his voice.

Only when he opened his mouth was it obvious that he was gay and American, with a strong Brooklyn accent. His voice was a funny mix of "New York" movie star with a bit of the George Michael lisp and dramatic rolling of the eyes thrown in whenever possible. Lucy wondered at first if it was a big joke, if he was doing his very best gay impression. But no, it was Carlos. And Lucy was delighted he was her work buddy. He was as straightforward as Genevieve was false and Lucy admired his natural talent for assessing a situation and grasping what had to be done.

They had hit it off when they'd met and he asked her where she'd got her emerald-green neck scarf.

"Topshop."

"Shut the fuck up."

Lucy laughed. "No, really. Topshop. Hi, my name's Lucy."

"Your name is Gorgeous, girlfriend," he told her. "Anyone who teams Topshop with Chloé and works it like Claudia Schiffer has my vote. Want to get some sushi?"

And from that moment Lucy knew she had at least one friend she could trust at the magazine.

The morning Lucy made front-page news, he had called and screamed down the phone: "You're a fucking star! It's always the quiet ones. You showed that bitch. Well done, baby. Champagne on me. Tell me all about it . . . no, don't . . . can't chat. Raymondo's kid from his marriage when he was straight is here. He's three and he's a friggin' psychopath. Save me every detail and I'll call later, OK? Ciao."

Lucy couldn't help but share a small sense of achievement with Max and Carlos. Amy had text-messaged her too: "My best friend the socialite, huh? U go girl! X".

But by the time her afternoon meeting with Hartley had come, Lucy was terrified.

What if he thought she'd courted the publicity? Gone out of her way to get attention?

She needn't have worried. He seemed to know exactly what had happened without her mentioning a thing. And he was so apologetic that she had had to encounter his vile ex.

When she arrived at Claridge's, Lucy had been escorted by a member of staff to a table for two. There had been no sign of Hartley.

The huge drawing room was almost full, mainly with ladies meeting up to talk about their friends. These were women in their sixties who looked amazing — thanks to a lifetime of pampering, Lucy guessed. You could almost tell some had got rid of their wrinkles with a facelift or two but the work was so discreet it left no trace, unlike the Los Angeles wind-swept look.

Lucy tried to concentrate on an enormous chandelier hanging from the centre of the ceiling and the imposing portraits of royals and dignitaries, but her mind was racing with thoughts of that morning's news.

Hartley was one of the most private people Lucy knew. He had never bragged of his wealth, title or connections and hated the idea of his personal life becoming public. Lucy, who also was intensely private, admired this for he certainly had plenty to boast about.

He had told her over dinner at the Michelin-starred Chinese restaurant Hakkasan how he'd fallen out with a close friend with whom he had boarded since he was nine because of the friend's obsession with fame.

"He'd stagger out of clubs every night knowing that photographers would talk about him — after all, he is the son of the woman who married a royal," Hartley had told her. "I thought that was stupid but he was my friend. What I couldn't forgive was when he tipped off some diary writer about where I was holding my birthday party. He knows my family. Having photographers camped outside was an intrusion — and it was not long after my father had died. That was unforgivable. I still speak to him but we'll never be close again."

Lucy liked Hartley's principles and the fact that his morals shaped the way he led his life.

Lucy wasn't like that friend. She hated the idea of fame, of being followed everywhere, of life becoming a circus. Although she had to admit she hadn't minded the *Mail on Sunday* headline one bit. But perhaps the fracas at Ascot had made it seem the only reason she was dating Hartley was . . . Oh God, what would he think?

Lucy loved Hartley's passion for his work. He had set up the Balmyle Foundation, a project which helped under-privileged youths get the training they needed to have a better start in life.

He spent three days a week in the small Chelsea offices off the Kings Road he had bought, and employed two full-time staff dedicated to raising funds and setting up projects to train apprentices who had dropped out of school with no qualifications. Normally it was down to family problems. Hartley had told Lucy about one girl whose mum was a heroin addict. Since her daughter was six, the mother had used her to pick up her drugs packages while she lay spaced out at home. By the time the girl was thirteen she was addicted too, having been offered her first hit by her mum. She was also being abused by her mother's boyfriend but, when she tried to tell her, her mum had slapped her across the face and called her a lying, jealous whore. She ran away aged fifteen and a year later came to the Balmyle Foundation for help. Two years on she was now clean and halfway through a secretarial studies course at college. Hartley used the girl, called Vanessa, as a shining example of what the Foundation could do. She often gave speeches at the fund-raising balls he held, her story never failing to touch the hearts of guests whose upbringing had been a million miles from her dark world. They forgot about sipping fine port and champagne to listen to her.

More than once Lucy had seen Hartley's eyes well up over dinner as he spoke of the lives he had helped change — and his frustration that he couldn't help hundreds more.

As well as the money he raised, he donated a tenth of his own income from various estates to his charity. Most endearing of all, he never boasted of his personal donations to friends — or indeed how hard he worked behind the scenes to raise cash. Even most of his close friends had no idea how much he gave and Lucy was touched he had bashfully confided in her. He knew more of the suffering of people whose lives could not be more different to his own than any of the pretentious waifs parading in Prada on her editorial floor.

Sometimes she caught herself daydreaming about a future with him. If only she could be like her sister, who lived for the next party, not looking and planning ahead. But it was hard to throw caution to the wind when you had been hurt before. She had trusted her ex blindly and felt such a fool for doing so. But Hartley had behaved impeccably and he was good company. Lucy found herself checking for text messages on her phone throughout the day, her heart leaping if Hartley's name appeared. He was clearly smitten by her, for now at least, hanging on her every word and showering her with flowers and compliments. Not all men are shits, Lucy told herself — something her sister had often reminded her of after "that cheating bastard" John.

Lucy had not given up on finding her soulmate. But, having turned thirty one, perhaps it was time she thought about stability, a lifelong partner.

The fact Lucy hadn't slept with Hartley was good, she reassured herself. Each time he had dropped her off at her Kensington flat they'd kissed, softly at first, with the tiniest touch of tongues. This had developed into passionate kissing, pressing into each other's bodies.

At first, Lucy had pulled away, perhaps out of fear of letting herself go. But the last time they had kissed it had been Hartley who broke off.

Maybe he was showing restraint out of respect and taking things slowly. Or maybe, as Max had suggested with that mischievous twinkle in her eyes, he was gay. Lucy had laughed. She would bet their Kensington flat on that not being a possibility. Each time they pulled up to her flat he had made her small pink nipples harden and she had felt a tingle between her legs that spread all over her body in anticipation of what was to come.

The last time she had seen him, Hartley had walked her to the door of her flat after supper and a gentle kiss had grown until both of them lost control for a few blissfully wild seconds, Lucy feeling excited at the warmth of his strong body pressing against hers. Hartley kissed her hard, pressing his mouth on to hers, letting his teeth sink into her bottom lip and creating a delightful second of pain, of wanting. God, she loved feeling wanted by him. Her longing heightened as Hartley brushed his hand over the thin material covering her hard nipples, sending a thousand tingles round her body. But as quickly as they had lost themselves in each other, the moment ended abruptly when a neighbour approached to let herself in through their communal main door. They had both composed themselves, flummoxed and red, Hartley giving a very proper and terribly British kiss as he said goodbye.

The extent of her desire for Hartley had taken Lucy by surprise.

"Hello, Lucy Lu." Hartley's booming voice came over her shoulder, making her jump.

Hartley had taken to calling her this pet name — and hearing it she instantly knew he was not angry with her.

Lucy, blushing slightly, smiled and stood up to kiss him on the cheek.

Settling down into their gilt-edged, pink-and-cream-striped armchairs, Hartley gave Lucy a wink.

"Battle of the socialites, huh?"

Lucy wished she could control the redness spreading across her cheeks.

"Darling, don't look so worried. I know what Bridget is like and I can imagine she was quite vile to you."

Hartley regretted ever going out with Bridget. Their families had known each other for ever and Bridget had always had a terrible reputation among his friends as a spoiled child who could be exceptionally rude. But when they met at a ball she had been utterly charming. She told Hartley she was often misunderstood, that she had been a brat but had grown to appreciate how lucky she was and would love to give something back. Perhaps she could play a small role in Hartley's charity work. He had warmed to Bridget and been determined to give her the benefit of the doubt. Before he knew it, Hartley was in a rather serious relationship with Bridget, who seemed to have endless plans for his weekends with her set, his set, with both of their families. He didn't mind really; she kept telling him she was just like his mother — quite the home-maker, always keen to please.

But Hartley soon began to realize she was nothing like his mother, for he could never use the words kind, generous and loving to describe Bridget. Her charm offensive began to falter until she was often just plain offensive. Once, after a few too many drinks, she told

Hartley how she had sabotaged a friend's chances of gaining membership to an exclusive polo club in Windsor by telling the president a few grossly exaggerated tales of him behaving badly at parties. Hartley was astonished by her poison. He knew he had to get out, no matter how often she told him they were two of a kind and a perfect match in every way.

"I'm so dreadfully sorry you had to go through that. All because of me, really. Do you forgive me?"

The relief on Lucy's face was visible. "Of course I do. I was worried you'd think this was my fault."

Lucy was overcome by a wave of emotion. Though they had been dating for less than a month, Hartley seemed to know instinctively who she really was, to trust her.

"Oh shush, Lucy Lu. I know what Bridget is like. You must wonder why I dated her. The thing is she was so nice to me at times. She really cared about our relationship." Hartley looked lost for words as he thumbed a button on his light blue Gant shirt. "But, well, I began to see another side. I . . . I knew she wasn't, you know, the One."

Reaching over, Hartley squeezed her hand.

Unlike some men she had dated before, he hadn't professed his undying love after two dates. He was warm and kind but had inherited the stiff upper lip of his upper-class roots.

What Hartley did — a squeeze of the hand, a warm look in his eye — meant more to Lucy than an outburst of phony emotion.

80

Perhaps she could love this man. Truly and deeply. She sensed he wanted to look after her, to protect her. How silly, she told herself, to be getting carried away so soon into their relationship. But didn't somebody once say that every girl visualized her wedding dress if the first date went well?

For as long as she could remember, Lucy had wanted to get married and have a family. She craved the security of a lifelong relationship; she had never known what it was to have the love of her own mother and father under one roof. She had been blessed with parents who loved her, indeed a mum who would do anything for her, and she thought of Fergal more as a second dad than her stepfather. But still, the situation had made her determined to get it right.

In retrospect, that's why she had stayed with her ex for so long. She felt a sense of loyalty, wanted to make it work and build something with him. This longing seemed to have made her blind for far too long to the fact that — as Max would say — he was an utter shit.

Lucy felt sure she would like the feeling of safety and security she was already starting to feel. Hartley was a simple, honest soul — not like John.

Lucy lost herself in the moment before realizing Hartley was asking her something.

"Lucy, I hope you don't think me too forward but, well . . ." Hartley suddenly seemed unsure of himself. "My friend Robbie has a place in Fife — he moved back recently from London. Charles and his girlfriend, Claudia, are going to stay with him for the weekend in a few weeks time . . . Lucy, I'd, erm, very much like to join them. With you."

Now it was Hartley who was blushing.

"Of course, I understand if you think it's too much." Hartley looked at the floor as his voice trailed off.

"Hartley," Lucy said softly, smiling when his eyes met hers, "it would be my pleasure."

He broke out into a relieved smile and laughed heartily.

"And I have an invitation for you," Lucy went on. "Clarissa has invited us for dinner. I kind of promised we'd go."

Hartley looked at Lucy. What had he done to deserve this beautiful, thoughtful girl?

She didn't seem to know how devastatingly gorgeous she was. No man in the room could keep his eyes off her. Yet she seemed blissfully unaware, making him feel like the centre of her world.

God, he hoped she felt a fraction of the feelings for him that he felt for her.

Those hips, that tiny waist, her long graceful neck. He felt the familiar tingling in his groin that came whenever he thought of her. He scrutinized her floral dress. Square-necked with not a hint of cleavage and a hemline below her knee. Refined and modest. So why was it the sexiest dress he'd ever seen?

No, he must act like a gentleman. Lucy was different from any girl he'd known. She wasn't obsessed with trading names of mutual friends, or finding out what societies and clubs he could introduce her to.

Hell, she was the first woman whom he'd really laughed with. She made fun of him, ruffling his hair and telling him his voice made the Queen sound common. She was constantly teasing him that no matter how long he took to get ready he always had the look of a dishevelled bumbler — and she told him that was one of her very favourite things about him. She was so stylish and feminine — more elegant than any titled girl he'd met.

He couldn't wait to take her home to Edinburgh, a city she seemed to love just as much as he did.

Lucy knew Edinburgh well. She'd lost count of the times she'd visited the castle on school holidays with her mum and Max. And she had seen a different side to the city when she had visited as a student and stayed with friends studying at the university. Walks to Murrayfield to see Scotland play England at rugby, and invariably lose in the Six Nations cup; taking in the wonderful smell of beer hops that settled like a welcoming blanket over the city. Like Hartley, she had climbed the Pentlands and Arthur's Seat. She had done her Christmas shopping in Jenners and Harvey Nics too. Maybe they had passed each other and never known.

She was constantly surprising him. Like last weekend, when he had complained he was feeling a little tired and longed to get back to Scotland for a few days.

She told him she knew just the cure. She would pick him up in fifteen minutes and he was to have a bag with a towel and swimming shorts ready. They had driven to

Hampstead Heath where Lucy took him to a large fresh-water pool she told him was a mixed-sex swimming area until October, when it got too cold.

"Come on!" She had tugged on his arm like a child to get changed.

Together they had jumped into the freezing pond. Lucy had laughed hysterically at the look of horror on Hartley's face when he hit the water.

"Don't worry; you'll heat up in a moment. Keep swimming. The shock to your system will do you good."

And it had. Hartley had felt invigorated — partly down to the swim, partly down to Lucy. They had had lunch in a nearby pub garden and ordered scampi and chips. Lucy, wearing no make-up, looked more beautiful than ever. She challenged him to the scampi competition — a long-running challenge she played with Max. The winner was the one who counted the most bits of battered scampi on their plate; the loser had to buy the drinks. Lucy had won with twelve pieces, telling him proudly her record was nineteen. She had decided to try a pint of Guinness for the first time and, after a gulp, declared it her new tipple of choice. She laughed as she thought of her twig-thin colleagues at the magazine sipping champagne and eating carrot sticks at parties, and watching aghast as Lucy downed her daily calorie intake with pint after pint of the tasty black liquid.

"Would you still love me with a beer belly?" Lucy had blushed furiously the moment she realized she had blurted out "love". They hadn't come close to talking of love.

84

Leaning over the wooden beer-garden table Hartley had kissed her firmly on the lips: "I would love you even more."

Hartley stirred his tea and smiled, enjoying the muted background noise of chattering and clinking cups around him. He knew already he wanted Lucy to be more than a fleeting girlfriend.

He could offer her a life of luxury and riches; she would never have to work and could have anything she desired.

He wanted to pin her down now and kiss those plump pink lips, to make love to her. The way she smelled was like a drug he wanted to inhale for ever. To kiss every inch of her creamy soft skin, her full breasts; to hold her to him while they made love.

But no, she would want to wait. And she was worth waiting for.

"Do I get to chaperone you to this dinner?"

"Of course."

"Well then, Lucy Lu, I wouldn't miss it for the world."

Chin Up, Chest Out

For an August day it was remarkably chilly.

Thankfully, Max was wearing new, matching, cream Calvin Klein bra and pants — respectable enough . . .

Oh God, there was nothing respectable about walking down the Kings Road in her underwear.

What the hell, onwards and upwards.

Max had worked with the photographer, John, dozens of times on different jobs — normally staking out some celebrity's house to catch them cheating.

John was a rosy-cheeked man approaching middle-age, with a shock of orange hair.

Max smiled as he instinctively transformed into snapper mode.

He'd done it hundreds of times, reassuring old ladies in his friendly cockney voice and getting them to smile while they waved their lottery cheque, telling topless or scantily-clad models they looked stunning — just relax and enjoy.

"Come on, Max, get that coat off and give me some attitude, darlin'."

Flinging her raincoat on the ground Max revealed her petite, toned, slightly tanned body with pert breasts and strong thighs.

And, oh bloody hell, nipples like coat hangers.

"Feeling the cold, Max?" John peeked out from behind his lens and grinned before continuing to click away. "OK, give me a smile."

Smile? Oh bugger it, I'm never going to see these people again, Max told herself as she made the effort to relax and look confident.

"Great, you've got a group of builders behind you. That's it, lads — point at her. Look amazed."

The men cheered and pointed for the camera, while Max negotiated the pavement slowly in the five-inch stilettos she'd borrowed from the fashion department, uttering under her breath, like a mantra: "The higher the heels, the smaller the thighs."

"Nice view."

What? Hold on. That's a slightly posh voice for a builder, Max thought as she heard a deep voice come from over her shoulder, while someone tapped on her back.

She turned her head and saw . . . Who was he? He looked familiar. She knew that voice. And she definitely knew the face. Was he famous?

Turning to face him, Max took in the man standing in front of her. God, he was handsome.

"Thanks," she said uncertainly. "Sorry, do I know you?"

The tall man with dirty-blond dishevelled hair was smiling. Well, actually, he wasn't but his bright green-blue eyes were twinkling with laughter.

"Kind of," he replied, holding her stare with supreme confidence. "The last time I saw you I said the same thing."

"I don't understand." He might be cute — very cute — but this guy could be a nutter. Yet he looked so familiar.

"That's what I said: 'nice view'."

Nice view. Of course! The guy who had shouted up to her as she climbed the VIP wall at *Man of Steel 4* — with a bird's-eye view up her micro skirt.

"Oh, you!"

"Yes, me." The man she'd noted was cute that night too — and no wedding ring.

"Tell me —" his eyes were twinkling like sapphires now — "do you have some kind of wonderful job that pays you to show men like me as much of your body as humanly possible?"

Max laughed out loud. She couldn't help herself.

"No," she said, looking up to meet his eyes and realizing he must be at least six foot two. "I, I don't normally do this."

"That's what all the girls say."

You're gorgeous! The voice in Max's head was so loud she wondered if he'd heard. "My name is Max. Pleased to meet you," she said, offering her hand.

"Luke," he said, taking her hand firmly. "And the pleasure is most definitely mine."

God, I fancy you, was all Max could think as she held his gaze. How often do I meet a guy I like? Never. Let alone one whose clothes I want to rip off.

"OK, Max, I'm all done 'ere." The photographer's loud cheery voice sliced into her thoughts. "I've got more than enough shots they can use. I've got to run to another job. You OK if I shoot off?"

"Erm, sure, John." Max turned to the photographer and kissed him on the cheek before turning back to . . . Luke.

Ask him for a drink, Max told herself. Ask him. He likes you. Or maybe he thinks you're a mad woman, a glamour model, a hooker. Why would he think you're a hooker? Oh just ask him.

"Tell you what, why don't I explain all over a glass of —"

"Luke."

What? Who was this? A tall woman wearing skinny jeans and skin-tight T-shirt was standing in between them.

"There you are. I told you to meet me at the Bluebird café."

Luke shifted uneasily on his feet, looking from Max to the girl.

"Sorry, honey, I just bumped into an old friend." Luke looked apologetically at Max. "Max, this is my girlfriend. Jenni, this is Max."

Max suddenly felt as stupid as she was sure she must look. Erect nipples, wobbly heels, bra and pants in the middle of the Kings Road. What a fool. What would Luke see in her when he had Miss Touching Six Foot, Skinny Blonde on his arm? Miss Pristine with a scary gap at the top of unfeasibly long legs poured into skin-tight white jeans.

Leaping sideways, she scooped her raincoat from the side of the pavement and hurriedly put it on.

Chest out, chin up, paint on the smile, she told herself.

"Ah, Jenni — I've heard so much about you," Max lied, catching Luke's eye and offering her hand.

The weakest, limpest handshake was returned by Jenni, who actually looked a little horse-like close up, Max thought. Always look on the bright side.

With a disdainful look that said, "You're not worth the dirt under my fingernails," Jenni smiled falsely. "Yes, hello there. Luke never fails to surprise me with the, erm, interesting people he knows."

Max sensed Luke had something he wanted to say, but Jenni, with impossibly big boobs for her tiny frame, was in no mood for chit-chat. Her voice was ridiculously plummy. Not at all like Luke's. He had a slight London accent. Jenni patted her hand on his stomach.

"Come on, Luke. I told you we have to be on time for the wedding planner."

Oh woopty, fucking doo. The only bloke she'd met for months whom she liked and he's marrying Jen the Stepford Wife. Was that a lump Max felt catch in her throat?

"Quite right, Jenni. I have to dash too. Luke, great to see you. Adios."

With that, Max clip-clopped off in her heels, tying the belt of her raincoat as tightly as possible.

Adios? Great parting shot, you moron, she thought as she hailed a cab. Note to self: why the fuck are you such a fucking fuckwit?

Settling into the back of a black cab, Max felt her mobile vibrate in her pocket.

"Hello?"

90

"Awright, doll? It's Sheri."

Shagger Sheri — just what she needed.

"Listen, I've got somefing to tell you."

"Sheri, can this wait?"

"No, it bloody can't. I'm pregnant. I'm only gonna have Kirk Kelner's baby. Tell me that's not a twenty-grand story."

Hubble Bubble, Toil and Trouble

Lady Bridget had been busy. After her run-in with Miss Lucy she had vowed to stir things up for her and had set about hiring a private investigator to find out everything there was to know about her background.

Turned out Lucy's mum lived in a terraced house on the waterfront in Broughty Ferry with a man who wasn't her dad. The investigator hadn't yet been able to find out who her real father was. But the facts spoke for themselves: her mum hadn't even married her father. Instead, she had hooked up with a local carpenter and had his child.

Perhaps she should forward Lucy's number to Jerry Springer or whatever chat-show host dealt with the infested, low-life stories of the working classes. Bridget had yelped in delight when the investigator had told her. Lucy might have taught herself to speak well but she was as common as the shell-suited families on morning television. Scum.

Best of all, her half-sister worked for the *Daily News* — a downmarket tabloid. The kind that delved into the private lives of famous people — the very thing Hartley despised. She was sure Lucy would not have told him about her sister's murky secret.

Lucy had got her claws into Hartley far too easily, but, now Bridget was armed with the facts, Lucy's run of luck was about to end.

She would be doing Hartley a huge favour. He had been taken in by this tart's string of lies. She was a gold-digger. Bridget just needed time to hatch a plan.

She didn't expect it to come in the form of a phone call from her friend Claudia.

Bridget had noted the anxiety in her so-called best-friend's voice during their conversation.

After making small talk about upcoming balls and which friends were trying to get pregnant/were pregnant/ engaged/had set a wedding date, etc., Claudia finally got round to the real reason for her call.

"Bridget, there's something I want to run by you."

"Yes?"

"First of all I want to say how much I miss hanging out with you and Hartley. I loved the whole double-couple thing we had — you two, Charles and I."

"Thanks, sweetie. You never know, we might have those times again."

"Oh yes, perhaps. Absolutely. The thing is . . . I don't want you to think I'm being disloyal in any way, but Charles has organized a weekend away."

Bridget guessed what was coming. "That's nice."

"Yes. Charles's friend Robbie, well, his family have an estate in Fife, near St Andrews, I think. Remember we always meant to go but never got round to it? The boys are always talking about playing golf at the famous Old Course. The thing is, Robbie has invited Charles and Hartley — you know what they're like: peas in a pod."

"Yes, sweetie." In the mirror, Bridget admired her black Chanel shift dress which came to just above her knees.

She was a good few inches taller than most of her friends and now, thanks to her Harley Street nutritionist's diet plan, she was at least a stone lighter. The diet had worked superbly, and it was worth suffering the cravings for carbs to look so good.

Her jet-black bob and pale complexion completed her look: exquisite. How dare Lucy say she had let herself go! Anyone could see the opposite was true. Lucy was plainly jealous of her grace, her standing.

"And, erm, Hartley has invited his new . . . his new, erm, girlfriend."

"That's the 'thing', sweetie?" chirped Bridget mockingly while stroking her large £10,000 diamond earring — one of a set Daddy had bought her from Tiffany's last Christmas.

"Um, yes. I do hope you don't mind, Bridget."

Bridget did mind. She minded very much.

She had brought Claudia into her very inner circle — introduced her to the Princes, for God's sake.

She had given her the number of her hairdresser, Pierre, who had made her strawberry-blonde frizz sleek with a chemical straightening perm, which was beginning to grow out. She had told her what labels to wear and how to wear them so she didn't look like the school geek.

94

And now Claudia was betraying her by running off for a weekend with that bitch. Claudia's problem was that she was too bloody wet for her own good. No backbone.

If any of her other girlfriends had been in this position they'd have called Bridget to offer to get all the dirt on Lucy over the weekend away. Not Claudia. She was one of those tedious people who believed in giving everybody a chance.

Bridget wanted to tell Claudia to have a great time because when she came back she'd find herself on far fewer invitation lists. Bridget would see to that. But for now she needed Claudia. She wanted the news that she had been gracious about the whole thing to get back to Hartley and his blonde tart.

"Of course I don't mind, Claudia. How long have I known you? Ten years. That's worth more than some weekend away, sweetie. And anyway, Hartley's new girlfriend has done nothing wrong. You're right to give her a chance."

There was silence on the other end. Claudia had been terrified of calling Bridget. In fact, Claudia was terrified of her full stop. Bridget's life consisted of bitching about people she didn't like, making sure she was on the best tables at the best balls and getting Daddy to make her life — and wardrobe — as wonderful as possible.

But Claudia had been a loyal friend to Bridget, partly out of fear but also because she tried to see the good in everyone.

"Perhaps she's insecure," she had often said to her boyfriend, Charles. "Maybe her rudeness is a cover-up for being unhappy."

"Maybe she's just a cow," was Charles's invariable reply.

Claudia had listened in horror as Bridget laid into Hartley's new girlfriend at Ascot a few days earlier.

Lucy was devastatingly attractive and, as far as she could tell, a natural beauty. Bridget had been awful and Claudia had looked at the ground throughout her tirade, beating herself up inwardly for being too cowardly to tell her to stop.

Lucy's put-down had been unexpected and mortifying for Bridget. Claudia admired this pretty girl who had remained so calm.

"Right. Well, that's jolly good of you, Bridget."

"Of course, sweetie. Was there anything else? I have a Deborah Lippmann French manicure at twelve."

"No, Bridget. I'll see you soon, hopefully."

"Yes, yes. Goodbye . . . Oh sweetie, one more thing."

"Yes, Bridget?"

"When are you going to Scotland? Just so I know when you can't do lunch."

"The last weekend of the month, Bridget."

"OK. Bye, darling."

As she put the phone down Bridget knew exactly what she would do next. She would destroy Lucy and enjoy every minute of it.

Sheri Comes Good Again

What a week.

Max had the potential scoop of the year on her hands: Shagger Sheri pregnant with Kirk Kelner's baby.

She'd wasted no time in racing back to the office to tell her boss.

"That's a belter, Max," Claire announced, leaping to her feet in anticipation of telling the big boss, the paper's editor.

Max felt the stares of her fellow reporters, who were envious it wasn't their story yet relieved the pressure to come up with a big exclusive was off them for a day or two.

It was said that Claire, four years older than Max and with thirsty brown eyes, would sell her grandmother if it meant getting a front-page. Having gleaned an insight into how she worked, Max was sure she'd throw in her grandfather too. But the result was she was known as one of the best showbiz journalists in the country, with a string of exclusives under her Gucci belt.

She cut an impressive figure, favouring classic suits — always in black and accentuating her waist. Her hair never changed: bleached almost white, a poker-straight bob in a severe centre parting with not even a millimetre of roots showing. This was some feat, given that a decade ago her hair had matched her dark eyes. Claire was attractive in a stern, perfected way, her look finished with bright red lipstick at all times.

As well as her own stories, Claire relied on her staff — Max and three other showbiz reporters — to come up with exclusives every day so she had a full list of four or five tales for the morning conference in which the executives planned what would appear in the following day's paper.

That morning's list had been on the light side.

"It's just what we need — someone pregnant with Kelner's baby. Fucking amazing."

That was the thing about working in a newsroom where scandal sold — even the women spoke like men who were trying to get their mates' attention after a few pints.

Claire, dressed in a trouser suit and Gucci heels, sat down and pointed a finger in the air.

"Hold on a minute. This is Shagger Sheri. Yes, she's brilliant for stories. But she'd also do anything to feed her coke habit. My mate at Elysium says it's worse than ever."

"Agreed." Max nodded. "It needs to be stood up before we can print it."

Standing a story up was journalist speak for proving it. Often, you could have the best story in the world but could never run it without verifying it through a reliable source: standing it up.

Otherwise the star involved would sue. Sheri had no reputation to protect or anything to lose with a story like this. Kirk Kelner might have been delighted with Sheri's sex-stud kiss-and-tell, but her allegation that he was the father of her unborn child would have to be verified. He would waste no time in suing or at least asking for a paternity test.

"Exactly. Max, there's only one thing for it."

Max had a horrible feeling she knew what was coming.

Uncovered:
Sheri in all Her Glory

It had taken a long time to convince Sheri to take the pregnancy test. Claire had insisted she used one of the home pregnancy tests — the ones you peed on to get a result, positive or negative — and that she did it in front of Max. That way Sheri couldn't doctor the results. This story was worth a lot of money and there was no telling what Sheri would do to get it.

"I've got to fucking piss in front of you?"

"Yes, Sheri. Sorry. It's at my boss's request. She doesn't know you as well as I do and she's nervous about paying anyone that amount of money — you asked for twenty grand."

Max thought it kinder not to mention the fact that no one with half a brain would trust Sheri in the same sentence as twenty grand.

Initially, Sheri had asked for twenty. Max had bartered her down to a more realistic price.

At first Sheri had refused point-blank to take the test.

In that case, Max had told her, no dinero.

"I'll go to the *Sunday Mirror*," she spat.

"Sheri, they'll just tell you the same and pay you a lot less."

So Sheri had eventually succumbed and shut herself in the small toilet of her Bermondsey flat with Max.

Handing her the test kit, Max, dressed in a black, sixties-style Warehouse mini shift dress and black-leather, knee-high Gucci boots, felt her cheeks flush as she perched on the edge of the bath and watched Sheri.

She could hear Sir Trevor McDonald now. "And the award for losing all self-respect goes to a journalist who watches coke-head kiss-and-tell girls urinating in front of them. Ladies and gentlemen, Maxine —"

Max's thoughts were interrupted by the noise of Sheri's trickling pee. She looked up and took in the pathetic figure Sheri cut: her tracksuit bottoms crumpled on the floor under her orange legs, her skinny, muscle-less stomach on show under a T-shirt emblazoned with the words "You Want Some?", which was cut off under her huge breasts.

Is this what Max's career had come to? Years of effort, tears, hard work — for this?

She had gone straight from school to the local paper, the Dundee *Courier*, with the DC Thomson publishing family, fitting in journalism night classes at college where she learned 100-words-a-minute shorthand and media law.

Then, aged twenty, she moved down south to Manchester for a news reporter position on a respected local paper.

She was named young local journalist of the year at the National Press Awards when she was twenty-three and promptly offered a job with one of the Sunday tabloids in London. And now, as a showbiz reporter, life was whizzing by in a flurry of free bars and canapés. Well, when she wasn't watching Sheri piss on a stick.

"Done," announced Sheri, waving the kit above her head.

Max's mobile rang before she could take it from her.

It rang three times before Sheri asked, with barely concealed irritation, "You gonna answer that or what?"

"No. If it's important they'll leave a message."

Sheri looked utterly devastated, dropping her gaze to the bathroom floor.

This pretty much confirmed Max's suspicion that Sheri had planned to trick her.

Sheri had shouted "Done" a little too loudly. Max guessed it was her flatmate Envy's cue to call Max, withholding her number. Sheri knew Max always answered her phone for work and a few seconds would be enough time to swap the kit for another (either tampered with earlier or peed on by a woman who was really pregnant) hidden somewhere in her loo. You can't trick a trickster, thought Max as she watched Sheri hoist up her pink Playboy thong and Juicy Couture tracksuit bottoms. How come she was tanned mahogany even on her hairless bits down there too?

A deflated Sheri handed the spatula to Max.

"It hasn't turned pink, Sheri — it's negative."

"I swear the test I did yesterday was positive."

Max didn't have the heart to tell Sheri she knew what had happened. As ludicrous as the plan to deceive Max was, in Sheri's desperate mind it was her only option. She needed money fast.

She had to look good and that came at a price — manicures, fake tan, hair extensions and designer bags. Maintaining her appearance was a full-time job. And she wouldn't let the other glamour girls who were regulars on her club circuit have the satisfaction of seeing her dressed in H&M rather than Dolce & Gabbana.

But most of all she needed the money to pay off her coke dealer so she could start getting credit again. Sheri knew she was taking too much but a line or two took the edge off and she needed that for the confidence to blag herself into VIP areas and chat up stars.

She'd finished her last lot of coke before Max came. She liked Max and was normally honest with her. But she really needed the cash. Anyway, if Max had printed her pregnancy story she'd have said she'd had a miscarriage a couple of months later and nobody would have been any wiser.

"Sorry, Sheri. I'm happy to stay and watch you do another test — this one might have been faulty — but I really can't pay you if it's negative."

Max wanted to give the money to Sheri — and insist she used it on a spell in rehab.

Sure, she looked her tarty best for the snappers waiting outside Embassy or Elysium but it took a hell of a lot of time and money for Sheri to transform herself these days. She was taking so much coke she shivered uncontrollably — even when immersed in a piping-hot bath — until she'd had a livener. Her eyes were sunken, her streaky-blonde hair lank.

Max did not consider Sheri to be her friend exactly — how could they be when their relationship was based on stories for cash? Sheri helped Max get good scoops and therefore give her boss goodies for morning conference, while Max helped Sheri make a living. For what, though? To snort more marching powder, Max thought sadly. She couldn't help but feel a little protective.

"Sheri, I was thinking that maybe with the next lot of cash you get you could go away for a bit. Even party girls need their rest. There are some lovely spas just outside London. Or rehab? It's all the rage with the A-listers. You might even get a famous boyfriend." Max hoped her tone was light enough so as not to sound like she was lecturing Sheri.

"Nah, babes. I'm fine for now. Maybe in a few weeks I'll 'ave a beach holiday or somefing."

Max knew she couldn't push it any further — it wasn't her place.

But Sheri didn't seem to have any real friends and Max couldn't help feeling sorry for her.

"Listen, Max, maybe I made a mistake with the test. Don't worry about it."

"OK, Sheri. Listen, I have to head off. Will you be OK?"

"Sure . . . Hey, Max?"

"Uh-huh."

"You couldn't lend me fifty quid, could ya? I'll pay you back next week."

"Sure," said Max, despising herself as she reached for her wallet.

Some Things Are Not for Sale

Max knew it was coming the moment Claire suggested they have a catch-up over dinner.

Word was out that her sister was dating none other than the UK's most eligible bachelor and that meant one thing: Max was in a position to bring huge stories to the paper.

"I know how important family and friends are," Claire told her over their second bottle of Pinot Grigio at Chez Gerard near Tower Bridge.

No, Max thought, you don't know how important family and friends are to me. She smiled at her boss through a mouthful of steak-frites.

Claire gently swirled the wine in her glass, brushing a stray strand of hair behind her ear with her other hand.

She looked at Max, her brown eyes so cold and serious. "But the thing you have to understand, Max, is that you, as a showbiz reporter, have a golden opportunity here. You are in the perfect position to bring in great stories — we're talking front page after front page."

Max fought an urge to stand up and shout at her boss that she was a blinkered bitch, asking her to tell tales on her sister. How dare she! But then that was exactly what Max had expected. It's what Claire had become, what the job had made her. Max looked and felt calm. Claire couldn't assess her reaction.

Putting her glass down, Claire clasped both her hands together as she pursed her MAC-glossed red lips together. A gesture, Max considered, that was meant to show just how honest and helpful she was trying to be.

"And it wouldn't be betraying your sister, Max. There are plenty of stories you could bring in that are positive. I mean, let's say he got engaged to Lucy. That would be a great exclusive."

Max raised her eyebrows and took a sip of wine.

"Or . . . or, if he was holding some exclusive party, you could get inside, get the goss. That would be great publicity for his charity."

Claire didn't want to let Max speak yet. She wanted to sell this to her as the career opportunity of a lifetime.

"You know what it's like, Max. There are always people willing to sell stories, so why shouldn't you benefit? More front pages, more salary increases. It's not like I'm going to be in charge of the column for ever. I'll be handing over the reins within a year, I'd guess. This is a job for someone with a younger liver, after all."

Max laughed. It was strange, this hard sell. When she had started out under Claire, she'd hoped they could be friends. She'd liked her boss's dry sense of humour and admired her ability to nail a great story.

But this only proved to her that for Claire the job came first, second and third. She was painting it like Max would be doing not only herself but Lucy and Hartley a favour by bringing Claire a daily list of their movements. Of course Max's career would benefit, but so would Claire's. She was the one who would walk into conference every morning with a great exclusive. Sure, she'd give Max credit, but she would also make everyone aware that she had been responsible for talking Max round.

"And I think you could be my natural replacement." Claire's tone had softened. But it was forced, intended.

Max wasn't so sure her boss wanted to relinquish her title just yet for an executive role on the paper, in the land of soft carpets.

That would involve a pay rise and more clout over the internal running of things but it would also mean giving up being recognized at every London party she attended.

Claire, like the others whose air-brushed pictures were published every day, was paid to write about celebrities and in doing so had become a minor star herself, courted on a nightly basis by PRs and music bigwigs at the Ivy, Momo, Cipriani. She had to hand over the baton sometime, but Max was pretty sure that talk of doing so soon was only a ploy to keep her hungry and keen.

"You're a great journalist, Max. I've been so impressed with your work. But, well, this could just be the thing that sets you head and shoulders above the rest. You never know, Lucy and Hartley might welcome having someone who can place positive stories about them. Or, if you wanted to keep it a secret that you were giving the stories, you could always change your byline — use a fictitious name on top of the stories you write about them. But the people who mattered at the newspaper would know it was down to you. You'd get full credit."

Like a barrister who'd just made the closing speech of her life to a jury, Claire leaned back in her chair, relieved and spent from making an argument she was certain would be accepted.

If only Claire knew how much Lucy meant to her, she would never even have thought of asking Max to do this. If only she knew their background, their story.

Max and Lucy's mother, Marjory, had fallen pregnant with Lucy when she was twenty. She hadn't realized the handsome man in his late thirties she'd fallen for was married, or that he already had two children. Peter Stirling told Marj he was a wealthy man and would look after their child. He offered to leave his wife and children for Marjory. She refused, telling him to go back home. Her heart had been broken but she would not be responsible for breaking up his family.

Peter had felt wretched about the situation and he came clean to his wife. Although she was devastated she didn't want a divorce and the stigma of being a single mother, which was undeniably still present in the late seventies. Patricia grudgingly agreed he should offer Marjory some maintenance money for the child and play a part in its life, though their family must always come first. When Lucy was thirteen, and as his sons already boarded in Kent, he suggested paying for Lucy to go to the nearby girls' school.

108

Peter's parents had left their estate to their only child, with money put aside in a trust specifically to pay for the education of any children he might have. Whether his wife liked it or not, Lucy qualified. On top of the school fees he secretly wrote Marj a cheque for £10,000 every year. Patricia never saw his accounts from his parents' estate and as a family they had more than enough money of their own.

Marj wanted the best education for her little girl but felt terrible packing her off when she was so young, although it was the age many girls started at the particular school earmarked by her father. She therefore left it up to Lucy to decide if she wanted to leave home. Marj explained to her daughter that the school would offer a world of trips, opportunities and new friends but that she could stay at home if she would rather. Mummy would miss her terribly but if she decided to go they would make up for lost time during holidays.

Caught up reading teen fiction that followed the adventures of a girl at boarding school, Lucy had jumped at the chance to go — what fun it sounded. And so Lucy's life took a turn that saw her mixing with privileged girls from all over the world. Her Scottish accent had quickly faded after her first year. Without intending to, she picked up the cut-glass English of the girls around her. Of course, Max had teased her for sounding posh when she came home for holidays. By the time Lucy returned to school she sounded a little Scottish again, then gradually this would fade once more. Lucy hadn't lived in Scotland since her schooldays, studying at Oxford then working in London, and, regrettably, she no longer had the soft Scots accent she loved.

The schooling arrangement suited her father, who visited her at school three or four weekends a year. Occasionally, she stayed at his five-bedroom house in Greenwich, in south-east London. Once a year, over a long weekend in winter or spring, she skied with the family, and in summer she joined them for a week at their villa in the quaint village of Lagrasse, in the south of France.

Lucy loved her dad and adored her two half-brothers, Ben and Luke, but never felt like she truly belonged, in no small part because of the frosty Patricia, who often barely hid her irritation that her husband's love child was joining their family unit.

Ben was five years older than Lucy. He was studious and for as long as she could remember he had had an air of gravity. He was darker than the rest of the family, with brown hair and eyes. The casual observer might have judged him a little stiff but Ben had always allowed Lucy to see his softer side. He shared with her his dry sense of humour and always let her know he was there for her.

Luke was completely different; as a teen he had looked like an extra from *The O.C*. He loved to find places to surf with friends — from Cornwall to Indonesia — and was permanently bronzed, his floppy blond hair streaked white from the sun. He was three years Lucy's senior but she often felt protective of him.

He was so fun-loving and trusting, open and charming. He reminded her of Max.

Lucy had tried to arrange a time when Max could meet her father and brothers but it had never happened. Max had moved to London only a few years ago and was always so busy. Lucy had invited her brothers to join them for lunch at their flat a year or so ago but it had to be cancelled when Max was sent to Dublin to chase some pop star. They rearranged a few weeks later but Ben had to pull out because of work. It would have made sense to invite Max to their villa one summer but Lucy had no doubt Patricia would be hostile and unwelcoming to Max and Lucy would not have her sister made to feel like an outsider. Nevertheless it was odd that Max hadn't met them. Now they were both in London, she resolved to arrange a dinner or lunch soon.

Lucy had loved school life, which passed in a whirl of captaining the hockey and lacrosse teams and gaining straight A grades. She was popular and in her final year was named Head Girl. When she was fourteen she had briefly succumbed to a bout of bulimia, just because it seemed to be the thing everyone was doing; her classmates competed to see who could lose the most weight.

But Lucy was quick to see how silly such games were, especially after spending holidays with Max. She never felt totally at home until she was back with her mum and little sister during holidays.

Max had come along a little over two years after Lucy. While carrying Lucy, their mum had met and fallen in love with a dashing Irishman called Fergal Summers. The feeling was mutual and Fergal, who ran his own carpentry business, said he would rather bring up another man's child and learn to love it as his own than risk losing Marj. Little did they know they would have another baby so soon.

The Summers Sisters were inseparable whenever together. Max attended the local school, Grove Academy in Broughty Ferry, where she lived with her parents right on the esplanade by the River Tay. She developed a slight local accent — nothing too strong but identifiably Scottish. Lucy loved being with her little sister. She told her she was like a breath of fresh air after a term with the boarders who obsessed over what ski resort they were going to at Easter.

Max smiled as she thought of Lucy, how close they had always been.

"Max?"

Shit. Max had let her mind wander. She'd glazed over, no doubt aided by the wine.

Max smiled at Claire. God, she was an intimidating woman. Attractive, talented, funny, but bloody scary too. Perhaps it was the wine, but Max wasn't afraid.

"Claire, I appreciate you looking out for me. I do. But no matter how much you polish the turd, it's still something I'd never do."

Claire sat forward, ready to speak.

Max cut her off. "Claire, there's nothing you can say. I'd leave the job before I ever brought in stories about my sister."

112

Claire lowered her head before looking at Max. She frowned and nodded slowly.

"Sure," she said. "I understand."

"You do?"

"Of course. I don't have a heart of stone, you know. Loyalty's important. Maybe not as important as exclusives, but then, hell, if we all agreed it would be fucking dull."

Max laughed. She realized how much she liked Claire, how much she had learned from her. A woman in her position had to be a little tough.

"Just one thing, though."

"Uh-huh?" Max asked.

"You'd better bring some kick-ass stories to the table on other celebs."

Max clinked glasses with her boss, making a toast: "To kick-ass stories."

As they ordered a third bottle, Max felt a sense of relief wash over her, tempered only by the realization that Claire was deadly serious.

Girls' Guide to a Night Out

Lucy smiled as she rubbed L'Occitane cocoa butter into her long legs.

She laughed out loud as she realized she was in fact grinning like a Cheshire cat.

Kneading the gooey lotion into her smooth skin she reflected on the last six weeks — that was how long she had been dating Hartley. She felt as excited as a schoolgirl with her first crush whenever she thought of him. She found herself daydreaming more and more of a future with Hartley. She couldn't believe how much she had fallen for him in such a short time. Most of the time it made her dizzy with happiness but sometimes she was terrified. She thought he had the same feelings, but could she be sure?

He was due to pick her up in an hour to take her to Clarissa's for dinner.

And soon they would have a long weekend away with his friends in Scotland.

She felt the fine hairs on her body prickle in excitement at the thought of spending the weekend with him in the remote castle. She longed for him to make love to her. Such a setting would be perfect.

Carlos had cornered her at work and demanded to take her for a coffee straight away so they could be out of earshot of Genevieve.

Safely in a booth at the local Starbucks he waved his hands in the air. "My God, girl, I've had to read about your new boyfriend and you in the bloody magazines. He's so eligible I'd go straight to date him."

Lucy laughed. "So I hear, Carlos."

"But he's not as beautiful as you, baby."

Lucy blushed.

"But tell me —" Carlos looked serious suddenly as he tightened his lemon-coloured tie then clasped together his perfectly manicured hands as if in prayer — "do you like him?"

"I do, Carlos, I really do," Lucy told him, catching his eye.

"And is he good to you?"

"So nice. I'm almost waiting for something to go wrong. It's all so . . . perfect."

"Honey, enjoy it while it lasts. And Lucy?"

"Yes?"

"For God's sake, get a friggin' diamond-encrusted Cartier before you break up."

Carlos erupted into laughter at his own joke before reaching for Lucy's hand and squeezing it.

"I'm messing with you, of course, baby."

Perhaps he was right. Perhaps Lucy should just enjoy how good it felt being with Hartley and stop hoping it wasn't too good to be true.

For the first time she felt like she was in a real relationship that was going somewhere, with someone she respected and who respected her.

She was inspired by Hartley's passion and offered to help in any way she could. His eyes had lit up and he suggested she take over planning his Hogmanay Ball for the Foundation.

"I've got a frightfully busy few months ahead, Lucy Lu. Mother needs some help running the estate. Since Father died I try to spend as much time with her as I can," he had explained. "You'd be doing me such a favour, darling."

Lucy hadn't hesitated and started at once to plan for the occasion. What with auction prizes, music, themes, speeches and so much more, her mind was jam-packed with lists of things to do . . . and she was loving every minute.

How wonderful, she thought, picking out her favourite baby-pink-satin camisole and matching panties from her bedside drawer, to feel wanted, appreciated, loved, respected.

An improvement on her last boyfriend, John.

She'd only realized her loyalty to John might be going unrewarded when she found a cheap red-silk nightgown under their bed. It definitely did not belong to her.

He had tried to laugh it off, telling her he was an athlete full of testosterone and had succumbed to temptation. He promised to be faithful in future. He told her she was the one he wanted on his arm. The most beautiful, sexy girl he had ever met, the most caring and loyal.

That night, Lucy had opened a bottle of Chardonnay then drank the whole lot before starting on a second. When Max came home from work she found her sister, for the first time in her life, wasted.

After explaining through a cacophony of slurs what had happened with the nightgown and John's reaction, Max was resolute.

"Lucy, that man's idea of foreplay is beating his chest and yelling, 'Are you ready for the big boy, little lady?' He's a pig. How fucking dare he do this!"

With that, Max had stormed through to the bedroom her sister shared with John — who rarely contributed to any outgoings in the flat — and, armed with scissors, cut up his new rowing gear. Then she cut all three of his Armani suits into small pieces.

"There," Max had announced, throwing all the bits of material into one of John's large Mulberry cases. She placed it outside the door with a note she dictated to Lucy so that it was in her handwriting.

Dear John,
   Sleeping with you is like having a front door fall on top of me, with the key still in the door.
   You're not worth it.
   Find a new flat and get a life.
   Lucy

Afterwards, Lucy had dissolved into a fit of giggles. "I love you, Max."

"I know, Luce. Come on, let's get you to bed. Tomorrow you get to experience the joy of your first major hangover."

John had bombarded Lucy with flowers, offers of dinner, holidays, the opera, everything. But she had remained resolute, with Max's help. As her little sister said, everyone needs a bad relationship to make them appreciate when a good one comes along.

She smiled as she thought of lovely Hartley, with his mouth full of marbles, floppy hair and rosy cheeks. She wouldn't have him any other way.

Lucy had laid out her outfit for the evening at Clarissa's on her pristine white Egyptian-cotton duvet. Summer was almost over but it was a gorgeously warm September evening, perfect for her lilac-chiffon Chloé shift dress. Letting it fall over her head she felt the soft fabric settle on her skin. Beneath her breasts the tightly gathered fabric flowed freely and loosely to just below her knees. Dusting some Benefit body shimmer over her legs she completed the look with matching lilac Miu Miu court shoes — a perfect combination to make her look young, fresh and sophisticated.

After blasting her hair dry she smoothed it with a little serum to highlight the wispy ends, which had turned almost white in the sun.

She patted a thin layer of Laura Mercier primer then tinted moisturizer over her face. A little cream blusher and a lick of Dior mascara — a freebie sample at the magazine — and finally a dab of Crème de la Mer mint lip balm and she was ready.

Lucy felt the familiar fluttering in her stomach as she heard the buzzer from the street-level entry to her flat.

Her heart jumped as she heard Hartley's trademark "Hello, Lucy Lu" over the intercom.

Hartley was a little early — Clarissa had invited them for seven-thirty and it was only just after six.

118

Excellent, thought Lucy. I'll open some champagne first and we can cuddle up on the sofa. When Lucy opened the door Hartley stood with his mouth slightly ajar. He couldn't help it. She looked incredible. Her white-gold hair floated over her shoulders. He wanted to grab her and take in its sweet scent. Her lilac dress set off her bright blue eyes.

Yet again he wondered how such a perfectly respectable outfit with a modest neckline and hemline could look so sexy.

"Lucy Lu, you look fabulous," he said over the long stemmed white lilies he was holding out.

Taking them from him, Lucy leaned forward and lightly brushed her lips against his. Taking his hand, she led him to the sitting room.

"Thank you, they're lovely. I'll put them in water and open some champagne?"

"Perfect."

Since meeting Hartley, Lucy had found herself gradually drinking more — a thimbleful compared to Max's trough — and often had a few glasses over dinner on school nights, which she had never allowed before. But she was enjoying being less rigid. She laughed as she remembered Max's description: "You're less anal these days, sis." Lucy was sure it had everything to do with being happy.

Hartley found Lucy irresistible. Whenever he said good-bye to her he counted the hours until he saw her again.

So sexy, yet somehow so pure. He didn't want to cheapen what he felt by overstepping the mark. He wanted to do things properly.

Hartley smiled as he sat back and took in Lucy's smell. It was everywhere, just like her style, scattered around the flat. On a canvas of creamy walls and carpets, throws and large pillows in rich reds and purples were dotted around the room, with a giant plum rug as a centrepiece under an ancient-looking, rectangular, low wooden table.

A giant oil painting hung on the wall facing him — a purple Buddha on sands of pink and red — adding to the exotic feel of the room.

Hartley guessed some of the decoration must be down to Max.

Lucy had admitted she'd been nervous about telling Hartley her sister worked for a tabloid. Max, she told him with pride, was one of the most talented young journalists in the country. She described how Max had won a prestigious award and been headhunted. And one day she wanted to be a foreign correspondent, exposing corruption in third-world countries or covering wars. Max, Lucy told Hartley, might make a living out of exposing stars. But she was the most loyal person she could hope to have as a sister. Yes, the fact her sister was dating the Earl of Balmyle could land her dozens of scoops for the *Daily News*. But Max would rather die than exploit her for stories. Lucy could not be more proud of her sister's achievements to date, she told him a little defensively.

Hartley had laughed, kissed Lucy on the forehead and told her to stop being silly. Max sounded like an amazing journalist with a glittering future. What twenty-something would turn down a showbiz reporter's role, mixing with the celebrities her readers were so obsessed by? And anyway, it wouldn't matter if Lucy's sister was a stripper (though his mother might object): it couldn't change how he felt about her. All Hartley asked for was honesty and that's what Lucy had given him. In truth, Hartley couldn't wait to meet Max. She seemed always to be out at some premiere or launch party when he called by the flat.

He had seen pictures of Max, who was pretty but not at all like Lucy. Her huge brown eyes and flowing chestnut hair made her look almost Italian, so unlike her fair, English-rose sister. A few days ago Lucy had started to say something about why they looked so different, but they were interrupted by a call from the Foundation.

Hartley still could not quite believe how Lucy had thrown herself into organizing the Hogmanay Ball. With strong Scottish ancestry, Hartley had been keen to celebrate Hogmanay Scots-style in London, and raise as much money as possible at the same time. Lucy seemed to revel in all the tiny details — champagne flutes tied with tartan ribbon round the stem, a ceilidh with an instructor to show everyone how to do the Gay Gordons, a piper to welcome guests. Was it foolish, less than two months into their relationship, to hope Lucy would one day relish planning their own wedding?

The thud of the flat door closing cut through Hartley's thoughts. Followed by a torrent of profanities.

"Fuck fuck fuck! I'm wet fucking through."

The door was flung open to reveal the girl in the pictures. It was Max. Although she was a little more bedraggled than in the posed family photos. Hartley couldn't help his eyes straying down to her jeans. Was that . . .? No, surely not.

"Hartley? Oh Christ. I'm sorry."

"Max?"

"Oh Jesus, meet the bloody Earl for the first time and I've peed my pants."

"I'm sorry?" Hartley wasn't at all sure he understood. Uncertain where to look, he tried to focus on Max's face, but couldn't help noticing her top: tight and black and torn right down the front to reveal a — God, her nipple. He was looking at his girlfriend's sister's nipple. He hadn't even seen Lucy's yet.

"Max?" Lucy appeared from the kitchen at the other side of the sitting room carrying two flutes of champagne.

"Oh Luce, I'm such a fuck-up." Max grabbed a red throw from a chair and hastily tied it round the huge dark wet patch which started above her crotch and spread almost to her knees. "Hartley, a pleasure to meet you. Let's shake on it once I've washed my hands."

"Um, yes, of course."

"Max, what on earth's happened? Have you been drinking?" Lucy asked with concern.

"I wish." Max groaned. "Oh God, I have to explain."

Max reached for a purple-velvet cushion and held it across her chest.

"Here's the thing. God, Hartley, sorry. The thing is my boss told me to stand outside the cinema in Leicester Square and wait for Tom Cruise. His latest film is premiering there tonight."

Max was distressed. This was not how she had hoped she would meet her sister's boyfriend for the first time. Lucy really liked him and Max wanted to make a good impression. Sure, he might learn after a few meetings that she was a liability, but fiddling with the throw to make sure her damp patch was covered? Classy.

She wanted to make Lucy proud, not embarrassed.

"Right, the thing is," she heard herself say, "Tom Cruise is famous for doing his walkabouts with the fans. And as there was no chance of an interview with the paper, Claire, she's my boss, figured it was the only way we could get quotes from him. So, to get a good spot — standing in front of his thousands of cross-eyed fans — she told me to get there at midday. These fuckers — shit, sorry, swearing too much — the fans . . . they travel from fucking Aberdeen and wait all night."

Max felt Lucy's and Hartley's incredulous stares upon her. She continued.

"I was in such a rush to get there I didn't have time to go to the toilet. I'd drunk a litre of water over lunch trying to be fucking — sorry — healthy. He was due at five-thirty. By four o'clock — four bloody hours — I knew if I didn't pee I'd be hospitalized with a burst bladder. I tell you, I was in agony, doubled up with cramps. I also knew that if I left I'd lose my place and have all hell to pay with the boss. The security guards had closed off the area. So, erm, I had no choice but to pee."

"You didn't?"

"Yes, Luce, I did. I'm ashamed to say I did. Another highlight in my career as a hard-hitting journalist. By the way, I got the chat with Tom so Claire was happy. I'm sure she won't care that a mad fan was so angry when Tom spoke to me she ripped my top and Tom got a full view of my left nipple."

"Oh Max."

"My new Sevens jeans are soaked in urine and, if that wasn't bad enough, the first time I meet Hartley he sees me having pissed my pants."

Oh God, Hartley was looking away. Maybe he'd dump Lucy over her disgusting, urinating sister. Bet Lady Bridget never peed herself.

Lucy and Max caught each other's eye as they became aware that Hartley was shaking.

"Oh . . . my . . . God," he gasped in between fits of bellowing laughter. "I don't think I've heard anything so funny in my life."

Uncovered:
What Really Happened at
Clarissa's Friday-Night Supper

Dinner at Clarissa Appleton-Smythe's was a success all round. Lucy had forgotten how well-connected Clarissa was, what with her ferocious ambition to meet Hartley. But then, Lucy had also forgotten just what a catch Hartley was — as a boyfriend or a friend. Counting him as a friend was on a par with knowing the younger royals. In some ways even better, because the people he socialized with were small in number and therefore exclusive. To Lucy, he had just become her lovely new boyfriend.

Clarissa treated maintaining her contacts book like a career. She regarded meeting the Earl of Balmyle as an accountant would regard winning the business of a new client.

Yet beneath her ambitious exterior Lucy had glimpsed a softer side to Clarissa, one that stuck up for her when Lady Bridget Beames had been so ghastly. Her heart was in the right place. Lucy sensed that, deep down, Clarissa saw the humour in her way of life too.

Clarissa had greeted Lucy and Hartley like long-lost friends when they arrived at her Putney town house.

Brimming with pride she shook Hartley's hand, introducing herself as "Clarissa Coldridge Appleton-Smythe" for full effect and making sure her fellow guests heard her introduce herself to Hartley.

Clarissa's house was exactly as Lucy had imagined. The decor and furnishings were fussier than the more minimalist look no doubt favoured by most in her stylish set. An overstuffed pink sofa with equally overstuffed floral cushions was surrounded by mismatched armchairs, a grand piano and solid dark-wood tables which looked very expensive. None of it would have looked out of place in a country home belonging to a fifty-year-old couple who kept the spare room for their daughter when she visited during university holidays. It was tastefully done in a chintzy way and so delightfully comfortable, filled with the delicious scent of a burning log fire. Mind you, it was a little balmy for a fire but Lucy guessed Clarissa wanted to perfect the feel of a homely manor. She noticed almost all the windows were open to counter the heat.

Lucy recognized Clarissa's dress from a photo shoot she had put together at the magazine, but the canary-yellow smock looked a little different on the pudgy Clarissa than it had on the skinny model with whom Lucy had worked.

"This season's Matthew Williamson, Clarissa? Now you're the trend-setter."

If Clarissa had had feathers they would have puffed out with pride as she twirled in front of Hartley and Lucy. "Oh Hartley," she said, composing herself, "you haven't met my fiancé, Clive."

126

Lucy had briefly met Clive at Ascot. She kissed him on both cheeks — after he had welcomed Hartley.

Clive was a small red-faced man with twitchy eyes. Perfectly pleasant but one of those people with whom conversation was always a little stilted. He was well put together, in a no doubt expensive lounge suit like his fellow guests, but he had an unremarkable air and would dissolve into any crowd.

Clarissa seemed as proud as punch of her other half. Having a fiancé, she told herself, made her more attractive as a guest. Females were always wary of single girls, viewing them as competition. And Clarissa was more in love with Clive than she had ever dreamed she would be with any man.

The seating arrangements had been planned meticulously. Hartley was next to Clarissa on one side and Lucy on the other. Philippa Bonner, heiress to the Bonner Publishing empire, sat opposite Lucy. Clarissa had known Lucy and Philippa would talk fashion immediately, leaving Hartley all to herself. Lucy was, after all, gaining a reputation for the terrific way she dressed, appearing in the mid-market and broadsheet newspapers and magazines when she stepped out with the Earl of Balmyle. And as Philippa loved to look good — and always did — she devoured Lucy's fashion and beauty tips like Clarissa relished society gossip. Lucy remembered Clarissa mentioning that Philippa knew Bridget, but there wasn't a hint of coldness, just delight in talking about clothes.

"Lucy, can you tell what I'm wearing now?"

Philippa, like all the guests round the table — four couples had been invited — was terribly well spoken.

Lucy was also well spoken but she had Max to thank for keeping her grounded, not carried away by thoughts of riches, of how many holiday homes/titles/horses she might acquire, like so many of the trust-fund kids.

Like Max, Lucy was able to talk to a prince or a plumber, while remaining true to herself.

The sisters had their mother to thank for that skill. She had always encouraged the girls to be outgoing and welcoming when they were growing up. "Be interested and interesting," she told them.

So many of the society set could only — and indeed wanted only to — talk to each other.

"Yes, I can tell exactly what you're wearing. Some people know computers, others rugby trivia. Me? I'm a slave to fashion."

"Do tell, then."

Philippa, a slender girl in her early thirties, was immaculately dressed. With a chin-length bouncy blonde bob and perfect complexion with a sweet smattering of freckles over her cheeks, she balanced looking perfectly groomed with looking very natural.

"OK." Lucy breathed in, looking Philippa in the eye as if about to start her round of questions on *The Weakest Link*. "Your cream blazer is classic Prada, perfectly tailored and timeless. Your summer skirt looks like it was bought to match the blazer but it is in fact Chloé — the multiple layers are a give-away, gorgeously feminine."

Philippa, delicately sipping her Chablis, looked delighted and wide-eyed as she took in Lucy's observations.

"Your pink pearls I'd guess are Tiffany, your tights are DKNY satin finish and your beige pumps are Prada."

Philippa, whose broad-shouldered boyfriend, Sebastian, was chatting about cricket to another male guest, shrieked with delight at her new friend's talent and asked if she would mind helping her pick an outfit for a wedding she was attending next month.

"I'd be delighted." Lucy smiled, spearing a piece of asparagus wrapped in Parma ham.

To her left, Hartley chatted to Clarissa, as a waiter served chateaubriand and some delicious red wine.

Miss Appleton-Smythe would later tell friends how the Earl of Balmyle found her hilariously funny — laughing heartily at all her stories. Hartley was, in fact, still chuckling over the image of Lucy's sister with her damp patch and exposed breast.

Lucy had warned him that Clarissa might seem a little scary, but she was sure she meant well. Hartley warmed to her. She seemed to relish having the right set of people at her Friday supper, but she was the perfect hostess — genuinely interested in Hartley and her other guests and attentive to their needs all evening. He was rather baffled, however, when she asked after his Aunt Brodie.

"Well, I, um, I'm not entirely sure I have an Aunt Brodie."

"Aha! You're right. She has always been called Bee — since she was a child."

"Aunt Bee?"

"Yes, her real name is Brodie but she never much liked it — thought it was a boy's name and insisted on a shortened version."

"Really? Well, you learn something new every day." Hartley had no idea how Ms Appleton-Smythe could have known such an obscure fact; she must have researched his family thoroughly in preparation for supper. He didn't know whether to feel flattered or scared of her considerable knowledge and couldn't help but chuckle as he caught the look of utter pride on his hostess's face. She seemed delighted to have been able to enlighten him. He found Clarissa's devotion to those around her quite charming. Granted, she perhaps paid him more attention than the others but she made time for everyone around her — complimenting a hairstyle here, asking after family members there.

Using the moments in which Clarissa tended to her other guests, Hartley looked at Lucy. She was talking to Philippa Bonner — Hartley's family had known hers since before he was born and he knew her well — and he marvelled at how Lucy made everyone feel so relaxed.

God, he couldn't wait until next weekend, for their trip to Scotland. Was it too soon, he wondered, to ask her to marry him? It was no time at all but already he felt he knew her, trusted her more than he could ever have imagined. He was in love, of that he had no doubt. Perhaps they could stop in Edinburgh on their way back from Scotland and pop in to see his mother; he was sure she would take to Lucy straight away. She had admitted, after he had split up with Bridget, that she had never quite trusted her.

Compared to Bridget, Lucy was Cinderella next to the wicked ugly sister. It had been less than three months since they met but he never wanted to let her go. God, she was beside him and he missed her.

The Plot Thickens

Lady Bridget Beames assessed the situation. The private investigator had found out almost everything there was to know about Lucy Summers. Somehow, she'd gone to a decent boarding school, though why in Kent when the family lived in Scotland she had no idea. Very suspicious. The carpenter who was the dad of her half-sister hack, Max, wasn't hers. The private investigator still hadn't been able to track down her own father as he wasn't on the birth certificate. But the investigator had travelled to Broughty Ferry and taken pictures of her stepdad leaving their local, the Ship Inn — very original — at closing time. The investigator had also managed to pull his birth certificate and the stepdad was born in Ireland.

Perhaps Blondie had got a scholarship because she was brainy and had her fees paid; she'd got straight As at A level and studied English at Oxford. How unbelievably working class, though, for her mother to have two kids so close in age by two fathers. Dundee had the highest teenage pregnancy rate of any city in the UK. Perhaps their family was normal there but it was not acceptable for someone of Hartley's standing to be associated with them.

It made Bridget's stomach flip when she found out Lucy was five years younger than her. Having children had become somewhat of an obsession, with her mother pointing out only the day before that fertility rates fall dramatically when women hit thirty-five. Mother could be such a cow. But she hardly ever questioned giving Bridget money whenever she asked for it, so she had her uses.

It pained Bridget to admit that Lady Barbara did have a point. She desperately wanted a baby and she had set her mind to it that it would be with Hartley. Lucy might be more fertile than her, and at thirty-one she no doubt wanted babies, but over Bridget's dead body would they be Hartley's.

Most of her friends had married well and had children, or soon would. She felt they were secretly laughing at her whenever they asked how her love life was or if she'd heard from Hartley. She was sure she had seen a look of pity flash across her friend Natasha's face last week at lunch. How fucking dare they! When she had been with Hartley, they had been the most celebrated couple in their set, indeed in London.

When they had broken up Bridget knew the importance of saving face and told her friends they had agreed to a break because they were both busy, but that there was every chance they would be back together before long. Bridget knew Hartley was too much of a gent to divulge the actual, awful truth of how one-sided it had been. But she was certain their friends knew what had happened. After all, she had told them just days before she was sure he would propose.

She desired with all her being to be the Earl's wife, with the prestige and recognition it would bring. Her mother had brought her up with a clear message: she should marry well and have children to make her family proud. The cooking courses and finishing schools that had peppered Bridget's teenage years were all booked by her mother with the intention of making her a desirable wife.

Yes, she had loved Hartley. She still did. When they split up a friend had drunkenly asked if she would love him if he had nothing, not a penny or title to his name. She had feigned a look of hurt and said of course she would. She almost convinced herself it was true, but of course it mattered — the peerage, the wealth, the family history. She had always wanted to find someone with all of that and so Hartley was her dream man. Anyone else who talked about finding the man of their dreams was deemed to be in love.

Now Hartley was with Lucy, she felt utterly humiliated.

Bridget's own bloody hairdresser, Pierre, had been gushing over a picture he'd seen of Lucy in *Hello!*. Style icon this, gorgeous hair that. She must remember to find a new hair stylist and tell her friends to do the same.

Lucy might have had a lucky start, having been to a good school and mixing with the right people, but she

134

was sure Lucy had been sparing with other details of her past.

It was time Hartley knew everything. But perhaps that wouldn't be enough. She had to be sure he was put off her for good.

Hot Off the Press:
Max's Night of Shame

Max groaned as her alarm sliced through her drink-induced sleep of the dead.

On the plus side, it was the alarm set on her mobile phone, so she hadn't lost that the night before. As she switched it off Max was conscious of a presence beside her. Slowly craning her head round, with more than a smattering of fear, she saw the back of someone's head. A man. With brown-black hair. Jesus, who the fuck was in her bed?

Think, think, she told herself. Where were you? The premiere of that American comedy, *I Can Do Anything Better Than You*. Then what? The after-party at Whisky Mist in Mayfair.

As with so many of the parties boasting A-list guests, there had been a tiny enclosure inside the VIP section — a Very-Very Important Persons' area pampering to the paranoia and self-importance of the big names. It had been guarded fiercely by beefcake guards.

Often Max had been the only journalist at a party to get in there too. Once upon a time the old pretending-to-be-on-the-phone trick had paid off. Another time she had sneaked into the kitchen of the five-star Lowells hotel in London, grabbed a tray of chicken skewers with satay dips and rushed out again before she was spotted. She had smiled brightly at the V-VIP guard and breezed in.

She had even talked her way out of an ugly situation when a rival reporter, terrified that Max would scoop her to a great story, had grassed her up for being a reporter to the bouncer; she had laughed it off as a case of mistaken identity.

Last night she had sneaked into the V-VIP area with fellow *Daily News* showbiz reporter Simon while the security guard dealt with a drunken guest trying to get in.

Then?

Shit, the evening got fuzzy after endless champagne . . . oh, and that ice sculpture with gallons of vodka pouring down it.

She and Simon had taken turns on it after bagging a chat with the film's leading lady, Java Hunter, at the bar. Buoyed by a few glasses of bubbly, Max had asked her if she was dating and Java had replied that no, she was single as always and considering turning lesbian. Joking or not, she'd said it, and Max and Simon had high-fived each other as they agreed her words were enough for a lead story on their column: "Java: I'll Be Lesbian" or similar. It would certainly be a welcome list-topper for morning conference. Claire and the other department heads always put their most exciting story first in the hope of putting the editor in a good mood. Java had left ten minutes later, before their rivals had got to her. Time to relax, they had decided — or rather, get buckled at the free bar.

Simon was one of the few reporters Max trusted. Unlike Jade on their desk, he wouldn't sneak into work half an hour early the next day to tell Claire about their scoop so that it would sound like it was his story and should therefore have his byline on it. No, Simon was a gem. He reminded Max of a young Ray Winstone, a swarthy Bromley boy who peppered every sentence with swear words, like rapid fire from a machine gun. He stood out from the immaculate world of showbiz, of fellow male writers clad in Armani and Paul Smith, who aspired to be like the celebrities they wrote about. Max found it hilarious to watch him talk to the plethora of gay PRs who represented the stars they wrote about, as perfectly preened as he was dishevelled.

Max loved working with Simon. She respected his honesty, his lack of agenda. He wanted to be a journalist because he loved uncovering stories, but had somehow wound up in the bizarre field of showbiz and decided to make the most of the almost nightly parties offering free bars. A bit like Max.

Occasionally, looking at Simon over the showbiz desk, Max had considered that he would make good boyfriend material — he never failed to make her laugh and he was the kind of guy who would play fair, no games. Then she'd spot the bulging belly or notice he was scratching his balls and picking his nose at the same time and realize she simply couldn't go there.

"Come on, Max, let's get wankered, shit-faced, pissed."

"Delightfully put as always, Si." Max laughed as she followed him to the bar and ordered shot after shot of tequila.

And? Oh no, oh God no. The PR guy . . . Andy? He had told her he knew celebrity stories that would make her hair curl.

Had he told her any? Something about a young actress taking coke and giving a blow job? Shit, who was it? And then . . . then what?

Max peeked under her duvet. She was naked. Fuck.

Looking over to her bedside table, she spotted a used condom beside her mobile phone.

Lying in bed with a random was worrying, but at least they hadn't exchanged body fluids.

Shit, she was as bad as Shagger Sheri. Worse. At least Sheri could remember the details. She'd never actually been unable to remember sex. A new low. And to think that until a couple of years ago she could count the men she'd slept with on one hand. She was certainly making up for it now, maybe fuelled by the drinking culture of her job. No, that was no excuse. Was she into double figures? Or rather, how far was she into double figures, she wondered, as a series of faces popped into her throbbing head.

Andy — or was it Adam? — turned in his sleep to face her. As she took him in, it came back to her. A drunken dance at the premiere, the lights coming up. Max had found him devastatingly handsome. Looking at him now, he still was. A chiselled face you might see on the front of *GQ*. His torso tight, toned, a real-life six-pack. He had suggested going on to a bar he knew that opened all hours ... They'd stayed there for a couple of drinks then headed back to Max's in a cab.

Andy/Adam and Max had been kissing passionately as she fumbled to open her flat door. Then they were inside and Max had pulled him towards her and had the deepest kiss imaginable. Her handbag fell to the floor as he pressed against her. She could feel he was rock hard against her.

Unbuttoning her shirtdress like his life depended on it, he pulled it off Max and groaned as he took in her perfect breasts. He unfastened her black lacy bra and with hunger in his eyes he craned his neck to reach her nipples. Unable to wait any longer, and keen not to wake her sister, Max took his hand and led him to her bedroom. As they fell into her bed, kissing all the time, Max felt the muscles of his face break into a smile.

"You are incredibly sexy."

"Thank you," Max whispered as she unbuckled the belt of his jeans and wriggled out of her black thong, running her hand over his perfect torso.

Grabbing him towards her, she arched her back as he entered her (yes, there had been a quick fumble for that condom, thank God). He had told her how wet she was, how she turned him on, how good she felt.

Jeez, he was hot. Max rarely had an orgasm after drinking a skinful, but she had one last night. So had he, with sheer ecstasy written all over his face. The thought of it made her shiver.

So the sex was great; he was gorgeous. Why the hell did she already know she didn't want to see him again?

140

What was wrong with her? Who did she think she was? She'd had sex, what was there to look forward to? Not for the first time, Max considered she had more of a boy's attitude in situations like this.

She had known before sex that Andy/Adam wasn't a keeper — he was gorgeous but she didn't want him as her boyfriend. She didn't know why, but she knew. She didn't get lost in his dark brown eyes; she didn't see his soul through those eyes. No doubt another lucky girl would fall madly in love with him. This hottie deserved no less. Funny how you could admire someone's sexiness yet know they were not for you.

Maybe I'm shutting myself off to love — like they say in the agony-aunt columns. Maybe I really do want to see him again — he's perfect — and I'm kidding myself so I don't get hurt. Nah, bollocks. I just don't want to see him again.

Fuck, he'd mentioned he was doing the PR for that new band, Roy's Iron DNA, who were going to be huge. Shit, she'd probably have to deal with him in future for interview requests and the like.

Moving a millimetre at a time so as not to wake him, Max edged out of bed slower than a snail with a full belly.

"Morning, gorgeous."

Fuckity woop woop, too late.

"Hey, good morning. How're you feeling?" Max chirped as sweetly as her mouldy-slice-of-bread tongue would allow.

"All the better for waking up to you." And with that he grabbed Max round her waist and pulled her to him. "You are even more beautiful in the morning."

Max was suddenly conscious she must have morning breath. She hoped he wouldn't notice she was ever so subtly pulling away from his grip.

He was undeniably cute. So how come she couldn't wait for him to go?

"Listen, I'm just going to fix us a coffee, OK?"

"Sure, honey."

Eugh. Max felt herself shudder at the words. She wanted him out of her bed and out of her flat. She wanted to clean her sheets.

The familiar panic that only a hangover could bring was descending — she often called it The Fear or The Madness as everything seemed so inflated in her mind the morning after.

Must stop mentally beating myself up with a hangover, she told herself as she noted her mouth tasted of a hundred cigarette ends. Must bloody stop chaining when pissed. The lungs take eight years to repair.

At least she had the day off, having worked the last Sunday shift. Each of the showbiz writers took it in turns to run the desk on a Sunday, then had the following Friday off for a long weekend. She had agreed to pop into the office around six for an hour or two, though, to check proofs of the showbiz pages and to cover Simon who had to leave early.

Pouring herself a glass of orange juice, Max noticed something on the kitchen table. A passport. Opening it up, she saw it was Lucy's. She smiled as she remembered taking their passport photos together, with Mum, a couple of years ago in Boots.

At the other side of the table was a note in Lucy's handwriting.

Dear Max,

I forgive you as always for waking me up in the middle of the night — though 5.30 a.m. is quite something even by your standards.

By the time you get up I'll be having brunch with my dad, then catching a flight from London City Airport to Dundee for a weekend with Hartley and his friends. Meeting the friends . . . must be serious!

If you need me, try the mobile — I'm staying at a country pile near the village of Peat in Fife — less than hour's drive from home! Hopefully the reception will be OK.

I'll bring you back a bottle of malt . . . hair of the dog.

I love you,
Lu

With the thud that only a hangover combined with a horrible realization can bring, it dawned on Max that Lucy had forgotten her passport — and as Lucy had told her a few days before, airlines were insisting on passports even to travel to Scotland, as part of some temporary security check. No passport, no flight, Lucy had told her.

Oh fuckity fuck. Right, think. How could she find out Lucy's flight time? Of course, the most organized sister in the world not only carried a personal organizer, she had a wall chart with her every move for the next year in her bedroom.

And there she found it, written in pink to indicate a social activity.

10 a.m.: Meet Dad for brunch, Grangemouth Golf Club
2 p.m.: Arrive at City for 3.30 p.m. flight to Dundee

Time now? 10.45 a.m. She remembered Lucy telling her that mobiles had to be switched off in the club — so she couldn't call her. If she jumped in a taxi to the golf club — it was where Lucy often met her dad and was, from memory, between their flat and the airport — she could meet Lucy and give her the passport.

"Rise and shine. I'm really sorry, something urgent has come up."

Max explained the situation to the bloke in her bed with as much drama as she could muster, her head keeping time to some messed-up symphony.

Max decided to leave the flat with him to give the story a realistic edge. It would spare his feelings to know that she really was in a desperate rush to get out and find her sister.

"Of course I'll phone you," Max promised as he handed her his card. She never gave out her own card, which had her mobile number, when she was sure she didn't want a sequel.

Scooshing deodorant under her arms and throwing mascara, lipstick and perfume into her Dolce & Gabbana black-leather bag, Max slammed her front door and bid farewell to what's-his-name before hailing a cab.

Tears for Fears

Yes, she'd put on the first clothes that came to hand, and her mascara and eyeliner had combined and expanded to make her look like a panda. But maybe she kind of pulled off that "just got out of bed" look.

Wearing a micro tartan skirt which only just covered her bum, a black Vivienne Westwood vest top and black-suede ankle boots, Max's clobber could almost pass for day wear. Well, if her job was as a lunch-time cocktail waitress in an uber-trendy yet slightly dodgy bar.

Max jumped out of the cab, gave the driver a twenty and asked him to wait. She'd only be a few minutes.

"Hello, miss, can I help you?" A gruff voice greeted Max as she breezed up to the entrance to Grangemouth Golf Club.

"Oh, yes, hello. I need to go inside and give something to somebody."

Max chided herself — she was sure she'd slurred at least half of her words. And she was even more sure the smell of alcohol from her breath and pores must have hit the man, who was dressed like a butler, like a body slam.

"I don't think so."

"Sorry?"

"I don't think so, young lady," the man with the posh voice was telling her. Taking in every inch of her, from her steel-capped toes to her ruffled hair, he straightened himself up and cleared his throat. "I'm afraid there must be some mistake. Our dress code is, erm, rather strict, miss."

"Listen, I know I'm dressed for a wild night in Ibiza." Max laughed as she tried to make eye contact with the posh doorman and win him over. As she heard herself speak she felt detached from what she was saying. Her Scottish accent had never sounded so broad. She felt so out of place.

"Thank you, miss. Our members expect a certain, erm, standard."

She felt like a tart. A dirty stop-out. How cheap she must look, with her tiny skirt and corset, her boobs thrust up and spilling out. The doorman must think she was like Sheri — after a rich golfer.

But she wasn't bloody Shagger Sheri, was she? She'd had a big night and smelled of pure alcohol, but so what? Did that give this jumped-up bouncer the right to make her feel unworthy of stepping inside his precious club?

The only person feeling sorry for themselves should be this nugget, for thinking he had a right to stand there and put anyone down. Even if Sheri presented herself before him dressed in a PVC catsuit, he should politely tell her to beat it rather than ooze the disdain he so clearly felt.

A sense of anger bubbled inside her as she readied herself to come up with a witty put-down for this plank.

"Nice view."

Max looked up and met the eyes of the man . . . the man who had said that before.

"Max?"

Luke. Just when she thought it couldn't get any worse, the man of her dreams had appeared. Granted, she could have sworn her heart actually stopped when she saw him. But what did it matter? He was engaged to Miss Perfect Tits and Teeth and would have white-haired, perfect children who would ski, play tennis and talk French before they could walk.

"Yes," Max said weakly, her tone a mix of resignation and fatigue.

"So it's true?"

"What?" Max said, barely audibly.

"You only ever leave your house half-dressed. Hey, I'm not complaining."

"Ha ha," Max said deadpan, with no sign of laughter.

"Listen, Michael," Luke addressed the doorman.

"Yes, sir?"

"I couldn't help but overhear your conversation with this lady. I'm sure Miss Summers will overlook the situation, Michael. You really had no reason to realize she is a very highly regarded journalist and my personal guest."

"Oh . . . oh — I-I do apologize, miss, erm, M-M-Miss S-Summers," Michael was stuttering profusely. "P-Please forgive me."

Before Max could take in the situation, Luke had put her arm in his and whizzed her through the entrance into the private members' lounge.

"How do you know I'm a journalist?" Max asked slowly.

Luke seemed not to hear. Stopping at a small table beside the bar he said: "Max, I would like you to meet my father, Peter." He gave her a beaming smile. "My brother, Ben." Another welcoming smile. He looked familiar. "Last but not least, my sister, Lucy."

The blonde girl with her back to Max turned round. As her face came into view Max saw it was . . . her sister.

"No, Luke, that's my sister Lucy." Max looked bewildered, suddenly unsteady on her feet as she looked uncomprehendingly from Lucy to Luke.

Peter and Ben had stood up and were kissing Max on the cheek. She returned the gesture as if on autopilot but her mind seemed frozen.

Finally, after what seemed a baffling eternity, Lucy spoke.

"Max, this is my brother Luke. You remember him from my photos? He's just been telling me how you met the other day. He recognized you from my pictures."

Taking the situation in, Max made a strange noise — half sharp intake of breath and half laugh. Lucy's brother? Oh Christ, she had thought he might have fancied her when all along he must have wanted to ask if she was his half-sister's sister.

Max's voice was thin and robotic, strangled in her throat. "Yes, I've met Luke a couple of times."

It was all too much for Max to take in. The impossibly gorgeous Luke, with his sapphire eyes, his broad shoulders and charm, was Lucy's half-brother.

Max realized with a jolt that this was the boy she had seen in family snaps over the years, skiing, diving and riding with Lucy. He looked so different to the chubby-faced teenager hiding behind his long dark blond hair. He had grown into his features, his face now handsome and strong, his body manly and firm, his shoulders broad. But those beautiful smiling eyes, they were the same.

"Oh Max, what a shock for you. I'm sorry. Luke was always a bit grungy as a teenager, a real surf dude. Ben's hardly changed, I guess, but Luke's so different . . ."

Luke was staring at Max, his eyes wide with concern.

"I'm so sorry," he said. "It dawned on me the first time I saw you — climbing over the wall at the premiere. Lucy's always talking about your exploits at the paper and she's shown me pictures. I tried to explain when I saw you again . . . but, well, Jenni . . ."

"Oh yes, please don't worry. It's fine. Funny, I suppose." Max tried to force out a laugh but it caught in her throat. This bloody hangover was reaching an almighty crescendo as she took in the situation — there was so much to compute it hurt her head.

Max wondered what must be going through Luke's head. How could one sister be so trashy, the other so elegant?

This was beyond weird. She made herself smile as she took in Lucy's dad and Ben. It was as if the old photos her sister had shown her were staring at her. Peter's hair was greyer, Ben's face had filled out a little, but they hadn't changed much. She could see the undeniable resemblance between Peter and Lucy — the bright blue eyes and strong cheekbones. Was there any way of turning this fiasco round so that she looked dignified? God, this was not the first impression she'd imagined making should she ever get round to meeting Lucy's family.

Taking a deep breath, Max composed herself. The sooner she spoke, the sooner she could get out.

"Finally we meet," she addressed Peter and Ben, who were still standing, looking at her kindly yet expectantly, "I'm Max."

Without warning Peter opened his arms and put them around Max, squeezing her tightly.

Fuck, she must smell like an unwashed beer mat.

"Isn't it just ridiculous we've never met?" he asked as he pulled away. "We've heard so much about you I feel like I know you already."

Max laughed, turning her head slightly so as not to knock him out with the vodka fumes. "Oh, you too. I think I've seen pictures of every family holiday you've ever had," she said, meeting Peter's eyes, hoping he would laugh, relieved when he did.

Ben leaned in and gave her a warm hug. "It's a travesty we've never before encountered the magnificent Max." He beamed.

"Oh I don't know about magnificent," Max replied, shifting from foot to foot.

"Please, you must join us for a coffee. You have time before your flight, don't you, Lucy?"

Before her sister could answer, Max cut in.

"That's so kind, thank you. I'd love to, really, but I'm in a bit of a rush."

Rush where? Shit. Think. Why would she be dressed for clubbing before midday?

"I'm on my way to an audition." Max wasn't exactly sure what would come out of her mouth but she was forming an idea as she said the words. "I have to audition for the new *Britain's Got Talent* — you know the talent show with Simon Cowell? It's for a feature for my paper . . . hence the get-up."

Peter, Ben, Luke and Lucy were smiling back at her. Peter was nodding, as if to say, "Ah that explains it."

So long as he hadn't smelled the alcohol she was sure must be oozing through every pore, he wouldn't think she was a raving alcoholic. Situation salvaged?

"Luce, sorry to barge in like this — and me looking like this." Max attempted a laugh again but managed only a whimper that caught in the back of her throat. God, this was draining. Maybe that's what actors meant when they described their last film as a labour of love. Max felt she deserved an Oscar nomination for this little performance. All she really wanted to do was drink a gallon of water, curl up in a ball and sleep in a darkened room.

Catching her reflection in a huge gold-framed mirror Max saw how awful she looked. Chapped lips, sunken eyes and smudged eyeliner — pathetic.

Looking around the golf club she felt naked in this quiet, calm room with expensive canvases on the wall and cigar cases behind the bar. Michael wasn't the only one who looked like he had a coat hanger up his arse —

a couple in the corner were sitting opposite each other and leafing through newspapers, their perfect posture matching their pristine outfits, with starched collars and fine-wool V-necked jumpers straight out of a *Good Housekeeping* feature from the 1950s.

Clearing her throat she managed: "Luce, you left your passport. I thought I'd better get it to you."

Handing it over, Max made a brave attempt at the motto that had seen her through so many mortifying situations: chin up, chest out, paint on a smile.

"Right, pleasure meeting you all. Hopefully we can meet again soon. Lunch, maybe? I'm afraid I have to dash now, though." With a flash of teeth Max turned round. They seemed like such nice people. She really would like to meet them all again, under different circumstances. But as for Luke . . . She'd been so attracted to him, Lucy's brother.

"Hold on, Max. Wait." Lucy was on her feet, following Max. "Thanks so much. Please. You sure you don't have time for a coffee?"

"No, Luce," Max said in a hushed tone so the others couldn't hear. "I feel as awful as I look. I have to go home. Have a great weekend with Hartley."

Concern and love were etched across Lucy's beautiful face. "You sure you're OK?"

Max forced a smile to reassure her sister, who looked so effortlessly elegant in her Marc Jacobs khaki trouser suit with cream silk shirt underneath. "Yes, anyway my cab is waiting."

As Max kissed her sister on the cheek and bid her farewell, she realized Luke was standing beside them.

"Yes?" Max asked him with a note of impatience, masking her humiliation.

"I'm heading your way. You live in Kensington with Lucy, right?"

"Erm, right."

"OK. It's the least I can do — you coming all this way to save the day. Let me pay the driver and I'll take you home."

The sparkling sapphires fixed on her once more — though now they were tinged with concern.

Before she could answer, Luke had walked out of the club house. Max kissed Lucy once more.

"Sorry, Luce."

"What for?"

"For being such a fuck-up."

"Shush. I love you, Max. I think you're wonderful and they do too."

Turning away, Max felt a lone tear roll down her cheek. By the time she was outside, she was crying uncontrollably.

"Hey. Max? What on earth is wrong?"

Luke, lovely Luke. With the Stepford Wife at home who would never reek of booze, wake up with a random, pee herself, watch someone else pee as part of her job, or any of the ludicrous things Max had done in the last few weeks alone.

Wiping away her tears Max tried to sound calm: "Luke, can you take me home now?"

"Of course. Let's go."

Here's Luke-ing at You

Normally, Max would have deflated the situation by making fun of herself and laughing it all off.

But she was exhausted, drained from the excesses of a life of free bars and celebrity vacuousness. Of people using her to get fame and her using them to keep up her reputation as a story-getter. What the fuck was it all about?

She sat in silence as Luke drove her home. She pretended to sleep in the passenger seat but her mind was racing.

Perhaps she had liked Luke from the moment she saw him because he looked somehow familiar. And now she knew why that was — he was Lucy's half-brother. Max was still in shock at the revelation. He didn't look like Lucy exactly, but there was something about him — in his sparkling eyes — that calmed Max, made her feel that she didn't want to be anywhere else.

How incestuous that she had fancied her sister's brother. It even sounded odd. Although Max and Luke were in no way related, so maybe it was OK. What was OK? That she fancied the pants off him? There was certainly no possibility in this little fantasy scenario that he even remotely liked her. At best he thought she was funny, at worst tragic. Not like Jen, waiting at home with a freshly baked low-carb pie or whatever the hell it was she ate that kept her skinny with big boobs.

Anyway, Miss Gap At The Top Of Her Legs was Luke's type — not Max the loose cannon, whom he'd only noticed because she was nearly naked on all three occasions they'd met. That and the fact he recognized her as Lucy's sister. No wonder he hadn't mentioned it in front of Jenni — he must have been mortified to have a family connection with her.

Max decided it was only polite to make a little conversation now they were nearly home.

"So," she chirped, chewing three bits of gum in a bid to get rid of her booze breath. "How are the wedding plans going?"

Luke, wearing baggy jeans and a crisp, close-fitting white shirt, managed to look smart and cool at once. The remnants of his rebellious surfing days were faintly present, yet he was so handsome and grown-up. His accent wasn't strong, but it was subtly from London. Whatever it was, it was sexy. He changed gear studiously before saying, "I'm afraid there isn't going to be a wedding."

Luke glanced over and caught Max's eye, almost shyly.

In spite of herself Max felt her stomach flip. God, he was handsome. Rugged yet beautiful, charming and cheeky.

"Really?" Max hoped she was veiling her excited curiosity with a deep concern.

"Yeah. I called it off," Luke continued, turning down his David Bowie CD.

"You did? Why?"

"Well —" Luke let out a slow sigh — "I'd had doubts for a while, but Jenni wanted so badly to get married. I guess I just went along with things." Luke caught Max's eye again. She wondered if the palpitations she felt might be nothing to do with him — and simply down to the fact that she'd downed her recommended weekly number of units in one session the night before.

"I see."

"Things came to a head when Jenni banned me going out with the boys last week. I was only allowed one night out — and I'd already used my quota."

"She didn't?"

"I'm afraid she did, Max. It's not that I'm some wild party animal. I'm just not ready to be told what to do. It's not like we have kids. We aren't even married. I guess I was scared of what was to come."

"I don't blame you." Max looked out of the window, recognizing the pretty tree-lined street as one close to her own. Town houses with window baskets of brightly coloured flowers whizzed by like a scene out of Mary Poppins.

"Do you think it's just a tiff? You think you might get back together?"

Luke didn't hesitate. "No, Max. I know we won't. Jenni was a great girl but not for me. I'd rather hold out and be alone than settle, you know?"

Max laughed, her eyes dancing with his. "Oh yes, I know what you mean."

Pulling up at her flat, Luke jumped out of the car to open the passenger door.

"Thank you, Luke."

Luke hugged her with a warmth that surprised her.

Pulling away he lifted Max's chin with his hand so her gaze met his.

"Max?"

"Yes?"

"Would you mind if I called you?"

"Of course not." Looking up at him, Max realized the sight of Luke took her breath away. But she must be misreading the signs. "Now we're family we should keep in touch."

"Max?"

"Yes, Luke?"

"That's not what I meant."

As Luke stared into her big brown eyes, Max forgot to speak. Or maybe she was speaking to him with no words. She couldn't tell.

Slowly, he placed his hand at the nape of her neck and pulled her to him. His soft lips cushioned Max's. She felt like she was falling and falling yet was safe and warm.

His tongue sought hers with real need, yet its touch was gentle.

Pulling away Max felt giddy. She wanted more.

Fishing out a business card from her bag, Max handed it to Luke, whose sandy hair shone around him like a halo in the September sun.

Kissing her on the forehead Luke said: "I can't wait."

Like a Bridget Over Nasty Waters

"Do I sound like I give a flying fuck how hard it is to get in or how cold it is? I could not care less about any of your moronic concerns. I'm paying you five grand for a day's work to do bugger all. Just take a photo and say what we agreed — how hard can it be? Now get in your car and get that bitch."

Bridget took a deep breath and exhaled. That had told the cretinous photographer. Now he would get on and do what she was paying him so handsomely to do — take a picture of Lucy and Hartley and make sure everyone in their cosy little group was in no doubt as to who tipped him off with their location: Little Miss Bimbo herself.

The only thing Hartley hated more than having his personal life in the press was disloyalty. And this plan should ensure he no longer trusted Lucy as far as he could throw her, which was hopefully all the way back to her working-class roots in Dundee.

Lucy deserved everything she had coming to her. Not only had she stolen the man everyone knew should be with Bridget, she had put Bridget down at Ascot, an incident still fresh, still rankling in her mind.

Bridget had been consumed with raw hatred when she saw Lucy that day. She hadn't been prepared for it at all. It winded her to admit, of course only to herself, that Lucy was indeed pretty, just as some columnists had said. And younger than Bridget. The tart probably had a game plan to snare Hartley and have his children. Bridget had to act now to put a stop to her fantasy before it became a horrible reality.

Of course, she was no match for Bridget, who outclassed her in every way, not least in standing and title. This tramp was an imposter from a grubby background. Looks and ambition could get you far in life. But it would not get her Hartley.

How Lucy must have laughed when she saw the newspaper the day after Ascot, with that hideous picture of Bridget pursing her lips next to a perfect image of the bitch. Bridget was sure her own friends had been laughing too. Of course, they called and told her the story had been written terribly unfairly, but Bridget could tell they loved every minute of it. Now it was her turn to publicly humiliate Lucy, and that couldn't come soon enough.

A Very Big House in the Country

The words "pile in the country" didn't quite do justice to the mansion Lucy found herself in somewhere near a tiny village called Peat. Robert had picked up the four of them — Lucy and Hartley, Charles and Claudia — from Dundee airport and taken them across the Tay River to Fife. Hartley had suggested they could fly back from Edinburgh and pop in to see his mum on the way. When he called to make sure she would be there, the housekeeper answered and said she had gone to visit a friend in Inverness and would be away all weekend. But still, the thought had been there and Lucy felt flattered that he wanted to introduce her to his mum. He spoke so fondly of her; she clearly meant a great deal to him.

"Perhaps if we have time we could visit my family," Lucy had ventured. "Mum lives half an hour from Dundee airport — or she could come to meet us there for coffee in the departure café."

Hartley beamed at the suggestion. Lucy could see it meant just as much to him to be asked to meet her mother as it had for her. "That would be wonderful, Lucy," he had told her.

Driving through St Andrews, Lucy wondered how Prince William had adapted to such a sleepy town after years of partying in London. Ha! He probably loved the tranquillity, the fresh air, the tiny boutique shops and unaffected locals. What was there not to like? Whizzing past the famous Old Course, Lucy found conversation in Robert's Range Rover flowed easily. They seemed simply to accept she must be a "good egg", as Hartley would say, because he was with her.

Lucy's boss, Genevieve, had practically salivated when she told her she was taking Friday off so she could have a long weekend in Scotland.

"Oh really, who with?"

"Oh Hartley's friend Robbie has a little place in Fife."

"Not Robbie as in Robert Mackenzie?"

"That's him."

"He split up with a friend of a friend of a friend when he moved to Scotland from London a year or so back."

Lucy looked over her shoulder to see if anyone else on the floor had noticed her boss's voice had moved up several octaves.

"He's single. Did you know he's single?"

Lucy smiled and said no as her boss rabbited on like a raver on acid about how she'd once met him . . . well, said hello . . . at some charity thing and thought he was gorgeous. Punching Lucy on the shoulder in a sisterly, jokey, but nothing-funny-about-it kind of way, she made Lucy promise to let him know she had a pretty single friend who would be perfect for him.

Since Genevieve had learned of Lucy's boyfriend, there had been a transformation in her behaviour towards her. Just months ago, she had treated Lucy as

162

the tea girl, with a frequent roll of her eyes followed by, "Oh Lucy, I could kill for a skinny latte . . . would you be a darling?"

The plum jobs like styling a vintage shoot she had either kept for herself, in the hope of snaffling a handbag or dress, or, when she couldn't be bothered working them herself, she carefully chose who would take her place, normally one of the girls who were well connected and who would repay her by inviting her to a party. Now it was Lucy who was being promised the shoot in Monte Carlo with Elsba, the model being tipped to take over the world, and a luxury skiing trip to write a commentary on slope chic and other glamorous jobs.

Lucy relished doing the best job possible on the increasingly high-profile shoots and interviews she was being given, but Genevieve's motive for this sudden change of heart grated. Lucy had no doubt her boss would have demoted her to tea girl by now if she could have, but the fact was that Lucy more than deserved her position as a writer. She made any article come to life with her description of clothes, her love of fashion shining through. But there was something about Lucy that made Genevieve uneasy. Rather than applaud her for bringing talent to her department, she had tried to hide from others on the magazine how good Lucy was, taking credit for herself instead where at all possible. But her ruthless ambition to know the Hartleys of this world seemed to have surpassed her dislike of Lucy.

Lucy had lost count of the times Genevieve had asked her a question ridiculously loudly so the other girls could hear. Quite often she bellowed: "You'll never guess who asked me out on a date last night! Go on, guess."

She insisted the girls guessed. When they had exhausted their mental list of eligible bachelors, Genevieve would shout out the name — some friend of a friend of a minor royal or similar. The girls had never heard of him but pretended to be most impressed. She was, after all, in charge of allocating trips and shoots for the writers. Lucy guessed that's why she wasn't on her boss's list of favourites: she didn't pander to the inane boasting.

The only person who showed less interest was Carlos. While Lucy was at least polite if indifferent, Carlos would openly mock Genevieve in front of her gaggle of assistants. Even they couldn't help but stifle giggles when their boss was at the sharp end of his tongue.

"Oh enough of the 'guess which millionaire fancies me today' game. Who the fuck cares?" he said once in his hardened, mock-macho yet clearly gay New York accent. "Get yourself a real man — one who works for a living — and beg him to give you a good seeing to. That would get the coat hanger out of your skinny ass."

Carlos had nothing to fear from Genevieve — she couldn't sack him. He was the best at what he did in London and, if it came to a choice, the publishers would choose him over her. Genevieve was exposed as the coward she really was when Carlos had made fun of her; she laughed nervously, pretending Carlos was sharing some in-joke with her.

"There's nothing to joke about," he told Lucy afterwards. "I smelled her out as the bullying phoney she is. I see the way she looks at you — she's a jealous fake."

Genevieve had learned from experience not to make boasts in front of Carlos again.

"Has Hartley shown you his third nipple yet?" Robert asked, taking his eye off the road for a second to address Lucy with a mischievous look, ending her thoughts of her peculiar boss and bringing her back to the present.

"Erm, no, Robert — I mean, Robbie."

Their host had insisted that Lucy call him Robbie, because being called Robert made him feel like he was in trouble.

"Look, Robbie," started an indignant Hartley, "I've told you before, it's just a birth mark."

"OK, Scaramanga," Robbie countered before he and Charles exploded with laughter.

You see, Lucy told herself as she joined in with the laughter, these people were no different. Yes they had more money and opportunities than most. But they also laughed at themselves. Who would have believed it: the upper classes had a sense of humour. Indeed, Hartley had made her laugh more than any man she had ever dated. Put him on a remote island and she had no doubt he could not only survive but also grow his own crops; she was equally sure, though, that he had never put on a load of washing without forgetting to remove a chocolate bar from a trouser pocket or to take out the red top that dyed his cricket whites pink.

Lucy imagined Hartley's friends thought so highly of their genuine, fun-loving pal that they welcomed a girlfriend who made him happy. Lucy chided herself as a wicked thought flickered through her mind: just maybe they disliked cruel Bridget and were thankful he had found a kinder, nicer replacement. Hurray! Then again, what if they had all glimpsed a softer, lovely side to Bridget? They would have had to look very deep inside, Lucy thought, to see any warmth within the Ice Queen.

In Robbie's big car, Lucy felt like Alice in Wonderland when she became a giant, speeding along the winding country roads, with miniature white cottages and dinky fields dotted with sheep.

She took in the delicious smell of burning wood as they drove up what she imagined was the drive to Robbie's house. After a mile or so she wondered if any drive could be so long. How did they maintain the spectacular gardens with perfectly trimmed hedges and rose bushes as far as the eye could see? And then they were there, in front of an awesomely imposing Georgian house. As she entered, she inhaled sharply as she looked up to a grand wooden staircase straight out of a Jane Austen novel. Paintings bigger than her adorned the walls — pictures of distinguished officers and delicate women with ivory complexions and trussed-up bosoms escaping their tiny bodices. Lucy wondered if these people were Robbie's relatives.

166

Most of the portraits looked so formal, but one caught Lucy's eye. A virginal-looking woman, no more than twenty, with blood-red lips, big sad blue eyes and beautiful dark hair which fell in loose ringlets to her waist.

Lucy smiled as she thought of one of her colleagues, Sophie, who wrote for the mag's diary section. She had had the most gorgeous long, black, silky hair but was so obsessed with having the latest look that she had chopped it as short as possible and dyed it white — all because the supermodel Agyness Deyn was gracing covers with the quirky style. Sophie suited the look — she was stunning, with a size zero frame most of the girls on the floor would kill for — and it made her look funky and edgy. Still, Lucy couldn't help but look at her at times and lament her glossy locks.

Hartley squeezed her hand. "This place has been in Robbie's family for centuries. His mum and dad are getting on and he's running the place now."

"Oh I see. It's stunning."

"Yes, it is." And so are you, Hartley thought. Seeing Lucy in such a splendid new setting was like seeing her for the first time. As he drank in her every detail, he wanted desperately to make love to her, to throw her on the bed upstairs and rip her clothes off. Just what he needed, a bloody erection in front of his friends.

"Right," he barked, while holding Lucy's brown-leather overnight bag in front of his crotch, "shall we drop our bags?"

167

Marching up the stairs, Hartley told Lucy he knew well the room they would stay in. He had boarded with Robbie and stayed for many a night over the holidays. His own family home in Edinburgh was just an hour's drive away.

"Here we are," he announced, throwing open a door. "Hartley's room."

Lucy let out a shriek of delight as she took in the room, which looked like it had been untouched for a century. There was nothing ostentatious about it; it was just quietly grand with a little dark-wood dressing table displaying a lady's brush and mirror set, and a four-poster bed with delicately embroidered pale blue covers.

She sat on the bed and bounced up and down. "I feel like Bridget Jones when Hugh Grant takes her away to a stately home for the weekend."

"I'd choose you over Renée Zellweger any day," Hartley said, joining her on the bed.

"Good. And don't do a Hugh Grant on me and run off with some totty like he did as Daniel Cleaver in the film."

"As if, Lucy Lu."

Hartley caught Lucy's eye. She saw something she hadn't seen before. What was it? Leaning towards her, Hartley moved his body to face hers. The power of his kiss stunned her. Desire, that's what she had seen. Raw lust. He wanted her. Thank God. There had been little more than kissing for weeks. She wanted him too, now.

She pulled him to her as she felt the wonderful throbbing between her legs. Manoeuvring herself on top, she lay on him, kissing him with an intensity she had forgotten or perhaps had never felt before. She felt Hartley's hand on her blouse, opening her top button and fumbling on the second. To hell with it, she thought, tearing at the front and ripping the fastenings apart.

Lucy couldn't stop kissing Hartley deeply, moving to his ear. She could tell he liked that and relished his groan and the swelling of a rather impressive erection.

Craning his neck up, Hartley took Lucy's right breast in his mouth and sucked her nipple while kneading the other with his hand.

"Oh God," Lucy moaned, pulling his T-shirt up and over his head.

"Lucy, I've never wanted anything more."

"Mmm . . ."

Pulling at her belt, Lucy knew she had to have Hartley inside within moments. She had to.

Her thoughts were jarred by a sharp noise, a knock at the door. "Guys, chop-chop, I've booked an early supper." It was Robbie. With a jolt, Lucy, straddling Hartley, turned round.

"Oh Christ, sorry you two."

Grabbing her cream blouse, Lucy clutched it to her breasts.

"Oh that's OK, we were just, erm . . ." Lucy's voice trailed off.

"Sucking on Hartley's third nipple?"

"Yes, sucking on Hartley's third nipple," she replied meekly.

She collapsed on Hartley's chest, her face scarlet red.

Hartley lifted his head an inch off the pillow, sheltering Lucy with his strong embrace. "Great timing as always, Robbie, you arse."

"Sorry, Scaramanga. But we're running late for dinner."

"Yes, yes, we'll be down in ten."

Sheri, Anyone?

Sheri took in her reflection in her bathroom mirror and almost cried. Her eyes looked tiny, surrounded by dark hollow circles no amount of concealer would hide. Her hair extensions needed to be redone — the bleached-blonde hair imported from Russia cost a fortune and chunks had fallen out, taking some of her lank locks with them. She looked as bad as she felt. Last night had been a new low. A paparazzi contact had told her where Justin Timberlake was staying — the Landmark hotel in London — and she had hot-footed it along to nurse a bottle of white wine in the bar. After a couple of hours, around midnight, Justin had come back from whatever party he'd been at, then walked straight past her and headed to his room. The boring bastard. Just as she was about to leave, a guy offered to buy her a drink. Sheri was pretty sure he wasn't famous, but he was wearing a Rolex so she agreed. Then he was joined by a woman who told her — when he'd nipped to the toilet — that she was his escort for the night. He was hoping Sheri would join them.

Dressed in a shocking-pink PVC miniskirt and cut-off white vest top which barely covered her boobs, Sheri wondered if they'd mistaken her for a hooker and prepared to tell this tart where to go.

"We've got plenty of coke, enough for a top night," the woman — Sheri guessed she was in her late twenties to early thirties — told her.

Sheri could think of nothing better than hoovering up a few lines. She needed it after the crap end to the night. She deserved it.

And so she followed the tall Scouser with dark hair and a square jaw, who was wearing a wedding ring and introduced himself as Patrick, to a room in the hotel, along with the woman, who was called Tasha. She had peroxided hair with split ends and later told Sheri her four-year-old was at home with her own mum, who thought she was out on a date.

Sheri asked for some coke before they got started.

After a couple of lines, as well as the bottle of wine — and the champagne Patrick had poured — Sheri felt invincible.

When Patrick told her he wanted to do all sorts of things to her and Tasha, Sheri told him he could do anything he goddamn wanted — after all, the coke was seriously good stuff.

And now here she stood the afternoon after the night/morning before, remembering what she had done in return for multiple lines of gak. Patrick had tired of straight sex pretty soon. As he whipped out another bag of the white stuff, Sheri agreed to anal. She had agreed to everything — kissing Tasha, oral with Tasha. And now she felt dirty, used and sore. What's worse, she was broke and no matter how much charlie Patrick had given her, his lack of fame meant she couldn't sell the story. He'd given her £300 in cash when she left but that wouldn't go far; she owed her dealer £2,000. How the fuck was she going to pay for her extensions? She might have to ask Envy to cover her half of the rent this month. As she felt the familiar onset of comedown palpitations, she knew one thing for sure.

She had to find a celebrity. Quick.

Power to the Max

Max felt on top of the world. She couldn't explain it, but somehow Luke had blown her away. His dancing eyes, that wonderful searching kiss. It made her stomach flip every time she thought of it. He liked her, he actually liked her. She hadn't misread the signs. And she liked him. Luke, the hottie. Granted, it was a bit weird him being Lucy's half-brother but, hell, they were in no way related. The thought had crossed her mind that Lucy might find it odd, but she was sure she would understand when Max told her how much she liked him.

Moments after she had left him following that wonderful kiss, he had texted: "I mean it. I want to see you as soon as possible. I can't wait."

Max had read and reread it, smiling like a maniac each time. Normally such keenness would have turned her off but this felt great. Well, when you really like someone, playing it cool is hugely overrated. She wanted to be told every day that he wanted her. Because, for once, she wanted him too.

Max replied with a lone "x" — OK, so the guy shouldn't play it cool, but she didn't want to get all gushing on him.

When, a couple of hours later, Luke's name flashed on her mobile, she was inexplicably struck by nerves.

Shit, what do I say? Shall I ignore it and call back when I've thought of a few witty lines? Shut it, you fuckwit, and answer the phone.

"Hello, Luke."

"Hi, Max. How you doing?"

"Good thanks, you?"

"Very well. Can I take you out for dinner tonight, eight o'clock, Islington?"

Max laughed. "Sounds like you've made up your mind."

"I have. You seemed like you needed cheering up and I'm the man to do it. Shall I pick you up?"

"No, I have to pop into the office. I'll come straight from work."

"OK, can you find your way to the Duke of Cambridge?"

"Sure, I'll Google it. See you there."

When Max arrived at her desk, Simon looked apologetic.

"Hope ya don't mind covering for me, Max, but I'm booked into this Alan Carr class to give up smoking . . . a-fucking-gain. I'll do it this time, though — at fucking £200 a pop, I'd bloody better."

"Try stopping swearing at the same time, maybe?"

"Fuck that."

So proofing the showbiz pages — making sure there were no spelling mistakes or errors after the subs had edited the reporters' copy to make it fit their design — was down to Max. Some England rugby player had issued a legal letter to all newspapers saying they could not refer to him pulling a transsexual unless they wanted a whopping law suit. Max had briefly referred to it as part of another story and the sub editors only

175

flagged it up to her as she was leaving. Hastily, she changed the copy with some other anecdote to fill the space and raced off to hail a taxi.

Not even bumping into the messenger boy she'd fantasized about had sidetracked her. Luke filled her thoughts.

Max had even forgotten her hangover and was sure she'd made enough effort to wipe away her tiredness.

She had chosen her outfit with great consideration, settling on a purple-satin sleeveless shift dress. It was pretty short, but it was too high-necked to reveal even a hint of cleavage, and loose fitting, only outlining the curves of her body when she moved — so it was more than respectable, she told herself.

Once inside the cab, Max emptied her bag of essentials on to the seat. She started with a dusting of Bobbi Brown bronzing powder over her cheekbones, a lick of YSL mascara after teasing her eyelashes skywards with mini curlers, a dab of Benetint on her cheeks and finally clear MAC gloss to cover her cupid bow lips. Ruffling her hair for a didn't-really-try-just-out-of-bed look, she surveyed the results in her mirror and was happy. You can do it, Max, she told herself. OK, so you don't have a gap at the top of your thighs like his ex, but is that really attractive? No, it's not; he bloody dumped her. She smiled as she thought of what her mum would tell her in such a situation.

"Max, be yourself. If you do that, he'd be a fool not to love you."

Leaving the driver a hefty tip, Max ran to the door of the restaurant. Well, pub. As she entered, she looked to the bar and there he was, looking right at her.

Luke waved with a welcoming smile and Max approached him, hoping her knees wouldn't buckle while holding his gaze.

"Hello."

"Hi, Max, you look great."

"Thank you." Shit, should she tell him that he too looked great? No, accept the compliment with grace.

They both started to say something, then laughed awkwardly.

"I hope you don't mind my choice of pub. They serve great food and I thought it might make a nice change from your normal showbiz hang-outs. Keeping it real wiv de north Londoners."

Max was aware that she was looking at his mouth all the time he spoke. She was inexplicably turned on and wanted to kiss him.

He was wearing a dark blue, V-necked, fine-cashmere jumper and those baggy jeans again. Above his dark brown belt she caught a glimpse of his white boxers peaking out.

Laughing, she said: "It's perfect." And it was. Ciders with funny names behind the bar, a fire in the corner she could imagine burning and crackling on cold winter nights, round wooden tables crowded by the laughter of friends and clinking glasses. Stuff starchy Nobu. This was lovely.

Max agreed when Luke suggested she try a pint of cider, which he promised was the best north of the Thames.

Settling at a table, they toasted each other with their pints and drank.

"Did you know," Max said, "it's seven years of bad sex if you don't look someone in the eye while saying cheers?"

"That I did not know, Max."

They laughed and ordered hearty food and red wine, catching each other every now and then with a look of curiosity mixed with elation.

Luke was eager to hear all about Max's exploits and she laughed as he lapped up her stories of meeting Angelina Jolie, Tom Cruise, Sean Connery, Nicole Kidman.

"The secret is not to be too impressed by the celebrities. Otherwise you'll end up asking them what their favourite colour is, and who wants to read that? The cheekier the question, the better the story."

Max loved that every fibre of Luke was concentrated on her — his eyes were dancing as he took in her words and she could almost feel the warmth of his body pulling her in.

Collecting her thoughts, she smiled. "Enough about me. What do you do?"

And Luke told her all about his job, training to be a human-rights barrister. Max was impressed and had so many questions for him that Luke asked if this was an interview for the paper.

"It sounds like you can really make a difference."

"It's a slow process, but that's the plan. To be honest I didn't get the grades to study law so got a general business degree and went travelling. There were only so many bars I could work in in Australia before I realized I had to have a vocation, something to believe in. I'd got a decent degree — a 2:1 — so I was accepted on a fast-track legal course for graduates. Somehow I got through that — I treated studying like a full-time job and it meant more to me than it would have done when I was eighteen. And now I'm taking more exams to be a barrister."

"So you can be one of those guys with the funny wigs?"

"Exactly, I get to play dressing-up every day."

Somewhere during their second bottle Max asked about his ex.

"It all happened so recently. Surely you can't be over her?"

Luke took her hand. "I don't want to sound like a shit. I'm not. But I was over her nearly a year ago. That's when I should have ended it but I thought I had to ride it out, weather the storm, make her happy. Trust me. I'm ready to move on."

And somewhere during their slightly drunken conversation, Luke told Max he wanted an all-encompassing love. One that blew him away, made him want to be with that person every moment of every day.

"My dad's friend met a woman and proposed three days later," Max told him.

"That's it. That's perfect."

Max agreed, with the qualification that three months might be spontaneous enough.

As the bell rang for closing time, Max was determined to leave. You like him. A lot. So why be too accommodating on the first night? If he's a keeper, it will be worth the wait and you don't want him to think you put out on the first night. But Jesus, she wanted to rip his clothes off.

"I should get a cab."

Luke stood up and lifted Max's coat. "Yes, of course. I'll help you get a car."

As they braced the chill of the first hint of autumn, Luke slipped his fingers through hers.

Max's thoughts raced — was this really happening? Did she feel more for this guy than all other men she had dated for six months? More than her first love, Alfie, when she was seventeen? She'd thought girls who gushingly told of how they "just knew" from the start it was love were deranged psychos. And was she really wet just thinking about kissing him goodnight? The feeling of having a hot-water bottle stuck between her legs would indicate the affirmative.

Luke turned to Max and looked at her. She didn't know how long she had been staring at him.

"I love the way you look at me," he told her.

Pulling her to him, he placed a hand to the side of her face and kissed her tenderly for what seemed a millisecond. Sensing him pull away, Max wanted more and moved forward, seeking the warmth of his breath with hers. They lost each other in a deep, longing kiss.

Max felt dizzy; everything was spinning when she pulled away.

Well, well, well, Max thought. Luke Stirling. He's the one for me. But shit, there was no getting away from the fact he was Lucy's brother. How would she explain that one to Lucy? Or her mum and dad? But there was something incredibly right about being here with him.

"It's impossible to get a cab at this time of night round here. Do you mind a ten-minute walk to a taxi stand?"

"Not at all." Max had a sudden craving for a cigarette — something that always came after a few drinks. Perhaps she should hold off. Luke might detest it. Hell, what was the point in being anything other than herself? Max had often thought that when you went out on a first date, you never met the real person — it was a projection of what the guy wanted you to believe he was. Only weeks, sometimes months, down the line did you glimpse the true man. They should come with a sign which reads: "This is not the real me. I will show you what a bastard I am on date number four."

"Do you mind if I have a cigarette?"

"Not at all. Sometimes I have a cigar after dinner. Do you always smoke?"

"No, it doesn't enter my head unless alcohol is involved."

"Every night, then?"

Max laughed as she rummaged around in her handbag for a lone cig she was sure she'd spotted earlier. Got it! It must have fallen out of a packet at some point.

Fishing out a lighter, she lit it and inhaled deeply. Then grimaced. Yuck, her perfume must have leaked on to the cig. One more puff and it might taste better.

"Eugh, it tastes of flowers," she told Luke, stubbing it out.

Taking her hand once again, Luke clasped it tightly as they made their way to the main street. They settled into a comfortable silence, Max wondering how it was possible to feel so at ease so quickly.

Shit, hold on . . . her legs felt unbelievably wobbly. She'd heard of going weak at the knees but her legs felt as though they were buckling under her. They were. Holy fuck, Max thought as her heart pounded against her chest. This isn't right. "Luke —" she started to say, but it was too late. Her mind went blank as she fell to the ground.

Gotcha!

Robbie had booked dinner at the Peat Inn, a restaurant renowned locally and beyond for its Michelin-star-quality food and unpretentious surroundings. The fivesome nestled into snug chairs round a low oak table where Robbie ordered five vodka martinis.

The place felt like a secret retreat in the heart of this beautiful countryside. It was surrounded by winding country roads with old-fashioned wooden bus stops sheltering women wearing headscarves and kind smiles.

Robbie looked across at Lucy. Hartley was his best friend in the world and Bridget had come as a bitter disappointment. He despised her but of course said nothing for fear of upsetting Hartley — and after all, maybe he had got Bridget wrong. He had vowed to share his concerns should they ever get engaged, but thankfully that had never happened. Bridget represented everything he loathed: snobbery, fake concern for the environment and charities, and utter self-obsession. She masked this cleverly by acting sickly sweet around Hartley, fussing over him, making plans, buying him presents every time she shopped. But Robbie had seen through the facade and witnessed on more than one occasion the sharp end of her tongue. Once, during a skiing trip in Italy, he had overheard a phone conversation she'd had with her father and was disgusted by the way she spoke to him. As far as Bridget was concerned the man who afforded her pampered lifestyle had, it seemed, no right to an ounce of respect or gratitude from his spoiled daughter.

So thank God for Lucy. He had just met her, but Robbie sensed she was worlds apart from Bridget. For starters, she didn't look as harsh. Her features were as soft as Bridget's were hard. Lucy was demure, almost shy, and yet full of grace and sexuality. Hartley was one lucky boy. Robbie was sure Lucy was altogether more gentle and genuine than Bridget. Though who wouldn't have been?

"So, tell me," Robbie addressed Lucy, taking a glug from his drink, "do you have any beautiful single friends you can introduce me to?"

Lucy smiled. Genevieve? She could think of nothing worse than going on double dates with these warm, welcoming people and her boss, full of questions about who was who, what new places the royals were hanging out in. She could think of other girlfriends she would far rather see Robbie with. Then again, what harm was there in setting him up on a date with Genevieve? If he hated her, there would be no repeat. But then again, that might turn her neurotic boss against her, and she would be back collecting the skinny lattes before she knew it.

"I can think of a couple."

Claudia, a quiet girl who seemed constantly to be preparing to speak but rarely did, joined in. Lucy recognized her from the day she met Bridget at Ascot.

184

She had assumed the strawberry blonde girl by her side was stifling a giggle as she looked at the ground during Bridget's tirade, but now she wondered if she had simply misread her shyness, for she seemed as gentle as her friend was brash.

"I have a few friends who would kill for a date with you, Robbie," Claudia told him. "You're quite a catch. And moving to Scotland has only made you harder to get."

Robbie laughed heartily, covering his face in mock embarrassment. "Oh shucks, Claud. They are after me for one thing and one thing only . . ."

Claudia looked at him, wide-eyed and expectant.

". . . my enormous manhood."

As the group of friends laughed, the waiter approached and signalled their table was ready. While Charles and Robbie caught up on news about mutual friends — they too were school friends — and Claudia excused herself to the Ladies, Hartley squeezed Lucy's hand under the table.

"Are you OK, Lucy Lu?"

"Of course. Are you?"

"Never more so. Having you here with my friends, it's divine. Sorry about earlier . . . you know, being disturbed."

"That's OK," Lucy said, smiling. "We have all weekend."

Hartley laughed and jokingly hit the air with a clenched fist like a winning jockey crossing the finish line. He kissed Lucy on the cheek as she laughed, then settled into conversation with his friends about old pals.

Claudia seemed relieved to have Lucy to herself and quizzed her relentlessly about fashion, endearing herself to Lucy by telling her: "I'm a bit of a geek, you see. I need all the help I can get."

The six-course tasting menu was delicious, with tiny tastes of local produce — salmon, pheasant and duck — washed down with fine wine.

"I do feel dreadful, about Ascot," Claudia ventured over sticky toffee pudding. "I was there, beside Bridget."

"I know you were, but you did nothing wrong. You can't apologize for the way others behave."

"Bridget did behave terribly. But I don't think she's all that bad."

Lucy smiled. "No, perhaps she's not."

When they were leaving at the end of the meal, Robbie smiled as he watched Hartley escort Lucy to the door. He had never seen him look so happy. And that made Robbie happy. Hartley had had it hard since his dad died — he felt responsible not only for his mother's happiness but for helping as many people as he could through his charity. It was about time he had someone to share his life with.

Stepping outside, they were blinded by a flash.

"What the hell . . ." Hartley started.

"Alright, mate, give us a smile."

"What?"

Charles instinctively lunged at the man who was in their faces, standing at the bottom of the steps and blinding them with his camera flash.

As Charles wrestled the camera from him, the man shouted in a thick London accent: "Oi, what's the problem? Lucy, you tipped my boss off — he said you knew we were coming. I don't want no trouble."

Charles let go of the camera as suddenly as he had grabbed it and turned to Lucy.

Lucy stared at the man, trying to compute what he had just said.

"Come on, Lucy, tell the big fella . . . I've come all this way."

"I have no idea who you are," Lucy said as loudly as she could. "I have no idea what you're talking about. Hartley?" Lucy looked at Hartley but he couldn't meet her eyes. "Hartley?"

He was walking to the car as the photographer scurried off into the night.

Confused, Lucy stood and watched as her friends, as if in slow motion, followed Hartley.

She got in the car and sat in the back beside Hartley. She took his hand but he pulled it away.

"We'll speak about this later," he said in a hushed tone.

"Guys, I have no idea who that was."

Silence.

"For God's sake, you think I told someone to track us down to a country restaurant in the middle of nowhere to get my picture in the paper?"

Robbie coughed in embarrassment. "No, I'm sure that's not the case. It's just . . ."

"Yes?"

"Well, as you say, it's not the sort of place you stumble upon. And . . . well, why would he blame you?"

Lucy looked at Hartley and caught something in his eye she wished she hadn't. It was the rawest, most painful look of hurt she had ever seen.

She turned away to look out of the window, her eyes stinging with tears.

Just Like Clockwork

Bridget was brimming with anticipation as she paced up and down her corridor for most of the evening, waiting for the photographer to call. God, she hoped their plan would work. It had to.

She had tried to relax and stop feeling jumpy by smothering her new Tanda range of anti-ageing products all over her face and body. It was more important than ever to look her best. If anything, she looked younger now than when she had dated Hartley — that chemical face peel had worked a treat — and there was no doubt he would be attracted to her again.

As she paced the hall, she put a hairspray can between her legs — a trick her personal instructor had suggested. Her inner thighs must have benefited from hundreds of metres of toning over the course of the evening.

When her phone rang around ten o'clock, Bridget surged to grab it, cursing as she put it to her ear and felt its coldness against the face mask she had forgotten was still in place.

"Did you get them?"

"Yes."

Bridget's heart leaped. He'd done it. She'd done it. Got Lucy. She zoned out as the photographer babbled on about the details. All that mattered was that her plan had worked.

She focused suddenly. The details. She had to know everything.

Cutting the man off, she barked: "Tell me again, where did you get them?"

The photographer's voice was shaky, partly down to the adrenaline rush from what he'd just done and partly because the woman on the other end of the line was the most terrifying thing he'd encountered — and that was saying something after he'd been a member of the ruthless paparazzi for fifteen years.

Normally, he would have told anyone as rude as this woman exactly where to go. But he'd be an idiot to turn down the money — he needed it. Yet it was more than rudeness; there was something chilling about the ice-cold voice with which he was doing business.

"I stuck out like a sore thumb hanging around the guy Robbie's house so I waited on a country road and followed them to a restaurant."

"And what did you say?"

"Just like you told me — I told Lucy to smile for the camera, she was the one who'd tipped me off she'd be there, I'd come a long way and all that."

Lady Bridget let a wide scarlet smile spread across her face. "Yes, yes, and what did Hartley do?"

"He just walked off."

"Excellent. Good boy. You'll have the cash by Monday." Lady Bridget had had two grand delivered to the photographer by a member of staff — and instead of the total of five grand they had previously agreed, she had upped it to ten — promising the remaining eight when the job was done. Of course, she hadn't given the cretin her name. She told him there was no need to know. He had readily agreed, eager simply to make his money.

"I'll have someone deliver it in cash — no cheques, no records. As you know, I decided to pay double to buy your word you will never mention this to a soul. If you do, I'll see to it you never work again."

Bridget let out a squeal of delight as she hung up. Lucy's little fantasy was over. People like her always got found out. She had done Hartley the favour of his life by making it happen so swiftly.

Bridget was euphoric as she opened a bottle of Taittinger. Well, a triumphant victory glass was the least she deserved.

She smiled as she felt the cold bubbles spread over her tongue. A warm sensation coursed through her body as her mind raced with thoughts of winning Hartley back. And of a masterstroke that would ensure Lucy went crawling back to where she belonged.

Ambi — Pure and Simple:
I'll Be There for You

The first person Max saw when she came round was Luke.

"Hello, Max. Are you OK?"

Max lifted her head weakly from what felt like a pillow.

"Where am I?"

"You're in hospital, Max. You collapsed."

"Oh Jesus . . . what happened?"

Luke stifled a giggle which, even in her confused state, Max realized was highly insensitive. She had never fainted or collapsed in her life. Was it a hernia? A tumour? The bastard.

"Sorry, it's in no way funny . . . it's just, well, it's a relief."

"What is?"

A nurse was standing over now.

"Don't worry, pet," came the Geordie voice. "You're going to be just fine."

Max felt a sense of panic rise within her. "What the hell is wrong with me?"

The nurse took Max's hand, and she realized Luke had been holding her other hand all the while.

"Well, pet, we had a look through your handbag for any medication you might be taking when this lovely man brought you in. We didn't find any but there was an Ambi Pur car fragrance in there and it had leaked all over the place."

Max could vaguely remember a hanging air freshener Lucy must have put in their car. Could it have fallen into her bag?

"Your boyfriend here told us you'd had a cigarette just before you collapsed and complained it tasted of perfume. We did a few tests and it turns out your body had gone into shock after inhaling the liquid. It's dangerous stuff to have in your body and you got a massive hit of it, petal."

Max looked at Luke, whose lovely eyes were smiling at her — but kindly.

"And the good news is," he told her, squeezing her hand, "you are a hundred per cent back to normal."

"That's right, pet. Your heart rate is back to normal and everything is fine — you just blacked out as your body went into shock. Are you feeling OK?"

"Yes, thank you," Max said as the nurse smiled. "Oh God," she said, almost under her breath after the nurse had left them.

"What? Are you OK?" Luke looked concerned.

"Yes, I'm fine. Apart from the fact you must think I'm an absolute moron. I can see why you laughed. I'm an idiot."

Luke was laughing again. "I think you are who you are and I like who you are very much."

"Quite right, Luke. Nothing like getting to know someone on a first date."

Luke's eyes were dancing with hers. "The nurse called me your boyfriend. I like the sound of that."

All is Not Well

Lucy's name flashed up on Max's mobile moments after she arrived home. She had been discharged from hospital soon after she had come round and Luke had seen her home safely in a cab. He had asked if she was sure she would be OK alone — Lucy was still in Scotland — and Max insisted she felt just fine.

"But I do want to see you again soon," she told him.

"Don't you worry about that. I'll make sure of it. I can't stand the thought of missing out on your next adventure."

Luke leaned over to kiss Max and she felt dizzy again, but it had nothing to do with the Ambi Pur. Every part of her body felt alive — and the hot-water bottle was back between her legs. Be good, it will wait, she told herself as she pulled away and said goodnight.

"Hi, Luce, how are you doing? How's Scotland?"

Silence.

"Luce?"

"Oh Max, it's awful." Max knew her sister and could tell from those few words she was trying not to cry.

"What's wrong?" Max could hear the panic rising in her voice.

"Oh I'm absolutely fine, don't worry. I just had a bit of a fight with Hartley and I wanted to come home. I'll explain when I see you. I'm on a sleeper train from Dundee — I'd missed the last flight and this was the only way I could leave straight away. Bad reception. It gets in at seven in the morning at King's Cross. Can you pick me up?"

"Of course I can. Sure you're OK?"

"Yes. See you soon. Love you."

"You too."

Sister Act

Max was at King's Cross station by 6.30a.m. She was worried about her sister. Aside from the time her shit of a boyfriend had cheated on her, Max couldn't think of a time when Lucy had had a crisis and needed her. It was always Lucy who guided Max, who made her believe in herself when she was down. She had a way of making Max feel like a wonderful person, even with the worst of hangovers. And Lucy told Max that without her, she would be another person — like the girls at her magazine. Max had taught her what it was to be yourself, to have a personality, to embrace life.

Max was shocked when she saw Lucy come off the train. She looked tiny, vulnerable and exhausted.

Lucy fell into Max's arms and sobbed — heaving sobs that seemed more powerful than her whole being.

"Come on, sis, you're safe now. Let's get you home and you can tell me all about it."

Back at the flat, Max tucked Lucy up on the sofa with a fleecy duvet normally reserved for Max's hangovers.

As Lucy told her of the events of the night before, Max was horrified. She was furious too that Hartley hadn't accepted she had nothing to do with it.

"What choice did he have, Max? When we got back to Robbie's he told me he needed time to think, that he didn't want to believe I would betray him when I knew that privacy and loyalty were so important to him . . . but he was at a loss to understand how a photographer would know where we were . . ." Lucy's voice trailed off.

"What? What else?"

"He asked if I thought you had something to do with it, because you work for a tabloid."

"He did?"

"You have to see his logic."

"I guess."

But Lucy knew Max would never betray her in any way — no matter how many brownie points it would score with her boss.

Lucy's voice was strangled, as she tried to hold back her tears. "I felt ashamed when I saw how he looked at me, how his friends looked at me, Max."

Max opened her arms for a hug but Lucy shrugged her off.

"But I also felt angry that he wouldn't just take my word for it. How could he think I'd do that? But Max, everything was pointing to me. He really had no choice but to at least ask for time to think. I just don't understand what happened."

Max placed her hand under Lucy's chin and raised her head so she could look in her eyes.

"Oh I think you do. This has Bridget's talons all over it. And I'll prove it if it's the last thing I do."

Lucy suddenly looked like she'd come out of a trance.

"Bridget? You think Bridget was behind it?"

"Absolutely. It's the only explanation. I've no doubt that she's evil enough and that she hates you enough — for Ascot and for going out with Hartley."

The thought had crossed Lucy's mind as she tossed and turned on her bed on the train trying to work out what had happened. But she had dismissed it straight away, certain she must be going mad. No one would do that, surely? The thought that someone could hate her so much made her feel sick. Lucy couldn't bring herself even to discuss the possibility with Max.

"God, I've been so wrapped up in myself," she said as brightly as she could manage. "I forgot to ask: what did you think of my dad? And Ben and Luke? He gave you a lift home, no? That must have been so weird for you. I can't thank you enough for coming out with my passport. Mind you, it wasn't quite the trip I'd hoped for."

Max thought about telling her sister how wonderful she thought her brother was. But it wasn't the time. Her Ambi Pur story could wait too. Lucy had enough to take in for now.

"Oh no worries," she said, adopting her best sing-song carefree voice. "I thought they were all lovely, Luce, just lovely. Listen, I don't want you worrying about anything, OK? Everything will be fine."

Lucy squeezed her sister's hand. "Thanks, Max."

In for the Kill

Bridget had thought about biding her time. It might seem obvious if she called Hartley straight after Scotland. But then why would he ever connect her with what had happened? She hadn't spoken to him since their split and as he was no doubt angry with Lucy it could be the perfect time to strike.

News of his break-up had spread like wildfire. No one really knew what had happened, but Bridget was quick to tell them that she had heard an appalling rumour — that Lucy had secretly called a member of the paparazzi and asked him to take photos of her and Hartley on their romantic break. Rumour also had it, Bridget told them in hushed tones, that she had struck a deal to pocket half the profits from the sale of the pictures. Perhaps her magazine job didn't pay enough to keep her in this season's Chanel, she wondered aloud in front of a group of girls.

"Of course, this could all be nonsense," she told them, "but it came from a very good friend."

Bridget's crowd assumed she meant Claudia, who had been on the fateful trip to Scotland. Eager to sound just as well informed, they told her they had heard something similar. Before the weekend was out, everyone was talking about Lucy's terrible betrayal.

Bridget decided that phoning Hartley might seem a little odd but bumping into him accidentally on purpose was a stroke of genius. It was all so easy given that Hartley was such a creature of habit.

She remembered how he would visit Columbia Road flower market in East London most Sundays. He would buy dozens of bouquets for his Foundation, to scatter around the place and cheer people up when they came there for help. Bless him, darling Hartley. Quite the sweetheart. Bridget wondered what kind of flowers she would like for their wedding. Lilies, perhaps — all white and pristine.

She also made a calculated guess that Hartley would visit the market that very Sunday. She knew how his mind worked. When he planned a weekend away he always made sure he was back in London by Sunday afternoon, to prepare for work at his charity. And when he was upset he would do anything to keep his mind active. So it stood to reason he would keep to his flower-buying routine.

She had sat waiting in a café for over an hour before she spotted him picking out roses from a stall. She had chosen a simple midnight-blue cotton shift dress from Whistles, teamed with a matching mohair cardigan, and toned down her make-up — instead of the bright-red lipstick she normally favoured, she had gone for a nude gloss. She wanted to appear as Earth Mother as possible, his friend in his hour of need. She had decided against wearing couture — it was the East End, after all, hardly Chelsea. She couldn't resist her dark blue Louboutin heels, though, which completed the look: understated but sexy.

"Hartley, darling. Hello!"

The Earl of Balmyle spun round and froze. After what seemed an age, he spoke. "Bridget. What a surprise. How are you?"

"Oh, you know, same old. Just buying some flowers to cheer Mummy up. She's not been terribly well."

"I'm sorry to hear that. Nothing serious, I hope."

Mother had recovered from the flu weeks ago, but Hartley need not know that, she told herself as she looked at the ground forlornly. "Oh I'm sure she will be fine . . . You have to keep positive."

Hartley smiled at Bridget, who beamed back at him.

"God, it's good to see you, Hartley."

"Thanks, Bridget, you too. Listen, I have to be getting along."

Bridget looked crestfallen. "Oh I was hoping you would join me for a coffee to warm up a little?" Noting Hartley looked unconvinced, she put on her best wounded expression. "What happened was an age ago. I'd like to be friends."

Hartley took Bridget in. She seemed different, softer somehow. Hell, it was a long time ago and he was the one who had ended it. He hadn't thought too highly of her by the end but it was rather decent of her to be so charming. The least he could do was to be civil. It was, after all, only coffee.

"Of course," he said. "Just let me get these and I'm all yours."

Yes, Bridget thought as she smiled sweetly back at him: you will be all mine. She had removed Lucy from the picture, making Hartley believe she had betrayed him.

Now she had walked back into Hartley's life, she was there to stay.

Family Comes First

Max didn't know how long she had been staring out of the restaurant window. She kept replaying the conversation she'd had with Lucy the day before. Having woken after their heart to heart about what had happened in Scotland, Max had been sure her news would cheer Lucy up.

"Luce, I'm in love."

"Of course you are, Max, until next week. Who's the lucky chap?"

"Luke."

Silence.

"Your brother."

"No, Max, don't even think about it."

Max was taken aback by the harshness in her sister's voice. Lucy, normally so calm, had turned to face Max and was confronting her with real hostility.

"What? I like him. He's wonderful."

"Don't you dare, Max. Is it just like the time you slept with one of my best friends and he still refuses to speak to me because you stopped taking his calls?"

"No, it's not like that."

"Or the time you did a runner halfway through dinner with the guy I know from work because he had a squint?"

"Luce, he was wearing shades when I met him. I hadn't realized. I didn't know if he was eyeing up the waitress or my tits."

"No, Max, you cannot do this — not with my brother. Family is everything, you know that. I can't let you hurt Luke. He's my brother, for God's sake. It's far too close."

"But he's lovely."

"Yes, Max, he is. But you drop guys as soon as you become bored. It's what you've always done since Alfie. How do you think that feels for them?" Max had never seen Lucy look so serious. "I know you don't mean to hurt them, but you do. I can't let you do that to Luke. I love him. You always come first, Max, but, Jesus, there are millions of guys you can date. Not Luke."

Lucy stared at Max, waiting for her to laugh, to agree that London was full of hotties and she was right — Luke was off limits. But Max wanted to scream that yes she was a fuckwit when it came to men, yes she had been careless with some men's emotions . . . but she had never felt the way she did about Luke. As she looked at her sister she thought about how much Lucy had done for her, for as long as she could remember. She had given her cash when, as a cub reporter, Max had reached her overdraft limit; more than once she had driven miles to pick her up in the early hours when she had drunkenly fallen asleep on the night bus and missed her stop; she had supported and loved her through every crisis — and there was always some drama in Max's life. She had never brought any of it up again to remind Max how indebted she should be, not once. Her support was unqualified and unquestioning.

And now Lucy was protecting her half-brother because she had no reason to believe Max would not tire of him like she had the rest. Max longed to tell Lucy that she craved love as much as anyone and thought, at last, she may have found it with Luke. But how could she do that when Lucy had been through so much? Half of London's socialites were probably bad-mouthing her for betraying Hartley even as they spoke. And the man with whom Lucy had imagined spending the rest of her life thought the very worst of her. No, for once Lucy needed her help. What was she supposed to do — pat Lucy on the back and say, "There, there, I know you've had your heart broken but guess what? I'm in love with your brother." Somehow, she didn't think so. Max knew what she had to do.

"Ah, you know me too well. Maybe you're right. Keeping it in the family would be a bit too weird." Max shrugged her shoulders as if to say "easy come, easy go" and hoped the act was convincing.

Lucy looked relieved, like a weight had been lifted from her shoulders. Max knew she had made the right decision. Lucy would always come first, especially now.

"OK. Good. I want you to find the right guy, Max, to be happy. But I doubt Luke is your Mr Right." The anger had gone from Lucy's face; she was smiling as she absent-mindedly poured a glass of orange juice.

Her coffee now cold, Max smiled as she thought of Luke. Perhaps she wasn't in love with him — she had spent so little time with him, after all. But she knew something was different. Maybe those hopeless romantics were right and you "just know" when the right one comes along.

But it was a chance she could not take. Not while Lucy was so fragile. As she felt her mobile buzz she fished it out of her handbag and saw a text message from Luke.

"Hello, Miss Ambi Pur. Can I take you out for supper tonight? x"

Max was overwhelmed with sadness as she deleted the message. If she ignored him, he might be hurt but it was the easiest way. He would soon forget. She couldn't meet him; she knew she could not trust herself to do anything other than be honest with him. And if he knew how much she wanted him he would not let her go.

Closing her eyes, Max took a deep breath and tried with all her strength to focus. She knew Bridget had to have been behind what happened in Scotland and she resolved to put her best investigative foot forward to prove just that. She desperately hoped it would stop her thinking about Luke.

For once, Max was grateful when she saw Sheri's number flash on her phone. She was bound to have some ridiculous tale to tell, and Max needed a distraction.

"Awright, sweetheart, I've got a cracker."

Max suddenly remembered something Simon had told her the other day after he had read two exclusives he'd been working on for months, in a rival paper: she should watch what she said over the phone. He was sure a journalist had hacked into his voice messages or even tapped his phone.

"You do? Where are you?"

"My place."

"OK, I'll jump in a cab and see you in twenty."

Thank God her expense account allowed for all the taxis she wanted, Max thought as she put on her new coat — a lightweight, military-style, full-length, navy Armani. It had cost more than Max had ever imagined she'd pay for a coat but reasoned Lucy could get some use out of it too. No matter how glossy and upmarket the mag her sister worked for, staff didn't enjoy the sort of inflated salaries and expense accounts of many of the tabloid hacks they looked down upon. Once they'd made the soft-carpet land of an executive post that all seemed to change, with no shortage of lunches and entertaining clients. If anyone put in the work, it was Lucy. Max had known her sister to be leaving the flat as she was returning from a bash at four or five in the morning — so she could catch sunrise for a fashion shoot; or stay in the office until midnight to speak to a fashion designer who was seven hours behind in Los Angeles. Max just hoped someone would reward Lucy rather than a work-shy clothes horse with an eating disorder just because she was related to someone important.

A clear cab run brought her to Sheri's flat within ten minutes. She climbed the stairs to her flat as quickly as her Topshop platform ankle boots — hell, she couldn't afford designer bloody everything — could carry her, and knocked on the door.

A breathless Sheri looked like hell again. With her lifeless eyes, skin as grey as that of a sixty-year-old smoker, lank hair with half the blonde extensions missing, she cut a tragic figure. No doubt she had been unrecognizable the night before when fully made-up.

"Quick, come in, you're gonna love this one."

Max walked through to the sitting room and noted it wasn't as neat as usual. There were unwashed wine glasses and coffee cups on the table, a square mirror on the sofa with the remnants of the white powder she was so partial to.

It was as if Sheri had read her mind: "Envy's away on a shoot — I've been lettin' me hair down a bit."

Max smiled to reassure Sheri but couldn't help feeling sorry for her. Beside the window hung a picture of Sheri aged seven or eight, dressed as a fairy. A beautiful, angelic, blonde little girl in wings and a tutu, with the world at her feet. So pretty, so happy. And now?

Everyone saw her as a fame-hungry user, which was true. But it was she who was being chewed up and spat out by the dark side of showbiz. Sure, every footballer she kissed and told on faced the wrath of his girlfriend for a few months. But the girlfriend's anger subsided in direct correlation to the number of Cartier watches and Gucci bags he bought her. Even if she did dump him, he still had his fifty grand a week job doing the thing he loved and clubs full of girls desperate to be with him. Sheri? She had no money, a coke problem of biblical proportions and an addiction to the seedy world of celebrity she had briefly inhabited. Where would it take her? Looking at her — pale, ravaged and skinny in her pink Juicy tracksuit — Max shuddered to think.

"So, what's the big story?"

Sheri took a deep breath. "Max, last night I shagged Billy Brown."

"Shut up."

"I promise you, on me mum's life."

"England captain Billy Brown?"

It was too good to be true. Arsenal and England captain, Billy, had the perfect marriage to Becci Brown, from girl group the Baby Dolls. She had just given birth to their second child, Sugar Plum, a sister for their two-year-old son, Tizer. They had been hailed as the new Posh and Becks, their marriage and fairy-tale life untouchable.

"Max, I know what you're finkin'. I'd do anyfing for a bit of cash now. You're right, I would. That's why I've been out the last three nights. Finally, thank fuck, I struck gold. I promise you. Couldn't believe me luck. He was so drunk, he didn't know what he was doin'. But I promise ya, Max, he was doin' me by the end of the night."

"Do you have any proof?"

"Semen stains still on me bed sheets — we came back 'ere. Get a DNA check?"

Max laughed in spite of herself. "Somehow I don't think he'd agree to a sample, Sheri. I wouldn't know where to start with that."

"Bloody get one of his hairs or saliva from a glass, I don't care. I bloody need the cash."

Max regarded Sheri. She was desperate. But Max knew Sheri well enough to know she was telling the truth. Maybe there was a way.

"Do you have his phone number?"

"Yeah," Sheri said, rummaging through her bag and fishing out her mobile. Max noticed she was starting to sweat, her hands were shaking. "I waited till he was out cold and called my phone from his phone so I 'ad the number. But then I passed out before I got a bloody picture of 'im beside me in bed. Max, I promise ya . . ."

"OK, don't worry. I have a plan. But we'll have to wait a week or two."

That's Why the Lady is a Tramp

Bridget drummed her nails on the dashboard of her Range Rover. She was running late for lunch with her girlfriends Fifi and Dorcas at Shoreditch House, a darling members' club with its own outdoor swimming pool, just like Soho House in New York. Daddy paid for her annual "all house" membership, which gave her access to Soho House in NY and London, Shoreditch, the Electric Rooms and a few others. He also took care of her membership at Maddox, Annabel's and the Ivy Club. Well, he wanted the best for his little girl and, God, it was hardly a fortune to Daddy.

She edited in her mind the story she would tell them. Bridget knew only too well the importance of getting it right. Whatever she said would have made its way through half their friends by that evening.

She would confide she had been spending most days with Hartley. What luck they had bumped into each other at the flower market. Fate, you might call it. Hartley had needed a shoulder to cry on and admitted he had made a frightful mistake and misjudged Lucy terribly. Of course, her friends would ask with wide eyes if there was a chance she would be getting back with Hartley. And Bridget would cover her face with her hands and tell them she shouldn't really say anything. "What?" they would squeal and eventually she would tell them they had a little drunken kiss the other night — "So who knows?" Yes, Bridget resolved, they must be left in no doubt that it was highly likely they would resume where they had left off. They must also see the new soft and sympathetic Bridget.

She smiled as the traffic lights for Tower Bridge turned green and she shifted into gear. Was the truth really that different? Hartley had not said a bad word about Lucy, only that he didn't know what to think.

Every fibre of Bridget wanted to scream at him: "Think the worst, you buffoon — she was a gold-digging, fame-hungry tramp who fucked you over." But she had learned her lesson. When Bridget had dated Hartley before, she should have been the embodiment of sweetness and light but had let her guard slip towards the end. Every woman put on an act until she had a ring on her finger, Bridget was sure of that. It was tiresome but needs must.

"Of course you don't know what to think, sweetie. Perhaps it had nothing to do with Lucy."

Hartley had been surprised at Bridget's response. She was so willing to give Lucy the benefit of the doubt, so perhaps she had moved on. She seemed so much kinder than he remembered. But Hartley had replayed the incident in Fife over in his head so many times and still could not think of another explanation. Beautiful Lucy. He had never even dreamed of being so happy. He kept his thoughts to himself. No matter what Lucy had done he had no intention of bad-mouthing her in any way. He had to admit it was a relief to have some female company — he missed Lucy so much, her femininity, her warmth, her laugh, her hair. No one could compare, but he was glad to spend time with Bridget and catch up on news of mutual friends.

He didn't mind in the slightest when Bridget asked if she might tag along the following weekend for drinks at Tramp with Hartley's friends. She told him she craved a night out — she too had split up with someone recently. He had moved to Hong Kong for work and they had both decided against a long-distance relationship.

"I have to admit I was terribly upset. I really liked him. But life goes on," she chirped. "And the best cure for a broken heart is oodles of champagne."

Hartley laughed and toasted Bridget with his mug of coffee.

Bridget laughed too. She had had no boyfriend since Hartley. But it was imperative that he think of her as a kindred spirit, facing heartbreak bravely just like him.

Hartley drank considerably more than normal at Tramp, determined to block out thoughts of his first encounter with Lucy at the club. Bridget timed her moment to perfection, planting a kiss on Hartley's lips at the bar when he had insisted on buying another bottle of Krug. She squealed with delight as she did so, drawing as much attention from onlookers as possible. Hartley hugged her warmly, buoyed by alcohol and the camaraderie of two friends determined to get on with life. When news spread of their kiss, Hartley would assume it had come from an eagle-eyed bystander — not from her. She could always trust Fifi and Dorcas to spread any kind of gossip. For good effect she would, of course, tell them not to breathe a word, but she knew for sure they would be on the phone within moments of air-kissing goodbye.

As Bridget pulled up to the private members' club, a thought crossed her mind and she was truly glad it had. She might have kissed Hartley but that was one hell of a way from where she wanted to be — sending out hundreds of invitations to their wedding. Perhaps there was a way to give him no choice. She had heard men talk crassly about a "rebound shag", when they had slept with someone to get over the end of a relationship. Having seen the drunken state of Hartley the other night, she was sure she could coax him into bed. Every man needed sex and he was no exception.

She must organize a little night out with a few friends, and copious amounts of bubbly and shots. She would be careful not to drink too much — but look as though she was — and ensure Hartley's glass was permanently refilled.

And what if she told him she was on the pill and there was no need to use a condom? Bridget had felt a mild sense of panic the other day when reading yet another magazine article repeating her mother's warning about the huge decline in women's fertility after the age of thirty-five. She would be damned if she was going to watch all her friends produce a litter while she looked like a barren spinster. Why should they get all the attention? There were only so many bloody "first lock of hair" holders she could send before it drove her insane. Accidents happened all the time for women on the pill. Hartley need never know she had never taken it in the first place. Fifi all but admitted on their last skiing trip that she had used the same trick to conceive on her honeymoon. A little white lie could lead to an unexpected surprise for Hartley. He was such a gentleman he would do the right thing and propose. He would have no choice. He was hardly going to have some bastard child and not marry the mother. It simply wasn't done.

It was not the sequence of events Bridget had hoped for, but there was nothing wrong with having a solid Plan B. They could marry straight away, when she was slim enough to squeeze into a breathtaking gown, or wait until after the birth — within six weeks she could be rake thin with the help of her trainer, nutritionist and a nip and tuck. With two people of their standing there would be no shame in marrying after having a child . . . so long as they wed eventually.

Time was ticking — and not just with her damned biological clock. The last thing she wanted was for that tart Lucy to bump into Hartley at some event and flutter her eyelashes at him. Bridget had put everything into winning Hartley over. It had almost killed her to smile when he talked about Lucy. She wanted to tell him never to mention that little slut in her company but instead she pretended to give her the benefit of the doubt — she can't be as bad as everyone says, she must be misunderstood. It was to Bridget's great annoyance that no one ever said a bad word about Lucy. Until, that was, Bridget had planted so many seeds of suspicion about her that people in their set couldn't help but gossip about how badly she had treated Hartley. Bridget's little plan to make her friends believe Claudia had told her all about Lucy's devious plan in Scotland had been a stroke of genius. The more she said it, the more people believed it. It had worked. The cause of Lucy's split with Hartley being his discovery that she'd tipped off a photographer was now repeated as fact in her set. Bridget had even seen snippets hinting at what had happened in the broad-sheet diaries.

That reminded her: now that she had a file on Lucy's family history from the private investigator she had hired, she really should make good use of it. It wouldn't do for her to simply blurt out everything she had learned about her scummy working-class roots to Hartley. That would be too obvious. Far better she remained the picture of innocence. No, much better to make sure the details got into the hands of a writer on a newspaper.

It was no less than Lucy deserved. Who did she think she was? Bridget was the one for Hartley. They were equals and he would come round to seeing this. She would simply be pushing him in the right direction. And the Earl of Balmyle desperately needed an heir.

As she smoothed down her Diane von Furstenberg deep-purple wrap dress (Shoreditch House was an exception to the East End) and applied a coat of gloss to her crimson lips, a smile spread across her face. The truth was she'd be doing Hartley a huge favour.

Exclusive:
Earl's ex Hides Humble Beginnings

Lucy knew something was wrong the moment she walked into the office.

Genevieve was clearly halfway through talking about her when she walked past her desk.

"Oh hi, Lucy. Are you OK?"

"Yes. Are you?"

"Are you sure?"

Lucy looked at the gaggle of girls gathered round Genevieve. She was an hour later than normal — having first picked up clothes for a shoot in the West End.

Tentatively and slowly, Lucy replied: "Yes. Has something happened?"

"You haven't seen the *Daily Mail*?"

Lucy felt faint. "No." It was as if they were speaking to her in a foreign tongue and all she could do was answer yes or no.

Practically leaping out of her seat, Genevieve marched over to Lucy's desk and laid a double-page spread before her. Lucy was almost too scared to look at it but knew she had to. Looking down, she took in the headline: Earl's Ex Hides Humble Beginnings.

Her mouth went dry as she read on. My God, her poor mother — she sounded like some bed-hopping hippy. And Max . . .

By the third paragraph, the words had blurred into one giant ink blob.

Looking up, she saw the huddle of girls gawping at her, waiting for her reaction — like scavengers circling a carcass. Christ, where was Carlos when she needed him? She couldn't see him anywhere. They would have liked tears best, she thought — that would have sounded most dramatic as they retold the story to friends over cocktails. Or a tantrum; that would have gone down well too. Lucy had no idea where the strength came from as she rose to her feet. Inside she felt numb. She clenched her fists as tightly as she could to stop them shaking with shock.

Lucy could hear Max as clearly as if she was standing beside her. Head up, chest out, paint on the smile.

"Come on, ladies, you should know by now not to believe anything you read in the papers."

And with that, Lucy picked up her bag and waltzed out of the office. She could feel their eyes burning into her as she left. She didn't care about them. It wouldn't surprise her one bit if they thought less of her for having the words "working class" linked to her family. That said far more about them than it did her. All she cared about was her mum and Max. The two people she loved and admired most had had their names tarnished for the world to see. It was bad enough that her name was dirt in certain London circles after the incident in Scotland, but how dare anyone drag Marj and Max through the mud.

Lucy took her mobile out of her bag. Shit! She'd missed seven calls from Max because it had been on silent. She punched Max's number into her phone.

"Hi, Luce."

"Have you seen it?"

"Yes."

"I'm so sorry."

"Don't be. Revenge is a dish best served cold." Max knew her sister didn't have enemies, with one notable exception. "It's time for Bridget to get what's coming to her."

A Time for Change

Lucy had called her mother straight after she had spoken to Max. She hadn't picked up so Lucy left a message. She wanted to be strong but felt ashamed that she had dragged her mother into this mess; she could not get the words out without sounding strangled.

"Mum, I'm guessing you know about the newspaper. I'm so very sorry . . . I love you."

Lucy sat on a bench down a quiet lane near her Mayfair magazine office. She could not face going back to work, with the girls whispering and watching. There were a couple of sweet girls on the floor. There was Sophie, with her hair freshly dyed jet-black in honour of another new supermodel.

She had actually cried for a full hour at work the other day because her prized Burberry blazer, which she'd blagged a few months ago and had refused to take off even when temperatures in the office had topped 30 degrees back in July, had been stolen from a nightclub cloakroom. Lucy had handed her a fresh tissue as she wailed that it wasn't about the cost but it was virtually a one-off and irreplaceable.

Sophie had run after her on her way out of the office and Lucy assured her she was fine and thanked her for asking.

And there was Penny, the fashion desk PA with shoulder-length dark blonde hair, a long face and severe rectangular glasses, which she changed on a daily basis to match her outfit. Lucy was sure she would have run after her too, had she not been on holiday.

But most of the girls were too scared of Genevieve to break free from the pack and try to comfort her without having at least some juicy news to take back to the boss. God knew what she had said about Lucy before she'd come into the office that morning to instil this level of fear about being too friendly to her. The thought might once have bothered Lucy but, hell, after reading a malicious article in a national newspaper, seen by millions, not only about herself but about her family, well, Genevieve's bitching was the least of her worries.

Lucy smiled wryly as she thought of the story in the paper. It made her sound like she was a fake — that she hadn't gone to one of the most prestigious girls' schools in the country, that she had put on a posh accent the moment she left her family council house. In truth she had lied about nothing — Lucy's voice, her interests, her friends, were the product of her background. And it was one of which she was proud. Yes, she had mixed with the upper classes. But she had all kinds of friends from all walks of life. And it was her sister and mother who had shaped her, made her happy to be herself. How shallow it all seemed; the very fact a newspaper would give up two pages to dissect her social status was utterly unfathomable.

Lucy felt the wind through her vintage Westwood cream-satin blouse and tight black jeans but she felt numb to its assault. A photo album of images of her mother flashed through her mind. Swimming naked with them in Cornwall when Max and Lucy were children, putting on plays for the return of her stepfather from work. Lucy had a biological father she loved but Fergal had been just like a dad, always making her feel equal in his heart to Max.

While he had worked hard to establish his carpentry business, Marj had marketed the company and it became a household name in Dundee and nearby towns in Tayside. But she had seen her full-time job as investing every ounce of energy into making her daughters happy and strong enough to take on the world. And this was how she had been rewarded.

And all because of Hartley. Lovely Hartley. She could not think badly of him through any of this. He was probably as bewildered as her, perhaps more so. While Lucy knew the details that had been published painted her wrongly as a ruthless liar, gold-digger and opportunist, Hartley knew no such thing. He must think of her as such a fraud. And yet she could not help but hope he had glimpsed the real her — the honest woman who loved him dearly. But it was stupid to think he would hold on to his impression of Lucy after all of this. And anyway, what did it matter? She had heard rumours and spotted a diary piece hinting that Hartley had started seeing Bridget again. The thought of him with anyone else, let alone Bridget, was too much to bear. It hurt like hell to think Hartley had moved on so quickly when she still thought about him all the time.

Carlos would know what to say. Shit, now she remembered: he was trouble-shooting in the Bahamas after a model had assaulted an air hostess on the way to a job there. No doubt she was high as a kite and would blame the stresses of work/lost luggage/a recent relationship break-up — or rather, Carlos would invent a kick-ass story to save her from community service.

The sharp ringing of her mobile cut through her thoughts. It was Amy. They hadn't spoken much since the evening they met Hartley at Annabel's. They had texted and emailed, promising to meet up soon, but Amy had a new project on at work which had her working late. Lucy had been busy too, at the magazine and — she smiled sadly as she admitted it to herself — falling in love.

"Are you OK?"

"Yes, thanks. Boy, am I glad to hear your voice. I take it you've seen the story?"

"I have. Don't worry. Today's newspaper is tomorrow's fish and chip wrapping, Luce."

Amy was relieved to hear her friend at least try to laugh. "Is there anything I can do?"

"There is. You can help me get very drunk tonight."

Exposed:
Truth by Text

Getting Bridget's mobile number had been easy. A journalist friend had given her the number of a dodgy contact who specialized in "pulling" phone bills — give him the name, date of birth, address of anyone and the chances were he could get not only their mobile phone number but their credit card details too.

Max had then bought a cheap pay-as-you-go phone. Armed with a new anonymous number — the last person she wanted to have her real number was the ghastly Bridget — she considered for some time what she would text.

There was no doubt in Max's mind that Bridget was behind what had happened in Scotland. She worked on the assumption that Bridget had paid the photographer. Lucy had told Max he had a thick London accent. He would hardly have travelled all that way for free — and Bridget could afford to pay him handsomely through the Bank of Beames.

Max could also assume that Bridget had sworn this man to secrecy — she could never be linked to the incident. Max's hunch was that Bridget had not so much as divulged her name to the man, for fear of him ever blabbing. But Bridget's control-freakery would have made it impossible for her not to bark commands at him by phone to ensure the job went exactly as she had planned.

Max played with the wording of her text before settling on: "This is my new number should you need me again. Your photographer friend."

Max knew it might amount to nothing. Bridget might suspect something was up and call the snapper's old number. But this trick had worked for Max before. She had bought a pay-as-you-go a few months ago and texted a Cabinet Minister she suspected of having an affair with a pretty student. "This is my new number, Cheryl x" it had read and . . . bingo! He had replied with: "I wish I was buried in your breasts right now." Ha! That had made the front page and a double-page spread inside. Cheryl had pocketed twenty grand, the politician — who professed publicly to being a devout Christian and family man — had been uncovered as a hypocrite and Max had been the toast of the newspaper. Everyone was happy — apart from the politician, of course, though he had managed to keep his job and his wife.

Sure, Bridget no doubt thought of herself as intellectually superior to almost everyone. But those who, like Bridget, had had everything given to them on a plate rarely possessed the cunning of those who had had to work for results.

Max's text was general enough for Bridget not to worry that it would catch her out — it was vague and ambiguous.

Max relished the task of trapping Bridget because it stopped her being consumed by thoughts of Luke. He had texted again. "Max, you OK? Would love to see you xx"

Poor Luke. If he had experienced half of what she had felt on their date, he must be bewildered as to why she was ignoring him. More than bewildered: utterly devastated. But it had to be this way. It would be disloyal to tell him Lucy was behind her decision to stop seeing him. He might blame Lucy, and Max would not risk coming between them. As her sister had said, family is everything. It was better for everyone if nothing was allowed to happen. He would soon forget.

Max was determined Lucy would never know how much Luke meant to her and resolved never to talk to Lucy about him. But she had had to confide in someone for fear of going mad, so she had called her mother a few days ago.

Marj had been quiet on the other end of the line. Max wished she could see her mother's face, to read her thoughts.

"I know I have to step back, Mum. It's just, well, I really liked him. But it's complicated." Max had chided herself — her words made her sound childish, like a schoolgirl with a crush. She hoped her mum couldn't hear the hurt in her voice.

"What do you mean, complicated?"

Max didn't want to make her worry. The last thing Marj needed was to be burdened with the knowledge that one of her daughters had fallen for her other daughter's half-brother.

227

"Oh I'll tell you another time, Mum." Max hoped she sounded more positive than she felt.

"Darling, what is meant for you will not go by you," Marj told Max, sensing her daughter didn't want to tell her more.

Max smiled. Her mum's clichés normally helped. But not this time.

And now, as she remembered that conversation, Max was so relieved that she hadn't told her mother any more: she'd still be reeling from Max's news when she was hit with the shock of today's newspaper article "uncovering" Lucy's murky past.

Murky, my arse, thought Max as she rubbed Clarins Beauty Flash Balm on her face in the hope of masking another late night.

Their childhood had been idyllic compared to half the girls Lucy had boarded with. Being sent away so their parents could do exactly as they pleased, or even move to another country, had left many of them miserable, with eating disorders and insecurities that followed them like a dark cloud for life. Max and Lucy had been loved by their mother and father — for that's what Dad was to both of them. Their mother would have stood for no less, but Fergal did it because he was a strong, decent man. God knew what his reaction to the article had been. He had hardly been mentioned — the only comments were that he was a carpenter, not one with a successful business, and that he was a "hard-drinking Irishman", which was a stretch of the truth given he enjoyed a few pints with workmates once or twice a week at his local and dinner out over a bottle of wine with Mum on Saturdays. Compared to most of the Irishmen she knew, that pretty much qualified as teetotal.

He was every inch the Alpha Male, seeing his role as providing for and protecting his family. He would be furious to think his girls had been hurt by the article. True to his Irish roots back in Armagh, on the country's borders, family was everything. And he was strong, so heaven help the reporter who was to blame for the story should he ever bump into Fergal Summers.

Her thoughts were interrupted when her specially purchased phone buzzed.

Max experienced the thrill of victory. The text was from Bridget. It simply said, "OK." It was enough, if not to prove her guilt, to point strongly towards it. Max hoped it would also be enough to make Hartley see how wrong he had been.

Lucy:
I Will Survive

Lucy rifled through her wardrobe like a woman possessed. She couldn't wait to get out, to laugh, to drink and forget, she hoped, about Hartley and that damned newspaper story.

Everything is bloody knee-length and below, she thought as she dismissed each one of her pristine outfits. Pastel-pink Matthew Williamson knit dress — too girly; chocolate-brown Stella McCartney wrap dress — too sophisticated. That was her problem, Lucy told herself — she was too damn sensible. Never drunk, always ladylike, conscientious, dependable. And where had it got her? No boyfriend and half of London thinking she was some manipulative gold-digger. It was time for Lucy to have some fun and she would start with looking through Max's wardrobe for an outfit.

She ran to Max's room in her dressing gown — her sister was out at some premiere or other — and opened her wardrobe. Lucy laughed out loud: it was as messy as hers was neat. Skimpy tops that had slipped off hangers lay on the floor; hangers were smothered in three or four dresses each, no doubt hung in a drunken stupor. It was always Max who came to Lucy for clothes, normally with a frantic brief to make her look smart enough to gatecrash a posh party. More than once, Max had returned a vintage Westwood blouse or cashmere blazer with a red-wine stain or cigarette burn, but she had always had the good grace to have it repaired straight away.

But tonight the roles were reversed because Lucy wanted to be a party girl. That said, Max's D&G bra masquerading as a top was taking it a little far. She could never wear a skirt that short, she thought as she browsed through her sister's wardrobe.

"Aha," Lucy said triumphantly as she spotted the dress she had often admired on Max. A Moschino metallic-silver number. Foxy. Yes, it was time for Lucy to dress the way she felt. And she felt she wanted to take a risk for once — to be young, free, wild. Hell, she would start by opening a bottle of wine. It was only 5.30p.m. and she wasn't meeting Amy for an hour, but after the day she'd had she deserved it. Lucy still hadn't heard from her mum, despite leaving another message. She resolved to call her again in the morning. Perhaps she could take a couple of days off work and drive home to see her. She desperately hoped Marj was OK. She was made of strong stuff, but that day's story wasn't just a surprise, the majority of it was made up — or at least spun out of control to paint Marj, Lucy and Max as something they were not.

Back in her room, Lucy switched on her iPod and smiled as Nina Simone's "Feeling Good" blared out of the speakers. She might not be feeling so good, but mind over matter was a powerful thing, she told herself. No point wallowing in self-pity. Those who thought less of her after the day's story were not true friends. Lucy, Max and Marj knew the truth and that was all that mattered. Lucy had toyed with the idea of ringing the newspaper and giving the editor a piece of her mind. But experience at the magazine had taught her that putting forward your side of the story made you look a little fame-hungry, and that's one thing Lucy was not. She wanted nothing more than to fade back into anonymity. In any case, ignoring the attention placed upon her could only make the story go away all the sooner.

Poor Max had called her in a state of high excitement that afternoon. Like a child with too many things to say in one breath, she had told Lucy that she had proof Bridget was behind the whole photographer affair.

"OK, so it's not concrete, but it's pretty damning and Hartley —"

"Stop." Lucy cut Max off. She had thought about nothing else but proving herself to Hartley. She had thought about it so much that she had realized there was absolutely no point. "Max, if I have to prove my innocence like this, I'm better off without him."

"What? No, Luce, you don't understand. It's the only —"

"No," Lucy interrupted her sister again. "It's not the only way. If he loved me and if he knew me half as well as I thought he did, there would be no need for this. But, Max?"

"Yes," came her deflated, faint response.

"I can't tell you how much it means, having you on my side. No matter how bad things are, having you batting for me always makes it better."

Lucy could sense Max soften.

"No worries, Luce. Are you sure?"

"Yes, Max. Swear you won't do anything with that text."

"OK."

"Max?"

"Yes, hand on heart, I promise. I kind of see what you mean — he should have trusted you all along."

It was a relief Max had seen her point of view, she thought as she lathered a layer of cocoa butter over her skin, followed by a dusting of Benefit body glimmer. Slipping the dress over her head, she closed her eyes until it settled on her body. She felt nervous. She had never had the raw confidence Max exuded, the wild streak of abandon. And here she was looking like . . . what? Standing in front of her oak-framed, full-length mirror, she took herself in. She looked like a young woman with a lust for life. Lucy laughed. That's just how it should be. The dress was hardly indecent — it was conservative by Max's standards, if not Lucy's. The neckline was high, skimming her collarbones and cutting across them in a straight line. The sleeves were full-length and flared at her wrists with dramatic effect every time she swished her arms. The stretchy silver fabric was neither skin tight nor loose but traced Lucy's toned body, showing off her flat tummy and full womanly breasts. It covered her bottom with a good few inches to spare. Quite respectable really. As she turned round and looked back into the mirror Lucy let out a yelp . . . there was no back whatsoever. One big plunging back-line, so low you could almost see the top of her bum. But, somehow, an exposed back was sexy; it wasn't like putting your breasts out there for the world to see.

Lucy slipped on a pair of Wolford matt-black-satin tights and strappy silver Gina heels. Normally £400, she had bought them after they were reduced by 70 per cent. A missing ankle strap had deemed them faulty, but Lucy had matched the material at a nearby fabric shop and had them looking perfect within hours.

She took a sip of the cold Pinot Grigio she had poured. It tasted good. Deciding on a wilder look than normal, she backcombed her hair a little at the roots for volume, then applied a liquid black eyeliner and grey shadow over her eye sockets. She highlighted her cheekbones with a dusting of Versace pink shimmer and dabbed a thick layer of clear MAC gloss on her lips.

Very sixties glam, she told herself as she turned from the mirror and drained her glass. She would enjoy herself tonight if it killed her. Sure, if she stopped for a moment to think of Hartley, she would probably break down in tears. The hurt was almost unbearable. But she had to be strong. The more she thought about what had happened, the more she started to feel hurt by Hartley. He couldn't really have known her if he was prepared to think she would betray him, even if all the signs pointed to her. Lucy wanted someone who unquestion- ingly believed in her. But then, did he have any choice but to doubt her? Stop it, she told herself. Amy has booked a fabulous restaurant. You are going to wine, dine, laugh, slur, dance and stumble home this evening. You are going to forget about Hartley and have fun, goddamn it.

Punching Amy's number into her phone, Lucy chose a black shawl from her wardrobe to guard against the evening chill.

"Aims, hi. I'm leaving now. I'll pick you up in a cab in twenty?"

Lucy grabbed her black-leather Prada baguette and left the flat.

Another Day, Another Doorstep

Max had been sitting outside the pop star Jay Conner's Hampstead house for two hours. At least she was warm; she was in Greg's van with blacked-out windows. Greg, a photographer with baggy jeans and shifty eyes, worked for the same paper. He moaned less than most of the snappers, but their conversation had dried up a good hour ago and Max studied the *Daily Express*. Not that there was much to study apart from a couple of thin showbiz stories and the obligatory front page about Princess Diana. What was it with the paper's obsession with her more than a decade after her death? Max browsed the sport pages. A poor knowledge of the big-hitting Premiership football players' names, their salaries and their positions let down many a female showbiz reporter. Football and celebrity were inextricably entwined, after all, Max thought as she nursed a polystyrene cup of lukewarm coffee from a café at the end of the road.

Max's boss had had a tip that Jay — whose second single had followed the first to the top of the charts last week — was in the grip of a serious addiction to the old Columbian marching powder and his dealer called by his house religiously on Thursday afternoons. As many stars who had found fame at a young age would testify, they had no idea how to handle the massive transformation. Jay's case was the perfect example. He had found himself on the guest list to every celeb party in London, with no shortage of hangers-on queuing to buy him drinks, offer a line or two and laugh at his jokes. Club owners would ask him to choose a girl he fancied and they'd bring her over — oh, and they could use the back room if they wanted. Having Jay in their club brought publicity money couldn't buy. Nothing was too much trouble when it came to making sure Jay became a regular. Just months before, he'd been stacking shelves at his local Tesco supermarket in Leeds. How the hell could anyone stay grounded in such a situation at that age? He was handsome in a messy-haired student kind of way — tall and slim with a mop of wavy brown hair girls would kill for. But he was in danger of becoming a two-hit wonder if he continued down this route.

Back in the world of newspapers, it would make a great story if Greg grabbed a picture of Jay welcoming the dealer at the door. And then, when he left the house, Max would pounce on him and ask Jay why a known dealer was visiting him. How the fuck will I know it's the dealer, Max had asked Claire.

"Just call me as soon as he goes in. Don't let him know you're there, and get a picture from inside the van. Then call me, describe him. Jay can't have many visitors with shoulder-length peroxided hair, head to toe in leather and riding a Harley Davidson, for fuck's sake."

Max wondered how Claire knew Jay's dealer. She knew that to get exclusives her boss would have some dodgy contacts; maybe she'd come across him in a club and he had tipped her off he'd be making a visit, and would be paid handsomely for the information. With no police on hand to search him, he couldn't be arrested — and he was probably the type who craved celebrity himself.

And so Max had waited, and waited.

She reflected on Lucy's insistence that she should not contact Hartley to tell him about the text she had received from Bridget. She could see Lucy's point of view. If Hartley thought enough of Lucy, if he really knew her, she shouldn't have to prove her innocence. Fuck him, Max thought as she looked over at Jay's house. Then again, he had made Lucy happier than Max could remember ever seeing her sister.

A bit like Luke, she thought with a wry smile as she remembered yet another text that had come from him this morning. She had deleted it without reading it. God, that had hurt. But what was the option? Tell him Lucy had warned her off because she was bound to fuck everything up like always? No, she had shut out memories of bad stories she had covered as a trainee — the smell of burning bodies after a horrific train crash near York, all those death-knocks, calling at the homes of parents whose child had just died to ask for a comment — so she sure as hell could block out Luke. It was only fair on Luce. She couldn't resent her sister for protecting Luke — after all, Lucy had always put Max first. The least she could do was return the favour by

238

putting Lucy first if this meant so much to her. Max tried to brush the thought away but she couldn't shake the feeling of hurt that Lucy had assumed she would mess things up with Luke.

Max's thoughts were interrupted by the buzzing of her phone in the pocket of her brown Paul Smith cords. It was Sheri.

"Awright, darlin'?"

"Tickety boo. What's up?"

"It's been a week, Max, can we do it now? Please, I need the money bad."

If Max left the photographer here, Claire would still get her picture — and she could always phone Jay's agent for a comment. Meanwhile, Max would have another, potentially brilliant, story.

"OK, I'll have to clear it with my boss to leave the job I'm on. But it should be fine so I'll be at yours in half an hour."

Once, Twice, Three Times
a Bloody Lady

It was all so bloody tiresome being nice all the time. Smile at this, laugh at that, don't ever say a mean word about anyone. How insanely dull. But it had to be done, Bridget reminded herself many times every day. She would not lose Hartley this time, even if it meant a personality bypass in the process. There was, of course, nothing wrong with Bridget's personality — people admired her for her honesty and humour. But she would be Snow White for a few months if that's what it took to get a bloody ring on her finger.

That bitch Lucy had, by all accounts, been sweeter than sweet. Claudia had chirruped on like a deranged nightingale about how lovely Lucy had been and how she simply couldn't believe she would be behind the photographer incident. Bridget wondered if Claudia was having a dig at her; perhaps she suspected Bridget had played a part. Doubtful, given that Bridget had been sure to keep up the saintly act in front of Claudia too. It was imperative that Hartley saw what a good friend she was and that she hadn't minded in the slightest that her very best friend had welcomed Lucy into their group.

240

"Oh yes, I gather she was a lovely girl," Bridget told Claudia. "I can't quite believe what she did. Poor darling Hartley."

Bridget's plan seemed to be working, albeit much slower than she would have liked. She had caught Hartley at just the right time. He was vulnerable and a little lonely and had welcomed Bridget, his fellow newly-single friend. But he had seemed wary at first of being anything more than friends. Bridget had been sure to let him think romance was the last thing she wanted too. But she had sensed a slight change in him over the last few days. Bridget had arranged dinner at the Ivy Club with Claudia and Charles — double dating, just like the old times. If there was a book to be written on sweetness and light, Bridget would be the author after that night. She asked Charles all about his deadly dull job as a trader and complimented Claudia on everything from her nails to her last-season Mulberry raincoat. When, a little merry at the end of the evening, she took Hartley's hand while leaving the restaurant, he responded by tightening his grip. And when he dropped her off they kissed on the lips. Bridget wondered if he had read the magazine she had left at his house. She had popped in to drop off a batch of delicious home-made cookies for him to try. (Her baker friend had made them but acting like a cross between Little Bo Peep and Nigella Lawson was her game plan.) And before leaving she had left several magazines, telling him they were for the waiting room of the Balmyle Foundation — often there were a few homeless types who popped in for a cup of tea, wasters that they were. This might cheer them up, she had told Hartley. And she had carefully left one of the magazines open at an article on the benefits of being a dad before the age of thirty-five. Subliminal messages, subtle prodding in the right direction was all he needed.

When she dropped off the cookies, Hartley had told her over coffee that he was glad she had been around.

"You've been lovely to me, Bridget, a real rock. Thank you."

"Oh darling Hartley, what are friends for?"

"You seem somehow different from before, Bridge. I don't know. More gentle, perhaps."

Bingo! Bridget had been waiting for this opportunity. The key was to make him think that she was never really as bad as he had imagined, that it was somehow in his head.

"Perhaps you are right, Hartley. But also, maybe you saw in me what you wanted to see when we dated. Sometimes, when we want a relationship to end, we make ourselves think our partner is not right for us . . ." Bridget left the thought hanging in the air like a wisp of smoke meandering to the ceiling, before cutting in. "Who knows, sweetie? So long as you know I am always here for you."

Hartley smiled back at Bridget. Indeed, she did seem so warm, so giving compared to the Bridget he remembered. Perhaps she was right. Maybe she hadn't been so bad. She was so sweet to her friends, so keen to make everyone happy. She was always asking how he felt, how his mother was bearing up in Scotland alone. Hartley knew it made a great deal of sense to be with

242

Bridget. But sense did not equate to love, the kind of raw emotion and passion he had experienced with Lucy. But look what that had brought him — utter devastation. Bridget had either changed or he had misjudged her.

Hartley had been a wreck after Scotland. He was still at a loss to explain what had happened. He felt so lonely and hated the prospect of having nothing but his own thoughts and company. So many times he had wanted to pick up the phone and call Lucy, to ask her what had happened. He had called once but hung up when he heard her answer message. Every day he hoped desperately to see her name flash on his phone. He longed to hear her voice.

He was thankful Bridget had been there for him when he was down. She reminded him that Lucy hadn't contacted him to explain the situation. She didn't say it unkindly, pointing out that poor Lucy must be mortified. After all, the evidence pointed so clearly towards her. Hartley had to admit Bridget had a point. Even when the story about Lucy's background had broken, Bridget hadn't judged, telling him that perhaps she was just embarrassed about her past — even though it didn't make her a terrible person. Hartley had read the article with an overwhelming sadness. He didn't care what Lucy was or what her family had, but the girl staring up at him from the newspaper seemed so remote now. They had shared so much during their time together and yet Lucy had never told him she and Max had different fathers, or so many other things. Perhaps he never really knew her.

243

A few days before the story appeared, Hartley had kissed Bridget. Poor lonely Hartley needed a woman in his life and it wouldn't be long before he wanted more than a kiss. Then there would be no going back.

The Sheekey Girls

Lucy groaned when Amy told her she had booked J Sheekey in Covent Garden for dinner. It occasionally boasted celebrity diners — and if there was one thing Lucy did not want it was to be in the vicinity of waiting paparazzi.

"Nonsense," Amy had told her in the cab. "The fish is the best in London and I am not hiding you away. Look at you!" Amy couldn't believe the transformation in her friend — she looked beautifully untamed with her backcombed hair and black eyeliner and her metallic dress showing off every inch of her body. "You're looking hot, Luce. Make the most of it. You've done nothing wrong, remember that."

Lucy shrugged her shoulders and smiled back at her best friend — next to Max, of course.

They had met at Oxford and formed a tight bond during the three years they studied English. Both girls had worked hard. Amy had a strong work ethic, which Lucy admired.

Lucy had loved their nights in, drinking wine or watching movies, and the times when Amy had shown her pictures of Kashmir. She had been blown away by its beauty and Amy promised that one day she would take Lucy to the beautiful north-west region on the

Indian subcontinent, which she described with its mountains and waterfalls as being like heaven on earth.

Walking into the restaurant, Amy giggled and whispered to Lucy over her shoulder, "You do realize every man in here is staring — and not at me."

Even the men on a romantic night out with other halves couldn't help but look as the girls were shown to their table.

Lucy laughed. "Aims, they probably all fancy you, you fool."

Amy always looked wonderful with minimal effort. Tonight's tight-fitting, black-velvet trousers made her legs look fabulous teamed with her impossibly high black-patent Gucci boots. A tight black-cashmere polo neck adorned with a string of chunky pearls accentuated her petite, girly frame.

"You don't think I'm too underdressed?"

"Enough modesty, Amy. You are sex on legs tonight; lap it up, girl. And anyway, we are going clubbing after this. Then we'll probably both feel overdressed."

As their drinks arrived, Lucy noticed her friend looked troubled and asked if everything was OK.

Amy smiled, a little sadly.

"Is it James? Has something happened?"

"I love him," Amy said, "I really do, but I've too much living to do to be a mum and wear floral dresses all day. I'm worried that's what is expected."

It was an odd thing to say, from nowhere it seemed.

Lucy looked at her friend. Amy was naturally stunning — the kind of girl who could wake up, pull on jeans and a T-shirt and still look amazing. She had translucent skin with big brown eyes and almost impossibly glossy black hair. Lucy knew James was proud of Amy and her achievements at work. But she also knew he would dearly love her to give up work and concentrate on breeding a new generation of de Vosses. And Lucy understood why that scared Amy; there was something of the free spirit in her that wasn't ready to be tamed.

James's background was poles apart from Amy's. He came from a long line of famous men; there had been many poets, barristers and politicians in the family through the centuries. James, a politician himself now, had often told Amy she had no need to work but she had insisted on continuing her career as a charity campaigner. Her job was to raise awareness about STDs — how they were spread, how to tell if you had one, how to get help and the like. She was in charge of a small team whose job was to come up with ideas for posters, TV and radio advertisements and increasingly clever viral-marketing campaigns. She also took part in workshops aimed at trying to help people come to terms with the sexually transmitted diseases that a dose of prescription pills would never clear up.

She loved her work, both the challenge of the creative side and feeling she was making a difference, no matter how small.

Amy was tracing the tip of her right index finger around the rim of her glass. When she spoke her voice seemed far away. "Sometimes I dream of travelling to Africa and working with people who desperately need help. Sometimes I just dream of travelling the world, going everywhere I can, for a very long time."

Tonight, Lucy knew how Amy felt. She had a desire to let go, be unleashed and live life without barriers.

As Lucy thought of what she could say to make her friend feel better, Amy looked around the bustling restaurant.

"Oh my God," Amy whispered over her cocktail menu.

"What?"

"Bloody Kirk Kelner is over there . . . and he's staring right at you."

Exclusive:
Billy's in the Brown Stuff

Max couldn't have hoped for a smoother ride with the Sheri story. She was still pinching herself at the result.

She had explained to Sheri that Billy Brown could be caught out with a phone call but she would have to wait a week or two to make the call so that what she told him sounded authentic.

Max wondered if Sheri had left the flat since the last time she saw her. She was dressed in the same pink tracksuit, only it was even baggier on her pathetic frame than before.

"Nice outfit," Sheri said, taking in Max from top to toe. "Paul Smith?"

"You've got it." Max felt embarrassed. Sheri's life was consumed by labels and guest lists. Here she was, with no proverbial pot to piss in, eyeing up Max's cord suit. On the one hand, Max had everything crossed, hoping that her plan worked so Sheri could net a tidy sum for the story. On the other hand, she knew it would only feed the lifestyle that was destroying her, which was a depressing thought.

"Are you sure he didn't know who you were?"

"Positive. I wore one of Envy's wigs that night — all my extensions are fallin' out. I looked half bald, so I had to. Anyway, when I saw him come out of Sketch he was all over the place — a right mess. The bouncer had fuckin' knocked me back cos I wasn't on the list. Bastard. His mate who's normally on the door lets me in for a little favour, if you know what I mean." Sheri winked at Max, her pallid skin wrinkling beside her eyes. "Whatever. Doesn't matter cos I spotted Billy, right? And I said, 'Mate, you want to jump in a cab with me?' And he just followed like a puppy."

Sheri's hands were trembling as she reached for a rolled-up £20 note on the coffee table. Chopping a line on the mirror, she looked up as if realizing for the first time what she was doing.

"Shit, you don't mind, Max, do ya?"

Max had seen it plenty of times, she just hated the effect it was having on Sheri. "No, not at all."

"The dealer's given me an extra week's credit — I assured him I've got a big story in the bag."

Kneeling on the carpet, Sheri bent over the table, the note in her nose, hoovering up two fat lines. She straightened up, wiping her nose.

"Right, so we gets back here and he's babbling like a crazy person. I puts on some porn — hoping that would get him in the mood and it seems to do the trick. We're kissing and he says he feels sick so I take him through to my bedroom, give him a glass of water. He's going on about how he's only ever cheated once before and I have to promise not to tell anyone. Of course, I say, 'Sure, honey, my lips are sealed.' He livens up at this and says, 'Not too sealed, I hope,' and he pulls me on top of him. He couldn't get enough of my tits . . .

250

mind you, compared to that scrawny cow of a wife, Becci, I suppose they are a treat. So I climbs on top . . . and there's no need to lie about this one, Max, he really is hung like a donkey —"

The coke seemed to have hit Sheri, who was animated now, her eyes wide and staring at Max.

"OK," Max interrupted, "I believe you, Sheri, but in the absence of hard evidence, let's make the call to him and then, if that works, I'll get all the details."

Sheri nodded obediently, sipping from a glass of water.

"Right, call from my phone," Max told her. "The number comes up withheld so there's no way of him tracing it or phoning back."

Max put an earpiece with a tiny mic inside it into Sheri's ear and pressed record on her Dictaphone.

"OK, so you remember what to say?"

"Yep."

After a few seconds Sheri waved her hand excitedly in the air, signalling Billy had picked up.

"Oh Billy, it's, erm, Sheri 'ere. You might not remember . . . last week you came back to mine."

Max had turned the volume on her phone to full so she could hear what Billy was saying.

"Oh, right. How'd you get my number?" He sounded guarded.

"You gave me it," Sheri lied, knowing he wouldn't be able to remember half the night. "Anyway, I won't keep you long, but I have somefing I have to tell you. My period, it was late when I slept with you . . . and it's still not here."

"What? You said you were on the fucking pill."

Bingo! An angry Billy Brown hadn't given a moment's thought to his reaction, so consumed was he by anger and shock.

"I am, darlin'," Sheri replied, giving Max the thumbs-up. "I am, but accidents happen."

"Oh for fuck's sake. Give me your number and I'll get one of my friends to call you . . . I'm sure we can arrange something." Max detected the guarded tone creeping back into Billy's voice. "Listen, doll, please don't say a word to anyone, OK?"

"Course, sweetpea." Sheri gave Billy a false number, changing a couple of digits of her own — the last thing she wanted was a footballer with a grudge getting his heavies on her — then she said goodbye.

The moment she hung up Sheri jumped up and leaped on Max, hugging her with everything she had. "You little beauty, Max. We did it."

Indeed they had. Max would have tomorrow's splash and Sheri would have the thirty grand they'd agreed on to pay off her dealer, stock up on supplies and kit herself out like a WAG once more. Max asked herself if she felt bad about uncovering Billy's exploits. After all, when the story went to print, he'd have a hell of a time — from his wife, his family and probably his manager, who liked his team to be cleaner than clean. Jeez, Max had cheated in her time so who was she to expose him? But then Max wasn't earning millions from advertising campaigns, sponsorship deals, TV documentaries and magazines by pretending to be Britain's Number One family guy.

A politician who banged on about family values deserved to have details of his exploits shagging his secretary or visiting a brothel laid bare. Likewise, Billy would be exposed as a hypocrite. As well the £50,000 a week he pocketed from his club, he'd made millions from his image as a family man. He'd picked up a £5-million pay cheque posing with Becci and their kids for Marks & Spencer, Gap and American Express in the last year alone, going on about how much he loved his wife and children in media campaigns. He'd even had the nerve to share some words of wisdom with the footballers who had been caught cheating, urging them to act as role models and turn their backs on temptation. Now his lies would be exposed.

Max called her boss to give her the news.

Claire wasn't one for showing much emotion over the phone or face to face, but her voice crackled with excitement and relief.

"Thank fuck for that. You know that tip I was working on? Well, turns out it's bollocks. We need a good story like this."

Max could imagine Claire biting on her well-chewed biro, typing an email to the editor spelling out the bones of the story, the phone cradled between her shoulder and chin. Every now and then she would pull her bleached white hair behind her ear, becoming a little impatient. She would be glad Max called but desperate to get off the phone so she could walk into the editor's office with the triumphant news. Sure, it wasn't her story but she would take credit for giving

Max plenty of time to work on it, to set it up, to wine and dine her contacts.

Max had learned much from observing Claire at work in the office. Like the phone stunt she used whenever she had to make a call to a PR or agent of a star, but really didn't want to have the conversation. Claire had taught her there was a way out.

With a really big story, reporters were obliged to run it by someone who represented the star in question the day before publication. This was, of course, fine if you wanted a comment on how the actor's movie had smashed box-office records or the singer's single had rocketed to number one. But there were some conversations Max dreaded having, like the one she would be having with Billy Brown's press spokesman very soon: "Hi, it's Maxine Summers from the *Daily News*. Having a good day? Good. Listen, just to let you know we're running an exposé in tomorrow's paper about how golden boy Billy has been shagging for Britain, outing him as a scumbag cheat and jeopardizing all those lucrative advertisements painting him as a family man. OK?"

The get-out ploy went as follows:

Take two phones, usually your mobile and a landline when in the office. Dial the number on both then, at the same time, press the "call" button on both, thus creating an engaged signal, putting you straight through to the answer phone. Leave a message spelling out what the story is and the evidence you have and . . . hey presto, deed done.

Of course, the PRs usually rang back. Max always took the calls, though some reporters didn't, reckoning they'd done their bit.

But at least the PRs had had a little time to digest the facts and there was less chance of them screaming like a banshee down the phone.

Max had transferred the trick into her personal life, cancelling dates or giving the "I'm really busy at work and won't be able to see you for a few weeks" speech to an answering machine. Cowardly, yes, but preferable to listening to some halfwit drone on about how he really cared for you and hoped you were both on the same fucking page.

Claire told Max she was a superstar. "The editor will love it. Well done, Max. I'll put you through to a copytaker."

Max was mid "Thanks, Claire" when she heard the click that signalled she was being transferred. Her boss would already be sprinting as fast as her Gucci heels could carry her to the editor's office.

"Hi, ready? OK. 'EXCLUSIVE by Maxine Summers: BILLY'S IN THE BROWN STUFF. England hero Billy Brown is today exposed as a love cheat. We can reveal the England captain has been playing away with busty glamour girl Sheri Jones. The news will devastate Billy's pin-up pop star wife, Becci, mother of their two children . . .' "

Max dictated the story expertly, breaking halfway to get a few more lurid details from Sheri.

After five hundred or so words, Max's story was complete and she called her boss.

"Spectacular, Max. I think we'll splash it and run on to a four/five."

This was as good as a story got: a dedicated front page and a double-page spread inside.

"Maybe you'll need more copy?"

"Don't worry. If I need more, I'll get Simon or Jade to knock something up."

Max was wary of such a scenario. She was less protective than most over bylines. But experience had taught her the hard way that a reporter might kindly offer to add a few facts to a story while she was out of the office doing another interview then, lo and behold, the next day their byline would appear alongside hers. Simon would never indulge in byline banditry, but Jade Stone, with her small, twitchy grey eyes and tight curly brown hair, was another story. She had famously done the dirty on her own boyfriend, a reporter for a rival daily, to get a scoop. After sifting through his text messages to see if he was cheating, she had stumbled across a story from a tipster telling him where Russell Brand was holding a secret party. Jade had gatecrashed the party the following night and bumped into her boyfriend, who promptly dumped her. Not that Jade cared — she got a great story that one of Russell's movie star pals had turned down a well-known girl band singer for a threesome with two waitresses.

As if reading her mind in the few seconds of silence, Claire told Max not to worry. "I'll see to it that there's only your name on it. It's a brilliant story and you got it — it's all yours. Now, treat yourself to something cold, fizzy and expensive — on me."

256

Maybe she had a heart after all.

"Max," Sheri said the moment she had hung up, "any chance of getting some of the money now?"

"Sure, Sheri. We can stop off at my office — I'll call the finance department and ask for an advance of, say, £500 in cash?"

Sheri nodded like a child who's been told she could lick the Angel Delight from the bowl.

"OK, and the rest will be in your bank within three working days, just like normal."

"Sorted. I'm gonna get me hair done right now and go out to celebrate. You wanna come?"

Max considered the prospect of partying with Sheri, watching her gyrate in a bikini top and hot pants beside the VIP section of the latest trendy club, seeing her drag off some footballer, like a python with an oversized kill.

Max decided she'd rather pour lemon juice into a paper cut while listening to a medley of Johnny Cash's most depressing songs. "Thanks, Sheri, but I've got plans."

Max had plenty of options — she could call Lucy and join her for dinner with Amy; she could head to a showbiz party with Simon and get drunk as a skunk. Hell, she could even have meaningless sex with whiffy Phil. Wonder if he'd started wearing deodorant?

She longed to call Suzie, who always had a way of making her laugh, no matter how awful she felt. But she was on holiday in Spain with David and had updated her Facebook status to: "Suzie is . . . pickled on sangria in Barcelona with her fiancé."

The last thing she needed was Max droning on about her broken heart. At times like this, she missed Suzie desperately.

Max wanted to be alone. Not quite true — she wanted to call Luke and tell him how much she thought about him, that she woke every morning with a dull ache at the memory of him.

She might have deleted his number from her phone but had forgotten they had become Facebook friends: she had received a message from him through the site back when she first started ignoring his calls and texts. She had deleted the message straight away.

Damn Facebook for showing pictures that had been tagged of him by one of his mates. She couldn't help clicking on one of the images and there he was. So bloody gorgeous, just as she remembered. No, even better. Max felt a stab of pain as she noted the girls in the background at some party. Attractive, blonde. Fuck, what if he'd moved on? She had given him no option but to continue his life without her, but it still hurt to see him laughing, to see him getting on with things. He looked so happy. And so fit. That was the thing about Facebook. It allowed you to spy on snippets of people's lives — the bits they wanted you to see when they were surrounded by friends, having fun. And sometimes, when you wanted to be part of that person's life, it hurt like hell that you could only watch on your laptop from afar, your stomach churning each time you saw them. Max considered deleting Luke as a friend but it was her last remaining link to him. She could kick herself for being so weak, but she couldn't cut the last tie.

She should be out celebrating tomorrow's splash, but Max the party girl just couldn't face it and that was most definitely a first. Max Off Booze shocker. This wave of sadness would pass. Luke would be a distant memory soon. He had to be — this feeling of loss was too strong to sustain.

Lucy Has an Admirer

Lucy and Amy had giggled like giddy schoolgirls when they spotted Kirk Kelner, before telling each other to get a grip and act like they hadn't seen him. There was nothing more pathetic than grown women drooling over a man just because he was famous.

"Not just famous," Amy had pointed out. "He's also the fittest man I've ever seen in my life. By far."

Lucy had laughed, stealing a last glance at the actor. "Agreed. He's divine. But enough about him. This restaurant was a great choice after all, Aims, and this lobster bisque is amazing."

Amy lifted her glass and clinked Lucy's.

"Here's to you, Luce — and the future."

Lucy felt the effects of their gin martinis and the bottle of Chablis, and revelled in the abandon she felt.

"It's got to be better than the last few weeks, Aims. Here's to both of us."

The girls caught up on each other's news over their main courses — Dover sole off the bone for Lucy and hake for Amy. There was so much to tell. James was desperate to marry. Part of Amy couldn't wait for the fairy-tale wedding she'd always dreamed of but the thought of a lifetime of school runs didn't do it for her.

"I love my job, Luce."

"I know you do but James isn't so stuck in the Dark Ages, Aims; surely he'd be happy for you to carry on?"

Amy drained her glass. "I don't think so. I'm over thirty, his mum is desperate for grandchildren and it's simply not the done thing for a de Vosse mother to work. It's modern in the very worst way to them. But it's just not me."

Lucy felt a surging sense of respect for her friend. Many women would jump at the chance to be kept for the rest of their days, the hardest decision they had to make being what kind of nanny to hire — an enthusiastic young French one or a sterner lady of a certain age because the more nubile option might turn hubby's head. Amy had never changed to fit with James's set. She stood out, with her Manchester accent, swearing when the mood took her to bring a story to life. Lucy had no doubt that's why James adored her — he had fallen for Amy as she was. Lucy couldn't believe he'd expect her to change who she was just because he'd decided the time was right to start a family.

As the girls gave their cards to the waiter, he smiled back.

"Mr Kelner has taken care of the bill for you."

"Mr . . ."

"Yes, Mr Kelner," the waiter said, with a hint of an Italian accent. "He hopes you do not mind. He has also asked for a bottle of champagne to be sent to your table."

Amy lowered her head to the table, then looked up at Lucy and spoke in a hushed tone: "Bloody hell, bloody Kirk Kelner has bought us dinner."

Hollywood star Kirk Kelner. The man Armani dressed for free because the clothes looked so good on him.

"Please tell him we would love to accept his champagne, and thank him for us," Amy told the waiter firmly.

"Very well, madam." The waiter nodded, marching off to Kirk's table.

"Luce," Amy was still talking in a hushed tone, full of urgency and excitement, "Kirk Kelner — the only man in the world I'd be unfaithful to James with . . . I've told him that, don't worry — is after you. He's bought us dinner and is making eyes at you like a lovesick school-boy."

"What's your point, Aims?"

"My point is . . . go and bloody say thank you. Now."

Of course he wasn't really after her. He had his pick. Mind you, she thought, looking over at his table, his dinner companion didn't look much like a date. Unless he'd taken a fancy to the more mature lady. She was a stunning woman — perfectly turned out, great skin — but must be over fifty or wearing well for sixty. And she looked far too poised and refined to lust after a toy boy.

God, Kirk was handsome. Hell, when would she ever contemplate not thanking anyone who had just bought her dinner?

"OK, I will."

Lucy was grateful for every sip of alcohol she had had since opening the bottle of wine at the flat. She needed the courage it had given her.

Floating over to the other side of the room, she felt detached from her body, like she was watching this surreal scene from above. Was this really happening?

"Hello, Kirk?" Shit, it was real, she thought as she heard the words come from her mouth.

"Yes, hello. Pleased to meet you . . .?"

"Lucy — Lucy Summers."

Kirk offered his hand and stood for a few seconds. He held Lucy's frozen gaze. He was overwhelmingly handsome, gorgeous. Better than on film. She was aware he was motioning to the other side of the table.

"This is my mother, Daphne."

Daphne offered her hand and a broad smile. "Charmed." She was even more stunning up close, all white teeth and luminous skin.

"I . . . I just wanted to thank you for your lovely gesture. It was very kind."

Kirk's eyes were twinkling, still fixed on Lucy's. "It was my pleasure."

Lucy felt she should be overcome with nerves and shyness. But somehow she felt alive, more sure of herself. Maybe it was the drink. More likely it was the fact that Kirk Kelner had bought them dinner. If that wasn't a boost to the ego, what was? And why be nervous? He was, after all, only human.

"There is, however, a catch." Kirk was studying Lucy. "I can't pretend my motives were completely selfless."

Lucy found herself smiling at him, intrigued by what was coming.

"The thing is . . . I'm on the guest list for a club nearby — my driver's waiting outside — and as hard as I've tried, my mother is refusing to even entertain the thought of accompanying me. So . . ."

Lucy raised her eyebrows, playing this fun flirting game with Kirk bloody Kelner.

"Would you like to be my guest? You and your friend . . .?"

"Amy."

"I'd be delighted if you and Amy would join me. I shall try to be as entertaining as is fitting for two such beautiful ladies."

What was a girl to say to such a proposition?

"Thanks, we'd like that."

Lucy couldn't wait to tell Amy.

Charity Starts at Home

It had all been so easy. A leaflet about the Moonwalk marathon in London in aid of breast cancer here, a "£5 a month could save an orphan's life" pamphlet there. Bridget had been sure to leave some charity paraphernalia behind at every opportunity. Last week, having popped into Hartley's flat to drop off some home-made Dundee cake (it could only do her good if he learned to associate her with his beloved Scotland — her mother's party caterer had actually made it but dear H needn't know), she had left behind a book on depression. Hartley had called her soon after she left, gingerly bringing up the subject of the book.

"Oh darling, don't worry. It's not for me. What have I to be down about? I'm a very lucky girl. That's why I've decided to do some voluntary work, you know, chatting to people who are a little less happy. But I'm doing some training first, sweetie — these things have to be handled ever so gently."

"Oh I see. That's, erm, lovely, Bridget. Good for you."

Bridget beamed with pride at the other end of the phone. Thankfully, he couldn't see the wicked smile that then spread across her face.

Yes, she had painted a rather saintly picture of her new self. In fact, when she was at his town house yesterday she had overheard Hartley tell an old school friend just how kind she was. When his mobile had started ringing she had kissed him on the cheek and waved goodbye before running down the stairs to the first floor as noisily as she could — then she had quietly retraced her footsteps back up to the landing to listen in.

"Bately, I really appreciate your concern . . . Yes, I know, but really, she's a different person . . . Yes, old chap, you're right, I do know best . . ."

Bloody Bately, the interfering idiot. OK, so she'd told a girl Bately was dating a while back that he had cheated on every girlfriend and that she would be no different. Actually, Bridget told her, she had heard whispers he'd been seeing quite a bit of an ex recently. She was only looking out for the poor girl . . . Mel, was it? Bately hadn't seen it that way. He had called her in such a rage he could hardly get his words out. He had, however, managed to convey his thought that Bridget had sabotaged the relationship because she was jealous. His girlfriend had finished things even though Bately insisted he hadn't so much as looked at another girl since he met her because he was smitten. He pleaded, he begged, but it was no use. He said Bridget was a spiteful bitch who couldn't stand the fact Mel had been an instant hit with their group of friends.

Mel was too much of a threat for Bridget, Bately had told her. They were around the same height and both had slender frames.

266

"But with one big difference," Bately had spat.

"What's that, sweetie?"

"Her face doesn't look like she's chewing a wasp."

Bridget had laughed. "Darling Bately, you are such a hoot."

She couldn't remember much more of the conversation. It was an age ago — just a few months after she'd started dating Hartley first time round. She hadn't banked on him holding a grudge for quite so long. Thankfully, Hartley had seen the light, she thought as she listened to him reassure his friend she was a changed woman. Dear H, she thought, as she heard him come out with gems like "everyone's allowed a second chance" and "she's in a much better place these days".

Simple phrases even his dyslexic buffoon of a friend Bately might understand. Psycho-babbling Hartley was falling for her all over again. And that simply proved what Bridget had known all along: they were meant for each other. Even if he didn't realize it at the moment, if he was "encouraged" to think about a future and family with Bridget, he would see it all made perfect sense.

Lucy Lets Her Hair Down

"Oh. My. God. Kirk Kelner wants to take us to a party? Are you joking?"

Lucy laughed. Amy's face was etched with delight, shock and fear.

"Not joking, Aims. Just me, you and Kirk Kelner. You don't think James will mind?"

"Stuff James, Luce, it's Kirk Kelner. If he wants our company, who are we to refuse? Of course, he really wants to be with you. Will I be in the way?"

"Oh please. He insisted you come. Anyway, he might be Kirk Kelner but he's still a stranger — I won't go unless you come."

"Luce, I was just fishing — of course I'm coming."

"Good."

"But I am going to bugger off if it looks like you two are hitting it off. I want a Hollywood wedding, Luce, the full works. Max and I will be bridesmaids."

"Yes, yes. I'm sure he'll have his pick of girls once we're in the club. He'll probably slip off with some gorgeous clubber barely out of her teens. Let's just have some fun."

"Exactly. And don't worry about the world knowing. I promise not to call everyone I've ever known tomorrow to tell them — although I bloody want to.

Just James and my mum, OK? I know the last thing you want is more attention."

"Thanks, Aims. Now let's party."

Amy was delighted to hear Lucy talk like this. Lucy always put others first, often before her own happiness. She never really let go or threw caution to the wind. Perhaps that had become a natural instinct, growing up as big sister to Max. Carrying her home after a night out, fielding calls from smitten exes wondering why she was ignoring them. Lucy was so used to being the sensible one, it came naturally to her.

If only she could see how bloody attractive she was, and started enjoying it. Maybe that's what was happening tonight. Lucy was enjoying herself. She was more vibrant than Amy had ever seen her.

She had been wounded so deeply by what had happened with Hartley — not just knowing that people thought she had set out to lie and trap him, but mostly because Hartley had believed the very worst of her. Amy was relieved to see Lucy picking herself up and having fun.

Kirk had asked them to join him at his table for a glass of champagne before they left for the club. Daphne, whose jade-green Chanel pencil skirt suit showed off her slender frame, was charm personified. She asked Lucy and Amy about themselves and said she was delighted to be leaving her son in the company of such intelligent and beautiful ladies. After twenty minutes or so Daphne glanced at her watch. With a flurry of air kisses she announced she really had to go and bade them goodnight.

Draining his flute, Kirk warned them that some paparazzi would probably be lying in wait outside the restaurant. He offered to call another car for them to leave five minutes after his exit.

"Otherwise," he said, "you might appear in some rag as 'Kirk's mystery girls'. I wouldn't want to embarrass you."

Lucy agreed. She was sure Kirk had no idea of the press that had followed her since meeting Hartley. Little did he know what a great story it would be for them — Lucy Lands Another Millionaire — painting her as . . . hell, who cared? At least this way, if they left in different cars, the press wouldn't get the chance. Lucy giggled as she read Amy's face. She could tell Amy quite fancied the idea of being splashed all over the papers with the world's sexiest man.

She'd love to see James's face as he picked up the paper with snaps of his fiancée on Kirk's arm. It would bring a whole new meaning to keeping him on his toes.

Kirk had been thoroughly charming to Amy, asking where she lived, commenting on her lovely jewellery. But his expression changed when he looked at Lucy. He couldn't stop taking her in — not so much in a sleazy way as with mounting curiosity. She was so different to the girls he'd been spending time with in London.

What a beautiful pairing they would make, Amy thought as she watched them. Both were almost impossibly gorgeous — tall, flawless skin, fair silky hair, bright white smiles.

270

Shortly after he left the restaurant, with instructions to meet him inside the Met Bar on Park Lane, where their names would be on the door, Lucy and Amy followed in a black Bentley.

"Not bad for a standby car," Amy laughed as they sped off.

Full of anticipation for the glitzy night that lay ahead, the girls watched the bright lights of Covent Garden whizz by in a blur.

Smitten Kelner Makes His Move

Kirk couldn't take his eyes off Lucy from the moment he spotted her in the restaurant. It was as if the rest of the room was a 2D cartoon and she was the only real thing in it. She was just his type: blonde, slim, so pretty. But the girls he was usually attracted to had had a great deal of help — hair extensions, fake tans that rubbed off on his Egyptian cotton sheets, acrylic nails. This girl seemed to be real. Daphne had followed his trance-like gaze.

"Oh yes, now that's the sort of girl you should be going for." Daphne had recognized Lucy at once. Although she hardly ever read newspapers she'd become quite addicted to the social diary column in the *Daily Mail*. That was Lucy Summers; she'd graced his pages almost every day for the past few weeks. And there had been some falling-out with her boyfriend, the Earl of Balmyle — she couldn't remember what it was about. Who cared? This girl was single and mixed with aristocracy — much more fitting than the string of near-prostitutes her son had taken to bedding. Honestly, if she read another story about him leaving a club with a glamour girl in the early hours, she would scream. What Kirk needed — for his reputation and for his own happiness — was a real lady. This one was stunning and also well connected. Daphne decided not to tell her son everything she knew about Lucy — after all, an over-enthusiastic mother was enough to put any son off.

"She is gorgeous."

Daphne couldn't help but laugh. Kirk looked just as he had when he was eight and she'd told him he could ride in a helicopter. He was transfixed, his eyes wide and dreamy as he watched Lucy glide to her table.

"Yes, darling, she is." Daphne was keen to get things moving. It would suit her very well for Kirk to form a relationship with Lucy. She had grown to like London very much and might even consider staying if she could meet the right kind of people — the sort she had read about in novels by English authors. Perhaps a charming widower who would take her to the opera and parties. Her own husband, Eddie Kelner — Kirk's father — had run off a decade ago and had gone through three younger models since, the fool. Some male company would be lovely. Someone who would treat her well, take her to places she had never been. "Darling, I have an idea. Treat her to dinner; let her know you are interested."

Kirk looked unsure.

"Kirky, otherwise you might never see her again. What harm can it do?"

Kirk smiled. "You are absolutely right, as always, Mom. I'll let the waiter know. Another glass of mineral water?"

"Yes please, darling."

"Good, I'll stick to the double scotches."

When Lucy had come over to thank him, Kirk was a little taken aback. She seemed to radiate some kind of unearthly glow. God, she was gorgeous. And that accent — incredibly polished without a trace of the London whine that had so quickly started to grate when he picked up girls from clubs.

Kirk was a little confused by the realization that he was in awe of this woman. Normally, he didn't give a shit. Ply them with champagne, tell them how beautiful they were, how lonely he got and — bingo! — back to his room for dirty sex. But this girl was something else. So polite, a little shy. Jesus, did she have any idea how stunning she was? Her friend was pretty too. They were like a different breed from the women he'd been hanging out with. Poles apart from one girl he'd slept with, whom he'd spotted just now as he came in . . . Sheri? She might be a fame-hungry gold-digger, selling stories about him, but it had hardly done his reputation any harm.

Kirk was delighted when Lucy and Amy appeared at the Met Bar. He wasn't a man who suffered from insecurity, but he had worried they might have had second thoughts and decided not to join him.

But here she was, once again the only luminous thing in the club. Her shiny dress clung to every inch of her. God, to see what was under that dress would be heaven.

"Hey, glad you made it." Kirk stood up as a bouncer lifted the red rope to let them in the booth.

Lucy had been to the Met Bar once before, for the party during London Fashion Week. Part of the

Metropolitan Hotel, it was one of the most famous celeb haunts in London, though fewer stars hung out there now compared to the 1990s, when Brit Pop was in full swing. Then, the Gallagher brothers would be snapped staggering out in the early hours, Liam brandishing a bottle of beer and giving photographers his signature one-fingered salute. These days it was more of a venue for rich businessmen in expensive suits drinking on their company's expense account. A string of newer clubs had most of the paparazzi lying in wait outside, hoping to catch the fresh blood of showbiz like Lily Allen and Amy Winehouse — the current caners of pop.

But tonight the bar was guest list only, in aid of some up-and-coming American DJ who had invited the uber-cool of London to his party. Lucy spotted one of the Kaiser Chiefs at the bar and . . . oh was that Kate Moss? It was! That's how you knew the DJ playing was cooler than cool — when he attracted the world's best-known supermodels to his gigs. And if there's one thing Kate did well it was tapping into the next big thing, whether it be fashion or music.

Lucy loved to people-watch, even though this was definitely more Max's scene than hers. Shit, this would be a great source of stories for her. But then she couldn't very well ask Kirk, who had been kind enough to invite her to this private party, if her sister, who worked for a tabloid, could come to write about him. Anyway, Max had said she was staying in for a night of hot chocolate and DVDs.

Kirk was devastatingly handsome. And so attentive. Didn't he realize Kate Moss was a few feet away? Or see the gaggle of pretty girls — all miniskirts, hot pants and hair — on the dance floor? He didn't seem to care. How could any woman fail to be flattered? And he was funny, not at all as self-important as one might have expected.

Amy was in awe of Kirk, laughing like a giddy schoolgirl at his jokes.

After half an hour or so she announced she had spotted someone she'd like to talk to.

"And no, I'm not being polite. I really have spotted someone I want to talk to," she shouted over the music to Lucy and Kirk.

Lucy deserved some luck, Amy thought as she watched Kirk drinking in every inch of Lucy with his eyes. But to have Kelner hanging on your every word? That was taking luck to a brand-new level.

Amy Makes Her Move

Sheri had had some offers in her time but this one took the biscuit. In fact, she could hardly believe what this woman was asking her.

"Have you ever had an STD?"

"Excuse me?" She stared back incredulously.

"A sexually transmitted disease."

"I know what a fucking STD is, you cheeky cow."

Sheri had hit the town with Envy to celebrate her windfall courtesy of Billy Brown. She'd squeezed in an appointment at the hairdresser's and felt great showing off her new mane of dark blonde extensions. The peroxide ones had been too hard to maintain as her roots came through. She looked altogether classy, even if she did say so herself. Her Fantasy Tan was much more realistic than the St Tropez she'd been using. And her royal-blue mini-dress with the zip all the way down the front made her look as skinny as any of the famous footballers' wives, but with a far superior cleavage.

Envy had got them into the Met Bar and it was brilliant — loads of famous people, big-name models and cool DJs. Bet they had some quality gear — top-of-the-range coke. She thought about making a run for it when Kirk Kelner came in — he might take issue with her kiss-and-tell. Then again, she had made him sound like the sex god he was far too drunk to have been. She had made eye contact with him for a second and, with just a whisper of a smile, she could tell he recognized her. He had quickly turned his attention to a member of staff who was showing him to a booth. Even though he had come in alone, he had seemed distracted, then totally focused on the blonde who joined him. She was stunning, must have been a model. Sheri had been making eyes at the DJ — apparently the next big thing, who looked the sort who'd be well up for a threesome with her and Envy — when some woman had tapped her on the shoulder. She was a pretty girl, even if she needed a bit more make-up.

Sheri couldn't understand why this woman was being so nice to her. She was shouting over the music, asking if she was having a good time, if she came here often.

"Look, darlin', I'm no carpet-muncher."

"Sorry?"

"Dyke. I ain't no bloody lesbian. At least not if no men are involved. Not interested, if that's what you're after."

Knowing she was looking h-o-t tonight, Sheri could hardly blame this bird.

The girl had apologized, insisting that's not what she had meant. She said something about her job and could she ask a personal question. Then, bang, asked if she had had a bloody STD.

She seemed to have sussed she was out of order from Sheri's reaction.

"Have I had a fuckin' what?"

278

"Oh God, sorry."

This bird was from Manchester, a Manc — the same accent as Liam and Noel Gallagher, but a bit softer.

"I don't think you heard me introduce myself. My name is Amy and I work for a charity that raises awareness of STDs and safe sex."

Sheri stared at her, then gazed over her shoulder, wondering if the DJ would have any coke.

"The thing is . . . How can I say this? I can help design posters about the dangers of chlamydia until I'm blue in the face . . . but it's almost impossible to get the attention of the young people they're aimed at."

Sheri looked back at her blankly.

"Sorry, I'll cut to the chase." Amy was grateful the music had quietened a little. "I recognize you; you've had a few, erm, relationships with famous people, yes?"

"What's it to you?"

"You are, well, a bit of a role model to some young girls who dream about going out with a famous footballer or pop star."

This was stretching the truth somewhat but working on the basis that flattery got you everywhere — and that she didn't want to be lamped by Sheri in the middle of the Met Bar — Amy continued.

"I've been thinking of getting a celebrity to front a campaign aimed at teens and young women but I've not come up with anyone I think they would really believe."

Amy could tell she had hooked Sheri, who was now nodding and "uh-huhing" as she spoke.

"And I thought that you, being a girl with real experience, could be perfect for —"

"Bloody right," Sheri cut in. "The stories I could tell you. I know better than most you can never judge a book by his cover — bloody footballers might look gorgeous, but I can tell you from itchy experience they might often have crabs too."

Amy laughed. "That's just what we need — someone with humour, who can tell it like it is and make people take notice."

Sheri had visibly perked up. "Well, I'm your girl."

A Drunken Lucy Makes Her Move

Lucy felt like a different person. When Kirk suggested another bottle of champagne, she knew the old Lucy would have said no. So she said yes. Amy had already left, to talk about a work project with a woman she'd met at the bar, checking first with Lucy that she was happy to stay on with Kirk.

"My mobile will be switched on, Luce. You call me if anything happens, OK?"

Lucy had reassured Amy she would call should something go wrong, but she was sure Kirk would be quite gentlemanly.

Amy blushed furiously as Kirk kissed her goodbye.

As the party wound down, Kirk suggested he get his driver to drop Lucy off at home before heading back to his hotel. When his charcoal-grey Jaguar pulled up at her flat, Lucy knew she should at most kiss Kirk and give him her number. But where had doing the right thing got her so far? No boyfriend, miserable and most probably despised by half of London's elite. And this wasn't just any guy, it was Kirk Kelner. One-night stands had never been Lucy's thing — mainly because she was sure she'd struggle to cope with no contact after sharing something which should be special. But hell, you should do everything once. And if you're going to have a one-night stand, it might as well be with Kirk Kelner.

Lucy realized this was the logic of far too much wine and champagne, but it also made a great deal of sense.

"Would you like to come up for a coffee?" Lucy couldn't believe she'd said it.

"I'd love to."

Kirk followed Lucy out of the car, said something to his driver and took Lucy's hand. She felt like a giddy teenager on a first date as she led the way up the communal stairs. She wondered if Kirk even understood the concept of a shared entrance. A man with a penthouse at the Dorchester for six months of the year and a mansion in Los Angeles probably had little opportunity to contemplate such a notion.

And yet she didn't feel self-conscious in the slightest. Maybe Kirk craved some normality in his fairy-tale life. She unlocked her door. As she stepped inside, Kirk pulled her round to face him. His warm lips were on hers, moving with her own. She felt his tongue on hers, soft at first, then searching, firmer. God, he was hot, she thought, brushing her fingers against his rock-hard stomach. Lucy took his hand and led him to her bedroom.

Shock of the Morning to You

"Fuck me, you're Kirk Kelner."

It wasn't what Max imagined her first five words might be that Friday morning. Of all the people she expected to see coming out of the bathroom, Kirk Kelner was not in the top ten. He didn't even register in the top ten thousand.

But Kirk Kelner it was. Max hadn't even been out last night, so she knew she wasn't still drunk and imagining things.

She was staring at him, he was staring back. This was surreal.

There was a knock at the door. Max looked at it, then back at Kirk. Another knock came, more insistent this time.

"Right, I'm going to get the door. Back in a minute . . . Kirk Kelner."

Was his being in her flat anything to do with her meeting him (and subsequently turning him over) at the premiere of *Man of Steel 4*? Doubtful, given there wasn't a flicker of recognition when he saw her, just a look of surprise. Had he stayed over with Lucy? Impossible! Man, this was weird, Max was thinking as she absent-mindedly opened the door.

"Fuck. Mum."

"Lovely to see you too, Max," Marj replied, kissing her daughter on the cheek as she stepped inside the flat.

Marj had by-passed the intercom system. A passing neighbour must have let her in or left the street door open.

Max looked back towards the bathroom. Kirk had vanished. She watched as her mum put a small brown-leather suitcase beside the sofa and unbuttoned her red raincoat. As she smoothed down her choppy sandy-blonde hair, she addressed her younger daughter.

"Honestly, Max, I'm as modern as you'll get for a middle-aged mother, but I'd far rather you greeted me with a simple 'Hello' than the F word . . ."

Marj's words floated over Max. Whoever said life was stranger than fiction must have lived through a scene similar to the one unfolding here.

Gathering her thoughts as quickly as her overloaded brain would allow, Max bounded over to her mum, kissing her cheek and hugging her. Then she headed to the kitchen.

"I'll pop the kettle on," she shouted over her shoulder in as carefree a tone as she could. "Nice cup of tea to warm you up? You should have said you were coming. What a lovely surprise."

"Surprise? After that newspaper article yesterday?"

"Oh . . . yeah."

"I would have come much sooner but I'm just back from Ireland with your dad. He took me for a treat for our wedding anniversary. Kept it a secret, bless him."

Max was wincing as she popped her head out of the kitchen door. "Shit. Sorry, Mum, I forgot . . . again."

"Never mind that. I left my mobile phone at home — you know me and mobile phones, Max — and I had about twenty messages. Lucy sounded like she was about to burst into tears. Anyway, she didn't answer her phone last night so I got a sleeper train down straight away. Do you know how expensive it is to fly from Dundee if you book at the last minute? And the train's so relaxing. I always get a good night's sleep — I think it's the motion. And here I am."

"Yes, here you are."

"Max, what's wrong?"

Shit. "What do you mean what's wrong?"

Marj was standing beside Max now, her kind blue eyes twinkling as they looked into her daughter's. "Max?"

What was the use? Max could tell Marj anything — she always had. Far better to say Kirk Kelner was in the flat now than have her scream and possibly collapse with shock when he burst out of Lucy's bedroom, which he could at any moment.

"Mum, you might not believe this, but Kirk Kelner is here."

"What? Where?"

"In Lucy's room."

Marj looked at Lucy's door, as if its large wooden frame held the key to this mystery.

"Kirk Kelner," Marj repeated to herself. "Kirk Kelner. Oh the one you wrote about, who was cheating on his wife? I still cut out all your stories, darling. There are folders of them in the loft. Has he come here for an interview? You must be doing well to get a big star like him to come to you. I thought you always did those things in hotels?"

Max didn't know how to explain, because she had no clue what was happening.

But without coming up for air, Marj continued, "Well, anyway, darling, if you have to do an interview I shan't get in the way. I should have told you I was coming. Lost my phone charger — aren't I terrible? I'm going to pop out and get some papers, have a nice coffee at that lovely little place round the corner, and leave you to it. I'll be back in an hour or so, OK?"

"OK, Mum."

"Will Lucy be here?"

"Erm, yes. I think she has the day off."

"Is she OK?"

"I think so." By the looks of things, very OK, Max thought.

Max kissed her mother goodbye. Only Marj could suggest popping out for papers having just learned Kirk Kelner was yards away. Of course she wouldn't have screamed had she seen him — she would have asked how he took his tea.

Max stood outside Lucy's bedroom, wondering if she should knock. Could Kirk really be in there with her? Half or totally naked? Max's heart pounded, though she hoped not as quickly as Lucy's had if she'd actually shagged Kirk Kelner.

Marj Has News

Marj fastened her raincoat against the chilly morning. Summer had gone so quickly, she thought as she made her way to the newsagent's. She would read the papers over a latte then head back to the flat. Honestly, those girls. Lucy had sounded so worried on the phone, fearful no doubt about the article in the paper. Marj wasn't in the least concerned what anyone thought of her or her family after reading it. If their judgement was to be clouded by such nonsense then they were not worth knowing in the first place.

What did concern her was that someone clearly had it in for Lucy and that would not do. Fergal had paced up and down the living room when she showed him the paper, cursing the press, the reporters and the world in general.

He had wanted to join her in London, to make sure the girls were OK but she had persuaded him to stay in Scotland to work on a big new contract he'd landed near home in Arbroath. Marj had something on her mind and had been meaning to visit her daughters soon anyway.

Marj looked at her Raymond Weil watch, a fiftieth-birthday present from her girls. It wasn't even eight o'clock yet. It was so early, but her sleeper had arrived at 7a.m. at King's Cross. No wonder she'd surprised the girls.

"What —?"

Marj stopped suddenly in front of a news stall. Was that . . .? It was. Lucy — on the front page of the *Daily News*.

Max's paper.

Marj lifted a copy. "Hartley's Ex Dates Kirk Kelner" screamed the front page, above separate headshots of Lucy and the actor.

"Hey, lady, you gonna pay for that?"

Marj wasn't aware that she was walking off with the paper. "Sorry," she told the man absent-mindedly, and rummaged in her purse for coins.

Thumbing to the inside pages, Marj took in the words:

LUCY COPS OFF WITH KELNER

Just weeks after her split with Britain's most eligible bachelor, the Earl of Balmyle, Lucy Summers has struck gold again, with Hollywood heart-throb Kirk Kelner.

We can reveal the ambitious blonde enjoyed a cosy date with Kelner, 39, who is worth an estimated £500 million.

A source said: "There was instant chemistry between Kirk and Lucy. Kirk has a reputation as a ladies' man but he's put that behind him — Lucy could be the one."

Lucy recently split with Hartley, the Earl of Balmyle, amid rumours of a falling-out after she tipped off a photographer to follow them while holidaying in Scotland.

But the fashion writer seems to have landed on her feet again after cosying up with Kirk during a private party at trendy London club the Met Bar.

Marj was struggling to compute the fact that the story in front of her was about Lucy. Her Lucy? She was still reading the details when she arrived back at the flat.

Mum's the Word

Max opened the door to her mother for the second time that morning.

"Hi, Mum, that was quick."

"It was, darling, but as it happens I had a little surprise on the way to the café," Marj said, laying her coat and bag on the sofa.

"You did?"

"Look." Marj held up her copy of the paper.

"Fucking hell."

"For goodness sake, Max, what's with the swearing?"

"Sorry, Mum. It's Lucy; she's on the front page."

"Yes, Max."

"Of my paper."

"You catch on quickly, Maxy." Marj's tone was playful. "You didn't know?"

"God, absolutely not." Max took the paper from her mum and peered at the front page. The story had Jade Stone's name on it. How the hell could she have known about last night? Max felt a rising fury. Her so-called colleague hadn't had the decency to even ring Max to warn her that Lucy was front-page news. How the hell had Jade got this story?

When Marj had popped out, Kirk had jumped in the shower and Max had grabbed the opportunity to grill

Lucy for every ounce of information. She had laughed because for once it was Lucy who was struggling to lift her head off the pillow; it was weighted down by the aftermath of the night before.

"So this is how it feels," Lucy croaked, raising herself up on her elbows as Max came into her bedroom.

Max ran out of the room and was back in again within twenty seconds, carrying a large glass of water. Lucy took it from her and gratefully downed the liquid. The ridiculous concoction of drinks from the night before had combined to give her the most almighty headache. It felt like a wrestler was doing squats while balancing on her head.

"So why the fuck is Kirk Kelner in our flat?"

Lucy pulled her duvet up to her chin. She looked as coy and giggly as a schoolgirl readying to replay the details of her first kiss.

She told Max in a hushed voice that she'd met Kirk at Sheekey's and gone to a club with him and Amy.

It felt surreal at the time and it still did, she said. Kirk had sent over drinks and asked them to party with him. What were the chances? Amy had left and Lucy suggested Kirk came up to the flat.

Max clapped her hands in anticipation, willing Lucy to tell her every juicy detail. But a knock had come from the front door.

And now Marj was in the flat, armed with the newspaper. Max marched over to Lucy's bedroom, followed by her mum.

Holding the paper in front of her sister, Max said: "Brace yourself, Luce. Somehow the story is out."

"Oh no." Lucy's voice was faint as she took in the front page.

"Hello, darling." Marj jumped out from behind Max and greeted Lucy, kissing her on the cheek.

"Hi . . . Mum," Lucy said, staring at her mum but failing to make sense of the overload of information unravelling in her bedroom. She was on the front page. And Marj was here. She'd bought the paper. "Max said you were here."

"Just as well I am, darling. The past hour has made an episode of 24 look terribly dull."

Lucy and Max laughed. What a bizarre situation for their mum to walk into.

"Hey."

Max, Lucy and Marj turned to the man who had entered the bedroom. With a fluffy white towel wrapped round his waist, his toned, tanned six-pack was on show, glistening with drops of water from the shower. He looked from Lucy to Max to Marj and seemed a little timid.

"Hello, there. I'm Lucy and Max's mum," Marj said, offering her hand to Kirk. In response he released his own hand from where it had been resting on the towel. As he reached forward, the towel fell to the ground.

Max and Lucy looked away, shielding their eyes with their hands, but not before Max had noted he was more medium-to-large in the underwear department than the "average" Sheri had described. Marj remained facing Kirk and picked up the towel for him.

The normally unflappable movie star looked flummoxed as he hurriedly tied it round his waist.

Not sure if it was yet safe to look back at Kirk, Max caught Lucy's eye. She looked stunned, almost baffled, as she tried to do the mental arithmetic: momentous hangover + Mum + front-page news + Kirk Kelner + his penis = utter bewilderment.

Marj turned round to her daughters then back to Kirk. As she turned once more to face Max and Lucy, she was shaking with laughter.

"Now that's what I call funny," she gasped, barely able to get the words out. "Max, let's make some tea. Leave Lucy and Kirk alone. Kirk, how do you take yours?"

"Erm, just milk, thanks, Mrs . . .?"

"You can call me Marj."

"OK, thanks, Marj."

Marj walked quickly out of the door followed by Max. As she shut it behind her, Marj doubled over, clutching her stomach.

"Stop it," Max told her mum as she fell to her knees. "It's too funny. I'm going to wet my pants."

Kirk's Crazy in Love

Kirk Kelner felt a little dazed as he sat in the back of his car. After calling his driver, he had been picked up from Lucy's a little after eight o'clock. He had missed his personal training session and massage but he didn't care. The trees and old terraced houses with their balconies and bright flowerpots whizzed by as he thought about what had happened. Numb, that's how he felt, but in a good way. It was as though his mind could only replay the night before. He didn't want to think about anything else.

Wow. That had to be the first time a girl had refused to sleep with him. Kirk hadn't been too pushy, he was pretty sure of that. But, well, he'd kind of expected that's where things were heading when they fell into Lucy's bed, kissing. God, she was hot. Those bright blue eyes and hair that smelled so good.

She'd been a great kisser too. He had felt her body through her shiny dress and hitched it up to her waist before pulling it over her head. God, those breasts; they were the most perfectly formed he had ever seen. Full, round and beautiful. She wasn't too skinny; some girls' angular frames reminded him of a boy's — not a turn-on. Lucy had seemed a little embarrassed and this had somehow touched him. He was so used to girls racing to get their clothes off to sleep with him that Lucy's uncertainty had taken him aback.

For years, Kirk had had his pick of girls, and not just the wannabes of the world like Sheri, who had sold her story. He'd had hot members of girl bands come on to him, offering a threesome with another member of the group. He'd had gorgeous young actresses, more famous for famous exes than any discernable talent, making all sorts of offers. They knew it would do their career no harm to be linked with a true Hollywood hitter. It was all so easy.

Inexplicably, he liked Lucy's shyness. He had kissed her tenderly but she had pulled away.

"I'm sorry," she had said softly, facing away from him. "I . . ."

Her voice had trailed off. Kirk placed his fingers under her chin and gently turned her face to his. "It's OK, whatever it is. It's OK."

Lucy smiled at him. "It's just that I . . . I've recently stopped seeing someone. Maybe it's too soon."

Kirk took Lucy in. His eyes were kind but full of regret. He smiled.

"I understand," he told her. "Listen, Lucy, I really like you. There's no need to rush anything. Hey, I'm the lucky one. I'm here in bed beside you, and I think you're amazing."

Lucy laughed.

"Would you like me to leave?"

Lucy took his hand and smiled. "No. Please stay."

Those words had made Kirk happier than he had felt after being given the green light to sleep with any girl.

"Kirk?"

"Uh-huh?"

"I really like you too. It's just . . ."

"It's OK, Lucy, I understand. Like I say, there's no rush."

"And Kirk?"

"Yes?"

"Remind me in the morning never to tell anyone I had Kirk Kelner in my bed and refused to sleep with him."

Kirk laughed. As Lucy put her head on his chest and moved her warm body to him, he inhaled deeply, taking in her scent.

Maybe the romantics were right, he thought now. Perhaps you really did know when the right one came along.

The Secrets of Jade's Trade

Max had called Simon a little after ten o'clock. She had the day off after working last Sunday, but he would be at the desk.

"Alright, mucker?"

"Hi, Simon. Can you talk?"

"Yep."

"You've seen today's front page?"

"Ah." Simon seemed to be collecting his thoughts. "Hold on a minute . . . Right, I'm in the corridor, no one about. Yes, I've seen it. You want to know how Jade got it?"

"Do you know?"

Simon laughed. "Course I do. As discreet as hardcore porn, that one. Wait . . . you mean she didn't run it by you last night before she filed her copy?"

"Nope."

"What a tart. Lucy's your sister."

Simon admired Max's discretion — she had never boasted about her sister dating that posh Earl and made it clear she wouldn't be divulging any details, no matter how much praise it might get her at the paper. What were brownie points worth when you'd sold a family member out, Max had told Simon.

"Right," he continued. "She knows I'm your mate but couldn't help boasting about her big story this morning. Apparently," Simon lowered his voice conspiratorially, "she was hanging around in Claridge's. You know the comfy chairs where you can have a drink and those nice cheesy nibbles and see everyone who comes in the main entrance?"

This made sense. Mick Jagger and a couple of the *24* cast were staying there. Panicking at her lack of exclusives of late, Jade would have sat in wait, hoping to witness something — an argument with a girlfriend or drunken conversations at the bar.

"Uh-huh."

"Well, in pops Daphne Kelner. She'd been out for dinner with Kirk. Jade saw her chance and went over to talk to her. Even tells her she's a reporter and — bingo! — daft Daphne gives her every cough and spit of what's just happened."

It all fell into place. There was no "daft" Daphne about it. Kirk's mum had known exactly what she was doing. After her son had been associated with the likes of Shagger Sheri, she would have been elated to see Kirk go for someone like Lucy. And after dating Hartley, Lucy couldn't be further removed from the Fake Brigade who stalked her son in clubs, with pound signs in their eyes.

"OK, thanks, Si."

"Don't mention it."

"Did you give up the fags?"

Simon dug a pound coin out of his pocket and slotted it into the vending machine. He pressed a button for a packet of salt and vinegar Snack-a-Jacks.

After he had been complaining about his growing gut, Max had told him they were far lower in calories than normal crisps and suggested he had a packet when hungry. He was averaging six packets a day.

"Did I fuck! Lasted half a day. It's this fucking job. How can anyone give up anything when life's a free bar?"

Marj Takes Charge

Surreal wasn't the word. Here was Lucy, explaining to her mum and sister why she hadn't slept with one of the world's most famous men.

"I'd had so much to drink — I was on a bit of a mission — and somehow, when I was kissing Kirk and my eyes were closed, I . . . well, I got a fright when I opened them and didn't see Hartley's face. It freaked me out a bit." Lucy paused and laughed. "God, now I say it out loud I feel a bit stupid. Kirk Kelner."

"Completely understandable, Lucy. It's not that long since you split up with Hartley. But Kirk — he is such a dish."

"Dish? That's so 1980s, Mum." Max laughed.

"Hey, Mum, you're being pretty cool about all this," Lucy said.

"What's there not to be cool about?" Marj asked, matter-of-factly. "For starters, you don't suddenly lose your sense of humour when you turn fifty. Secondly, Hartley is bound to see what he's missing when he reads how you attracted the attentions of Kirk Kelner."

"Or, given Kirk's reputation with the ladies, he'll think I'm just another notch on his bedpost," Lucy offered. Thoughts of Hartley had been the main reason she hadn't slept with Kirk. But thoughts of all those stories — the nanny and the kiss-and-tell girl among them — hadn't been far from her mind either. He had made her feel special, but maybe he excelled at making all the girls feel like that.

"True, darling," Marj replied. "I bet he's used to girls being rather, shall we say, accommodating?"

"Or," Lucy added, "Hartley could just think I'm a millionaire-chaser. That's how I'm portrayed in the paper."

Lucy hadn't mentioned her encounter with Philippa Bonner a few days ago. She had been standing behind her in the queue at Starbucks. Lucy had tapped her shoulder and said hello.

Philippa had looked back slightly blank, smiled weakly and said: "Oh hello."

Odd, thought Lucy. She had been so friendly at Clarissa's supper, drinking in her fashion expertise.

"It's me, Lucy Summers. We met at Clarissa's."

Lucy could tell by the coldness in Philippa's eyes that she had needed no reminder. She didn't want to talk to Lucy.

"Oh yes," she replied with a fake half smile. "Oh . . . my turn to be served."

And with that, Philippa turned to the counter, paid for her coffee and left without saying goodbye.

Lucy was shocked. Philippa had seemed to genuinely like her when they first met. Clearly the thing she really liked was her status while dating Hartley. Oh God, Philippa's family had known Hartley's for years. Was this a sign he hated her and was so distraught that his friends couldn't even bring themselves to acknowledge Lucy?

While Philippa's reaction had come as a surprise, Lucy had only met her once. Far more upsetting was that she hadn't heard from Clarissa for weeks. Lucy had always known Clarissa was eager to get to know her because of Hartley, but still, she thought she had glimpsed the makings of a real friendship. She had been sure Clarissa enjoyed her company; Lucy had certainly warmed to Clarissa. Was it possible she had been discarded so casually because of rumours that had spread?

Cutting through Lucy's thoughts, Marj said in a chirpy tone, like she was talking about the weather, "Granted, it makes last night sound premeditated on your part — like you sought him out — but from what Max says that's down to a bitter writer." Marj fluffed up the cushions on the sofa then turned to face her daughters. "We ladies have to rise above this nonsense. I did not bring my girls up to worry about what people think. If they change their opinion of you because of something they read, it says more about them than it does about you."

Bloody bitter, scheming Jade, Max thought. She could almost forgive her for not running the story by Max. After all, she would only have tried to persuade Jade not to tell their boss about it. As Jade was one ambitious woman, she had clearly put her career above any respect she had for Max. That was to be expected from someone like Jade, but she couldn't forgive the vicious way in which she had written about her sister, portraying her as a fame-seeker when nothing could be further from the truth. Of course, if confronted, Jade would put the blame on the sub editors. It was their job to polish the copy to make it sparkle, as though you were trying to get the attention of a guy in the pub who'd already had a couple of pints, and had to lure him with your first two sentences; then they had to cut the copy to make it fit into the allocated space. But Max had long suspected Jade was simply a nasty piece of work. The fact that Max had landed a string of big exclusives recently had eaten away at her and she would do anything to get one over on Max.

"I know, Mum, but —"

"No buts about it. It's better to be talked about than not at all. The people who matter know the truth. Anyway, for goodness sake, there are worse things people could write than describing how Kirk Kelner is smitten by you. In life's big pond today's front page is but a drop, darling."

Lucy laughed. "I guess."

The power of Marj's positivity was infectious. Somehow she had a way of making everything better.

Bridget Thinks on Her Feet

That little tramp. Lucy Summers had wasted no time in snaring Kirk Kelner. Bridget had to read the first few paragraphs several times before she believed them. Of course, she never normally read such rags but Dorcas had rung her that morning to say she'd heard Hartley's ex had pulled Kirk Kelner.

Dorcas's voice had sounded teasing on the phone, like she was goading Bridget by telling her Hartley's ex must be stunning if she could pull someone like Kelner.

Bridget had played it down, saying with a laugh, "Oh you know the tabloids. They probably said hello to each other and they've made a story out of it."

The last thing Bridget wanted Dorcas to know was how much she detested Lucy.

"Then again," Bridget added, "I wouldn't be surprised if Kirk was interested in Lucy. She is quite stunning, after all." It had almost killed Bridget to say that but she was most pleased she had. Dorcas had been silenced. Now she could only tell the friends in their set that Bridget seemed to have no bad feelings towards Lucy, quite the opposite in fact.

"So, erm, how are things going with Hartley?" Dorcas had asked when she had finally collected her thoughts.

"Oh darling, it's as though we've never been apart."

Ha, that had got her. Bridget couldn't wait for Dorcas to spread that little gem around. That would get everyone talking. She prayed the rumour mill would go into overdrive if everyone thought she had started up where she had left off with Hartley.

Her mother had been spreading the word within her own set too, which was excellent as it consisted of many of her own friends' mothers. She was subtly letting them know her daughter was once again close to the Earl, dropping into their conversations details of where they had been for dinner or the latest on Hartley's Foundation. Mother would be pleased with how Bridget had handled Dorcas.

Dorcas's news of the front page had simply confirmed Bridget's suspicions that Lucy was a gold-grabbing slut. She was no better than the wannabes who hung around clubs waiting for their chance with stars. Hartley had made a lucky escape.

But Bridget couldn't help feeling a rising sense of irritation. Who did Lucy think she was? The picture they had of her on the front page was stunning — a fact Bridget hated to admit, even to herself. What if Hartley read the article and wondered what he was missing? Why couldn't Lucy just go away? With Lucy in the limelight with Kirk Kelner, Hartley would be forced to think about her all over again. Bridget must ensure she planted some key bits of information in his head.

Yes, Bridget could well have spoken to a friend who was in Sheekey's last night and witnessed what a fool Lucy had made of herself. She was all over the actor like a rash. Excellent. And anyway, it probably wasn't far from the truth.

Hartley is Stunned by Splash

"I've arranged for a few friends to come round for supper tonight, sweetie. Mel and Tom. Oh and Philippa will be there."

Bridget and Hartley's families had known the Bonners since they were children. Philippa was a good friend. She had been eager to report her sighting of Lucy the other day. Annoyingly, she said Lucy still looked good. Bridget had hoped the flattering picture of her in the paper had been an old image and that she had let herself go. It would have made Bridget's day to hear she'd piled on a stone or had broken out in spots since her split with Hartley. Never mind. Philippa had given her an icy reception. Hopefully, Lucy was getting the message: she was not welcome in their circle.

Claudia was another matter. Bridget had had no choice but to give her a severe warning.

She had decided to give her mousy friend another chance. Instead of completely cutting her off, Bridget had realized Claudia was still of use. After all, her father was president of Daddy's golf club and got them those fab tickets to the annual Spring Ball.

Just the other day she had invited Claudia to her house for an early supper — all protein, no carbs after 2p.m. was doing wonders for her weight.

Bridget had made a passing comment about Lucy — how trashy she was, what with setting up the photographer and now chasing after her next meal ticket, Kirk Kelner.

"Poor Hartley had a lucky escape there," she told her friend knowingly.

"Now, Bridget," Claudia had said, rather bravely Bridget thought, "I know it looks like she must have been behind the thing in Scotland, but I can't believe it was her. Honestly, Bridget, if you'd seen her afterwards . . . She was a wreck. She seemed so lovely. It just doesn't seem the sort of thing she would do."

Bridget felt her anger rise with every pathetic dribbling word that came out of Claudia's feeble mouth.

"How dare you?" she said, looking at Claudia with disdain.

She stood up, thumping her glass of water on the table in front of her. If the table had been glass instead of solid oak, it would have smashed to pieces.

"You have the gall to defend this slut even when she has betrayed Hartley? I have known you for years, I have helped you in every way I could — taking you to the right places, helping you get over your geek chic, if I can even call it that." Bridget was shouting now, her face reddening through her pale matt foundation. "You've known this imposter for two minutes and come into my house and tell me how wonderful she is, how happy she was with Hartley. How fucking dare you?"

Claudia looked down, her face bright red and full of fear. She looked like she would burst into tears at any second.

Bridget was now incandescent with rage, screaming so hard that specks of spit were flying from her mouth. "If it wasn't for me he'd still be with that little bitch, still thinking she was sweetness and fucking light. I'm the one he should thank, you should all thank, for making him see the kind of thing she'd do —"

Bridget stopped suddenly. Shit, she'd almost told Claudia about Scotland. She was so sick of playing the angelic card that sometimes she just wanted to be congratulated for being so bloody clever, for opening Hartley's eyes. But no, that wouldn't do. Got to keep up the act. She'd nearly let it slip. Claudia wouldn't put two and two together, though. She looked too bloody terrified to take her next breath of air, let alone work out what Bridget had done.

Bridget took a deep breath and exhaled, then another. She sat down and ran her fingers through her sleek black bob. She did not need such stress.

Claudia didn't say much except to apologize, as she should. Bridget made her promise not to even think about having contact with Lucy and never to bring her up again unless she had something of interest to report.

"I expect loyalty from my best friends," Bridget told Claudia when she had calmed down.

Claudia had nodded and smiled.

Bridget was now drumming her fingers on her cup as she stared at Hartley. He wasn't paying her any attention. A workman had left his copy of the *Daily*

News on the table beside them and Hartley had spotted Lucy's picture on the front page. Well, it was as good a time as any. It saved Bridget bringing the topic up herself.

She watched as Hartley leaned over and picked up the paper. She gave him time to take in the words.

"Oh darling, is that the story about Lucy?"

Hartley looked up as though he had just noticed Bridget was there.

"Ah yes. How funny. I didn't realize it would make the papers," she lied.

Hartley looked down at the headline then back at Bridget, confused.

"My friend Jasper called me this morning to say he had seen Lucy in Sheekey's last night and she had been all over Kirk Kelner." Bridget lowered her tone to almost a whisper. "Apparently, she tipped the waiter and asked him to send a note over — with something very suggestive on it." Bridget grimaced for effect.

Bridget watched Hartley's expression and saw a fleeting sorrow in his eyes, replaced by a duller sadness. This was very good news. The more wounded he was, the more likely he was to fall into bed with Bridget, especially after the few drinks that she would ensure he had that evening.

"But, sweetie, I didn't want you to think I was gossiping — I take no notice of such stories. But there it is for the world to see."

Could this be the same sweet girl Hartley had known? Had Lucy blinded him with an act? It was so odd that she was on the front of a newspaper — the

310

Daily News — the one her sister worked for. Had they colluded to get her on the front page? Hartley didn't know much about newspapers but surely Max would know if her sister was the main story of the day? Lucy had seemed so resistant to attention when he was with her. Was that a sham too?

"So, sweetie — supper tonight. You can come?"

Hartley nodded vacantly, agreeing to whatever it was Bridget was asking.

Marj Comes Clean

Marj had loved seeing her girls in London. They had spent a glorious weekend together, catching the Thames riverboat to Greenwich, buying each other little gifts from the handmade jewellery stalls there, taking in Jersey Boys, a musical in the West End, and having cosy nights in when she cooked their favourites: fish pie, her special prawn and pea risotto with mint, and rich bread and butter pudding with vanilla custard.

"Just as well you don't live here all the time," Max had told her, "we'd be fattened up in no time."

Fergal joked he knew it was dinner time when he heard the beautiful sound of a fork piercing a microwaveable lid. Cheeky thing — that only happened once or twice a week when she was in a hurry to get to her yoga class.

Marj had chosen one such night, when the girls had finished supper and were curled up on the sofa in their pyjamas, watching television, to tell them about her operation. For a moment or two she built up the courage to tell them. She didn't want to spoil the night — they looked so happy. It might have been two decades ago but had so much changed from when she'd tuck them up on the sofa at home with a cosy fleecy blanket? Then, she had watched them, all rosy-cheeked and full of anticipation, as she handed them mugs of milky hot chocolate. She knew she was blessed to have such beautiful girls who loved not only her but each other so much. She knew that then and she knew it now.

"Girls, I have something to tell you," she said, pressing mute on the remote control.

They looked up at her expectantly, their sweet-featured faces blank canvases. Part of Marj didn't want to tell them. She loved being there for them, sharing their funny stories, helping when things went wrong. She was there to worry about them; that's what mothers were for. She never wanted that role to be reversed. And yet she had told her girls they could tell her anything — secrets were only kept between those who never truly trusted each other — so it was only fair she applied the same logic to herself.

"Before I tell you, you have to know that everything is OK."

Max's brow furrowed, her big brown eyes suddenly apprehensive. Lucy looked frightened.

"A while back I found a lump in my breast." Marj heard her voice like it was suspended, her words hanging like a wisp of cigarette smoke in the air. Suddenly she felt a lump in her throat. She knew she had to speak quickly, tell them everything. She had to make them see everything was going to be fine.

"I had a biopsy and it was breast cancer . . ."

Max's eyes had filled with tears. Her chin was shaking uncontrollably as she fought with everything she had not to cry. Lucy looked uncomprehending.

313

"I didn't tell you because I wanted to have the operation first. I hope you understand. I didn't want you to worry until I knew more . . . Anyway, I had the lump removed — they call it a lumpectomy. A mastectomy is when you have the breast off. It was as good news as I could have hoped for. I'd caught it early and it was a slow-developing grade of cancer. It hadn't spread to my lymph nodes — you have them under your arms. The doctor said that was crucial to knowing the cancer hadn't moved on elsewhere around my body. He was hopeful — more than hopeful — he'd removed it all."

Marj hated watching Max and Lucy battle to take this in, to grasp what she was saying.

"I'm having a little treatment, radiotherapy, at Ninewells Hospital when I go back to Dundee. But that's more of a precaution, to make sure I've got all the . . . all the . . ."

"Cancer?" Lucy asked, quietly.

Yes, cancer. Marj nodded. No matter how simply she put it to the girls, no matter how bright a picture she tried to paint, there was no getting away from that word. When Marj had first heard it in the doctor's surgery she felt like she had been given a death sentence. She had grown up in an era when the "C word" was whispered over garden fences.

When she was a little girl, Marj remembered her own mum telling her friend in a hushed tone that one of the neighbours, Vera, had the "C word", as though, if she actually said the word, it might spread. Marj never saw

Vera again. That's the way it seemed to be with anyone who got the "C word".

"It's not like it used to be," she said as brightly as she could. "The doctor was even able to tell me the chances of it coming back. And you know what? After the radiotherapy there's a ninety per cent chance it will never return."

"Really? That sounds good," Max whispered, straining to speak. Somehow, she had managed to keep in her tears. She could cry later, she told herself, not in front of Marj, who needed to see in her face that things were going to be OK.

"Well, let's put it this way, Max. Ninety per cent in an exam would be a top-band A grade, right?"

"Right."

"So, my chances of being OK are top-band grade A. The doctor even recorded what he said to me after the op so I could play it back whenever I needed reassurance."

"Dad? How's Dad?" Max asked.

"Oh your dad is the best man in the world. He's been my best friend through it all; he made me feel more beautiful than ever. He wanted to come and see you, but I thought I'd like to tell you myself, have a little bit of girl time."

Max gave a lopsided smile of reassurance and it melted Marj's heart.

Lucy was on her feet. She was crying; she couldn't help it. She put her arms around her mother and hugged her as tightly as she could. The distinctive floral

315

smell of Paris perfume hit Lucy, its familiarity filling her with happiness and sadness at once.

"You should have told us," she whispered.

"Sorry," Marj said into her daughter's soft hair.

Lucy pulled away, wiping the tears from her eyes. "It's OK, I understand why you didn't."

Max tapped Lucy on the shoulder. "Room for a little one?" she asked.

Lucy stepped back, keeping one arm around Marj and putting the other around her sister. The three women stood there, holding each other, in the sitting room of the Kensington flat. At first they cried but eventually they smiled.

Marj was right. Everything was going to be alright.

Marj Makes Her Move

Marj had seen the pain in Lucy's eyes when she talked about Hartley. Lucy had thought the world of him. Knowing that he believed she had set up the photographer was tearing her apart.

After her weekend in London, Marj had Monday to herself while the girls went to work, then she caught a train to Dundee. She found getting the train a real treat; six hours of reading newspapers and books and watching the beautiful countryside whizz by was bliss.

Marj had done a little research on Hartley on the girls' computer in the flat. Google. Such a wonderful invention. She had written the address for the Balmyle Foundation in her Filofax and planned her tube journey there.

She remembered Lucy telling her how Hartley spent Mondays at the Foundation, planning the week ahead.

Marj was a great believer in looking your best at all times. While other mums had encouraged their daughters to cover up and lay off the make-up, she had told Lucy and Max there was no shame in making the most of what you had. A little bit of lipstick could transform a tired face; a bright little dress was so much more cheerful and feminine than a baggy jumper. Now more than ever, Marj was of the belief that life was for living and making the most of what you had.

She wore a jade-green cashmere V-necked jumper and black-linen trousers from the Per Una range at M&S and Russell and Bromley tan-leather loafers. There was no point tottering up and down those huge tube escalators in perilous heels, after all. They matched her lovely Prada bag, which Lucy had given her last year.

A designer had gifted it to her as a "thank you" for a piece she had written about their new collection. Lucy had more than enough bags, she told her mum. Marj hadn't banked on the reaction her new accessory would get on her yoga night out — the girls had touched and admired it as though it was a celebrity. Nowhere sold Prada in Dundee.

Money had been tight when the girls were young. Fergal was a proud man and insisted Peter's money was for Lucy's education but that he would provide for their family. And he had. He had worked hard to build a reputation as a reliable and talented carpenter, working for a medium-sized local firm in his twenties before setting up on his own. Marj had put her all into keeping the books and marketing the company. Now Summers Carpentry was an established name in Dundee. They had a workshop in the west end of the city just off the Perth Road, showcasing the beautiful wooden furniture he had lovingly carved. And he employed a small team of workers to take on jobs — from carving tables and chairs for a new quirky restaurant to commissions from the council.

318

All that hard work had paid off. More importantly, the Summers family were as close as ever.

Marj's hair was newly washed and fell naturally round her heart-shaped face. She wore a little make-up — Stila tinted moisturizer, a lick of mascara, a hint of cream blush and a light plummy lip gloss.

"Hello, I wonder if you can help. I am interested in donating money to the Foundation." At Hartley's offices just off the Kings Road, Marj addressed the young receptionist brightly.

The girl had a trendy lopsided fringe; her hair was coloured purple, her nails neon green.

"Of course," she replied cheerfully. "Would you mind taking a seat?"

Marj smiled and sat on one of two pink sofas. She took in the beautiful smell of the white lilies that were speckled with pink, fully open and spilling out of a huge vase. She picked up a brochure and recognized one of the faces on the front as the receptionist's, although she had orange hair in the picture.

Shona, 19, came to the Foundation 18 months ago seeking help for her drug addiction, which had led her to a life of crime. After successfully completing a rehab programme she has been clean for over a year and now works here at the Foundation.

Marj looked up and saw Hartley in front of her, smiling and offering his hand. She recognized him from her Google search.

"Hello, I'm Hartley," he said pleasantly. Not announcing his title or surname, Marj considered, said a great deal about Hartley.

"Hello, Hartley. I'm Marj. Very pleased to meet you too." She smiled back at him.

"Please, let me show you through to my office," Hartley said, holding open a door at the side of the reception area.

Marj sat opposite Hartley on a soft dark-green leather armchair. The room was small and welcoming, the scent of a large bunch of red roses filling the air.

"So, Shona tells me you have been thinking about getting involved with the Foundation. That's wonderful news. Can I get you a tea, or coffee, perhaps?"

Marj couldn't help but like Hartley. He was incredibly well spoken, almost comically. He seemed so open and warm.

"Oh no, I'm fine, thank you."

He smiled back at Marj as a silence descended upon them, neither sure how to continue. To think that just a few days ago she had been Googling Hartley's name to find his Foundation's address. And now she was sitting here in front of him. She just had to tell Hartley the truth. He might think she was a meddling mother, but it was a chance she was willing to take. She was here for Lucy.

"So, how did you hear about the Foundation?"

"My daughter."

"Oh really? Has she worked with us? I know most of the people involved here. What's her name?"

"Hartley, my daughter is Lucy Summers."

Don't Luke Back in Anger

Try as she might, Max couldn't stop thinking about Luke. She had thrown herself into work and partying in the weeks since Marj's visit, but still he consumed her thoughts. He must think her awful, ignoring his texts and calls. As much as it hurt, Max knew she couldn't talk to him. Cutting him out was her way of coping. But she hated to think of how confused and hurt he must have felt. She hadn't heard from him for at least a fortnight so guessed he must have got the message. Poor Luke. Jesus, all Max really wanted to do was see him and experience that wonderful high again.

Marj's news had been such a blow. She had made everything sound so positive but Max couldn't escape the realization that her mother had been through something quite terrifying. She was very close to Marj, as was Lucy, and couldn't stand the thought of anything happening to her. She couldn't wait to spend time with her family in Scotland over Christmas. But for now she had to clear her head; she needed a new project.

There was only one thing for it. She had to remove herself from London, and she could think of nowhere better to go than the city that never slept. She resolved to fit in a trip before Christmas.

For the past three years Max had worked in New York in April, covering Scotland Week for the paper. As she was a "sweaty sock" or Jock, as the English guys in the office fondly called her, she would be best for the job — and what a job it was. The Scottish government set up a series of events like the Scotland parade down Fifth Avenue, with clans gathering in a march.

Last year Max had interviewed Sir Sean Connery in his hotel room before the annual Dressed to Kilt fashion show and, for the first time, had been star-struck. Even in his seventies, he had more presence in his pinkie than Brad Pitt and Tom Cruise put together. When he sat down wearing his kilt, with his legs placed wide apart, Max asked him if he was a true Scotsman, and had melted when he raised one eyebrow just like when he played James Bond in Dr No.

"Yesh, Max, of coursh I'm a true Shcotsman," he had told her in that shexy voice.

She might not meet Sir Sean this time round, but the Big Apple would be just the ticket.

Clarissa's Back

Lucy smiled as she read the invitation that had arrived in the post. She had almost forgotten about the Hogmanay Ball. Her heart had pounded when she first saw it — could it be from Hartley? Reading an accompanying handwritten note, she felt sad and happy at once. It was not from Hartley — how silly of her to even imagine it would have been. It was from Clarissa. Lucy was touched. After not hearing from Clarissa since her Friday-night supper, she'd assumed her friend had ditched her.

As her mobile rang, she saw Clarissa's name on the screen.

"I was just thinking of you."

"Lucy, darling. Did you get my invitation?"

"Just got it. Thanks so much."

"Listen," Clarissa's tone was urgent, breathless, "you must have thought I'd abandoned you. I've just heard all the news. Are you OK?"

"Where have you been? Mars?" Of all people, Lucy was sure Clarissa would have known every ounce of gossip.

"Almost," Clarissa said. "I was trying to keep it a secret — surprise everyone, but you have to know. Otherwise you'll think me a terrible friend."

Lucy was intrigued.

"I've been to Thailand. You know that famous spa — the one the stars swear by?"

"Uh-huh."

"Well, I booked in for a three-month course. Boot camp, if you like. The full works, Lucy — colonic, leeches, you name it. I'm getting married next summer and I didn't fancy looking like Nelly the Elephant for the big day. I feel like a new woman. I'm a size 10 for the first time since I was ten. I'm terrified I'll put it all back on, though, so I've booked in with a personal trainer and nutritionist to keep me on track." Lucy could hear Clarissa inhale, coming up for breath in her excitement. "So, they insist on total escapism and that means no phones. It was bliss. But I come home and hear what you've been up to, young lady. My, my, I want to hear every single detail . . . Oh God, I don't mean that — not with what happened with Hartley. That sounds awful. But Kirk, I mean . . . Oh. My. God."

Lucy laughed. She had forgotten how fond she was of Clarissa.

"I promise I will tell you everything." She paused. "I was worried you had thought the worst and, well, you know . . ."

"Banished you from being my friend? Oh please." Clarissa bellowed, "It takes more than that to get rid of me."

Lucy was happy to have Clarissa back in her life.

"Oh darling, before you go, will you come to the ball?"

324

Lucy frowned. "Clarissa, I'm not sure. It's so sweet of you but . . . well . . ."

"It's Hartley's ball and you're scared of bumping into him?"

"Well, yes. I mean, not scared exactly . . ."

"You don't want him to think you are chasing him?"

Lucy had to admit it was the first thing that crossed her mind when she thought about accepting the invitation. He must already think of her as a calculating man-eater; why else would she go to his ball if not to see him? And coming face to face with him again would be so painful.

As if reading her mind, Clarissa cut in. "Listen, you are my guest. I would like you to be on my table. My friend is on the committee this year. I'd be going even if the Earl of Balmyle did not exist. It's nothing to do with him, Lucy. It's a fabulous way to see in the New Year and help raise money for a good cause. I will not take no for an answer."

Lucy smiled. "OK, OK."

"But, Lucy? One more thing."

"Yes?"

"Obviously, Hartley will be there so you must look even more fabulous than normal."

Lucy must be a distant memory to Hartley now. She had seen him photographed leaving a charity auction at Christie's with Bridget the other day. Genevieve had relished placing the photo, in a magazine, inches in front of her as she sat at her desk.

"Dearie me, Lucy, that must hurt. No?" she had whimpered.

Lucy didn't have the patience to pretend. "A bit," she replied, flatly.

Genevieve looked flustered, surprised by Lucy's honesty.

"I'll tell you what hurts, Gen Gen." It was Carlos, sweeping her aside as he stood behind Lucy and rested his hand on her shoulder. "What hurts is the fact you look like Ugly Betty in those Versace heels and knee-high socks. Kate Moss might pull it off, but not you, girlfriend."

With a dismissive hand he brushed Genevieve away like a pesky fly while Lucy lowered her head to her desk, trying not to laugh.

Muttering something about how Bridget was wearing the new Stella coat in orange and it looked great on her, Genevieve teetered back to her own desk, as self-conscious now as she had been self-assured just moments before.

The girls in the office had crammed around Lucy's desk on the Monday after the story had broken about her and Kirk.

Penny, the fashion desk PA, was so excited her glasses (small, rectangular, red Prada to match her Versace red jeans and Aquascutum blazer) steamed up as she elbowed through the little crowd to the front of Lucy's desk. Sophie, who had grown her hair a little longer and bleached it again, gave up all pretence of work for the morning to badger Lucy with questions, her normal facial expression of serious fashionista replaced by a giddy excitement.

Genevieve had sat quietly at her desk throughout, doing her very best to look busy. After drumming her fingers impatiently on her mouse pad all morning, while the girls crowded round Lucy, she snapped, telling them they were paid to put a magazine together, not gossip about who'd pulled whom.

"She's jealous of everything about you, Lucy," Carlos told Lucy matter-of-factly, when he arrived later that day. "The way you look, the way you dress, your popularity with the other girls. And now you're centre of attention for pulling the man she has as her screen saver? Ooooo, she's angry and jealous."

Now Genevieve was away on a three-week holiday in the Bahamas. The general rule was that no one could take off more than two weeks at a time but, as she told anyone who would listen, she was the boss and so stressed out she needed some "me time". Word had it in the office she'd gone by herself on a freebie from a luxury holiday company. One of the girls had overheard her on the phone promising a write-up in the travel section and asking if the flights could be upgraded to first class. It was odd, Lucy thought, given that they had a travel editor, Liza, who dealt with all such features. She offered writers trips to spas or to tropical locations in return for writing about them in her pages. When lots of editorial staff applied for a plum trip, she pulled a name out of a hat to be fair.

The other girls in the office relished the opportunity to moan about Genevieve's constant blagging, but Lucy couldn't care less. She was relieved to be able to get on with her job without an agenda. Genevieve hadn't left anyone in charge. She'd had three deputies leave within a year and currently had no second-in-command. But Lucy found herself being asked to do most of Genevieve's tasks by the overall boss of the mag, organizing not only her own shoots and interviews but also the main diary for the other girls, to make sure every important social and fashion event was covered. She had to admit, she enjoyed the responsibility.

Of course, the girls on the floor had been desperate to find out every snippet of information about what had happened with Kirk. Days after the newspaper story they were still grilling her at every opportunity. Lucy blushed furiously, terrified she would look boastful.

How did it happen? What's he like? Did you sleep with him? Is he hung like a donkey? The questions were fast and furious, her colleagues intrigued at this latest turn of events. Without Genevieve, there was a feeling of fun on the floor that was normally lacking.

Lucy batted the questions off as best she could, assuring them she didn't sleep with him. A goodnight kiss was all he got. And yes, OK, he was a great kisser.

Indeed he was, Lucy thought as she remembered how he had pulled her head to his, pressing his lips to hers. Then had come the flick of his tongue. She had felt his torso, impossibly solid beneath his top. And yet Lucy had been thinking of Hartley when she'd had Kirk bloody Kelner in her bed. She must need her head read.

She had frozen in horror when she saw the front page that day but Max had made her see the funny side.

Marj had too. She seemed somehow more relaxed than ever before when she visited for the weekend. She had always been the cool mum at school, the envy of pals, who would admire her trendy clothes compared to their head-scarved, Laura Ashley-clad mothers. Their mums visited them at weekends in their brand-new Range Rovers, dripping in diamonds. Then Marj would turn up having caught the train from Dundee, looking fresh and fun next to the Stepford Wives.

Carlos had also helped. Of course, he had demanded the unedited version of what had happened with Kirk.

He had bombarded her with texts demanding all the juicy details.

She agreed to spill the beans over dinner at Cipriani, after coordinating a shoot at Tate Modern. Carlos had choked on his Chianti when Lucy explained why she hadn't had sex with Kirk.

"Are you out of your friggin' mind? Kirk Kelner wants to sleep with you and you say no? Tell me you're shittin' me."

"Carlos, I couldn't. I kept thinking of Hartley. I was drunk . . ."

"Girlfriend, I could be in a five-year coma and still muster up a twitch of consent if Kelner came knocking." Carlos angrily took a bite from a piece of bread. "Fuck, you're driving me to carbs after six o'clock."

"Not carbs after six o'clock, Carlos. How will I ever forgive myself?"

"Very funny. You didn't ever sleep with Hartley either, did you?"

"Well, no, but nearly — I mean, I tried."

Carlos put his hand on top of hers. He had the air of a man who was about to impart solemn words of wisdom.

"You are in grave danger of sealing up, Lucy. You already qualify for that American cult of reborn virgins — no sex for a year and you get membership."

Lucy laughed.

"It's not funny."

"Come on, if I don't laugh I'll cry. Most girls regret sleeping with someone — not the other way round."

Carlos seemed to mull over the thought gravely, popping an olive into his mouth.

"There's only one thing for it," Lucy told him.

"Uh-huh?"

"Make up for it next time I see him."

Carlos clasped his hands together as if he'd decided on the best path to world peace. "Excellent, you're talking sense at last. Bonk his brains out, girl — it's Kirk fucking Kelner. But for God's sake, Lucy," his eyes widened, his tone lowered, "whatever you do, use a condom. I read he slept with that kiss-and-tell freak, you know the one — all tits and tangerine skin. Who knows where else he's been."

Lucy laughed. "Good point, Dad. I promise."

Lucy hadn't forgotten Kirk's reputation but, as long as she was careful, what was the harm? And where had being sensible got her so far? If she couldn't have fun now, she might end up regretting it. And Kirk Kelner was hot. He had a history, that was for sure, but anyone

330

could change and he was always so respectful and gentlemanly towards her.

The friends fell silent as the waiter poured more wine, Carlos catching a pained look in Lucy's eyes.

"You really liked him, huh?" Carlos looked serious, searching Lucy's face.

"Hartley? Yes. I do. I mean, I did." She felt a lump in her throat. How ridiculous. While Hartley was swanning around with Bridget, not giving Lucy a second thought, she was hankering after him.

Kirk was the fairy tale — impossibly handsome, with a jet-set life of glamour and glitz. Hartley was handsome in his own way but probably a bit like Eddie Izzard in comparison to the Hollywood star. It didn't matter. Lucy smiled as she thought of the way he always appeared slightly unkempt, with an untucked shirt and those rosy cheeks. She missed the way he sucked in his tummy in front of the mirror when he thought she wasn't watching. Sometimes she'd wake and he was the first thing she thought of, making her wonder if she'd been dreaming about him. Lucy couldn't shake the dull ache of longing for him and wondered how the hell something so good could have ended so unexpectedly.

Carlos squeezed her hand.

"He doesn't know what he's missing."

Lucy smiled. "It's OK, really. Anyway, Kirk texted this morning."

"He did?"

"He's invited me to a party next week. You want to come?"

The debonair, calm and collected Carlos Santiago was suddenly twelve years old, brimming with excitement.

"Do I? Hell, yeah. But be warned. If I so much as sniff a gay gene, he's all mine. Raymondo will understand."

Lucy laughed. She was feeling much better already.

She was looking forward to seeing Kirk again. How could she fail to be flattered?

Sheri Toasts New Start

This bird had looked posh with her glossy bob and pearls but she was alright, Sheri thought as she clinked glasses with Amy. She was really pretty, with skin the colour of creamy caramel and big brown eyes. She was a right laugh too, with her Manc accent. Sheri would rather speak like that than the way she did, like the stereotypical Essex good-time girl.

"Cheers, here's to you."

"To us," Sheri said and took a sip of champagne. It was delicious, cold and fizzy. What a few weeks it had been. Since she'd met Amy at the Met, things had moved quickly. They'd gone off to talk about this STD campaign Amy was in charge of. All Sheri had really wanted that night was to pull someone with a wad of coke — preferably a star so she could make a packet from the story.

She'd been irritated by Amy at first. She was in the way of her eye contact with the DJ. But then she had listened to what Amy was saying.

It was the first time anyone had talked to her like that, like she mattered.

Amy was right; the public did want someone to tell it like it was. And when it came to sex, Sheri knew a thing or two. She had left the club with Amy and had a drink at a quieter bar.

"So you really think I could be your poster girl?"

"I really do, Sheri."

"But I'm not doing anyfing that'll make me look like a slut."

"Far from it. You'll have to be honest and admit you've been careless, picked up an STD or two, but now you've learned your lesson."

"Gotcha. Well, that seems fair. Young girls ain't easily fooled — they'll only listen to someone who is real."

"Exactly."

Sheri's hands were shaking slightly. She wanted a line really badly. Coke or, even better, MDMA, which she'd tried last week. It was true what they said, it gave you far less of a comedown than charlie. But she wanted to be here with Amy too. She seemed nice. And she was offering her a chance to do something other than make cash through sex.

"Listen, Amy, I appreciate the offer and all, I really do. But I've got to pay the rent. Do I get paid for this?"

"Of course. You'd be working for us and it's only right you'd be paid. I'll check with my boss to make sure you get a decent rate. It won't make you rich but it will be a regular income. I have to warn you, it will be tough. There will be photo shoots, interviews, visits to schools, talking to experts — all in a day's work."

"I ain't afraid of grafting."

Amy had noticed Sheri becoming a little agitated and shaky. She had a good idea why.

334

"Sheri, I don't want you to take this the wrong way." Amy inhaled. "We can't afford to be associated with anyone who might bring bad press to the charity."

"All my press is bad." Sheri laughed.

"No, that's not what I mean. I want you to hold your hands up and admit to your mistakes — it makes you human. I want you to tell people you've been daft, forgotten to take precautions and had one-night stands. But there has to be a positive message — that you've turned your life around. If it was to get out that, say, you are taking drugs, the press would tear us to shreds. It would be 'Sex Charity Pays For Shagger Sheri's Next Fix'. They'd have a field day."

"Right." The elation Sheri had felt just moments before drained away. How could she stop? What would she do? Stay in and drink green tea at night?

She desperately wanted to make a go of it, to change her life, but all she could think about was coke. As Amy talked, she was making a mental list of all the various names she knew for it: coke, charlie, gak, chang, powder . . .

Amy seemed to detect her change in mood. "I'm not saying you have to be a nun. Hell, if you shag a footballer that's fine — so long as you're telling the world you used a condom. And you tell them through the charity. There can be no more kiss-and-tells if you work with us. You'd be our ambassador."

Sheri liked this girl. She had balls, that was for sure. If someone had told Sheri an hour ago she'd be sitting next to a woman telling her how to live her life, to stop shagging stars for a living, she'd have told them to fuck right off. But that was just it. Why would she want to carry on doing that? No matter how badly she wanted a line, maybe she wanted to get back some self-respect even more.

"I'll help you," Amy had told her. "We work with brilliant rehab centres that take in women who come to us for help. Sometimes they've been living rough and sleeping with guys for money. They'll help you and it won't cost you a thing."

A lone tear trickled down Sheri's cheek, taking a line of mascara with it. She hadn't realized how similar her job description was to a prostitute's until she heard Amy talk about them. Fuck, what was she doing?

As Sheri brushed the tear away, she let out an embarrassed laugh. "Count me in. It's time for a change anyway."

"Good," Amy said softly, taking Sheri's hand in her own and squeezing it. "You won't regret it. This is your new start."

And here she was just a few weeks later. Amy had called her the morning after they had met and told her she could check into rehab that afternoon if she wanted. Sheri wanted it so much, though she was terrified of leaving the very life she needed to put behind her. Sometimes the thing that holds us back is fear of leaving the known, Amy had told her. What was she? Her fucking guardian angel? Whatever she was, Sheri was glad she had come along when she did.

"To us," Amy agreed as she sipped her champagne at Dover Street Wine Bar. She took Sheri in. It was the first time she had been out of rehab and she'd be checking back in that afternoon. She'd be out in a few days and then become a regular out-patient. Things were going well and the therapist had said she could have a glass of bubbly to celebrate her new job. A lot of coke addicts couldn't drink alcohol as it set them off on a drugs binge. But they reckoned Sheri was addicted to coke and was not alcohol-dependent, so one glass was OK. She looked different, with a fraction of the caked-on make-up she had worn when they first met. Her blue eyes were brighter and less bloodshot, her skin shinier. She looked like she was recovering although she was still tired, her eyes sunken. There was a way to go but Amy could see a pretty young woman trying to get out. She had already come so far from the jittery girl with dead eyes who was so on edge. Amy hoped she could watch a full transformation, that Sheri would stick with her and the campaign. Her boss had thought it was an inspired idea to sign Sheri up. She would be worth ten multimillion-pound government campaigns aimed at young people. She would talk to them, not down at them. He had been a little sceptical when Amy assured him she wouldn't bring scandal to the charity, but she had persuaded him to give her a chance. If she messed up, Amy would shoulder the blame.

"Next week the hard work starts. You'll be speaking at schools, colleges and prisons and launching our new campaign aimed at teens."

Sheri was excited and scared. She desperately wanted a new start. She needed it. What was the alternative? Selling kiss-and-tells in her fifties, having lost half her nose to coke? Did she really want to live to regret every day that passed since Amy had offered her a way out? Amy had taken a chance on her when no one else would and that had touched Sheri to her core. She wouldn't let her down.

"I can't wait," Sheri said quietly. She meant it.

The Earl's Eyes are Opened

Hartley had sat in his office for a long time after Marj left all those weeks ago.

"Don't worry," she had told him. "I'm only here for a little chat, to clear up a few things."

She looked too young to be Lucy's mum, and so different from his own mother, who seemed to have had grey hair for as long as Hartley could remember.

His mother was a statuesque woman and attractive in her own way — slim, tall and always perfectly turned out. But Marj seemed from a different generation. Her skin looked so soft. She had the traces of laughter lines round her eyes and mouth, which hinted at her age, but still, she looked great. Hartley remembered the newspaper article he'd read just a few days ago — the one Bridget had shown him — about Lucy's background. It painted her family as some kind of Jerry Springer Show fodder and Lucy as a manipulative fantasist who lied about her past. It was clearly nonsense. The woman in front of him was poised, articulate and full of grace.

She had Lucy's colouring, with bright blue eyes and thick blonde hair, but was smaller, petite like Max.

"I see." Hartley didn't quite understand but the woman sitting opposite didn't seem angry. On the contrary. She was smiling, trying to put him at his ease.

339

"As I said, I've just come for a chat."

"A blether, as they say in Scotland?" Hartley couldn't believe he'd made a joke. It certainly betrayed how nervous he felt. Damn, he should have dressed more smartly. She must think him terribly casual in his chinos and checked shirt.

"Exactly, a blether," Marj replied, repositioning herself on the leather chair and leaning forward slightly. "Hartley, Lucy has no idea I am here. It's not like me to do anything like this. I don't interfere."

She paused, as if to make sure Hartley understood. He nodded, willing her to continue.

"I've noticed that Lucy is very unhappy. I understand this has something to do with your split and something that happened in Scotland."

Hartley shifted in his seat.

"Of course, as Lucy's mother, you would expect me to take her side in the matter." Again, Marj was smiling kindly and Hartley found himself reciprocating. "But the truth is that Lucy is the most loyal daughter a mother could hope to have. What you think she did, well, it's beyond her."

Hartley looked at the floor then back at Marj. He sensed he would add nothing by talking.

"Now, I am not here to paint my daughter in a wonderful light so that you two get back together. I'm afraid that ship has sailed, my dear. Take away the cruel newspaper stories and the tag she seems now to have as some kind of predator, what really hurt is that you didn't believe she was innocent. You didn't trust her."

Hartley felt his chest tighten.

"As I say, I'm not here to suggest a reconciliation. I just want to clear my daughter's name. She can cope with people turning against her because of something they read — it's not pleasant but these people were never true friends. But not you. She expected more from you."

Hartley looked out of the window. Hearing it put as simply as this was painful. He wasn't hearing anything new. He'd thought the same things over and over in his head. And yet he hadn't called Lucy. He should have spoken to her; it shouldn't have come to this.

"Thank you," Hartley said, speaking over the lump in his throat. He felt ashamed that this woman had had to come to him. She had no sinister agenda; she simply wanted to make him know how badly he had hurt her daughter.

Hartley stood up and took a deep breath. He walked around his chair and leaned on it.

"I never fully believed she was behind it," he told Marj, a hopeful tone in his voice.

"No, but you never fully believed she wasn't."

Hartley looked deflated. She was right. He came back to the chair and sat in it heavily.

"Far be it from me to tell you what happened that night. But there's something you should know."

"Yes?"

"Max, my other daughter, saw how low Lucy was when she came back from Scotland. She put on her journalist hat — a cunning little thing, she can be — and found something out, about what really happened, involving a certain Lady friend, I believe."

Hartley felt his blood run cold. Bridget.

But she'd been so nice about Lucy for weeks. She'd been so attentive and caring, a million miles from the Bridget he had remembered. His friends had warned him not to be taken in by her but he had told them that people change; everyone is allowed a second chance.

Why hadn't he applied that logic to Lucy and given her the benefit of the doubt?

Jesus, please, no. Bridget couldn't be behind this.

For weeks after they started spending time together, nothing had happened between him and Bridget. Hartley didn't want her; he wanted Lucy. All those times he had picked up his phone and thought about calling her, before bottling it . . . Why hadn't he grown a pair of balls?

And God, he'd had sex with Bridget the other night. The thought of her being behind the photographer in Scotland was almost too much to take.

Marj was talking but his head was so crammed with horror he was struggling to listen.

"Max linked Bridget to the photographer in Scotland. Armed with the proof that Lucy had no part in what had happened, Max wanted to come to you, to make you see. Lucy told her to forget it. She made Max promise not to contact you. Why should she have to justify herself to you?"

Oh God, Hartley thought, what have I done?

"I am so sorry," he said, looking Marj straight in the eye, his eyes filled with remorse. He hurt so badly he thought he might crumple there in front of her and wail for days. How bloody stupid he had been.

"How . . . I mean, Bridget — she wasn't even there." Hartley said the words as they came into his head.

"That's not my business. I came only to make you see that Lucy is the girl you got to know. I couldn't stand for you not to know the truth."

"I should never have doubted her," he said quietly.

Marj felt sorry for Hartley. She wasn't angry with him. Of course Marj wanted her girls to find someone who could take care of them, to protect them and love them. She couldn't give a stuff for Hartley's money or title. It would bring a certain comfort no doubt and that was a huge bonus, but what mattered was the man. Fergal had taught her that. She liked what she saw in Hartley. But there was no getting away from the fact he had not stood by Lucy.

"From what I heard, you jumped to an obvious conclusion. We all make mistakes. Perhaps it's a mistake me coming here. After all, I am doing this behind Lucy's back. It's not easy, you know, being a parent, loving your children so much you never want them to hurt. Of course they will — no one can control that. But it's not fair that you think the worst of my daughter when she did nothing wrong."

Hartley looked forlornly out of the window, at the cold, dark winter sky, and wondered how this could have happened. How had he managed to lose the woman who made him feel like he would burst with joy every time he thought of her?

Marj was speaking again, her voice still soft. "As for that other article — the one about our family. We have nothing to hide, Hartley. I fell pregnant when I was twenty to a man I loved. I discovered he was married. He wanted to leave his wife but I said I wouldn't be the one to split a family. It was tough — the stigma of being a single mum three decades ago was huge. I fell in love with another man, Fergal, the best man I have ever met, and he is Max's father. His own father abandoned him when he was young and that made him doubly determined to make sure he was always there for his girls — that's how he sees them both. It turned out Lucy's dad was a wealthy man and he offered to pay for her to go to boarding school. There you have it — the big mystery about Lucy's accent is solved. Hardly qualifies for an episode of *CSI*, does it?"

Hartley didn't know whether to laugh or cry. Had it mattered to him when he saw the article? He remembered being hurt by it — assuming she had lied. But she had never misled him in any way.

Marj stood and picked up her handbag from the floor.

"I must go," she said lightly. "I hope you don't mind me coming here."

"Oh God, not at all. I can't thank you enough. Is there . . . I mean to say, do you think there's anything I can do?"

"I'm not sure," Marj admitted. "That's not my business either."

Marj held out her hand and shook Hartley's with real warmth. She leaned in and kissed his cheek.

Reaching the door, she turned back suddenly. "Oh Hartley?"

"Yes?"

"Did you see the story about Lucy and Kirk?"

"Yes."

"Nonsense. Well, ninety per cent of it. Max found out that Kirk's mum placed the story in the paper — doing her son's PR, if you like, trying to get him away from the reputation he has with glamour girls. It was Kirk who chased Lucy and things went no further than a goodnight kiss. You know why?"

Hartley shook his head.

"Because she couldn't stop thinking about you."

Marj was pleased to see a huge smile light up Hartley's rosy face.

. . . And Now for Max

Marj had no idea if she had done the right thing visiting Hartley.

Perhaps it was her breast-cancer scare that had made her realize her girls' happiness meant so much to her.

At least Hartley knew the truth now.

Then there was Max.

During her stay with the girls, Marj knew something was wrong. Max wasn't her normal carefree self. Marj couldn't remember ever seeing her daughter so down.

The other night on the phone she had tried once more to speak to Max about the guy she had briefly mentioned, the one who was clearly the cause of her sadness.

"What's up, Maxy?"

"Nothing."

"There's something."

"OK, something. Just that guy I liked."

"Didn't he like you back?"

"He does, but it's too complicated to be with him."

"He's not married?"

"No, no."

"Engaged?"

"No."

"Because engaged isn't married, Max. A girl in my yoga class fell for someone when she was engaged, so she left her fiancé for him and is blissfully happy now."

"No, nothing like that."

"You liked him?"

Marj heard her daughter's voice catch in her throat as she desperately tried not to cry when she said, "I think I loved him."

Marj had wanted to take her sobbing daughter in her arms. She seemed suddenly so young and vulnerable. After a few moments, she heard her daughter the actress, the selfless young woman who didn't want her mother to worry. "Thanks, Mum. Don't worry. You know me, I'll be fine."

Marj could imagine her daughter using every ounce of willpower to paint on that funny smile she'd always worn to reassure her. She didn't want to push Max. She was sure her daughter knew she would always be there for her, and took comfort from that.

The conversation had played on Marj's mind, though, and she called Lucy soon after.

"Lucy, is Max OK?"

"Sure. Why'd you ask?"

"She's terribly down, not like her at all."

Max down? There must be some mistake. She was fine. For once it was Lucy who was all over the place, splitting up with Hartley, splashed over the papers.

"She is cut up about a boy."

Lucy laughed. As if. Her little sister down about a guy? "Mum, this is Max. She breaks the hearts — not the other way round."

"Not this time."

There was something in her mother's tone that made Lucy stop. She put down her work notebook. She had been absent-mindedly chatting to Marj while jotting down questions to ask Alexander McQueen about his summer designs, after Carlos arranged a last-minute meeting with him later that week. It was a huge coup for the magazine, as he wasn't doing any other interviews, and testament to Carlos's reputation in the industry.

"Mum, I know everything about Max's life. We live together. She tells me everything, you know that."

It was true, Max and Lucy had no secrets. That had always been their way.

"She said there was someone she liked and wanted to be with, but she couldn't be — the situation was too tricky?"

Lucy was taken aback. She didn't have a clue. There was whiffy Phil and that PR guy she'd regretted, but no one else. Except Luke.

But that hadn't been anything; nothing had happened. What was it Max had said? She had agreed there were plenty of people to have a crush on other than Lucy's brother.

Lucy tried hard to remember how the conversation had come up. It was just after the photographer in Scotland. Lucy hadn't been herself. She remembered being very angry with Max for suggesting she liked her brother. "Luce, I'm in love." That's what she'd said. And that Luke was wonderful.

"Not Luke?" Lucy asked her mother as the thought formed in her head.

"I don't know, Lucy, but she's devastated it couldn't work out . . . You don't mean your brother Luke?"

"Yes."

Lucy waited for her mother to laugh at how ridiculous the very thought of Luke and Max was.

"A handsome boy," Marj said, almost to herself. She had seen hundreds of photos of Luke and Ben over the years. She had invited them to stay in Broughty Ferry but their mother had told them that would happen over her dead body. Such a shame. They were Lucy's family; they should be part of her life in Scotland. "And you always say how wonderful he is."

"He is. But he's my brother."

"He's not Max's brother."

Lucy raised a palm to the ceiling in protest. "Mum, you can't be serious."

"Why not?"

"What happens when it all goes wrong and Max decides he holds his fork the wrong way or buttons his shirts too high and dumps him? It's just all too close, Mum."

"I don't know what happens if, Lucy, not when, that happens."

"It becomes as awkward as hell, Mum. Luke gets hurt and I feel awful every time I see him. Neither of us knows what to say and our relationship suffers. He's my brother. You understand."

Marj was quiet for a few seconds before replying, her voice calm and considered. "And do you think, given the value your sister places on family, she would risk dating him if she didn't really think there was a chance?"

Lucy's brow furrowed. She hadn't thought of it like that.

"She's devastated, Lucy."

"Really?" The question came out as a squeak with Lucy's voice catching in her throat. Had she really been so consumed with her own problems she'd missed how Max felt?

"She's not incapable of finding love, Lucy. She wants it as badly as you or I or anyone."

Lucy felt her cheeks flush. She was overcome by guilt. Of course Max wanted love. Lucy had only ever wanted her sister to be happy and find a great guy. That's what Luke was. Max had ditched men because they weren't right — what was wrong for holding out for someone who was? And what if Luke was that person? Marj was right; Max wouldn't risk dating Luke if she didn't really like him. God, it had probably taken guts for her even to admit she liked him and Lucy had been so vile, caught up in Hartley and Scotland. Some big sister.

"Mum, I told her to stay away. I gave her no choice in the matter."

"Lucy, you are always there for Max — don't beat yourself up. That's probably why she put your feelings before her own happiness. You've had quite a time of it — she knows that."

"But Mum, I must have been totally wrapped up in myself . . . I didn't even realize she was down."

"Lucy, Max has been trying to protect you. You know Max — the best actress in the world when she has to be."

Marj imagined her daughter's face at the end of the line, those blue eyes full of remorse.

"Listen, Lady Macbeth was wrong: what's done can be undone. Talk to Max."

"She's just gone to New York."

"When she gets back, then."

Lucy had a better plan. She would speak to Luke.

Bridget Plays the Waiting Game

Hartley had been in such a state on the night Bridget had ensured he got exceptionally drunk. She had practically dragged him out of the cab and into her house. Her plan had been easier than she had imagined. She had invited bloody Bately and his new girlfriend for supper — she had wanted Hartley to see just how charming she was with the man who had clung to his stupid grudge against her. Philippa had come too, with her boyfriend, and Bridget was careful only to ask her all about her meeting with Lucy when no one was listening.

After supper Bridget had suggested they head to Maddox for a few drinks. She much preferred Annabel's but Maddox was livelier and she wanted Hartley drunk. Bridget had been a member when it was called Noble Rot, before it was taken over by Fred Moss.

It had been the unofficial social headquarters of London's blue-blood set and still attracted quite a few in her circle. Bathed in dim red lighting, a table on a Friday night in the minimalist black-and-red Sammy Chams-designed interior cost £1,000 including champagne and a hostess, and was more New York than the old-country-house feel of Annabel's or glitzy Tramp.

She had ensured Hartley's glass was constantly topped up over dinner and noticed he was drinking like a fish. Bridget had an inkling as to why he was on such a mission: he had been looking and acting rather vacantly since he saw Lucy on the front page earlier that day. Although it irked Bridget to see how much reading about Lucy and Kirk had bothered him, the timing was perfect. She simply made sure he drowned his sorrows that very night. Lucy, the little tart. Bridget couldn't have hoped for a better situation. Now he saw how cheap she was, desperate for any man who was famous just weeks after splitting up with him.

Bridget had put up with the terminally dull Bately and his new girlfriend, who looked like a horse. A slim horse, but a horse nonetheless.

She smiled sweetly at their stories and jokes. This time she would get it right. She would be nothing other than charming to all his friends. Well, for the time being. She could think of better things to be doing than feigning interest in Bately's latest mountain climb for charity, but she would be rewarded for all her hard work.

Hartley maintained his thirst throughout the evening. Come one o'clock in the morning he was struggling to stay awake so Bridget asked a waiter to call her a cab.

It wasn't easy getting him to bed — he kept muttering incoherently about nonsense, mentioning Lucy a few times. He was out like a light as soon as his head hit the pillow and somehow Bridget got his shirt and chinos off as he lay snoring. She pulled the duvet

353

over his body, took her clothes off and slipped in beside him.

Bridget set the alarm on her mobile phone for 4a.m. — on vibrate so he wouldn't hear. She placed it under her pillow so she would feel it buzz. When it did, she pulled at one of Hartley's sideburns, remembering it was a particularly sensitive area. He stirred and opened his eyes.

"Darling, you were coughing in your sleep, almost choking. Are you OK?"

"Oh sorry . . ." Hartley's eyes had a thick glaze of drunkenness still covering them. "Yes, I'm fine."

Bridget smiled and kissed his cheek before climbing on top of him.

"Don't worry. I'm on the pill," she whispered in his ear while making him hard. He was too confused to object. Bridget was certain he had wanted to anyway, but he was shy and needed her to make the first move.

The best bit was that Bridget had timed it to perfection. She had read up on the best times to have sex when trying to conceive and she slept with Hartley bang in the middle of the optimum days, thereby increasing her chances spectacularly.

Bridget had wondered every day since then whether she could be pregnant. She was sure she had waited long enough and resolved to buy a pregnancy test.

New York, New York

Max felt the surging thrill of New York as her cab pulled up at her hotel on 54th and Seventh. She soaked up the atmosphere, the cacophony of car horns, yellow cabs everywhere, people of all nationalities striding confidently, walking tall. Somehow, folk seemed more assured in New York. They looked up to the sky-scraping buildings with wonder while Londoners kept their heads low, cloaking themselves in anonymity. Max thought of the *Sex and the City* episode where Carrie considered that perhaps the great love of her life wasn't a man, but NYC. Did people feel like that about London, with such passion and longing? But then London had its own breathtaking beauty. Who could fail to be moved by the dazzling sight of the architecture, the history and romance of the place?

There wasn't a city in the world that could compete with the views from the London Eye, when you were 135 yards above the River Thames in a capsule with a 360-degree panorama. You could see the Houses of Parliament, St Paul's and Hampstead Heath. Even Windsor Castle on a perfect day. Twenty-five miles of streets, churches and palaces grown from Roman times.

Max loved the cab journeys that took her over the Thames bridges, relishing the landmarks so many people walked past every day, immune to their beauty: Westminster, so ominous and eerie against a charcoal winter sky; the familiar shape of the Oxo Tower, lit up and inviting.

And now she was in the Big Apple it was time for her own fresh start. What to do first? Order pancakes with maple syrup and corned-beef hash in a diner? Shop on Fifth Avenue? Armani Exchange always offered cheaper stock than back home. Max needed some casual clothes — maybe Abercrombie & Fitch opposite Trump Towers for a tracksuit . . . mind you, everyone seemed to be plastered in A&F these days. She liked the look of the new Ed Hardy range. Or maybe going back to old school Nike or Adidas for a trackie and T-shirts was called for. Must get bloody fit, she thought as she pondered the last time she'd had a cigarette. Fuck, that made her want one, what with the adrenaline of being here. A beer and Marlboro Light would be perfect. Then another thought crossed her mind: she hadn't thought about Luke for at least half an hour.

Max couldn't help but feel angry with herself. During the six-hour flight, she hadn't stopped thinking about him. Something about flying always made her horny as hell and she kept replaying fantasies in her head where he ripped her clothes off, told her he had to have her there and then . . . God, she so wanted that to happen.

But what she really craved was just to be with him, have him hold her and make her feel there was no need to look for anyone or anything else any more. Those eyes, that smell.

356

She tried to replace him with other guys in these imaginary scenes but it was useless.

Max lay on her queen-size bed at the Wellington Hotel. The room was clean, modern and basic. There was no point in a luxurious suite that cost a fortune — New York was the one place where you never saw much of your hotel room. She didn't unpack but wanted to get out and do something to stop thinking about him.

She had always been able to move on, close a chapter and start again, It was a skill she had perfected — maybe to rid her of the memory of the sleazy things she'd done to get stories. And she had found it easy to all but wipe the memory of being with a man from the moment she decided she didn't want to see him again. Alfie was the exception, but still, she hadn't thought about him as much as she was thinking of Luke. And she hardly knew him. Shutting things out was her speciality. Why couldn't she do it with him?

Luke wasn't the only reason Max did not want to be alone. The memory of what she'd done two nights ago still made her face burn in shame. Sure, she could blame it on wanting to forget about Luke. But the truth was she had gone too far. Max had been invited to London's biggest radio station's annual awards. It was a midday start, at the Hilton on Park Lane, and she hadn't held back at the champagne reception or on the wine over lunch, when her glass had been steadily refilled. Afterwards, she made polite chat with rival reporters from the other papers at the free bar.

"I heard Jade screwed you — didn't tell you she had a story on your sister?"

God, they loved it, the drama, the gossip — it's why they were good showbiz reporters. Sure she was like them, like any girl who pored over *Heat* magazine to find out the latest on J-Lo or Madonna. But she never got star-struck, which was just as well. What was the point in meeting George Clooney or Julia Roberts if all you could do was dribble and tell them how wonderful they were, the most incisive question being what their favourite colour was? The secret was to think of a dinner lady who'd just finished work and was on the bus to pick up her son from nursery. What would she want to read — what would make her day? She was tired and worried about the bills. What would it take to make her forget all her problems? Max called it her "well, fuck me, I never" line — the nugget of gold a star came out with during an interview. As soon as they'd said it, Max knew it would be the first sentence of her story — the line that would hook the millions who read it.

No matter how big the star they were only human, and what separated the good reporters from the best was the ability to ask cheeky questions.

The sub editors would take that "fuck me" line and come up with a catchy headline. Sometimes their efforts fell nothing short of genius, like the time George Michael was caught with his pants down in a public toilet, inspiring the famous *Sun* front-page headline: "Zip Me Up Before You Go Go", in place of his famous eighties song, "Wake Me Up Before You Go Go".

There hadn't been many stars at the Drum Radio awards. Max had spoken to a couple of soap stars and a finalist from Simon Cowell's *X Factor* show before deciding to get smashed. One of her rivals, the tall slim brunette with a little acne who slept with stars' lackeys to get her exclusives, told Max with her stale tobacco breath that she'd heard a great bit of gossip: Joe Jacobs, the Managing Director of Drum, London's biggest radio station, was on the singles market after dumping his stunning Russian wife. Joe was in his late thirties, devastatingly handsome and a regular in the *Guardian*'s Top Ten of the most powerful men in media.

"He's not only the most eligible guy in this room, he's the hottest thing in London. When word gets out he's single . . . Shit."

"What?"

Cat was grimacing, her face red. "I've only gone and told you, my fucking rival, about a great story. That's my exclusive for tomorrow. Shit, I must have had too much wine."

Max touched Cat's arm. "Don't worry about it — your secret's safe with me."

"That'll be a first for a showbiz reporter," Cat replied, raising her eyebrows.

But Max had no intention of shafting Cat. The circuit was too small — she'd no doubt need her help at a premiere in the future. Many a time, Max had been desperate to go to the toilet or make a phone call but was too scared to leave the line-up of journalists waiting to talk to the stars so had stayed put. If only she'd had a friend to keep her place, she might never have peed herself in front of Tom Cruise.

"Look, I promise. I've got a couple of little stories — the *Britain's Got Talent* guy Jimmy has signed up for *Chicago*, the musical. So there, you know my secret too and you're to keep schtum as well, OK?"

Cat laughed and held out her hand. As they shook on it, Max decided what she was going to do next: pull Joe Jacobs.

She was more than a little drunk, not to mention bored, so why not? Max cast aside the reality of the situation — that she was doing it to make herself feel better. An hour didn't go by when she didn't think of Luke. Her heart jumped every time she received a text, thinking it could be him. Of course, it wasn't. If he had felt half the chemistry she had on their date, a fraction of the attraction, he would have been bewildered as to why she had blanked him. He must think her an utter shit.

A challenge was what she needed and Drum boss Joe was it. If she couldn't have the man she wanted she would have the man everyone else wanted. Then maybe she'd feel better.

It had been easier than she imagined. She spotted Joe at the other end of the room. Buoyed by the mix of bubbly, wine and a couple of gin and tonics, Max confidently walked over, tapped him on the shoulder and said hello. He smiled at Max as he took her in and said he was sure they had met before. As always, he looked dapper in an immaculate suit — pinstriped navy, Max guessed Armani — with a crisp open-collared lemon shirt and trendy brown lace-ups with slightly pointed toes. His hair was dark brown, an inch or two longer than that of most men in the room, with a slight curl. It gave him the look of a suave Italian.

Max was glad she had opted for a glam look despite the early kick-off. She was wearing a Miss Sixty short black dress with a light fringe at the hem, which swished at the top of her thighs as she moved. Shiny black tights and black Carvela heels with a slight platform completed the look which flattered Max's petite frame. Her make-up was a little heavier than her normal minimal daytime look, with a hint of black eyeliner and pink blush to accentuate her cheekbones.

"A couple of times," Max replied. "Not properly, though; we've just said hello."

Max could tell by the way Joe was struggling a little to focus that he was drunk too. Maybe he was letting his hair down after his split.

The rest of the afternoon and early evening were a blur. Joe had told her he was delighted she had interrupted the chat he was having with an utter bore of an accountant who worked for Drum. As late afternoon slipped into early evening, Joe suggested they get something to eat in Whisky Mist, a restaurant and bar in the hotel. They skipped the food and ordered mojitos. Max lost count after three.

"Where are you staying tonight?" Max asked.

"Here, at the Hilton." Max had figured so — the big media bosses were often booked into the swankiest of London hotels, even though their own homes were a few miles away and their town pads even closer.

Max's next memory was waking up next to Joe in his hotel room — a surprisingly boxy room.

"Morning." He smiled lazily, leaning on his pillow, his chin resting on his hand.

"Morning," Max managed. Why exactly had she done this? To make herself feel better. And did she? What bit of sleeping with a still-married man was it she'd imagined would make her feel better? And no, consuming enough alcohol for ten guests was no excuse. She couldn't actually remember having sex with him but she had a sketchy memory of pulling each other's clothes off when they got to the room. Now they were both naked and his smile was saying, "That was fun last night."

"I don't normally do this," she said slowly.

"Do what?" Joe was still grinning, a little smugly Max thought.

"Sleep with men I've just met."

Joe raised an eyebrow as if she'd told him something amusing.

"And I've never . . ." Max felt her voice trail off, conscious suddenly of a huge lump in her throat. "I've never . . . slept with a married man."

That had always been a deal breaker for Max, sleeping with men who had a girlfriend, fiancée or wife. What right did she have to break exclusives of "cheating rats" if she cheated with said rats? Mind you, it didn't stop half the showbiz reporters she knew from exposing stars for taking cocaine even though they struggled to make it through a showbiz bash without several discreet trips to the toilet.

"Really?" Joe said, stroking her arm lightly. "I'd have thought that was pretty common in your job."

Max looked at Joe, unsure she'd heard him correctly. She swallowed and the taste of pure alcohol was still in her mouth.

"In my job? I'm a journalist, not a hooker."

Joe laughed. "Some might say they're not so different when it comes down to it."

He stopped as he registered that Max looked deadly serious.

Max sprung out of bed, ignoring the dizzy spell as her feet touched the thick carpet. Pulling on her pants and clothes, she picked up her bag and stopped at Joe's side of the bed.

"Max, I was only joking." Joe was sitting up in the bed. "Anyway, we didn't actually have sex. We just fooled around. I left you for a couple of minutes to order champagne on room service and you passed out."

Well, at least that was something, Max told herself. But she still felt pretty low.

She tried to smile but couldn't. Why should she pretend nothing bothered her, as she always did? When Max told Joe she had never slept with a married man, she had expected him to say, "Oh but I've split up with my wife and I really like you."

How stupid. Act like a tart, then expect to be treated like one, Max told herself. Not that she wanted to see Joe again. But she wanted him to somehow assure her he wanted her.

Joe looked at Max's face, his expression quizzical. Max didn't give him the chance to ask whatever question he was forming in his mind.

She walked out of the hotel room and ran to the lift, struggling to see the button for the tears that had filled her eyes.

Here in New York, Max still felt the sting of shame when she thought about that night. She couldn't even bring herself to tell Lucy. She knew her sister wouldn't judge her as harshly as she was judging herself. But she would know it was something Max would never normally do and she would worry about her.

As if almost sleeping with a married man wasn't bad enough, Max had since learned he had a three-year-old son. Joe kept his family life pretty private but a story about him in a media trade mag had jumped out at her. When asked what the most important thing in his life was, he had answered his little boy.

When Max wasn't beating herself up about Joe, she was dreaming of Luke. What a mess.

Max looked at her watch. It was 7p.m. Too late for shopping but just right for partying.

One of Carlos's exes worked at Soho House, one of the most exclusive members' clubs in the city, originally set up as a place for media types to hang out. Media didn't extend to tabloid reporters and staff went out of their way to stop hacks joining, but her entry along with a few friends was guaranteed, thanks to Carlos. Max had only met Carlos a couple of times but they had taken to each other straight away, swapping celebrity gossip. He seemed to think so much of Lucy that nothing was too much trouble to help Max. When Lucy had mentioned to him that Max was going to New York, Carlos had insisted he guest-list her for a couple of clubs. He knew what Lucy and Max had been through with Marj's news and wanted them to know he was thinking of them.

But Soho House would wait. She was here to catch up with real friends in real bars. Max was never short of good company in New York. So many of the childhood pals she had got to know over the summers when she visited her dad's relatives in Ireland had moved to the Big Apple.

She hadn't seen Sean, Connor or Cath for a couple of years but had kept in touch with their news through friends and their drunken pictures on Facebook.

New York was full of Irish — from clubs and bars to the police department and fire service. If you knew enough of the right Irish people, you could get anything you wanted twenty-four hours a day — alcohol, great food, dancing. Jeez, no wonder she liked to party — being half Scots and half Irish, what chance did she ever have of leading a quiet life and ordering a Diet Coke at a free bar?

Just a few streets away in a Manhattan bar, friends awaited with a pint of Guinness with her name on it.

Lucy Makes Amends

Lucy wondered how she couldn't have noticed Max had been down. When she looked back over the last few weeks it was obvious. Max had been quieter, deflated even. Lucy may have had more drama in her life than she ever imagined possible, but it was no excuse.

At least now she could try to make amends.

Lucy had also been blind to the fact that Max and Luke were well suited. Hell, maybe it would end in tears, but who was she to put a stop to things before they even started?

Any guy would be lucky to have Max. So she'd broken hearts along the way. Luke was probably no angel either; she just didn't know every intimate detail of his love life as she did with Max.

Lucy had arranged to meet Luke at Selfridges for lunch and a little Christmas shopping. The huge department store reminded her of the excitement she felt as a child at this magical time of year. Lucy wrapped up against the December chill in skinny jeans, Max's Armani coat, which she had left behind for Lucy to wear while she was in New York on account of having lost so many expensive pieces of clothing on her travels, and a cream-cashmere polo neck. Wait until she told the girls in the office she'd picked it up for £30 while food shopping in Tesco.

Sitting at a small table in the bustling café, picking at their shared platter with chopsticks, Lucy noticed her normally carefree brother seemed a little awkward.

She had told him all about Kirk Kelner and how she was going on a date with him in a few days. He had laughed and clinked his glass of fresh orange with her glass of sparkling water. He had told her how he was trying to curtail partying over the Christmas holidays to study for his next bar exam. But behind the pleasantries something was missing.

"Luke, I don't know how to say this, so I'll just blurt it out and hope it comes across OK."

Luke studied his sister's face like a poker player trying to read his opponent. "OK," he said slowly.

Lucy took a deep breath.

"I know about you and Max."

She paused, hoping this would clarify the situation.

"Me and Max?" Luke was calm, as if mulling the words over in his head. He smiled wryly. "There's nothing to tell. I got the message a while back — after she ignored my umpteenth text and call."

Lucy sat up straight in her chair. "That's it. She didn't ignore you. Well, maybe she did, but it was all my fault."

Luke cocked his head slightly to the side, quizzically.

"You see, I told her to stay away from you. God, I was such a bitch. I told her to go after any guy she chose but not you."

Luke narrowed his eyes. "You did?"

"Yes, but not because of you . . . I mean, you're great. But that's my point. I didn't want her to hurt you or for things to go wrong and our relationship to suffer. I mean, it wouldn't be the most pleasant of situations if two of the people I love most in the world ended up hating each other . . ."

Lucy let the words trail off, unsure what to say next.

Luke had put his chopsticks on the table and was sitting back in his chair. "Right. OK. I think I understand. But Luce, Max has her own mind. She could have persuaded you, talked you round, if she thought enough of me."

"No," Lucy blurted out, "that's just it. I'm ashamed to say I didn't give her that option. I was so caught up in my own problems — I'd just come back from Scotland having had the most awful time and I'd split up with Hartley. Max knew I was on the edge. She felt guilty because it's always me helping her — well, it's not, but that's how she sees it. She was scared of hurting me."

Luke was resting his chin on his hand. His expression had softened. Lucy sensed he wanted her to continue.

"It's only when I look back over these last few weeks that I realize how down she's been. She's always so happy — singing, partying, laughing. That's all been missing. My own little sister and I've been totally unaware. Trust me, for a guy to do that to Max she'd have to feel a lot for him. And she does — for you."

Lucy paused.

"I feel like a prize bitch."

Luke laughed loudly. It felt like a release of emotion he had tried so hard to bottle. He had convinced himself that the way he felt about Max had been in his imagination. Or, if it had been real, patently it had been one-sided. Suddenly, he caught the sadness on Lucy's face. He took her hand and squeezed it tightly.

"Lucy, I'm not laughing at you. I'm laughing because I'm happy to hear what you just told me. You are anything but a bitch. This is probably the first time in your life you've not been aware of everyone else's feelings before your own. And to be fair, you have had a crazy time of it."

Lucy looked relieved and smiled back at Luke.

"Really? You don't think I'm awful for warning her off you like that?"

"I think you did it for the right reasons. You were protecting me. But guess what?"

"You don't need any protecting?"

"Exactamundo, sis. And guess what else?"

"I don't know."

"I really like Max too."

No Rest for the Wicked

It was a joy to catch up with friends who had nothing to do with media. They had chosen the Scottish-themed St Andrews bar off Times Square. Soho House could wait. Drinking Guinness with her pals Sean, Connor and Cath, who worked in New York selling the sports channels to bars in the city, was much more fun.

"Whiskey chasers?" Sean bellowed over the Proclaimers' "I'm Gonna Be" in the background.

"Why not?" Max replied, clapping her hands.

It never failed to amaze Max how her friends' accents grew more Irish each time she saw them. They had lived here for over a decade but sounded more Irish than most of their friends back home.

"Ah it's simple," Sean told her, downing his pint and picking up a full one. With dark auburn hair, brown eyes, freckles and a growing beer belly, there was no mistaking Sean's Celtic roots. "I have Irish friends who were born in New York and sound as comically Irish as Brad Pitt in the film *Snatch*. They work in Irish bars, they have Irish friends and family here. They never talk to Americans."

Max laughed. "You're joking."

"On me maither's life, Max, it's the truth."

"Anyway, when are you moving out here, girl?" asked Cath, a curvy size 14 with magnificently full breasts, curly strawberry blonde, shoulder-length hair which fell into pretty wisps around her face, and those blue Irish eyes.

"Yeah, the place was made for you, and we know all the bars that'll serve you at any hour," Connor piped up. He was just an inch or two taller than Max, with curly brown hair, bright green eyes and the solid frame of a feather-weight boxer.

"Just what I need." Max laughed.

She had to admit, she had often thought about moving to New York. She would miss Lucy, her parents, Simon, Suzie and a few other girlfriends, but the change would be wonderful for a couple of years.

She picked up her shot and toasted: "To us."

As the dram hit the back of her throat, Max felt her phone vibrate in her Seven jeans pocket (she'd washed them three times after the Tom Cruise incident and was certain they were now pee-free).

Claire's number flashed on the screen.

"I'll just be a mo — it's my boss — too noisy in here, better go outside." Max walked quickly to the door and answered. "Hi, Claire."

"Hi, Max, how's New York?"

"Wonderful." It wasn't, however, a wonderful sign that her boss was calling her when it was almost 2a.m. her time. It must be serious.

"Max, I know you're on holiday but here's the thing . . . I've just had a tip that Beyoncé's throwing a party tonight — some charity do with a guest list that reads like a copy of Who's Who."

Max knew what was coming. She happened to know the paper's New York correspondent was off on honeymoon.

"You know Paul's away?"

"Uh-huh."

"Well, I'd ask an agency reporter in New York to cover it but you're much better. If anyone can blag in, you can."

Flattery. Great. Max knew there was no way out. All she wanted to do was switch off and listen to her friends' sing-song voices in a cosy bar.

"I'll send you details of the address. You have your BlackBerry?"

"I do."

"Great. I really appreciate this, Max."

"No worries."

There was no point in telling Claire she had plans. On a Richter scale of care factors, her interest would be zero.

"Oh Claire, what time does it start?"

"Nine."

"That's in twenty minutes."

"And it's black tie."

"I'm in my jeans — I don't have time to change."

"Sorry? Oh Max, I think the line's breaking up. Good luck, thanks again."

A Close Shave for Max

Half an hour after speaking to her boss, Max pulled up at the Hudson Hotel, one of New York's coolest celeb hangouts. Shit. The entrance was teeming with security.

Max knew the only way she could pull off getting-inside was to muster all the confidence she had.

In the absence of a ticket, supreme self-belief was her only option.

Max employed the old phone trick, speaking into her mobile while striding up the red carpet past a line of animated photographers. For once, someone really was on the other end of the line — her sister.

Shit, was that J-Lo they were taking snaps of? It was. There was no mistaking that perfectly rounded bottom jutting out from her tiny waist.

No matter how top-secret the party, a team of security men outside the Hudson was always going to attract the paparazzi. And here they were, feasting on the A-listers like hyenas on prey, salivating over the thought of how many thousands they'd make from a night's work. The British tabloids alone — the *Daily News*, the *Sun*, the *Mirror* and *Star* — would pay premium prices for the best shots. They could hardly ignore them while rivals splashed them all over the front page. No editor would risk the resulting drop in sales.

Right, deep breath, chin up, chest out, Max told herself as her heart raced.

"Excuse me, ma'am," a burly Spanish-looking man had stepped in front of Max. "We have a private function here tonight."

Max let out a groan of frustration and spoke into her mobile. "Honey, hold on a minute, OK? I'm just speaking to the security man."

Max smiled at the man.

"Hi, I'm well aware of what's on tonight. I'm Beyoncé's PA."

Max watched as the man took in her attire. In jeans, tan Ugg boots, black-wool poncho and tartan scarf, she couldn't have looked more different to the women teetering to the entrance — all sparkling ball gowns with fishtail finishes and faux fur coats to fend off the December cold.

She laughed, her breath turning into white puffs as it hit the freezing air. "Do I look like I'm here to join a black-tie gala?"

The bouncer looked impatiently at her.

"I have Beyoncé's speech here. She's addressing a room full of people in ten minutes and I've got the list of people she has to thank."

"Sorry, lady, no ticket —"

"No ticket? Of course I don't have a ticket. I was all set to watch TV and have a quiet night in."

The bouncer frowned.

Max lowered her voice. "Look, that's Beyoncé on the phone. She's going fucking nuts in there. If she doesn't have a list of who to thank, she'll look like a prize tit."

374

The man's brow furrowed as though she'd just spoken to him in Gaelic.

"You know, asshole . . . she'd look like an asshole. And if I explain she didn't have it because I got to the hotel on time but the doorman wouldn't let me in, well . . ."

Max let the words trail off, keen not to make any threats that might get his back up.

"Look," she said, holding up her mobile. "She's on the phone now."

Max had edited Lucy's entry in her phone during her cab ride and replaced her name with Beyoncé's.

The bouncer's eyes widened as he saw the star's name on the screen.

"Would you like to say hello?" Max asked with more than a hint of sarcasm.

The man looked unsure. Max had forewarned Lucy to put on her best American accent if needed.

As if on cue — which it was — the sound of a woman shouting came from the phone. "I need that fucking speech — now. I'm on stage in five minutes."

The man looked as if he'd been told he'd just won the lottery, but could only collect the winnings if he hacked off his right leg: utterly confused, star-struck and scared.

"OK, baby, don't you worry. I'm coming."

Max put her phone in her pocket and took a step towards the door. "OK?" she asked the bouncer.

Logically, a suitable compromise would be if he suggested making sure himself that the notepad got to Beyoncé, and Max left.

"I've got to see her and calm her down," Max said, walking away from him.

Shit, he was coming towards her.

"We're all going to be in serious shit if I don't get this to Beyoncé right now."

The man froze. There had been a downturn in work of late. A couple of years back he had been booked by the security firm almost every night but now people seemed more cautious when it came to throwing money around. The last thing he needed was to be sacked by the biggest event-protection company in the city.

Max felt a rush of adrenaline as he stepped back. She'd done the impossible — got past a crack team of bouncers who looked like they were on leave from SAS training. Yes!

Max walked behind a crowd of guests, following them up the escalator into the bar area, which was bathed in pink light.

Taking a glass of rosé champagne from a waiter's tray, she took a gulp. Right, where were the stars?

"Ladies and gentlemen," a man's voice boomed, "I bring you Miss Beyoncé Knowles."

The crowd applauded as the singer-turned-actress took to the stage. Jeez, how was it possible for any woman to look so good? She had curves in exactly the right places. Beyoncé thanked a host of people and talked about the charity the party was in aid of — orphans in Africa.

Max slipped to the back of the room, conscious of how different she looked to the glamorous guests. While

Beyoncé spoke, Max texted Lucy: "Thanx 4 being a gr8 Beyoncé".

Right, where were the stars? Sticking out like a sore thumb in jeans, she could be thrown out at any minute, so best make the most of her time.

Fuck, what if a star recognized her? It was unlikely, given that she was in New York, but what if movie star Mac Ford was here? It was the sort of thing he'd be invited to and Max had no doubt he would remember her.

She hadn't realized quite how much he despised hacks until she met him at the premiere of chick flick *Annie Goes To Hollywood*, when she introduced herself as a reporter. There he was, all posh English accent, dazzling smile — and the perfect gentleman, charming every film bigwig and society beauty in sight. And the moment Max told him who she was, his eyes froze in horror; he mumbled, "Do excuse me," with his mouthful of marbles and left with an expression of such discomfort he may well have touched cloth before making it to the toilet. Maybe he still hadn't got over being caught cheating on his wife with a hooker, and the very mention of a tabloid filled him with disdain.

Buoyed by the free champagne, Max had run after him and doubled up in fits of laughter while chasing him round and round a giant plant.

She had felt perfectly justified the following day in slating him in the paper. She wrote him an open letter asking if he knew what a tosser he was, accepting millions for a movie then refusing to spare journalists a few moments of his time to publicize it at its global launch party.

Thankfully, Max remembered he was shooting a film in London now.

Max concentrated on Beyoncé's speech. Annoyingly, she wasn't making some astonishing announcement. That would have been perfect: stay in the party five minutes, pick up a gem of a story then leave.

Oh there was Will Smith. Bloody hell, Oprah Winfrey. As the speech ended, the attention of guests was no longer on the stage.

Max's heart was racing again — a mix of fear of being uncovered and of leaving the party without a story. She could hardly call herself a good journalist if she left this little celeb-fest with nothing to tell Claire.

Then it happened. Charlie Jackson, the bad-boy actor who had just finished a lengthy spell in rehab, turned round and smiled at Max. Under his nose were the unmistakable remnants of coke. Max guessed he'd been so eager for a line he'd been unable to wait until the speech ended and had covertly had a little sniff.

Six months ago, Max's boss would have said, "So what?" if she'd told her Charlie was back on the drugs. But just last week he'd done a TV interview on *Tonight* with Jay Leno, watched by millions around the world, claiming he was off the devil's powder for good. With tears in his eyes he had told Leno he was a changed man after finding God. When he needed a burst of energy the strongest thing he touched now was Lucozade. And with the Lord's help, he had said, turning to face the audience with his hands clasped together as if praying, he would stay clean one day at a time.

Rapturous applause followed. The Americans loved a sound bite, especially from a ridiculously handsome actor with blue twinkling eyes and fluffy blond hair, still boyish in looks having just turned thirty. He had simply lost his way and how wonderful to have him back in the fold.

Suckers. What a story that he was back on it.

It was totally unprintable, though, as her word against his. She needed a picture.

Slowly, slowly, Max prised her mobile from her pocket. She knew what she had to do: get a picture of his snowy nose. Then there would be nothing to stop the story being printed.

Max smiled back at Charlie, dubbed the new Robert de Niro a few years back after a string of stunning performances in dark, moody movies. The offers of work had dried up of late, though, as word spread about his erratic behaviour on set.

Max gave him a wide, beaming smile. She held his gaze, hoping to hell it would distract him from the fact she was edging her phone to his eye level and pointing it at him. It would only work if she got him face-on.

Click. Flash. Fuck. She hadn't realized it would flash — must be on automatic because the room was dimly lit.

Charlie's eyes stared blankly at Max, like a camera focus whirring into action. High or not, the realization of what had happened spread over his face.

Max turned, bumping into — shit — Jodie Foster. No time to ask her what life was like since coming out as a lesbian.

Max ran to the escalator. Fuck. It was the one that brought you up to the bar. Where was the down one? Fuck it. Before she knew it, Max was running down the mechanical stairs that were moving upwards, racing against them to make it to the bottom.

At last, at the bottom, she jumped on to the solid floor, dizzy. She didn't look back. She knew they were after her. Charlie had too much to lose by letting her go armed with the photo. It was the last thing he had expected at this exclusive party. Max slammed her body against the door, her weight opening it. She ran down the red carpet, sprinted across the road and down the street. Thank God New York was always so damned busy. She merged into the crowd and slowed to a walk. When she got her breath back, she was overwhelmed by relief.

Hartley Sings the Blues

Hartley felt stupid but more than anything he felt ashamed. Here he was, founder of a charity he had lovingly created, the very charity that existed to give people a chance. So why couldn't he have given the one woman who meant so much to him a chance? He was a hypocrite.

All the while he had thought Bridget was being so kind and non-judgemental about Lucy, she was really playing the long game. Hartley felt sick. He had slept with Bridget. He barely remembered it, but God, how could he have been so stupid? For weeks she must have been plotting, ever since . . . since — Hartley felt a shiver down his spine — Scotland. Lucy hadn't been behind the photographer episode, of that he was sure. He could tell Marj wasn't lying. She had admitted she thought it was too late for him and Lucy; she simply wanted to clear her daughter's name.

He hadn't given Lucy a chance; he saw that now. But was there any way he could be wrong about Bridget? He had been in a bit of a daze after reading about Kirk and Lucy in the newspaper, but since Marj had come to see him it was as though he could see Bridget clearly for the first time since he had bumped into her at the flower market.

He remembered Jasper Whitaker telling him that night at Clarissa's supper that he was leaving for Dubai within days for at least a few months, something about a horse-racing opportunity that had come up. Hartley made a call to a friend to make sure Jasper was indeed still in Dubai and yes, he was. So how could he have been "the friend" Bridget had said was in Sheekey's that night and spotted Lucy all over Kirk like a rash?

Hartley remembered little things — like the time Bridget had told him she was going on a course to learn how to speak to people who had depression and a friend had casually remarked he'd met her that very day at a polo match. He'd brushed it from his mind as some misunderstanding on his part. But the only thing he'd misunderstood all along was Bridget — she hadn't changed at all.

Marj had said that Max had even proved Bridget had been behind the photographer at Peat, that somehow she had linked her to him. Hearing her say it, he had no doubt it was true. He'd been stupid not to give Lucy a chance and idiotic to put any faith in Bridget.

He called Robbie. He had to talk to someone.

"I didn't think Lucy seemed the type to stitch you up," he told Hartley. "And it comes as no surprise that Lady Muck had something to do with it. She always was vile. I heard on the grapevine you've been seeing her?"

Hartley was silent.

"Look, I didn't want to put my size tens into your business but I was speaking to Charles the other night. He called to say Bridget had thrown some kind of hissy fit at Claudia. She was taken aback at Bridget's hatred for Lucy. Even by Bridget's standards it was pretty frightening, he said. Claudia said she all but boasted about being behind the photographer."

"Bloody hell, you should have told me," Hartley said, his voice more resigned than angry.

"I probably should have, old man, but I'm hardly Bridget's biggest fan and I didn't want you to think I was out to get her, not if you were happy with her . . ."

The friends were silent.

"But Hartley?"

"Yes?"

"It took all the willpower I had not to call you. I really do think she's a nasty piece of work. I'd made up my mind to tell you when I next saw you — these things are better said face to face."

"Sure, Robbie, I understand. It's just . . . I thought she'd changed," Hartley said meekly.

"She's done a good job on you, that's for sure."

Hartley felt sick again. "I'm an imbecile."

"No, you're just too trusting."

"I think it's too late for me and Lucy, Robbie. How the hell do I make up for any of this?"

"Well, flowers and chocolates probably won't do the trick, right enough . . ."

Robbie felt for his pal. He didn't have a bad bone in his body. He couldn't really be blamed for assuming Lucy was involved in Peat. Whatever Bridget had organized, she'd done it pretty convincingly. Even he had thought there was no other explanation. And yet Lucy had seemed so unassuming, happy just to be there with Hartley. He had desperately hoped they would make a go of it — and that Lucy had an identical twin sister she could put his way.

"Is there any way you can see her again?" Robbie asked.

"Well, I heard she's coming to the Hogmanay Ball." Hartley could scarcely believe it when one of the Foundation committee members had given him a list of guests and Lucy was on it, on Clarissa's table. His heart had leaped. Maybe it was a sign she didn't hate him too much — after all, she knew he was going to be there. But then what if one of the men on her table was her new boyfriend and they were madly in love? It was no less than Hartley deserved.

"OK, well, that's a good sign. It's your ball so she can't despise you too much. There's only one thing for it."

"There is?"

"Yes. Tell her the truth at the ball — how you dialled her number and hung up more than once, everything. Let her know how sorry you are."

Hartley couldn't help but think anything he said would be futile. Why would she want to even speak to him? But still, Robbie was right; she did know he'd be at the ball. Maybe there was a chance.

"And Hartley?"

"Yes?"

"Remember, I'm coming to the ball too, you big girl, so I'll be there to hold your hand."

"Bugger off," Hartley said as he put down the phone.

The Luke of Love

Max had sent her picture of Charlie to Claire's mobile straight away. Her boss was delighted. As Max had taken the photo herself there was no chance of any rival papers having the same story. Indeed, as no other journalists had been inside — Max was sure of that — Claire could bill it as a "world exclusive". Max added Claire's name on the byline. Many journalists wouldn't but it was newspaper etiquette to credit a writer who had contributed to the story and, after all, Max wouldn't have had an exclusive without Claire's tip. She had no doubt that Claire would have added her name to it in any case.

Max had sent the copy on her BlackBerry, hamming it up for all its worth.

Charlie's Back on the Charlie
Exclusive by Maxine Summers and
Claire Roberts

It was the ticket they all wanted, the hottest showbiz event of the year — and our girl made it inside to bring you all the news.

We can exclusively reveal that Hollywood mega-star Charlie Jackson — who just last week vowed he had overcome his deadly addiction to cocaine — is back on the Class A drug.

Our girl caught the actor, who has starred in gritty blockbusters including *Russian Roulette* and *My Name is Carl*, with a nose-full of the stuff.

And she even got the picture to prove it.

It was the early hours back in the UK, too late to make that day's paper. Claire could use it as her list-topper for tomorrow's conference.

In fairness, Claire was a decent boss. She would credit Max with the story — of course, pointing out she had received the tip about the party in the first place. But still, newspapers were full of bosses a lot worse than Claire, who was undoubtedly talented.

Max was elated but suddenly overcome by tiredness. It was 11p.m. — 4a.m. UK time — and she was jet-lagged. She called Sean, who told her he was still with Cath and Connor in the same bar, and joined them for a nightcap. Max had one drink then apologized for bailing out so early — it certainly wasn't like her.

She'd treat them to dinner at Soho House during her stay. Or rather, her company would. After telling Claire about the picture, her boss had insisted that she spend her expenses like there was no tomorrow while in New York. Who was she to refuse? And Max loved to mix the two — glam hang-outs with friends she adored.

Max hailed a cab back to the Wellington. She couldn't wait for bed. As she asked for her key at reception she realized she was slurring slightly. The drinks had gone straight to her head, mixing with fatigue to make her feel a little giddy.

"Hey."

Max froze as someone tapped her on the shoulder. Shit. Had the doormen from the Hudson tracked her down? Would a scene involving handcuffs and police follow?

Max slowly turned round.

"Luke?"

It was him. It really was. Luke was standing in front of her, all twinkly eyes and ruffled hair. God, he was gorgeous.

Was he here to work? On holiday? Why did he look happy to see her when she'd ignored him? Max should be embarrassed for the terrible way she'd treated him. But there was something about the way he was looking at her. Those bright blue-green eyes were laughing again.

"What are you doing here?"

Luke was calm. She liked that. God, he was hot. How come he was so calm? Why here? Max felt her heart rate rise, her face redden. How could she not freak out?

"I'm here to see you."

"Me?"

"Yes."

"You've come to New York to see me?" Max wondered if her heart had actually stopped as she said those words.

"Yes. Lucy told me that you do in fact really like me and that you callously ignored me because of what she said to you."

"She did?" How did Lucy know that?

As if reading her mind, Luke cut in. "I think your mum might have had a gentle word." Luke's eyes were smiling kindly.

"I see." It was beginning to make sense. Max had never been able to hide the truth from Marj. Or Lucy, normally, but she'd had so much on her mind.

"Have you been waiting for me for a long time?" Max asked.

"Not really — a couple of hours, but I've had a few beers and the *New York Post* to keep me company."

"Oh OK."

Luke suddenly seemed a little less sure of himself, shuffling on his feet. "You don't think I'm a mad stalker coming all this way to see you? I believe that if you want something you should just go for it . . ."

Max laughed, throwing her glossy brown hair back. She looked up into his face. "You know what Lucy said . . . that I really liked you?"

"Uh-huh."

"Well, why would she go and lie about a thing like that?"

Luke smiled down at Max.

God, she wanted him. "I'm so sorry for ignoring you . . . I really didn't want to, it's just . . ."

Max desperately wanted to tell him how she'd done it for Lucy, but how could she? She couldn't blame Lucy; that would be cowardly. The last thing she wanted was to be the cause of Luke and Lucy falling out.

388

Luke was leaning in towards her. He was whispering to her, telling her it was OK, he knew everything.

He gently brushed Max's hair from her face and his lips, so soft and warm, were on hers. She moved in closer to his body. She felt his tongue on hers. She wanted all of him.

Max had no idea how long she lost herself in him for — seconds, minutes? She pulled away, suddenly aware people were watching.

Luke was grinning. "They must be thinking, 'Get a room.' "

Max laughed. "Just as well I've got one, then."

An Even Closer Shave for Max

It turned out Luke had booked a room in the hotel too.

"I'd like to spend the night with you," he told her. His confidence was overwhelmingly sexy. "I don't mean . . . you know . . . but I've come all this way and I just want to be with you."

Max could think of nothing she would prefer to being held close to him all night. Mind you, she wasn't entirely sure either of them would be able to hold back.

Luke told her he'd come to her room in twenty minutes. He wanted to jump in the shower first.

Thank God, thought Max. She could freshen up too. And shave her legs. She had a waxing appointment booked for next week in London but the last thing she wanted was for Luke to feel her hairy legs. Thankfully, she'd brought a razor.

Stepping into the shower she let out a scream as the freezing water hit her. Jumping back, she gave it a moment to warm up. After lathering her hair with shampoo, she rinsed it off while hurriedly rubbing hotel soap all over her body. At times like this she wished she'd packed her best soaps and creams, like Lucy did wherever she went. But who could have foreseen Luke would turn up? How wonderful. Almost too good to be true. Max considered that it was a peculiarly pessimistic human trait to worry that things were going too well and to wonder what was round the corner. Enjoy the moment, she told herself as she washed the film of soap off her body.

Max launched herself out of the shower and quickly towelled herself dry. She brushed through her hair. No time to dry it — hell, the tousled look could be sexy. Max brushed her teeth, applied a light coat of mascara to open her sleepy eyes and rubbed in a little face cream.

He was really here. He'd flown to New York just to see her. Max was overcome with anticipation and excitement as she sprinted in little bursts around the room, picking up clothes she'd discarded about the place and shoving them under the bed.

She pulled on her cream-satin nightie, which only just covered her bum. A little indecent without pants, she thought, rummaging through her suitcase for her La Perla cream thong. A scoosh of Jo Malone Lime, Basil and Mandarin, nice and fresh.

"There, done," she said aloud standing in front of the mirror. "Shit, no, my legs," she muttered, racing through to the bathroom. Turning on the shower she put her right leg over the bath and started shaving. No bloody shaving cream. Ah well, needs must. Done. Now the left leg.

A knock at the door.

Shit.

"Just coming," she shouted.

Two more lines. That's it. Good.

Max turned off the shower and ran to the door.

"Hey," she said, opening the door, a surge of confidence rising within her. Luke had come all this way for her. There was no point in worrying if he liked her as much as she liked him. He clearly did.

She kissed him lightly on the lips and stepped back. He followed her in. Max was standing a few feet away from him. She wanted to look at him, make sure he was really here. He was wearing those baggy faded jeans and a light blue T-shirt. He was so effortlessly sexy.

Max looked at his face. Something wasn't right. He looked panicked.

"Luke?"

"Jesus, Max."

God, why did he look disgusted, like he was about to faint?

He was staring at her legs. She looked down.

Blood was gushing down her right leg. A bright-red stream from just above her knee down to her foot. She must have nicked herself with the razor.

Luke stepped towards her, his face etched with concern.

"Max, what have you done?"

"I've shaved my legs, Luke. Just not very well," Max ventured sheepishly.

He looked at her face. He guessed that guilty expression hadn't changed much since she was a toddler. He bellowed with laughter, doubling over.

Straightening up he looked at Max.

"You are adorable."

Max laughed back. "Well, that's one way of seeing it."

Luke picked up a white towel from the bed and wrapped it round her leg. They assessed her wound and realized the outlet for all that blood was nothing more than a teeny cut.

"I'm OK," she whispered.

"Good," Luke said, scooping her up and laying her on the bed.

Game Over

Bridget had never been so angry.

Hartley had been ignoring all her calls. Eventually, he had phoned her.

"At last. Where the hell have you been?"

Bugger. She'd let the sickly-sweet act drop. The bastard deserved it; but still, she had to sound concerned rather than angry.

"Hello, Bridget."

"Darling, sorry, it's just . . . I've been so worried about you. Did you have to go to see your mother in Scotland, sweetie?"

"No."

Something was wrong.

"Bridget, I know about everything."

"What do you mean?"

Hartley's voice sounded deeper than normal, more serious.

"I mean," he said purposefully, "your little game is up. I think you were behind the photographer in Scotland."

Hartley let the words hang, imagining Bridget's cold eyes taking them in.

"And I suspect you have been behind much of the bad-mouthing of Lucy, not to mention her 'murky' past that ended up in a newspaper."

Think. Quick. How could he possibly know, Bridget asked herself. She had left no trace of evidence.

"What on earth are you talking about, Hartley? My game? What game? Why are you saying these things?"

"Enough, Bridget, enough." Hartley sounded more bored than angry.

"Look, there's obviously been some misunderstanding." Bridget was scrabbling for words, talking quickly. She had to keep him on the phone. "Has one of your friends said something? I know Bately never liked me — he's making it up."

"It's got nothing to do with Bately," Hartley replied evenly, his voice as cold as steel.

"OK, it's Lucy, isn't it? She'd do anything to get you back. Did it not work out with Kirk Kelner, huh? She's a cheap little slut who's playing you for a fool."

Hartley laughed. "Now that's more like it, Bridget. The real you, the poisonous Bridget, had to come out sooner or later."

The cold realization dawned on Bridget that she had let her guard down. But what did he expect? "Sorry, Hartley, it's just . . . I can't stand to see you get hurt. And that's what she'll do to you."

"Hurt?" Hartley shouted. "Hurt? I'll tell you what hurts. Hurt is what Lucy felt when you set her up in Scotland. Hurt is what she felt when I turned my back on her. Hurt, you self-obsessed witch, is what she most probably felt when she read a totally fabricated story about the past you thought she should be ashamed of. Hurt is what her family felt when they read the lies. Hurt — that's the emotion Lucy felt when half of

395

London was calling her a gold-digger. And hurt doesn't even begin to cover what I feel at losing someone I was deeply in love with."

Bridget, for once, was lost for words.

Still, what real proof did he have that she'd done these things?

"I am furious you think I have anything to do with any of this," she told him indignantly. Anger — that would confuse him.

"I no longer care. Goodbye, Bridget."

"No, wait," Bridget pleaded. "We have to meet. You'll know I'm not lying when you see my face. I'm still coming to the Hogmanay Ball?" she half asked and half demanded.

"Do what you want," he told her. "You won't be on my table but you have plenty of friends taking tables. I can't stop you coming."

Bridget was panicking. She had never heard Hartley say a cross word to anyone. He hated conflict of any kind.

"I'll cook us a lovely dinner tonight, your favourite: lamb with honey and mint sauce. And we'll talk everything through, OK?"

Bridget's heart pounded as she prayed he would say yes.

"Bridget?"

"Yes, darling?"

"I'd rather prise out my eyeballs with a blunt spoon. Goodbye."

Lucy's Unexpected Blow

Kirk's eyes were closed tightly as he concentrated fiercely on the expert oral he was being given by this little platinum blonde. Carli, her name was. Kirk had asked his manager to sort out a hooker to come and give him head.

His mom had told him how Lucy had dated some dude with a title and that she was the kind of girl he should be going for. Daphne wasn't wrong. Lucy was exquisite.

She was just the type of girl he would like to date. Sure, if things went well he'd stay faithful but, hell, this was their first date and he hadn't had any action for weeks — well, at least a week. His manager was always telling him how he could sort out girls, no matter how last minute. So he had taken him up on the offer. Afterwards he would spend the evening with Lucy. That hair that smelled so good; those long legs; God, those wonderful round breasts. And she didn't put out at the pop of a Cristal champagne cork either, which was novel.

"Yeah, that's it, baby . . ."

Kirk put his hands on the back of her head. He was close, so close. He opened his eyes.

Fuck.

Lucy.

"Fuck."

Kirk raised his hands from Carli's head and raised his palms, like a man caught by cops trying to show he was unarmed.

Carli stopped, unsure why her famous client had suddenly deflated. Wait till the girls heard how she'd blown Kirk Kelner.

In one swift move Man of Steel himself would have been proud of, Kirk jumped to his feet while turning 180 degrees in the air. With his back to Lucy he hurriedly pulled his trousers from around his ankles and fastened his belt.

Kirk started to turn to Lucy, inching his way round as though, if he did it slowly enough, the whole scene would disappear, like a giant farce that had only been in his head.

Lucy was still there, half turned towards the door she had just entered.

"Lucy," Kirk managed.

Lucy turned to face him, hardly able to meet his eyes. Her face must be purple. This was beyond mortifying. She couldn't bring her eye level higher than Kirk's chest.

He was silent.

"Lucy," he started again, stepping towards her. Carli had slipped off to the bathroom.

Shit, he was coming towards her. Quick, think. "Kirk, I'll let you get ready. See you in the bar downstairs."

Lucy was out of the door before she'd finished her sentence.

Zip Me Up Before You Go Go!

Lucy pushed the elevator button. She pushed it again. Hurry up and get me out of here, she thought as her face burned and her hands shook. She had never been so shocked or embarrassed.

"Lucy. Lucy!" Shit, too late. Kirk was breathless and running down the corridor. "Wait, please, I can explain."

I doubt that very much, Lucy thought, though her mouth was too dry to form any kind of response. The only slightly feasible explanation might be that he was actually filming a scene for his new movie, which was of the soft-porn genre.

She turned to face Kirk. He looked as mortified as she did.

A man appeared behind him.

His manager, Jed, who had a smaller suite beside Kirk's, had heard his door slam, followed by his star client's raised voice.

Kirk turned to Jed, his expression changing from apologetic to furious.

"Jed, did you not tell Lucy to meet me an hour later at the bar downstairs?"

"No."

Kirk looked like he was going to hit his manager.

"Why the fuck not?"

"Because you told me not to. You said you'd rather text her yourself."

Lucy had spoken to Jed a few hours ago. He had called to ask if she would like to join Kirk at seven in his suite for a glass of champagne before they headed out for dinner. Then they would go on to the party where Carlos would join them. Lucy could remember Jed explaining clearly that the reception had her name and would give her a room key. The suite was so large and what with Kirk's love of rock music at full blast, it was best she let herself in.

"Fuck. I thought you said you'd do it." Kirk's head was bowed, his shoulders stooped.

"No. You were insistent on calling Lucy yourself."

Jed looked at Lucy, as if noticing she was there for the first time, and smiled painfully and remorsefully at her.

He lowered his voice, in an attempt to shield Lucy from what he was saying. "You said you wanted to look like a normal guy and text yourself," Jed said through gritted teeth.

"Fuck," Kirk repeated. Now he remembered. He'd asked Jed to get him a girl for some quick relief and that he'd call Lucy and ask to meet an hour later. But as soon as the conversation was finished, the second part of the plan was out of his head. Kirk's manager sorted everything for him — girls, clubs, clothes, you name it. Shit, he should have remembered to call Lucy. He was just so excited at the thought of the girl Jed had promised him.

The fact the girl had sneaked off to the toilet when Lucy came in, like she was the one who should be ashamed; the fact she looked like a thousand other girls with bad roots and long blonde hair — these were all give-aways that she was a hooker. Standing there in a pastel-pink wool wrap over a black-velvet dress, the material tight over her long thighs, Lucy looked breathtaking, as full of grace as Carli wasn't.

"Lucy, I'm so sorry you had to see that."

Lucy had no desire to argue back. She wasn't angry, just bewildered. She could hardly make a scene as the wronged girlfriend. This was supposed to be their first date, or perhaps the second if the Met Bar counted.

If it hadn't been for the scene of genuine confusion that had just played out between him and Jed, Lucy might have assumed this was a weird sex game where Kirk liked to have his date walk in on him with someone else.

"Listen, Kirk," Lucy congratulated herself inwardly for finding a voice, "I don't know what to say."

"I can explain."

"You can?" Lucy was looking forward to this one.

Kirk looked at his manager, as if for inspiration, then back at Lucy. What would he explain? That he was horny and decided to pay for a hooker to satisfy him so that he could behave well with Lucy? Because she was the kind of woman he wanted to be with and not just for sex. Hell, he was Kirk Kelner and had anything he wanted on speed dial. Somehow he didn't think the truth would go down too well.

Then again, in the absence of any other bright ideas, what did he have to lose?

"Will you join me for a drink downstairs, Lucy? Please. We'll have a chat and then if you want to go home, I will understand."

Lucy considered her options. Kirk looked a little pathetic, no matter how devastatingly handsome and famous, standing there in the corridor pleading with her. Perhaps having a drink would make him feel better. She certainly needed one.

"OK, but I deserve the finest champagne after that little scene."

Kirk smiled ruefully. "Make it a magnum."

Lucy Sees the Funny Side

Lucy couldn't help but see the comedy in the situation.

She had just listened to Kirk's explanation of what had happened. Somehow, she didn't feel as awkward as she was sure she should. It was like listening to a friend tell a funny story about someone else.

While pouring Cristal into her flute, the two of them in a cosy booth beside the main bar, he had explained how much he liked her. And that's why he had asked Carli to come round. He avoided the subject of whether Carli was paid help, though Lucy was sure she was.

"The thing is," he told her, looking in her eyes, "it kind of shows how much I think of you. I wanted to respect your wishes and take things slowly. I guess I just thought this would be some kind of release."

Lucy covered her mouth with her hand, stifling a laugh. She couldn't help it. Little did he know she had made up her mind to sleep with him. As Carlos had said, sleeping with Kirk Kelner was unlikely to turn into something she'd regret.

"Quite right. Kirk, I'm terribly flattered by the whole thing."

Kirk seemed to grasp how ridiculous what he had said was — that getting a blow job from someone else was somehow a show of affection, like lighting candles round a bath or scattering petals on a bed.

He concentrated on Lucy again, determined to win her over.

"But I'd love to be faithful, and I can be. I know I can."

Kirk could smell her hair, all fresh and fruity. She had crossed her long legs, so sexy in black patent heels and sheer stockings. Maybe they were tights. He hoped they were stockings.

Lucy was keen to take the sting of humiliation out of the situation.

"I'm sure you can be faithful," she said, putting her hand on top of his. "But listen, maybe we both need a little time. I'm just out of a relationship and you are going through a divorce."

Kirk nodded, unsure.

"Maybe it's a good thing you're having a bit of fun — getting it out of your system."

Lucy hoped she was being convincing. What she actually thought was that there was no way on earth she could so much as kiss him on the lips with the image of that blonde bobbing up and down between his legs.

But she had to admit she almost saw the logic of his argument about why he'd done it. He was Kirk Kelner, after all. Everything was on tap. And she believed him when he said he wanted to act properly with her. It was almost flattering — in a severely twisted kind of way. She couldn't wait to tell Max.

Kirk had taken her hand in both of his. "But Lucy, I could be faithful to you. I would be. You're different."

Lucy breathed in. Here she was turning Kirk Kelner down. If anyone had told her this was how the night would play out an hour ago, she would have laughed. Every woman she knew lusted after him. He was the screen saver on computers around the world; he was the man most voted as the one you'd cheat on your husband with. He was gorgeous, perfect. But now he was seedy. Lucy had caught him tonight by fluke, but how many other times had he done things which made that scene look tame in comparison?

That aside, she was still in love with Hartley, no matter how painful that was to admit.

She sighed. "I need some time."

Kirk looked at her with his big blue eyes. She didn't think he was acting, though that's what he did so well for a living. "I've blown it, haven't I?"

Lucy couldn't help but be touched. This wasn't acting. It was a man who knew he couldn't help himself. Even if he wanted to have a loving, monogamous relationship, Lucy wasn't sure he would be able to refuse temptation all the time.

"No, these things happen." She laughed. "Well, not normally to me. I just think we've both got a lot going on right now."

Kirk smiled thinly. He had blown it; he knew he had.

"But Kirk?"

"Yeah?"

"I like you. You're a great guy."

Kirk looked happier. One day, she thought, when I've wiped the image from my mind, I could forget where he'd been long enough to kiss him. It could be a long time coming.

"You still want to go to the party with me?" Kirk asked hopefully.

"You bet," Lucy said firmly. After all, she could hardly let Carlos down.

Lucy Sees Clearly Now
the Pain Has Gone

Lucy squeezed Carlos's arm.

"Can you believe we're here?" she asked him.

"It's amazing, Luce. You are, officially, my favourite friend."

Kirk had explained that his lawyer, Al, who ran a huge practice specializing in representing celebrities on both coasts — New York and Los Angeles — as well as London, held an annual party for clients and their guests. A thank you for all the money they'd spent. What with the number of libel cases against newspapers, magazines, film companies, not to mention their speciality of representing multimillionaire clients in their divorce cases, that amount of cash was not inconsiderable. Normally, Al threw the bash in LA but had decided on London this year. Many of his American-based clients had flown over for it. Kirk had told Lucy that some stars had been known to dump their attorney in favour of Al's firm after hearing about the ridiculously extravagant parties. That and the fact Al and his two partners were known for their balls of steel in court.

Al had hired Home House, the exclusive London members' club, for the night. It was a huge venue over several floors. Lucy and Carlos had been there before — on shoots or for parties, but tonight it was hardly recognizable. Each floor was themed. Everything on the first floor was purple. From the body paint on the near-naked waitresses serving canapés, to the silk sheets draped on the walls. A four-piece jazz band played in purple suits, their music soothing and mellow. Lilac bubbles floated around the room, making it seem other-worldly — like the guests had floated to heaven for a party.

On the second floor, where Lucy was standing with Carlos, the theme was orange. There was a huge glass tank of orange balls in a corner, like the ones you used to dive in as a kid. The room was fragranced with orange blossom and cocktails were clear with twists of orange peel. Waiters with amazing torsos wore shorts like *Baywatch* lifeguards, with orange Santa hats on their head to get into the spirit of Christmas, now just days away.

"This is awesome," Lucy whispered to Carlos. She was used to extravagant parties but this really was something else. She kept spotting new intricate details. She must remember to find out who the party planner was. Maybe she could hire them for a big shoot.

Lucy waited until Kirk had excused himself to her and gone off with Al, to be introduced to a few guests. Al's decision to hold a pre-Christmas bash in London was in no small part down to Kirk. He was set to spend a fortune with Al's firm in a very high-profile divorce case and Al was keen to let him know how much he valued his custom. As Kirk had based himself in

London for the last few months, what better way to demonstrate his generosity than bringing the party to him? It also did wonders for his relations with employees at his London branch — a relatively new office with a small staff. Slowly they were starting to take big clients from established rival English firms.

"You are never going to believe what just happened." Lucy was leaning into Carlos's ear, her voice dripping with dramatic urgency.

It was all the encouragement Carlos needed. His eyes wide, he half whispered and half hissed back: "Tell me, tell me. Have you already had sex in his hotel room? Is that why he asked you to meet him there? Did he fling you on the bed and make wild passionate love? Tell me he did."

Lucy controlled her fit of giggles by taking a deep breath, then placed her hand on her chest as though vowing what she was about to tell him was true.

"I walked in on him sitting on a chair facing me with his trousers round his ankles, his legs apart, getting a blow job from a girl. I think she was an escort."

"Nooooo," he half shouted.

Lucy put her finger to her lips: "Shhh."

"Fuck. Me. Hard. That is insane."

Lucy was laughing so hard, she was almost crying. She couldn't find the breath to explain any more to Carlos. Spotting an empty orange sofa he moved over to it and tugged on Lucy's arm so she followed. She looked fabulous. Carlos could never imagine her having anything other than the curvaceously perfect frame that made her look good enough to eat no matter what she wore, even if all the office girls were obsessed with being stick thin. Lucy was tall and elegant and that little Chanel black dress was divine, showing a hint of cleavage with a hem just above her knees. Perfectly refined and yet so sexy. She had gone for the classic Chanel look, with bold red lipstick and pearls.

Carlos clapped his hands and ooohed and aaahed through Lucy's tale of what had happened. This beat any story on Popbitch or Holy Moly.

Kirk had been gone for at least twenty minutes. Lucy didn't mind one bit. She loved telling Carlos everything and had to admit it was hilarious. When he'd got every last detail out of her — doing so in a huge rush in case Kirk came back — he settled contentedly back on the sofa and took in the hot waiters surrounding him.

"Ah, heaven," he sighed.

"You're taken. Raymondo, remember?"

"No harm in window-shopping, sweets," he told her sternly.

As always, Carlos looked remarkably dapper. A chocolate-brown Prada suit was set off perfectly against a lemon shirt and fashionably thin brown tie.

She had settled into a comfortable silence with her friend, sipping their Cointreau cocktails and soaking up the scene of decadence around them. The female guests looked so spangly and festive — women always made a special effort when Christmas was approaching. Lucy spotted the new Dior party gown, skimming the floor in rose-petal silk, before realizing its owner was none other than supermodel Agyness Deyn, who had fronted recent campaigns for Armani and Burberry.

410

The music mogul Simon Fuller, who had discovered the Spice Girls, was chatting in a corner to Emma Bunton, who was keeping it real in a glittery, girly, gold prom-style dress from Monsoon, with the new and not-so-affordable Jimmy Choo gold wedges.

And there was Simon Cowell, pretty short in the flesh with surprisingly broad, square-ish shoulders.

Lucy spotted Kirk, who had dressed down in navy Armani jeans, brown lace-up shoes and a black-lambswool V-necked jumper. Perhaps he had intended to put on a suit before Lucy had caught him unawares. He'd left his room to chase her straight away, after all. She found the sight of him rather surreal. Here he was, looking every inch as gorgeous as he did on the billboards and magazine covers — his tousled dark blond hair, that flawless lightly bronzed skin, all-American smile and perfect body. And she was his date. But was she? The body language of every woman in the room screamed they wanted him — they stood with their feet pointing slightly in his direction, their heads thrown back to laugh in an attempt to look like they were the life and soul of the party while desperately trying to catch his eye. The truth was that Kirk Kelner was everyone's date at a party. Women would replay the smouldering look he gave them — imagined or not — for months or years to come. And there was no getting away from it: Kirk loved the attention.

She was aware he kept looking over at her, checking she was OK. Of course she was flattered. But really, how could she ever date this guy? Many a woman would put up with anything to date him, but Lucy had met him just twice and already knew he paid for blow jobs. Hardly a way to kick off a honeymoon period for any relationship.

Lucy remembered something Marj had told her: you should never judge your success by your pay packet. The same could be applied to partners. It was wrong to somehow think yourself important or special because of the guy on your arm.

As much as she enjoyed his company — not to mention the admitted ego boost of Kirk Kelner pursuing her — she could imagine life would be far from easy with him. No guy looked that hot without dedicating a huge part of his waking hours to his image. Having your boyfriend spend more time in front of the mirror and in beauty spas than most high-maintenance women wasn't the sexiest thought in the world, but then it was in his job description to look the best he possibly could. There was something else that bothered Lucy. It wasn't the attention he got from girls; it was the fact that he clearly wasn't ready to give that up. He thrived on it, like a drug. She couldn't help but find that deeply unattractive, in spite of his heavenly looks.

Lucy had no doubt he had told her the truth when he said he desperately wanted to settle down and that he could be faithful. Whether or not he'd admit it, though, a bigger part of him wasn't ready.

Lucy sighed. "Tell me, Carlos, could you ever be with a man you'd seen getting a blow job from a prostitute?"

412

Carlos mulled the question over in his head, as if considering whether Burberry had outshone Prada at London Fashion Week.

"No. But in the case of that little stud muffin," he said, nodding his head in Kirk's direction, "I might have to make an exception."

"Well, I don't think I can," she told him quietly, soaking in every inch of Kirk Kelner — the man she would never sleep with. She couldn't, not now.

She smiled brightly as Kirk approached, apologizing profusely for taking so long.

"Al insisted I meet everyone. I'm so sorry," he said, addressing Lucy and Carlos. She couldn't fault his manners.

"Not at all, Kirk," Lucy said, standing up from the sofa she'd been sharing with Carlos, who immediately headed for a tray full of cocktails held by a near-naked waiter.

"Kirk," she said, looking at her watch, "it's midnight and I've got an early start at work. Would you think me a terrible bore if I went home?"

Kirk's shoulders sank. "I really did blow it."

Lucy put a hand on his shoulder, aware she was being watched like a hawk by Takira Freshwater, the pretty party girl and socialite who had dated a famous singer among others.

She was oddly reassured that Kirk would at least get laid. If Carli was anything to go by, that's just what he needed.

"No. Not at all. But some of us have a day job." She smiled.

"OK," Kirk said, brightening slightly. "But let me call you a car."

Lucy squeezed his arm. "Thank you." She turned to Carlos. "Carlos, I'm going to head off. Do you want to come?"

Carlos looked from Lucy to Kirk.

"Please," Kirk told him, "stay and party with me — you're more than welcome."

Carlos mock-sighed. "Well, if you insist, I suppose I could manage another hour or two."

"Excellent," Kirk replied, swiping an orange-tinged drink with tangerine feathers from a passing waiter. Any friend of Lucy's was a friend of his. After all, the way to a girl's heart was through her gay best friend. Admittedly, that ship may well and truly have sailed after Lucy's little discovery earlier that evening.

Even so, this particular gay friend was one of the best-dressed men Kirk had ever seen — maybe he could pick up a few tips.

Kirk excused himself to walk Lucy downstairs. He would ask his driver to take her home then return and wait for him to stumble out and on to another club or back to his hotel suite.

"Lucy, I really am very sorry. Not to mention embarrassed," he told her as the driver held open the car door.

"Please don't be," she told him, kissing his cheek. A kiss on the lips would be a step too far — God knew where they'd been. "You're Kirk Kelner and you can get away with more than most."

Kirk couldn't help but laugh.

414

Slipping into the back seat of the Jaguar, she said: "Don't worry. You're not getting rid of me that easily. I'll call you later in the week, OK?"

Kirk beamed back. "I'll look forward to it."

Excellent, he thought as she pulled away. Not only do I still have an albeit remote shot with the lovely Lucy Summers, there is a hot one-night stand this very evening to look forward to. What's her name? Takira? Clearly up for it. In fact, there are so many girls gagging for me at the party that a threesome or foursome may not be out of the question.

Flying Without Wings

Max smiled as her plane took off from JFK airport.

She knew she would never tire of replaying her night with Luke and that the six-hour journey would fly by.

They had had just one night and the following day together then Luke had to get back for his mum's sixtieth birthday party. She still couldn't believe he had come all that way to spend twenty-four hours with her.

Max shivered as she remembered. It hadn't been like sex with whiffy Phil or anyone else she could think of. Yes, there was passion and longing, but she had felt an odd sense of vulnerability too. He had pushed her back on the bed and kissed her so softly. His fingertips had rested on her collarbone as he seemed to take in her scent. His other hand brushed the hair from her face as he stopped kissing her to look in her eyes. They were kissing again, with abandon now, his warm tongue seeking hers.

Max felt his muscular stomach under his T-shirt — his skin surprisingly silky and warm. He groaned slightly as he felt the firmness of her breasts, pulling her to him and sliding her nightgown over her head.

There was a blur of unfastening his belt, pulling off his jeans and feeling him pressing against her. He moved his leg across and pushed her legs slightly apart.

416

Max felt her body tense in anticipation. He was kissing her again, longer and deeper.

As he entered her Max had gasped. Opening her eyes she saw he was looking right at her. Max felt as though her body had melted into his, pulsing against him.

They made love slowly. Luke watched as Max's face softened, her eyelids drooping, her round breasts flushed, her nipples pink and puffy. Carefully, he drew her towards him and cradled her, holding her close. He kissed her and felt her smile as he did so.

They had slept there in each other's arms until the morning. When Max woke she thought she would burst with happiness. Lying next to him, she felt like she had everything to look forward to. So her job didn't fulfil her? Then she could change it. Max could be and do what she wanted. Funny how things seemed simpler when happiness was thrown into the equation. But as she lay with her cheek against his chest, she was gripped by a sudden panic. Could Luke put up with her? Sure he'd found her Ambi Pur moment funny and her shaving-legs catastrophe hilarious, but would he tire of her disasters day in, day out? Would he disapprove of her partying? Was she really girlfriend material? There was only one way to find out — and that realization was exciting and terrifying at once. She had gone through her twenties without giving much thought to the guys she dated. And now she was faced with someone she couldn't get enough of, she couldn't stop thinking about him. Maybe she would turn into some Bridezilla nut job she'd always mocked, planning their wedding on the second date. Nah, not her style. But still, there was nothing wrong with a little daydreaming of what lay ahead — romantic holidays, great sex, nights in front of the fire.

Max laughed out loud as she remembered the shock she had while waiting in the departure lounge of JFK airport. Sheri had texted a picture to her mobile phone of a giant billboard in Piccadilly Circus, starring the one and only Shagger Sheri herself. Sheri had told her she'd been asked to front some STD campaign, but Max had thought little of it.

Seeing Sheri's image made her well up with a sense of pride. She looked amazing. Maybe that was due to airbrushing, but still, wow.

Max had zoomed in on the image to see Sheri was totally naked on the billboard, save for a giant crab covering down there, her arms crossed over her chest, her hands neatly covering her nipples.

A gorgeous male model dressed in a football strip was standing beside her, laughing as he held up a condom. The words above their heads read: "Make sure his laugh is the only thing that's infectious. Be safe: use a condom."

Max dialled Sheri's number.

"Awright, doll?"

"All the better for seeing you in Technicolor all over Piccadilly Circus."

"The billboards only come out this morning. They're all over the place — Hyde Park, Canary Wharf, Newcastle, Glasgow — you name it. Do I look OK?" Sheri asked breathlessly, her voice full of excitement.

"You look absolutely amazing."

"Fanks, Max."

"So, how are you?"

"Great. Been in rehab the past few weeks. Bloody hard going and, don't get me wrong, there are times when I could murder a line. But as they say: one day at a time."

Max unexpectedly felt a lump in her throat. Maybe she'd gone and done it: found her own way out of the hellhole of celebrity kiss-and-tells.

"Sheri, that's brilliant. I . . . I'm proud of you." Max felt the words catch in the back of her throat. "Listen," she said, swallowing hard, "I'm spending Christmas in Scotland. I'll give you a ring when I get back."

"OK, Max."

"I guess this means no more kiss-and-tells from you, young lady?"

"That's the plan," Sheri said cheerfully. "Max?"

"Uh-huh?"

"Thanks for everyfing."

"What do you mean? I've not done anything."

Sheri's voice was quieter. "Nah, you were a good mate. I know you were just doing your job and all. I could tell you wanted me to get clean. And now," Sheri sounded brighter, "that's just what I'm tryin' to do."

That had made Max happy, full of hope that Sheri really could turn things round.

With just two days to Christmas, Max was flying directly to Glasgow, where she would catch a cab to Queen's Street station and a train to Dundee. Claire had allowed her to take Christmas off to be with her family, so long as she worked New Year's Eve and New

Year's Day. Just one reporter manned the desk during the Christmas period, and the showbiz pages were mostly pre-planned and not news-reliant, so Max would cobble together a New Year showbiz quiz from the celeb news that year. Her shift would finish in time to join Lucy at the Hogmanay Ball. Lucy's friend Clarissa had asked if she would like to take a friend or two after a couple of people had dropped out.

Max had called Lucy the morning after Luke arrived, when he had popped out to buy some coffee and croissants for breakfast in bed.

Lucy had squealed in delight as she heard how happy and excited Max sounded.

"I'm so pleased," she told Max. "I had no idea how much you liked him. I thought he was just . . ."

"Another one who'd bite the dust?"

"I guess . . . Sorry."

"Jeez, would you stop apologizing? If it wasn't for you this wouldn't have happened. Thank you."

"You're welcome."

Max could tell from her sister's tone that she really was delighted. There never had been any pretence or games between them.

"Would you like to take him to the Hogmanay Ball? Clarissa still has a spare seat."

"That would be great, Luce, thanks."

Seeing in the New Year with Luke — Max could think of nothing better. She had started to ask Lucy what the latest was with Kirk, but Lucy had to go — work called.

420

Two nights later, on her last evening in New York, Max received an unexpected update on the state of her sister's relationship with Mr Kelner.

She had been with Sean, Connor and Cath in Soho House, treating them to champagne cocktails then fine red wine to wash down their steaks: the works. And all on her newspaper expense account. Claire had texted Max to tell her sales had gone up by 60,000 on top of their normal 2 million on the day her picture of Charlie Jackson appeared on the front page, under the headline "Charlie's Back On The Charlie". He had been forced to issue a statement through his publicist in Los Angeles, who admitted the actor had had a temporary relapse and was back in rehab. Well, he didn't have much choice, having been caught in the act.

As they sat at their table, Max's phone bleeped. She felt the thrill of excitement at the thought it could be Luke again. He'd texted a few hours earlier saying he couldn't wait to see her again. God, she was turning into character in a Jane Austen novel. It was Lucy's number on the screen. Clicking to see her message, Max's face dropped.

"Are you OK?" Connor asked. "You look like you've seen a ghost."

Max looked at him, dazed, then back at the text.

"FIRST DATE WITH KIRK KELNER . . . WALKED IN ON HIM GETTING BJ FROM HOOKER!!!!! Luce xxxx"

"Oh. My. God," Max said, showing them the text. She laughed as she watched their expressions.

Max tried to call but went straight to the answer phone.

Another text message.

"Can't spk. C u in Dundee Xmas eve and will tell all. Safe home. x"

"God," Sean said, draining his glass, "it's never dull in the Summers sisters' household. If one's not catching Charlie Jackson with a nose full of coke, the other's catching Kirk Kelner with his pants down."

Max shook her head in disbelief. "I know, I know, you couldn't make it up if you tried — story of my life."

Judging by Lucy's text, whatever had happened with Kirk, she saw the funny side. What a story. If Lucy had been Jade's sister, this would be front-page news.

Still, Max hoped Lucy was OK. Here she was, walking on air, and Lucy was trying desperately to get over Hartley. Then again, she was hardly struggling in the looks department — Kirk Kelner was testament to that.

Max had caught a few hours' sleep after dinner with Connor, Cath and Sean before catching her flight. She looked out of the plane window, then closed her eyes again and thought of Luke. Even the way he smelled turned her on. She'd read somewhere that humans had an inbuilt sense of smell to determine who would be a good partner. So, say Max's genes determined she could have heart problems, she'd subconsciously sniff out a guy with strong heart genes to cancel this out and give their babies the best chance of survival. Max wondered what whiffy Phil's odour said about him. Hey, maybe it meant he had acute hearing and some lucky girl with a history of deafness in the family would find him irresistible.

As the plane touched down in Glasgow, Max knew she should feel exhausted — she'd had hardly any sleep while in New York. But she had so much to look forward to — not least catching up with pals in Dundee — that she was buzzing. Her old hang-out, Fat Sam's nightclub, was calling. Stuff the Met Bar and the Ivy — you couldn't beat five floors of fun with Bacardi Breezer on special offer. Now that's what she called a night out.

Testing Times

Bloody whining carol singers, Bridget thought as she fought her way past last-minute shoppers to get into the pharmacy. It was Christmas Eve and she was livid she had been denied the best present of all. She had taken three pregnancy tests to see if her plan had worked. All were negative. Bridget cursed the fact that the opportunity to sleep with Hartley again hadn't arisen before he decided to cast her aside. How dare he! She was the best thing that had ever happened to him.

But all was not lost. Her friends weren't to know when she last slept with Hartley. Creating the rumour that she could be pregnant was a stroke of genius. Hartley wasn't to know she wasn't expecting, either — lots of women didn't find out until they were a few months gone.

She had confided in Dorcas that she had decided to take a pregnancy test, asking her tearfully over the phone if she would mind coming with her to the chemist. Her doctor was only doing emergencies over Christmas and this didn't qualify, his secretary had told her, suggesting she buy a home pregnancy test.

How very Jerry Springer, Bridget had told the gormless woman.

She'd need moral support as she queued with all those methadone addicts she'd read about. She had told Dorcas how she'd had a little drunken accident with Hartley. They had got carried away, were careless and now she feared the worst.

She could trust Dorcas to tell everyone who mattered within a ten-mile radius of Fulham about that little gem of gossip. She might not be carrying his child but at least news would be out that her relationship with Hartley had well and truly left the shores of friendship. It was not the game plan Bridget had hoped for but she had no choice. Hartley had all but banished her from his life and had ignored her many calls. This was the only way she could think of to get him back. If he believed she was pregnant, he would have no choice but to let her back into his life. In fact, he would have no choice but to marry her. It was the only decent thing to do and she could count on him to do the right thing. All she needed was the chance to sleep with him again, then it really could happen.

Annoyingly, Dorcas looked like she'd lost weight, her frame undeniably svelte under her Vera Wang cashmere wrap in duck-egg blue. Bridget consoled herself with a swift look down at her friend's Mulberry loafers. Dorcas had always had fat ankles: fankles, she liked to call them when talking about Dorcas to others in their set.

Must remember to chew every mouthful of Christmas dinner thirty-two times, Bridget reminded herself, to start the digestion process in the mouth rather than the stomach.

Bridget bought two tests, just to be sure, she told Dorcas. She wasn't quite ready to give her friend the result just yet so made an excuse about wanting to get Christmas out of the way before taking the test.

Dorcas had nodded sympathetically and Bridget air-kissed her goodbye, her eyes full of sincerity as she thanked her for being such a good friend.

Back to Blighty

Christmas at home had been fun. As always, Marj had cooked the most magnificent turkey dinner and clucked like a mother hen as her girls told her they looked forward to the feast all year.

Fergal had been in charge of the wine selection, something he excelled at after taking up a tasting course at Dundee College. The guys at work had ribbed him something awful when they found out, but hell, now he knew his Merlot from his Montepulciano he was laughing all the way to his modest cellar — well, outhouse in the garden.

When she arrived home, Max had asked her parents if she could listen to the recording the doctor had given Marj of his prognosis after the op. They understood her need to hear the facts word for word, and the hope he had given them. Marj laughed and told Max she'd leave her to it; she knew the speech off by heart she'd listened to it so often. But Fergal sat beside Max on the sitting-room sofa while the CD played. He watched his daughter tenderly. He knew only too well how much she needed to be reassured her mother would be OK. They both loved her so much.

Max smiled as she listened to the doctor. He handled the situation perfectly, his voice kind but firm. He said there were no guarantees but, with the radiotherapy, she had given herself the best possible chance of the cancer never returning.

Max felt Fergal's hand on top of hers. She looked up at her dad and saw what she needed to see. Yes, he was worried, but more for his daughter. He was telling her Marj would be OK. Fergal wasn't the kind of man who told her he loved her every day, but he showed it every time he looked at her, every time she told him she'd broken a big story. He was less vocal than Marj, strong and quiet, but, just like their mother, he had always willed her and Lucy to make a mark on the world.

When Lucy arrived home, Marj couldn't remember ever feeling so contented. Her little family unit under one roof.

Marj was relieved to see Max back to her normal carefree self. And Lucy seemed in good spirits, happy for Max and full of life as she told her sister and mum the latest episode in the Kirk saga: walking in on him in his hotel suite.

"Really. All the magazines are full of this oral-sex stuff. I'm sure we didn't have it in our day," she told her daughters, who couldn't help but laugh. "Oh I'm as open-minded as the rest but I'm not so sure he's right for you, Lucy. You can get over many things in a relationship, but that sight in his hotel room? I don't think so."

"Me neither, Mum," Lucy agreed.

After Christmas dinner, Marj told Lucy she had visited Hartley — she couldn't keep it from her any longer.

428

Lucy felt a pang of emotion as her mum told her what she'd done and admitted she was terrified Lucy'd think her a meddling old fool.

Lucy shook her head. "Not at all, Mum. If the last few months have taught me anything, it's to cherish the people who will stick by you, no matter what. You were only trying to help."

Marj smiled and squeezed Lucy's hand. She had seen the flicker of hope in her daughter's eyes when she told her how Hartley had reacted, how he looked as though he would cry and how he admitted he felt ashamed at believing she could have betrayed him.

"Mum, I wish he'd believed me too. I don't know if I could ever be with him, knowing what he was prepared to think of me. But, well, Bridget did a good job setting me up — anyone would have come to the same conclusion."

Fergal had come to join "his girls" as he loved to call them for mince pies round the roaring fire.

Their mother had looked a little tearful as she waved them off at Dundee airport. But she had Fergal, who, Max and Lucy agreed, was even more adoring of his wife than they could ever remember.

They had laughed as Marj told them that, before she knew if she'd need a mastectomy or chemo, he had assured her he'd love if she were bald or had five breasts or one. But everything was going to be OK.

Now the sisters were back in their Kensington flat. With the Hogmanay Ball just two nights away, Max was trying on her gown. She had always admired on Lucy a stunning Dior number in deep-purple velvet and her sister had offered to have it taken up a few inches for her. Max may have been a little more petite in frame than Lucy but the fabric clung to her as though it was made to fit.

The high peep-toes she had found in Karen Millen were exactly the same colour and Lucy told her they looked like this season's Gucci.

"I love it," she squealed while parading for Lucy.

Lucy had her eye on a YSL gown that had been used for a shoot for the mag last month. A designer at the fashion house had promised she could borrow it for the ball.

As Lucy began to explain what it looked like, their intercom buzzed. Lucy smiled as she heard Clarissa's voice. She couldn't wait to see her — it had been an age.

Lucy opened the door and was greeted with a flurry of air kisses.

She couldn't believe her eyes. "Bloody hell, Clarissa, where's the rest of you? You're . . . so . . . slim. You look amazing."

"Ha! Tell me again," Clarissa roared, twirling in front of Lucy. "To hell with humility, I'll never tire of hearing those words."

Lucy was astonished. No wonder the A-listers queued to stay at the Thai spa. Clarissa was half the woman she remembered; her wobbly tum and bum had vanished. She could be no more than a size 10. And she looked healthy, her small waist accentuating still-womanly breasts and hips.

Max teetered over in her gown. "Hello, I'm Max, Lucy's sister."

"Wow. You look divine," Clarissa told Max, taking her in. "That dress is to die for . . . and the gorgeous gene clearly runs in the family."

Max blushed as she took Clarissa's coat.

Sitting beside Lucy on the sofa, Clarissa was waving her hands excitedly. "So, you like the new body? I tell you, I don't think it will last too long. I've already given in to a cream cake or two."

Lucy laughed. "You look amazing. And speaking of things we shouldn't have, would you like a glass of Prosecco? It's nearly New Year, after all."

"Oooo, yes, please."

"Don't worry," Max shouted through from her bedroom, where she was changing into her jeans and a T-shirt. She'd get it, so the friends could catch up.

"Anyway," Clarissa told Lucy, "as I say, I don't think I can keep it off for long. That's part of the reason Clive and I have decided to get married sooner than planned — on Valentine's Day. What do you think? Of course, it's not just about me not looking like Nelly the Elephant; it will be so romantic too. But I might as well make the most of being slim. If we wait until summer I'll no doubt be the size of a house."

Clarissa relished watching Lucy's expression. "That's wonderful! Valentine's Day is perfect."

"You can come?"

"Of course." Lucy smiled.

Clarissa beamed, thanking Max as she gave them both a flute.

"Mmm, lovely," Clarissa said as the sweet honey bubbles spread over her tongue. "I tell you, this near-starvation thing does the trick but, my God, it's dull. This tastes like nectar."

The girls clinked glasses, with Max leading the toast: "To us."

Clarissa suddenly looked serious and turned to Lucy. "Now, what of your love life, young lady? Kirk Kelner? Should I be buying a hat for your Hollywood wedding?"

Lucy grimaced. "Not quite." She looked at her sister. "Max, why don't you tell Clarissa what happened? You tell it so well."

Max clasped her hands. This was a story she would never tire of telling. And as she built up to the bit where Lucy caught him with the blonde bobbing up and down, Clarissa's facial expressions were a picture.

"Noooo! Really?"

"Really," Lucy and Max chorused.

It took Clarissa a while to recover before reassuring Lucy that film star or not, she could do better. Clarissa looked trendier than normal. Clearly, she'd had to buy clothes in a smaller size and had opted for a new style at the same time. She wore dark denim high-waisted jeans and a crisp Anne Fontaine white wrap-around shirt. There was still something of the thrown-together look about her, but that was part of Clarissa's charm.

Lucy noted the absence of Hartley's name in the conversation. Perhaps Clarissa had heard he was back with Bridget and didn't want to hurt her.

"Don't worry," Lucy told her. "I read the magazines. I know Hartley's back with his ex."

"God! That vile excuse for a woman we met at Ascot. How could he?" Clarissa boomed.

Lucy looked into her glass, then caught Max's eye. She could mask her feelings from most people but not Max. Max knew Lucy was still hurting. And Clarissa had sensed how much Lucy had liked Hartley at her supper. Lucy had been dating him for only a few weeks, but her face came to life when she talked about Hartley and that had touched Clarissa.

Clarissa didn't have the heart to tell Lucy the latest gossip — that Bridget might be pregnant. She had heard the news through a friend of Dorcas King, who said she'd been with Bridget when she bought a pregnancy test. Clarissa was sure her friend had told her because she knew she had become friends with Lucy and Hartley when they were an item. Hartley had seemed so lovely — warm and unaffected. Why would he ever be with Bridget after Lucy?

It would do no good to tell Lucy the news, which might not even be true. God, if it was, poor Lucy. No matter how brave a face Lucy put on it, Clarissa could see her friend was in pain.

"Anyway," Clarissa said brightly. "Enough of men. Are you looking forward to the ball? It's only two nights away. And Max, you're coming too? With Lucy's brother Luke?"

Max nodded, aware how odd it sounded.

"My, my, it's hard to keep up with you two," Clarissa said, draining her glass.

The Times They are a-Changin'

Lucy woke on New Year's Eve with a strange feeling. Her stomach was tight with anticipation, a mix of nerves and excitement about the ball that evening.

What would it be like to see Hartley again? In spite of herself, her heart had leaped when Marj told her how sad he'd looked when she spoke to him. But things had changed. He had moved on; that much was clear. God only knew what he thought about her and Kirk.

Lucy had realized Kirk wasn't exactly boyfriend material that night in his hotel room. Her doubts had been reinforced a few days later when the News of the World splashed on "Kelner's Five In A Bed Orgy". Two of the girls, one nineteen, the other twenty-three, had revealed all about their "sordid night of passion with the insatiable star".

Lucy didn't feel jealous, not even disappointed. It simply confirmed her suspicions.

Carlos had partied with him until five o'clock the night she had left them at Home House. He told her how Kirk had disappeared to the toilets at regular intervals and come back with his eyes wilder, his jaw more clenched each time. Kirk had been charming to Carlos all night, complimenting his outfit and asking for his number so he might call to arrange lunch. Fuck, he was ridiculously gorgeous, Carlos thought as he looked up into Kirk's flawless face. His long eyelashes that curled upwards around his sky-blue eyes, his smooth bronzed skin, that strong jaw . . . The dream of every straight woman and gay man. It wasn't like Carlos to get star-struck — that's why he was so good at what he did, telling A-listers exactly how they'd fucked up and why he was the man to bail them out. But who wouldn't meet their ultimate wet dream and be a little flummoxed? Thanks to Lucy, he wasn't too in awe, though; he just couldn't get the image of a bottle-blonde with bad roots bobbing up and down, Kirk's trousers round his ankles. And that ridiculous visual picture somehow made him human. Still Adonis, but flawed nonetheless.

Kirk had made a big play of telling Carlos he was ready to settle down with the right woman and how much he thought of Lucy. It wasn't lost on Carlos that many straight men were aware the best way to a girl's heart was through her gay best friend. But by the time Carlos left, Kirk was stroking Takira Freshwater's thigh.

Lucy hoped she could keep in touch with Kirk and be friends because she enjoyed his company. But she wasn't convinced Kirk was a friendship-only kind of guy. He had sent her beautiful white roses the morning after. Lucy had smiled as she read the card: "Lots of love, Kirk . . . the guy who hopefully didn't blow it."

Lucy texted to thank him but was sure they both knew deep down that blown it was exactly what he'd done.

Onwards and upwards, as Max would say. Tonight would be fun. She hadn't spent New Year's Eve with Max for a few years, with Max usually heading to Scotland to party with Suzie while Lucy stayed in London with Amy or other friends from university.

Even better, Luke would be there too. If only she could shake the nerves she had at the thought of seeing Hartley . . . He probably wouldn't even notice her; he'd be too busy organizing things and fawning over Bridget.

Lucy had received a call the night before to say the YSL dress had been delivered to her office. She had also received another call, from her editor's PA, asking if she could pop in for a chat with the editor and managing editor. The two big bosses. The PA assured Lucy there was nothing to worry about. But still, being summoned on New Year's Eve, when most of the staff were enjoying a few days off, was most unusual. Granted, there was no such thing as a two-week holiday over the festive period when it came to magazines and periodicals. They still had to get their regular edition out. But the executives usually took New Year's Eve off, and stayed off until the third or fourth of January.

Lucy told Sarah, the PA, that midday was fine. She had to go in to pick up the gown in any case. She had booked an appointment with her favourite hairdresser, Taylor, just off Kensington High Street, for 2p.m., having decided that pinning her hair back would best complement the dress.

As Lucy applied a coat of mascara and mint lip balm, she cringed when she recalled the night before.

She had arranged to meet up with Amy for a drink at Dover Street Wine Bar. Amy looked a fright — full of the winter flu, her nose red and eyes puffy. Amy told her she'd been determined not to cancel because they hadn't seen each other since she'd left her with Kirk at the Met. They'd texted here and there but nothing made up for hearing all the juicy details face to face. Amy's face was a picture when Lucy told her the blow-job story, which she now felt she'd told a hundred times. In her shock, Amy launched into a coughing fit, spluttering and gasping for air. When she had regained her composure, Lucy insisted she go home. As lovely as it was to see her friend, she was clearly in need of a good night's sleep.

Lucy had made her way back to the flat. She'd expected to be out for the night, not home by nine. On the plus side, a night watching TV in her pyjamas with Max beckoned.

She wasn't quite prepared for the scene that greeted her upon entering the flat: Luke and Max, half undressed on the sofa. As they hadn't heard her come in, they were on the way to becoming fully undressed.

Lucy considered slipping out again unnoticed but as she shifted on her feet Luke, who was on top, saw her over the sofa and froze.

"Shit. Lucy. Hi."

Max craned her neck up and smiled. "Oh, sis. Hi."

Lucy covered her eyes with her hands. "Don't worry. I didn't see a thing." The back of the sofa would have hidden them ... but the mirror on the opposite wall reflected everything. Her brother and sister at it on the sofa would be for ever burned on her retinas.

"Sorry, Luce. I thought you were out for the night?" Max was hastily pulling her jumper on and sitting upright on the sofa, while Luke stood up. His jeans were around his ankles with only his boxers protecting his modesty. He was shuffling towards his T-shirt, which had been abandoned at the other side of the room. Then — wallop — he tripped over his jeans and thudded to the floor.

Lucy caught Max's eye and both sisters laughed.

Catching her breath, Max managed: "Sorry, Luce, this must be really weird for you."

It was. Max and Luke. Lucy was still trying to get her head round it. But she knew one thing for sure. She'd never seen Max so happy. And that made everything more than OK.

As Luke got to his feet, he was laughing too.

Lucy blushed now, as she remembered. She had to admit that it was hilarious as well as embarrassing.

Max, of course, had gone out of her way to make sure everything felt as normal as possible and insisted she fixed a bite to eat for them all.

"Well, cheese on toast — as far as my culinary skills go, I'm afraid, Luke. Lucy got the domestic-goddess genes."

Luke smiled back at Max. He'd hardly stopped smiling since New York. Max was unlike any girl he'd met before. A little whirlwind of fun — and yet at times he saw a quieter side, one that was reflective about what was happening between them. He longed to find out what she was thinking during those moments. Her expression told him it was something similar to what was going through his own head: was this really happening? The speed and intensity of it all seemed surreal, but wonderful.

As they sat round the table, Lucy marvelled at how natural Luke and Max were as a couple. It felt as though the three of them had been eating toasties together on winter nights for years.

In the back of Lucy's mind had been the fact Luke and Max had been ripping each other's clothes off less than an hour before, so she politely excused herself to bed.

When Luke's mobile rang, Max kissed him on the cheek, whispering, "I'll leave you to it," and knocked on Lucy's door.

"Luce, I'm worried. I can't stop thinking how you must be freaking out — your sister getting it on with your brother."

Lucy took her little sister in her arms and held her close. "No," she said into her sweet-smelling hair. "Two of the people I love most in the world are making each other happy. That's wonderful."

Max pulled away and looked at Lucy. She could tell she meant it.

"Thanks, Luce. Love you."

Mother's Ruin

When Max returned to the sitting room, she could tell from Luke's expression that something was wrong. He looked perplexed, maybe a little angry.

"What's up?"

His mind was somewhere else as he turned his head to Max.

"Sorry . . . what?"

"What's wrong? You look kind of . . ."

Luke shook his head and looked at the floor. He took a deep breath and ran his fingers through his hair. Patting the sofa beside him, he asked Max to sit down.

Not a good sign, Max thought. Jeez, she knew things were going too well. She felt a rising sense of panic. What was wrong?

Putting a hand on Max's knee and turning his body towards her, Luke's face became softer as he seemed to take her in.

"Don't look so worried," he told her, his brow furrowing with new concern. "No one's died. It's just . . . well, my mum."

"God, is she OK?"

Luke let out a laugh. "Oh she's fine. The thing is, I told her about us the other night. Actually, I told the whole family — Dad and Ben too. I knew they'd be

440

fine. So long as I'm happy, they're happy. Dad admitted it was a bit weird, but it's not like we're related. And he'd been quite taken with you that day at the golf club."

Taken with her? That was far more than Max could have hoped for; she had just prayed she didn't come over as some raving alcoholic stop-out.

Luke was serious again. "But my mum . . . well, she hit the roof." Luke took Max's hand. "She said some awful things — to me, my dad — things she should never have said and that can never be taken back."

Whatever Patricia had said had clearly hurt Luke, who looked wounded at the memory of her words. The situation was unexpected for everyone concerned but what a turn of events for Patricia. Lucy had often confided to Max how uncomfortable she felt in her company. She made no effort to conceal her displeasure that she had to have anything to do with Lucy, seeing her as an inconvenient reminder of Peter's adultery all these years ago.

While Peter, Ben and Luke were warm and kind, Patricia sounded like a bit of a snob, whenever possible letting Lucy know she looked down on her family in Scotland. Patricia never actually said it, but she didn't have to, Lucy had said.

Max squeezed his hand, willing him to go on.

"It's not that she's a bad person, Max. It's just . . . she really resents what happened, even now. I think she's the reason we never met you or Marj. She wouldn't have it. So, God, you can imagine how she feels. The one thing that might bring the families together . . ."

"I understand," Max told Luke quietly.

Luke smiled, taking a deep breath. "Anyway, we had an argument. I told her I was spending New Year with you at the Hogmanay Ball. She said over her dead body — she'd arranged some family gathering."

"Oh I didn't know. You already had plans?"

"No, no, I don't. Ben's not going either. It's for a few of their couple friends, really, and a few relatives. I'd have got out of it to be with friends anyway. But she's turned it into an ultimatum, painting it as a straight choice: you or her."

Max's shoulders drooped; suddenly she felt tired. How awful to put Luke in this position. Patricia sounded like a nasty piece of work. But she was his mum. Sure, he might not have the kind of relationship she had with Marj, but still, you can't change your family. What if he decided to put her feelings first?

Luke lifted her chin with his finger. "Hey, don't look so sad." His bright blue eyes were wide and looking into hers. "I know what she's doing is wrong. Sometimes there's no reasoning with her. I tried to but she wouldn't listen." Leaning in to kiss her forehead, he whispered, "Don't worry. Everything will be OK."

Max smiled. She hoped with everything she had it would be. But making Luke choose between his mother and a girl he'd known for a few weeks? How could that ever work out OK?

442

What Goes Around . . .

Lucy pulled up to her office car park in her shiny black Z4. A luxury she probably didn't need but, hell, you were only young once and she shared the costs with Max.

Her heart leaped as she spotted the dress hanging in the corner of the office. It was by far her favourite gown from any of the shoots she'd been part of since joining the magazine. The model had had to have it pinned to fit her tiny frame. Today there would be no need for pinning as Lucy was a good two sizes bigger. She just hoped it wouldn't be too small.

"Lucy, Colin and Sherman are ready for you." Lucy turned round and saw Sarah smiling. Lucy was suddenly nervous, her stomach tight. Head up, chest out, as the little one would say.

"Hello." Lucy smiled at the men, who looked unusually casual, dressed down in jeans and jumpers. They had clearly come into the office just to meet with Lucy. She had opted for bootleg brown-moleskin trousers she'd picked up from a trendy Kings Road charity shop, brown LK Bennett ankle boots and a coffee-coloured lambswool polo neck.

The men kissed her cheeks and wished her a belated merry Christmas.

Colin, a Mr Darcy-style character, always immaculately dressed, pretty posh and terribly polite, perched on his desk. As managing editor, he had overall control of staff matters on Lucy's magazine as well as a couple of other publications in the company. He was married with young twins, much to the disappointment of half the female staff.

Sherman, the editor, sat opposite Lucy on a two-seater sofa. He was a charismatic Liverpudlian, with floppy dark hair and big brown eyes. He had been quite the ladies' man a few years back, with rumours of female staff receiving generous redundancy packages after their office romances had turned sour. But since being appointed editor, Lucy guessed he'd been warned off any more indiscretions. He was now engaged and displaying the early indications of being in a comfortable relationship: the beginnings of a belly and a few grey hairs.

"Lucy, thanks for joining us," Colin said warmly.

Lucy hoped she didn't look nervous. She'd had few dealings with the men. They met regularly with Genevieve, to discuss fashion ideas for the mag, as well as with the heads of the various departments, health, travel, beauty and so on. With Carlos too, of course, who was paid so well in part to offer advice to the men on matters of PR, celebrity relationships and marketing. Why speak to Lucy? Were they going to sack her?

"First, we want to say how well we think you've managed while Genevieve has been on holiday," Sherman told her.

Bugger. The blow of a sacking was always cushioned by a compliment — everyone knew that.

"Yes, absolutely," Colin agreed. He paused before continuing. "The thing is, Lucy, we've been watching Genevieve for a little while now. The bottom line is that we're not happy with her performance. No doubt she's a talented woman but she is not delivering the ideas we need to put us head and shoulders above the competition."

Sherman took the baton.

"That's right. Word reached us that she had taken a freebie holiday and promised to write about it. As you can imagine, Liza, the travel editor, was none too happy when she found out. It compromises her severely as it's her job to do such deals with holiday companies."

Lucy nodded. She understood what they were saying but had yet to fathom how it involved her.

"It was quite wrong of Genevieve to arrange her own deals like that," Sherman told Lucy, Colin nodding in agreement. "But, to be brutally honest, we would have turned a blind eye if she was a fantastic fashion editor. The point is, she's not. We suspect that any good ideas she has in conference are those of her staff, though she rarely gives them credit. We've voiced our concerns to her and she's been defensive. We have concluded she's out of her depth."

Lucy couldn't shake the feeling she was part of some conspiracy, talking about Genevieve behind her back. Though why Lucy should feel bad in any way, given Genevieve's general vileness towards her, was beyond her.

"We met with Genevieve this morning," Colin offered. "We voiced our concerns and offered her a very generous deal. A pay-off, if you like."

This was typical of the media world. As soon as someone displayed signs they were either past their best or failing to live up to expectations, they were seen as dead wood and disposed of in haste. From what Max had told her, newspaper editors were even more ruthless.

Looking back, it really was only a matter of time before this happened. Genevieve talked a good game but rarely delivered any dynamic ideas. Even her organizational skills left much to be desired; she often forgot to put an important event in the diary and relied on agency writers and staff to cover it for her.

"So," Colin continued, looking at Sherman, "we have talked it over and decided to offer you the job of fashion editor."

He let the words hang in the air, gauging Lucy's response.

"Yes," Sherman said. It was quite a double act they had going. "As we say, we've been impressed with your work. We've been watching you for a while. You've got on with things quietly, you haven't sought glory and we think you will be a fantastic fashion editor."

Lucy hadn't expected this.

"Thank you. I'm very flattered."

"Of course," Sherman said, "it is a demanding job. You'll be in charge of six writers and you'll have a shared PA. As you know, our standards are high."

Lucy nodded.

Sherman and Colin stood and offered their hands, congratulating her on her new job.

She couldn't help but ask: "And Genevieve? Has she left?"

"Yes," Colin said. "We've told her that we will, of course, give any help we can. But there's no need for you to feel bad. We wanted her out. It was time she went. And, well, we do feel you are much stronger for the role."

And there it was. No more being sent out for lattes and watching publishers' nieces take the plum jobs. Lucy was the boss. She couldn't wait.

"You should know how well thought of you are on the floor," Sherman told her. "'Professional' is a word that often crops up with staff when talking about you. And Carlos Santiago, well, he is well and truly the leader of your fan club — and he's not a man who is easily impressed. We asked him for his thoughts on how you would compare to Genevieve as head of fashion and he left us in no doubt as to your attributes."

Colin laughed. "I think the comparison in taste and style he made was Ugly Betty with Claudia Schiffer."

That sounded like Carlos. He'd kept that one quiet, but maybe he hadn't wanted to raise her hopes. Then again, she did remember a recent conversation when he'd winked and told her that great things lay ahead for her.

Lucy shouldn't be giving Genevieve a second thought. She had no doubt she wouldn't consider Lucy's feelings if the ankle boot was on the other foot.

But Lucy resolved to call her former boss and offer to buy her lunch, to show there were no hard feelings.

Fergal had always told her that making it to the top required guts and drive, but she should never compromise who she was. And that was a good person, he had told her. One who knew how to treat others well, no matter how badly her peers behaved.

She would tell Genevieve she could call her any time, perhaps offer her articles on a freelance basis. In truth, Genevieve had been lucky to land a cushy cash package from the magazine. She'd failed to deliver and been paid to go. Lucy had no doubt that within a few months Genevieve would turn up on another mag with a fancy title. That's the way it often worked: the good workers stayed and grafted their way up the ranks while others who talked a good game flitted from one publication to another, landing great jobs by trading off their last title. More often than not, new employers took their CV at face value. They would assume they were up to their last job title and hire them with high expectations. So often they had been forced out of their last job too, either sacked for poor performance or under pressure to leave because they felt out of their depth.

When staff didn't deliver, they were brushed aside within a year.

Yes, Genevieve had been vile but how much of that was down to crushing insecurity?

"Oh we've decided to double your current salary," continued Colin. "You were overdue a hefty rise in any case but this will bring you in line with the other heads of department. Hard work deserves reward. We are very excited about this, Lucy, and if things go as well as we hope, we have plenty more ideas about how you can rise further within the magazine."

She felt a little dizzy with all this information. Her dream job. The money was beyond her expectations. Maybe she'd be able to treat Max to outfits and dinners now. But it was the opportunity more than anything that was so exciting. She'd had no idea she was being watched. As she shook their hands, Lucy beamed at them.

"Thank you so much. I won't let you down," she told them.

She felt like she was walking on air when she left the office. She couldn't wait to celebrate at the Hogmanay Ball.

The Time Has Come

Lucy squeezed Max's hand. Without her sister at her side she'd have been a bag of nerves walking into the grand entrance of the Grosvenor for the Hogmanay Ball. But Max somehow gave her confidence, as she always had.

"I can't actually believe how beautiful you look," Max had told her as she walked out of her bedroom in her gown. Lucy was relieved that, minus the pins, it fitted perfectly. The thin cream-satin fabric clung to Lucy's curves, accentuating the swell of her breasts and her long legs. It skimmed the floor, her deep-red Manolos just visible when she walked.

While most women would have immersed themselves in Fake Bake or St Tropez tan to carry off the paleness of the dress, Lucy's fair but peachy skin worked perfectly, giving the illusion her entire body was glowing. Her hair had been loosely pinned up with a few of the finer white-blonde locks falling at the side, framing her face.

Her blue eyes sparkled, expertly outlined with the finest black line; her lips were plump and rosy with berry-red gloss and liner. Lucy had matched her nails with her shoes and accessorized with a delicate necklace, the centrepiece a ruby with tiny diamonds around it — the finest costume jewellery Lucy could find and a dead ringer for the real thing.

"No bloody wonder you wanted that dress. If Hartley doesn't realize what he's missing when he sees you in it, every other guy at the ball will."

"That's not the point," Lucy chided Max with a grin. She was grateful for the compliment which settled her stomach a little.

"Course it's not," Max told her with a knowing wink. They both knew it did no harm whatsoever to look one's stunning best whenever in close proximity to an ex.

"Max, you look fabulous. Luke's a very lucky boy."

Max did a twirl for effect, showing off the dress which seemed to have been moulded to fit her perfectly. The deep-purple velvet bodice accentuated her tiny waist, before flowing to the ground, folds of the luxurious fabric catching the light as she moved.

"Cheers, Luce. Right, let's get this mutual appreciation society on the road."

And now the Summers sisters were making their way into the ballroom. Luke was meeting them there, as were Clarissa and Clive.

Lucy felt odd knowing Hartley would be there. How differently things had panned out from her expectations of the Hogmanay Ball a few months back. She had been so excited at organizing the bash, revelling in the finer details of tartan ribbons and Scottish dances. Now she was single and attending with her sister, who was falling madly in love with her brother. Lucy looked at Max and squeezed her hand.

Max smiled back. "OK, sis. Now we've arrived the party can start."

Max might be working the next day but she didn't have to be in until 11 a.m. and it would be an easy ride so long as a member of the Royal family didn't go and die or something. She would have a good few drinks — hell, it was Hogmanay, after all. Just not so many that she'd be dizzy focusing on her computer screen in the morning. And definitely not so many she thought she'd faint in morning conference — that was never a pleasant experience. And then there was Luke. It was the first time she could remember being anywhere as anything other than single. She'd been scared a boyfriend would suffocate her, stop her chatting to people at parties, would roll his eyes as she had another cocktail. But she didn't feel like that with Luke. It took her by surprise to acknowledge the butterflies in her stomach at the thought of seeing him again.

He had called her that morning to say he had spoken to his mum. Max felt her heart flip as he said the words. She had convinced herself Luke would decide he simply couldn't jeopardize his relationship with his mother and would pull out of the ball. Even if he did come, Patricia might have planted a seed of doubt about their relationship with all the vile things she'd said.

"Max, I thought a lot after I spoke to you. I couldn't stop thinking about how hurt you looked when I told you about my mum . . ."

Max tried hard to concentrate on what Luke was saying, but she was gripped by a horrible feeling of dread. The truth was that Luke meant everything to her. But what if the saying "what goes around comes around" was true and, by some stroke of karma, this was the retribution she deserved for being so careless with the emotions of guys over the years? Maybe she didn't deserve to live happily ever after.

"It hit me that there was only one thing I could do."

Oh fuck.

"I told Mum that if she was going to make me choose, it would be you."

"Me?"

Luke laughed. "Yes, of course you. She should never have made it into a choice in the first place. I told her I wanted you to meet my family, and I dearly wanted to include her but, if she refused, I'd be taking you for lunch with Ben and Dad in the New Year."

"Oh my God. What did she say?"

"Not a lot. I think Dad had stood up for himself for once too and told her he would stand by me if I wanted to be with you. Ben too."

"And . . ." Max's voice was quiet and worried as she took in what Luke had been prepared to do for her. "What does that mean? What will she do now?"

As overwhelmed with relief as she was, Max didn't want to be the cause of him falling out with his mum.

Luke's tone was lighter now. "Oh I think everything will be OK. If I know my mum, she'll come round. Even she knows what she did was wrong. And she knows now how I feel about you."

"And how's that, Luke?" Max asked playfully.

"I think you know, Miss Summers."

Max smiled. How wonderful. Their relationship was not up for debate. With anyone.

With Luke in the picture, things seemed to make more sense. Max knew she would soon leave behind the world of showbiz and parties, but she also realized what a kick-ass ride it was, and that it was one she should make the most of for a few months while she figured out what it was she wanted to do next.

Hell, if she didn't hanker after doing something that might make more of a difference, being a showbiz reporter was the best job in the world.

As Lucy and Max walked into the grand hall, they were immersed in the buzz around them. A sea of dresses — sparkly, black, backless, puff-skirted — mixed with the men, so smart in their tails and a few kilts dotted around the room. Champagne glasses clinked and the din rose to the high ceiling.

A man stopped the sisters as they approached steps leading down to the main floor and asked their names so he could announce them. Again Max squeezed Lucy's hand.

"Ladies and gentlemen," the man's deep voice boomed, "Miss Maxine Summers and Miss Lucy Summers."

As the words fell on the ballroom, the chatter of the guests subsided a little. Some people stopped and stared, others were nudged by a friend encouraging them to give their full attention to this unexpected guest. Some chatted on, oblivious to the fact the Earl of Balmyle's ex had just walked in, even though by all accounts she should be far too embarrassed ever to be in the same vicinity as him.

Lucy's stomach flipped. She hadn't anticipated quite so public an introduction to the hundreds of guests.

She glimpsed a woman quickly turn back to the group she was with, shielding her mouth with her hand while they lowered their heads to hear what she was saying.

As the sisters walked down the stairs, Lucy couldn't help but wonder what was being said: had she no shame? Was she here to have another go at snaring Hartley? Oh did you hear he's back with Lady Bridget?

Most of the crowd didn't know Hartley, or may have met him once and passed that off as a friendship with the Earl. But friends of friends in higher places ensured they were kept up to speed with the latest in his personal life.

"Darling!" A loud, robust voice rose above the crowd. It was Clarissa, who had gone for her trademark slightly garish choice of outfit — a lime-green, off-the-shoulder, full-length gown in raw silk. Her new svelte figure and slight tan from the Thai retreat combined to make her look like a pretty guest who stood out from the rest for having the confidence to wear something other than the staple flattering black number.

Clarissa kissed Max and Lucy, telling them they'd caused quite a stir when they walked in.

"Of course," she said, "all the women are seething with jealousy — you look like two models."

Blushing, Lucy took two glasses of champagne from a passing waiter's tray. She gave one to Max and made a toast.

"To a wonderful Hogmanay."

"To Hogmanay," Clarissa and Max repeated triumphantly.

The Lady is Not for Turning

Bridget was seething. She knew she looked fabulous. That was a given after preparing for the ball for weeks. She was down to her target weight, which was no small feat considering the party season had been in full swing for weeks. She'd stuck to champagne all December, surviving only on a little protein — prawns, fish or chicken — with salad. She had booked in for weekly facials with rich Crème de la Mer treatments and her skin was glowing. Her hair was glossier than ever in a perfect black bob that framed her face.

All that effort and every head had turned to see that little tramp Lucy Summers. What the hell was she doing here anyway? She'd heard a rumour she would be sitting at a table with Clarissa Appleton-Smythe — a name that had cropped up a few times recently. Philippa Bonner had mentioned Clarissa was getting married soon and the wedding was expected to be a rather grand affair. It might do to try to become friends with her at the ball. If Clarissa had any brains she'd invite Bridget to the wedding. She was, after all, Lady Bridget Beames, the highlight of any guest list and a huge attraction for the society magazines, which might carry a piece on the marriage as a result.

When Lucy had made her grand entrance, Bridget had been speaking to a group of friends she'd known for years — brothers Barnaby and Barclay Morrison and their cousin, Courtenay. She had been the centre of attention, accepting graciously their compliments on her black Vera Wang satin gown. She felt divine in the dress that had cost Daddy a small fortune. The neckline was high at the front, skimming her collarbones in a straight line, and low at the back, showing off the muscles she'd worked on with her trainer. It swept the ground with the trace of a train. An emerald choker she'd borrowed from her mother completed a truly regal and breathtaking look, of that she was sure.

Yet the boys had cooed like idiots when Max and Lucy Summers had been announced.

"Wow, are they sisters?"

"They're gorgeous."

"Is the blonde one the one Hartley dated? She's stunning."

Morons.

Barnaby looked a little sheepish as he realized what he'd said. Bridget had just been telling them that she and Hartley were an item once more and things were going well.

They had no reason to know the truth, that Hartley had been so angry on the phone. He would come round, of course he would.

Bridget had smiled back at them.

"Oh dear. Poor Hartley," she said, and they looked at her quizzically. "I shouldn't say anything but it's so unfair," she said, with her best pained expression. "He was so hoping she wouldn't turn up. He's told her over and over again to stop pestering him but she won't give up."

Bridget was buoyed by their silence as they seemed to turn over in their heads what she was saying.

"It's just so callous," she continued, lowering her voice to let them know they were in her inner circle of trust. "She tricked him with the photographer that time in Scotland so she could make money and now she's still after what she can get from him. Someone in his position is so vulnerable to that sort of woman. She's been in the papers since they split, you know, for sleeping with other famous and rich men."

Ha! Bridget surveyed her friends' faces. Not so smitten with her now, were they?

"Excuse me, gentlemen," she announced, preparing to spread this little gem of a story she had made up quite spontaneously. "I've just spotted a friend I've not seen for an age. Save me a dance, darlings, won't you?"

Hartley Goes Public

Lucy looked across the table at Max and Luke. Somehow it made her feel overwhelmingly proud to see them together. Good people deserved to be with good people and they were two of the best.

Lucy was aware of a few furtive looks over dinner from other tables, but she didn't mind. As they had walked to their table, Max had told her to walk tall. They knew the truth and that's all that mattered, she'd told her.

Lucy had glimpsed Bridget during dinner. Amusingly, she had been placed at a table near the back of the huge ballroom, far away from the stage where a jazz band were quietly playing throughout dinner and where Lucy guessed the after-dinner speeches would be made. It struck Lucy as most odd that she wasn't at the top table with Hartley. Perhaps Bridget had insisted on being placed at a particular table of note with some blue-blooded lord or the like.

And here Lucy was at Clarissa's table, which was placed respectably close to the top table. As she spotted Hartley her stomach flipped with that gut-wrenching feeling only seeing someone you love, or loved, can bring. Had he seen her? Lucy concentrated on not looking in his direction and instead chatted to Clive — financial markets couldn't be all dull, could they?

As he speculated on next year's property prices, Lucy's mind drifted. She noticed how many of the ideas she'd suggested for the ball had been used. Each table had the name of a Scottish clan and the linen table cloth and the tiny tartan ribbons around the stems of every crystal glass were of that clan's tartan. Their table was Maxwell, with a bright orangey-red tartan. The top table, bigger than the others to accommodate a few more seats, was Lucy's favourite: the dark greens and blues of the Black Watch tartan.

Dinner was exactly as she'd suggested. There was a starter of three dainty scoops of "haggis, neeps and tatties" with a brandy sauce, then Aberdeen Angus steak for main followed by the Scottish dessert of Cranachan with oats, raspberries and cream.

Even the band mentioned in the programme was the ceilidh five-piece she had recommended.

The spirit of how she imagined the night would be was there. Lucy put the thought to the back of her mind. How could she read anything into a few ideas? Hartley simply wanted to make it a successful night and had remembered a few of her suggestions. So what?

As coffee and shots of whisky were served, Hartley took to the stage.

God, he was handsome. Lucy remembered the delicious feeling of being in those strong arms — so safe and peaceful. And who could fail to love a man in a kilt, especially one with strong calves like his? Lucy caught Max's eye and lip-read her sister asking if she was OK. Lucy nodded, hoping her smile masked the sadness that she suddenly felt.

Hartley delivered his speech with supreme confidence. God, that was sexy. The audience laughed heartily at his jokes and looked moved as he talked about the Balmyle Foundation, while images of the young success stories flashed on a large screen behind him.

Lucy was aware he had stopped talking.

"And finally," he said, after a considerable pause, "there is something I would like to say. Anyone who knows me will realize I'm rather a private person so this is most out of character. But I've thought long and hard about it and there's something I have to say to someone here, in front of you all."

Lucy felt the sting of tears in her eyes, the choke of hurt in her throat. He was going to propose to Bridget.

"Her name is Lucy Summers."

What? Lucy felt the heat of eyes upon her. Oh my God, was this some kind of public shaming?

The crowd stirred, unsure of the reaction they should offer. A ripple of applause spread from the top table. Was that Robbie from Peat clapping enthusiastically? It was!

Clarissa's hands were clasped as if in prayer, willing Hartley to continue. Max looked like she was watching a tennis match, gazing from Hartley to Lucy.

Hartley took a deep breath.

"I am aware that some bad things have been said about Lucy in a very public manner. This is the only way I can think of putting things right — even in some

462

small way — publicly, that is, before you all. I encourage you all to tell others what I tell you here tonight."

Like a singer making a key change, Hartley's voice shifted. It was softer, crackling with emotion. "The truth of the matter is that none of it was true. I won't go over what has been said, but I can assure you that dark powers lay behind what you may have heard. For Lucy Summers," his voice was louder now, brighter, "is the most beautiful person I have ever had the pleasure of meeting. She is beautiful both inside and out. I will be eternally sorry I ever doubted her."

He was now looking straight at her.

"Lucy, I was very lucky to have you and very stupid to ever lose you."

Hartley let the words hang in the air. Max wiped away a stray tear, followed by another. Luke smiled at Lucy before turning to Max and brushing a wet cheek.

"That's all, folks. Thank you for supporting something so close to my heart by being here. New Year is just an hour away. I wish you all health and happiness when it comes."

As Hartley made his way back to his table, the room erupted in applause, with glasses clinking and heartfelt cries of "To Hartley".

Lucy was dumbstruck. Of all the things she had expected him to say, that particular speech wouldn't have made the Top One Thousand list.

Did this mean . . . What about Bridget? Did he know she'd been behind it all? Of course, even if he did, he was too kind to say so in front of all these people.

Lucy's mind raced, her heart thumping. Clarissa looked fit to burst with happiness, jumping out of her seat and kissing Lucy on the cheek.

"I knew it, I just knew it," Clarissa gushed. "A man doesn't look at you the way he looked at you and suddenly fall out of love. Lucy, go and speak to him. You must."

Lucy turned round in her seat to face Clarissa. "I promise I will. But look," she said, nodding towards Hartley, "everyone wants to talk to him. I'll wait a little."

Lucy glanced over at Hartley's table. He was surrounded by guests shaking his hand. But, for a second, he was staring right at her.

Two's Company . . .

Lucy chose her moment to speak to Hartley. She had spotted him walking away from his table towards the restroom. Thankfully, she timed it perfectly, walking towards him as he came back out.

She wasn't sure if what she was feeling was nerves. The only thing she was certain of was that she felt alive, with Hartley in front of her, getting closer. He was smiling. She had been sure she would feel nervous when she saw him but his speech had changed everything. God, it was good to see him again. And he wanted her too.

"Hi," she said softly.

"Hello, Lucy." Hartley wasn't sure he could say anything else. She took his breath away. Lucy looked like she didn't even belong in this world; there was something so incredibly beautiful about her whole being. That creamy skin merged with the satin of her gown, those pink lips, the sexy flush of her cheeks.

Lucy wanted to bottle that image, the way he was looking at her so tenderly, longingly.

But no, his face had clouded suddenly, like he had seen something awful. He was looking over her shoulder. Lucy turned. Bridget.

"Hartley," she said, ignoring Lucy and placing herself between them. Hartley stepped back.

"I am mortified and humiliated. I'm going home, so I'll cut to the chase."

Hartley's eyes narrowed.

"No matter what you might have said up there about that . . . woman," Bridget turned slightly to Lucy as she said the word, "there's something you should know."

Bridget stepped to the side, repositioning herself at right angles to both Lucy and Hartley, who were facing each other. Hartley looked Lucy in the eye. He said nothing but Lucy thought she understood his expression. It was strong. He didn't want to say anything to Bridget. He would let her speak, but she didn't matter any more.

"In fact," Bridget said cockily, "there's something you should both know."

She looked irritated that neither was asking her what this thing she had to tell them was.

"I'm pregnant." The words came out staccato, like machine-gun fire. Rapid, horrible, awful.

Slowly, Hartley looked at Bridget then back at Lucy. It was Lucy he addressed calmly.

"Lucy, I slept with Bridget once, a few weeks ago."

"Yes, you did," Bridget said indignantly.

Hartley's face was emotionless as he turned again to Bridget and talked to her for the first time.

"Bridget, I suppose there may be a slight chance you are telling the truth, though I very much doubt it."

Hartley's voice was even. It seemed as though he had almost expected this. He was ready. Bridget's posture changed, her bony shoulders dropping slightly. Still, her face was like steel, hard and determined.

"Oh you do? Maybe I've known for months and not told you."

"I can't quite imagine you keeping that little secret to yourself, Bridget." She certainly didn't look pregnant, Hartley considered as he took in her skinny frame. "If you were, I'd be there for the child."

Hartley looked at Lucy again, his eyes softening. His expression changed the instant he looked back at Bridget.

"But I'm ninety-nine per cent certain you are not pregnant. If, by some chance, you are, you should know something, Bridget. Even if you were the last woman on earth I could never be with you again, let alone love or respect you."

Bridget let out a mocking laugh. "If I was pregnant you'd have to —"

"No," Hartley cut her off angrily. "No, Bridget, I wouldn't have to do anything. Nothing could make that happen. Now, please, leave us alone."

Bridget looked at Hartley incredulously, her face crumpling as his words registered. She took Lucy in with a look of unbridled hatred.

Hartley's eyes were once more on Lucy. He stepped towards her and took her hand, pulling her away.

As they walked off, Bridget felt tears of humiliation sting her eyes. She stood there for a moment, watching them. When she looked around, everyone looked so happy, so bloody happy.

Hartley leaned in to Lucy. He'd forgotten how good she smelled.

"I'm sorry you had to hear that."

Lucy could see things clearly, as they really were. She was sure Bridget was not pregnant. She had slept with Hartley, that was all, and that was in the past. Lucy turned to him, his face just an inch away. She could almost feel his warm breath. Her smile told him everything he needed to know.

The Final Countdown

"Five . . . four . . . three . . . two . . . one."

Max pulled Luke to her. They kissed, lost in each other.

"Happy New Year!" came a voice from the stage.

"Happy New Year," Luke whispered in her ear. The people, the colours, tables — it was all a blur. He could see only Max.

"I love you." The words escaped Max's mouth before she knew it was what she was thinking. She put her hand to her mouth, blushing furiously. Hardly playing it bloody cool, she chided herself.

Luke threw his head back, laughing at her expression. "Don't sweat it, kid. I love you too."

Max threw her arms round Luke's neck and he hugged her, lifting her off the ground. When she landed, she looked round. Lucy was at the other side of the table with Hartley.

"Five . . . four . . ."

Lucy heard no more. She felt as though she had melted into Hartley. They were kissing. She wanted him. She had him. Nothing else mattered.

Pulling away, she looked over at Max.

Taking Hartley's hand, she led him over to her sister and Luke. They hugged each other and kissed.

As Max embraced her sister she said in her ear, "I'm bloody terrified."

Lucy looked into her little sister's beautiful big brown eyes.

"Me too." She inhaled deeply, smiling. "But ready too."

"Exactly, Luce. Let's do it."

What Happened Next

Bridget ran to the restroom in floods of tears. After reapplying her scarlet lipstick and powdering her nose, she bumped into Barnaby Morrison on her way out. He was very drunk and paid her another compliment. Bridget remembered he was the grandson of a famously wealthy shipping magnate, a friend of mother's. Suddenly, her evening was looking up.

Clarissa invited two new friends to her next Friday-night supper. She looked as proud as punch as Hartley taught her the steps to the Gay Gordons. Later, she politely refused when Lady Bridget suggested they meet up for lunch.

Sheri texted Max to wish her a Happy New Year. She felt on top of the world, having been asked to front the STD campaign for a whole year following initial positive reaction. She had allowed herself a few glasses of bubbly at a friend's party but stayed off the white stuff. God, it was tempting, but, as her sponsor said, one day at a time.

Marj and Fergal saw in the New Year by stripping all their clothes off and running into the freezing waters of

471

the Tay opposite their home. Hell, you only live once, Fergal told Marj before they took the plunge. He laughed as his wife waded in, screaming, "Life begins at fifty-two."

As they drove to the house of one of James's MP friends in Kew to see in the New Year, Amy asked her fiancé if he would consider travelling with her for a few months. He told her they were too old to play at being gap-year students, he couldn't put his political career on hold and they really should crack on with getting married and starting a family. She smiled at him sadly. She knew it was over.

Carlos Santiago accepted Raymondo's marriage proposal on the stroke of midnight. It was the second offer he couldn't turn down that day: Kirk Kelner had asked him to help shop for a new wardrobe the following week.

Kirk Kelner saw in the New Year in his hotel suite with a magnum of champagne, a pile of coke and hot Swedish twins. Next year he'd settle down a little. But for now, God, he loved being Kirk Kelner.

Acknowledgements

Thank you . . .

Diana Beaumont, my literary agent at Rupert Heath. Without your patience, experience and gentle prodding I doubt *Scandalous* would ever have been completed . . . especially during that six-month bender when I didn't write a word.

Alex Armitage, who introduced me to Diana with the words, "You should think about writing a book."

My editor Kate Burke for making this so much fun from the moment you said yes. For the title, which came to you in a dream, the changes you suggested and for being a cool cat.

Clare Parkinson, who made this flow with an incredible eye for details and, thankfully, for time lines. Thanks also to Sarah Hulbert and Francesca Russell.

I am thrilled to be with Michael Joseph and Penguin. It's a dream come true.

Those who have given me chances along the way, keep me in work or are kindred spirits. Some tick all three boxes. David Dinsmore, Craig Latto, Richard Melvin, Mike Graham, Billy Boyle and Annie O'Hare. There are more of you and I thank you.

Barrie Musgrave and Mark England for changing my life.

Everyone at the *Sun* and *Scottish Sun*. There are

many of you who taught me so much but special thanks to Rebekah and David for choosing me as your first graduate, fellow grad James, Fergus and my showbiz mentors Dominic and Victoria.

For your generosity in making *Scandalous* even more special and fun, Chris Palmer and David "Willow" Williams at Ladbrokes and Andy Agar at Why Not.

Ah, dear friends and muckers, by its nature, this novel may contain observations that have been borrowed, OK stolen, along the way. I hope a collective thank you — or sorry — will suffice. When Suzanne married Hartley Beames, well, come on, it was too good not to inspire the names of two characters. To the Dundee High School Class of '95 — Brodes, Zoe, Ali, Sal, S-J, Sus, Claire — and the boys, not least Barnaby, Paul, Guy, thank you for friendship, beds (especially during the recent nomad stage when my car was my home), drunkenness and loyalty. Ails and Charlie and all my friends from Edinburgh Uni. There's only one Ali Mackie.

My grandfather David "Papa" Maxwell, you are the best man I know.

My beautiful little sister, Holly Maxwell-Stevenson, you rock. And, of course, Alan.

This book is dedicated to my mum, Anne Maxwell-Stevenson, for bringing me up and making it so much fun. You made me see anything is possible and make me laugh more than anyone else in the world. We stick together like jube jubes.

How lucky I am to have you all.